THE LAST RED DEATH

Iraklis – a mysterious Greek terrorist group. A rogue offshoot of the Communist Party. At its head, a man with many names who has been in exile for ten years. Alex Mavros – a half-Greek, half-Scottish investigator. A man driven by the desire to find his missing brother. Grace Helmer – an American who saw her father murdered when she was a child. Iraklis was responsible. Now Iraklis is back – and Grace Helmer employs Mavros to track down her father's killer. From Athens to the mountains of the southern mainland he unearths clues from the past with a dangerous legacy in the present...

Please note: *This book contains material which may not be suitable to all our readers.*

THE LAST RED DEATH

THE LAST RED DEATH

by

Paul Johnston

Magna Large Print Books
Long Preston, North Yorkshire,
BD23 4ND, England.

British Library Cataloguing in Publication Data.

Johnston, Paul
    The last red death.

A catalogue record of this book is
available from the British Library

ISBN   0-7505-2166-X

First published in Great Britain in 2003 by Hodder & Stoughton
A division of Hodder Headline

Cover illustration by arrangement with Hodder & Stoughton

Published in Large Print 2004 by arrangement with
Hodder & Stoughton Ltd.

Magna Large Print is an imprint of Library Magna Books Ltd.

Printed and bound in Great Britain by
T.J. (International) Ltd., Cornwall, PL28 8RW

Dedicated
to the staff of the Polykliniki Athinon
with boundless gratitude and respect;
and, in particular, to Yannis Yiakoumelos,
Hans Katsifotis and Miltos Seferlis,
true heirs of Hippocrates

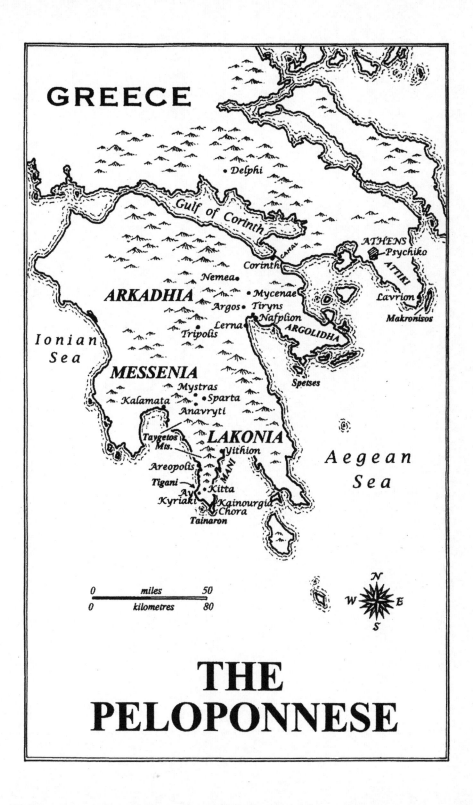

GREECE

Delphi

Gulf of Corinth

ATHENS
Psychiko

ATTIKI

Corinth

Nemea

ARKADHIA

Mycenae

Argos   Tiryns

Lerna   Nafplion

Lavrion

Makronisos

Ionian
Sea

Tripolis

ARGOLIDHA

MESSENIA

Mystras

Kalamata   Sparta

Anavryti

Spetses

Taygetos
Mts.

LAKONIA

Vithion

Aegean
Sea

Areopolis

Tigani

Ayi
Kyriaki   Kitta

MANI

Kainourgia
Chora

Tainaron

0   miles   50

0   kilometres   80

N
W   E
S

THE
PELOPONNESE

AUTHOR'S NOTE

Modern Greek is less inaccessible to English speakers than many imagine, but readers will save themselves headaches by noting the following:

1) Iraklis (stressed on the final syllable) is a transliteration of the Greek name that has come into English as Heracles. (The Latin form, Hercules, is probably more common.)

2) Greek masculine names ending in -os, -as and -is lose the final -s in the vocative case: 'Spyros, Kostas and Dhimitris are singing the national anthem.' But, 'Sing the national anthem, Spyro, Kosta and Dhimitri.'

3) Feminine surnames are formed differently from masculine ones: Nikitas Palaiologos, but Veta Palaiologou.

4) The consonant transliterated as 'dh' (e.g. *Dh*imitris, Argoli*dh*a) is pronounced 'th' as in English 'these'.

Prologue

19 December 1976

There was a hunter's moon. During the day, the north of Athens had been caught in the clear air and chilled like the stony bottom of a mountain lake. Snow gave the upper slopes of the surrounding mountains a deceptive glaze, their pitted surfaces and lethal chasms hidden beneath a soft white carpet. But when the sun had sunk behind the massifs of the Peloponnese, the cold tightened its grip even more, and the moonlight sucked colour and substance from the buildings. People hurried home, their backs bent and their breath flaring, anxious to get inside, as if the city had suddenly become a realm of ghosts.

The suburb of Psychiko, characterised by diplomats' residences and the mansions of wealthy businessmen, was near the imposing mass of the Pentagon, the American-inspired headquarters of the Greek Ministry of Defence. There was no shortage of senior military personnel in the neighbourhood, the tree-lined pavements ringing with the regular pace of well-polished shoes every morning and evening. But not now. It was almost midnight and the street named after the former King Paul was quiet, the moon glinting between the street-lamps off the roofs of luxury cars that were beyond the pockets of all but the best-connected Athenians.

Squeezed between a Mercedes station-wagon and a dusty Land Rover whose door was emblazoned with the words 'British School at Athens', the stolen Honda 250cc motorbike was almost invisible, its rider and passenger crouching low.

'What do you think?' The bearded young man at the controls looked round at his companion. 'Five minutes?'

'Maybe less. The traffic isn't too heavy tonight.' The pillion-rider glanced at his watch. 'Are you ready?' His dark eyes glistened in the reflected light as he examined the other's face. 'Are you ready to strike a blow for your people?'

The driver's eyes dropped for a moment, then met the passenger's again. 'Of course, Michali.' He gasped as he felt a sharp pain in his side.

'No names, Odhyssea.' The dark-eyed man's expression was unchanged, the skin still loose around his heavy moustache. 'At least, no real names.' His lips formed an empty smile. 'I am Iraklis, the hero, fighting for his birthright against injustice and the forces of reaction.' He withdrew the knife and watched as the man at the controls went slack, his breathing gradually coming under control. 'I am Iraklis, and together we are undertaking the twelve labours.' He nudged the man in front. 'Isn't that right, Odhyssea?'

'That's right.' The rider didn't turn round.

Iraklis raised his head cautiously and looked up at the apartment block on the right-hand side down the street. The target's home. The lights on the second floor were on behind thick curtains;

16

he could see faint lines at the edges of the balcony doors. The wife was there, along with the child and a Filipina servant – the watcher had confirmed that earlier. He tried to suppress the apprehension that had been mounting in him. Not about the mission: he had no misgivings about what they were about to do. His parents and their unjustly slaughtered comrades were entitled to a lifetime of missions. Nor was it the target that concerned him – the American was an invader, an enemy of the people. It was her. He steeled himself as he thought of the woman he had seduced; the woman who, in turn, had broken down his defences and almost diverted him from his purpose. Until his controller, hard and unwavering, had made him see reason. Iraklis picked up a sound to his rear. 'Keep down,' he whispered. 'They're coming.'

The pair dropped lower, their ears cocked, as the sibilant engine noise of a Chevrolet approached. As soon as the car was past them, its lights moving slowly down Vasileos Pavlou Street, they took black Balaclavas from the pockets of their jackets and pulled them down over their faces. The pillion-rider leaned forward and looked round the Land Rover's tail. The Chevrolet driver was inching into a space in front of the apartment block. The second the lights were switched off and the doors opened, the motorbike roared into life and swerved out into the street, skidding to a halt by the American car.

Both men jumped off the bike, the rider running round the front towards the chauffeur, who was fumbling under his jacket for a weapon.

Iraklis went to the back of the car and grabbed the occupant of the rear seat by the collar of his raincoat, dragging him out on to the pavement. Before the American could offer any resistance, the blade of a combat knife was at his throat.

'Deal with him,' Iraklis said to his comrade, nodding at the chauffeur.

Odhysseas had already relieved the bulky man with the crew-cut of his service automatic. Without hesitating, he smashed the butt of his revolver into the American's face, then clubbed him on the back of the neck as he went down. He sprawled motionless on the pavement.

'Bravo,' Iraklis said.

'Do it,' Odhysseas said hoarsely. 'Get it over with.'

The American was kneeling on the ground, his head twisted round at Iraklis. 'What do you want?' he said in English. 'I'm a diplomat.' He swallowed hard. *'Eimai Amerikanos ... dhiplomatis.'*

Iraklis gripped the man's fair hair with his left hand and forced his head back, the flat of the blade pressed hard against his throat. 'I know who you are, Trent Helmer,' he said, in heavily accented English.

A metallic noise close by made all three men look round.

'Trent?' The woman's voice was discordant. 'Oh, my God, Trent.' She stopped on the marble tiles outside the apartment block when she saw her husband's attacker tense, her hands moving to her mouth and her face contorted in horror. She opened her mouth to scream but no sound came. She leaned forward, the flaps of her

18

dressing-gown parting to r
nightgown.

'Stay back, Laura,' the Ar

'Oh, my God,' his wife
But her eyes were no lon
They were fixed on his a..
she said, stepping forward ..
you, it can't–' She broke off a.
masked man with the knife raise his ..
her.

'No,' she groaned, when she realised h..
daughter was watching from the bedroom
window above. 'No, Grace, no, no...'

Iraklis took in the little girl. Her face and
braided blonde hair were all that showed
between the curtains. Her skin was pallid in the
moonlight, the expression on her face vacant and
unreadable. Her eyes were on the well-honed
knife held to her father's throat.

'Do it,' Odhysseas said, swinging the gun
towards the woman. 'Do it now or I swear I'll
take out his wife.'

For a few seconds Iraklis was motionless. Then
he lowered his eyes from the upper storey and
shook his head at the woman.

Before anyone could move – the child at the window, the woman on the tiles outside, the masked
rider beside the comatose chauffeur, the diplomat
on his knees – the assassin whipped his knife along
the bared throat. His victim toppled slowly
forward, blood jetting out over his white shirt and
grey suit, and on to the smooth paving stones.

As Iraklis stepped away, he took a small piece of
carved wood from his pocket and dropped it on

19

omat's juddering back. Then, with the
f the widow in his ears and the solemn
the child burning in his eyes, he swung
over the pillion and wrapped his arms
d the driver.

a few seconds they were swallowed up by the
oonstained night.

1

18 December 2001

Alex Mavros was sitting at the window with the curtains half drawn. In the weak morning light the shapes on the Acropolis were unclear, columns jutting up like the bones of a whale that had somehow beached itself on this rocky prominence five kilometres from the coast. The sun was over the ridge of Mount Imittos but its rays were struggling to break through the layer of pollution hanging over Athens, the year-round traffic fumes boosted by the heating oil burned in thousands of apartment blocks throughout the winter. Mavros shook his head as he watched a gangly kid on a moped accelerate hard up Pikilis, exhaust blaring.

'What's the matter with you?'

Mavros turned his head towards the bed. Andhroniki Glezou's tousled, highlighted hair had appeared above the covers, her eyes sticky with sleep but restless as ever.

'Nothing,' he replied, in a low voice. 'You'd better get going, Niki. It's after seven.'

'Shit. I've got a meeting at eight.' Niki stood up and came over to the window, her legs bare under a T-shirt with the logo 'Olympic Games, Athens 2004 – Game Over'. 'What is it, Alex?' she asked, an edge to her voice. 'Let me guess. Your job? Your brother? The city? Me? Which one's bugging you today? Or is it all of them?' She gave him a sardonic glance and pulled the T-shirt over her head.

Mavros tried to keep his eyes off Niki's firm breasts and white thighs as she got dressed. He didn't want to make it too obvious that he still found her physically attractive. Their relationship had always been stormy, but recently it had been going off the top end of the Beaufort scale too frequently for comfort.

'Well?' Niki demanded. 'Oh, for God's sake, grow up, Alex. What have you got to complain about? I have clients with real problems, life and death problems.' She was a social worker who was involved with immigrants and refugees.

'Give me a break, will you?' he said lamely, aware that nothing he came up with would strike a chord with her when she was in this mood. 'So I've got a melancholic side. I'm not asking for sympathy.'

'Just as well,' Niki said, moving to the door. 'I haven't got time for sympathy.' She stopped, came back and picked up a file from the bedside table. 'I'm going to my place tonight. I need some clean clothes.' Her expression softened and there was a hint of a smile. 'I'll expect you by nine.' She moved away again. 'Don't let me down, Alex.'

Mavros watched her go, then sat down on the bed. Niki was always setting him challenges. It was the way she exerted control and he didn't like it. Maybe he'd stay away from her flat by the sea in Palaio Faliro tonight for all the hassle that would bring. It was about time he made a stand.

He felt his eyes closing. This had been happening to him a lot in the last couple of months. Ever since he'd come back from a gut-wrenching case in the islands, he'd been waking up in the small hours and unable to get back to sleep. Then, as soon as Niki left for work, he would sink into vivid dreams; dreams from which his long-lost brother Andonis with his piercing blue eyes and sad smile was rarely absent. Recently he had been plagued by scenes of his early childhood – the park, streets around their home, the beach – when he had clung to his older brother's hand for all he was worth.

Mavros struggled but soon succumbed to the pull of the other world.

The Fat Man was not happy.

'Can you believe this, Alex?' he grumbled, flicking a cloth ineffectually at the crumbs on his sole customer's table. 'The old woman's insisting that I take her back to the village for Christmas. In the name of Marx, I don't want to have my balls frozen off on that accursed mountain.'

Mavros gave him a tight smile. 'What will your regulars do without you?'

'Screw you.' The café-owner glared at him and shifted his bulk closer. 'Anyway, what's your problem? If it wasn't so cold, I'd guess a mosquito had got right up your arse last night.'

Mavros looked around the dingy establishment, the paint blotched with mildew in the corners and the dusty windows streaked with condensation. For most of the year he sat in the small courtyard to the rear, but that was out of the question now. Not that it was much warmer inside. The only source of heat in the café was an ancient diesel *somba* that smelled worse than the average lorry even on its lowest setting, which was what his thrifty friend always used.

'Got anything to eat?' he asked, looking across to the chill cabinet.

'All right, don't tell me, then,' the Fat Man said bitterly. 'I've only known you since you were a snot-nosed brat, I've only served you coffee for decades. What do I care about your pathetic little troubles?'

'Christ, Yiorgo,' Mavros said, raising his eyes to the cracks in the ceiling. 'For a Communist you make a hell of a fuss about personal relationships.' He couldn't help smiling at the Fat Man. It was true: they'd known each other for as long as he could remember. Although Yiorgos Pandazo-poulos was nearly twenty years older, he'd been a loyal comrade of Mavros's father and had always had a soft spot for the boy. Even when Mavros had shown no interest in joining the Party and had worked for the Ministry of Justice – anathema to the Left – before setting himself up as a private investigator, the Fat Man had stayed close. That didn't mean he gave Mavros an easy time.

'So, have you?'

'Have I what?' the café-owner demanded.

'Have you got anything to eat, idiot?'

The Fat Man lumbered away behind the counter and reappeared with a small plate. 'My beloved mother decided to change the routine

24

this morning, not that she bothered to tell me. Instead of *galaktoboureko* she made a tray of *kataïfi*.' He put the plate down with a crash. 'You can imagine the trouble I had with the early-morning trade.'

Mavros leaned forward and examined the portion of honey-drenched shredded wheat. He didn't mind. All Kyra Fedhra's pastries were delectable, but her custard pie was famed throughout Monastiraki. He took a forkful and felt the pores on his face tingle as the sweetness kicked in.

'That's better,' he said, when he had finished and drunk a glass of water to clear his palate. 'You're going away for the holidays, then?'

The Fat Man raised an eyebrow. 'Still not going to tell me what's eating you, eh? Yes, the General Secretary has spoken and I have to close up for a week.' He shook his head. 'God knows what's got into her. Maybe she thinks this is her last chance to see the family hovel before she—'

'That'll do,' Mavros interjected. 'Your mother's got years ahead of her. Why do you have to bring that up, Fat Man? Some of us have just had breakfast.' He picked up his dark blue worry-beads from the metal tabletop and flicked them across the back of his hand.

'Oh, I get it,' Pandazopoulos said, nodding his bald head slowly. 'I get it. You've been thinking about Andonis, haven't you?'

Mavros looked up and then away, his shoulder-length black hair partially obscuring his face. 'And if I have?' he asked, his voice almost inaudible. 'What's wrong with that?'

The Fat Man leaned over the table, his heavy body blocking out what little light was being admitted by the windows. 'Nothing's wrong with that,' he replied quietly. 'I knew Andonis too, Alex. I knew him better than you. And I know he wouldn't have wanted you to be plagued by his memory after ... how many years is it now? Thirty?'

Mavros met his eyes. 'Thirty next year. He disappeared in 'seventy–two.'

'Of course he did,' Yiorgos said, suddenly distracted. 'Of course he did.' He twitched his head and came back to himself. 'You have to let him go, Alex. You have to move on.'

Mavros ran his fingers along an eyebrow, then stood up. 'That's what everyone says. My mother, my sister, Niki–'

'And how is the delightful Niki?' the Fat Man said, a wicked grin appearing on his thick lips. 'As even-tempered and unselfish as usual?'

'Lay off, Yiorgo,' Mavros said. 'Niki has her own problems.'

'Yes, she has, Alex. And you're the biggest of them.' The café-owner grabbed his arm. 'Get rid of her before she does you some serious damage.'

Mavros shook himself free. The Fat Man had only met Niki once – she'd appeared at the café one morning in a flaming temper because Mavros, entangled in a tricky blackmail case, had failed to show the night before. She had given Yiorgos several original ideas about what to do with his customer and his pastries.

'Go to the good, my friend,' Mavros said, as he headed for the door, unwilling to discuss the tribulations of his love life any further.

'Hey, wait a minute,' the Fat Man called. 'I almost forgot to tell you.'

Mavros turned, a nervous look on his face. 'You almost forgot to tell me what?' It wouldn't have been the first time that Yiorgos had omitted to mention something significant to do with Mavros's professional activities. He didn't like potential clients coming to his home so he told them they could find him in the café. Sometimes his contacts sent them to the Fat Man's direct. 'You haven't antagonised a juicy capitalist by any chance, have you?'

The Fat Man was grinning again, a lascivious look on his slack features. 'Certainly not, Alex. Though I think she was American.' His eyebrows moved like a pair of lively caterpillars. 'And she wanted you, only you.'

'Jesus, Yiorgo, what age are you? Who was she?'

The café-owner shrugged. 'I don't know. She wouldn't leave a name.' He licked his lips in an exaggerated fashion. 'What I can tell you is that she was a real knockout. Tall, blonde and perfectly arranged. Lovely smile too, and...' He paused for the *coup de grâce*. '...and there was no trace of a temper whatsoever.'

Mavros gave the Fat Man the *moundza* with both hands, his palms open in the traditional gesture that consigned the recipient to hell. 'So what happened to her?' he asked.

Pandazopoulos extended his chin. 'Don't ask me. You know how much English I have. I think she said she'd be back later.'

'A blonde American?' Mavros said to himself,

as he moved off. He looked over his shoulder. 'Give her my number if she shows up again, will you?'

'Oh, yes, you can be sure I'll do that,' the Fat Man said, nodding avidly. ''Bye, Alex.'

Mavros raised a hand and went out into the cold.

The woman had been standing by the french windows for a long time, taking in the hull-like form of the Acropolis as it crested the waves of office and apartment blocks. The Parthenon was sublime – she'd gone up to it after she made the unsuccessful visit to the café Tou Chondrou – but she preferred the smaller Erechtheion at the side. It was a confusing complex of cellars and vaults but the Caryatids were what made it for her, even though they were replicas. Six women supporting the weight of the roof instead of columns. She had been captivated by the slender but powerful forms, left legs slightly bent at the knee to give an impression of paradoxical repose, their bodies outlined under the folds of their tunics. Strong women in this city of macho men – she'd provoked stares and whistles from the moment she walked out of the hotel, but there was nothing new about that.

She stepped back from the glass and looked around the spacious suite. The hotel had been a mistake. She'd booked herself in because she wanted a central location with an international name, but this place was a monstrosity – a pair of wide panels at a slight angle to each other, taller than the unexpectedly low buildings of the city

28

and as unsightly as a free-standing wall in the middle of a park. It was about to close for refurbishment in advance of the 2004 Olympics and it had the run-down air of a beach resort at the end of the season. That wasn't all that was wrong with it. As soon as she'd got in from the airport the previous day, she'd gone for a stroll around the neighbouring streets. It hadn't taken her long to realise that she was in the middle of the embassy district. The American compound, guarded even more obviously than usual in the aftermath of the terrorist attacks of 11 September, was further up the avenue that ran past the hotel. The embassy had brought everything back to her like a hammer blow to the heart.

It wasn't as if she hadn't known what to expect. Her father's death was why she had finally returned to Greece after twenty-five years. But being here, walking past the buildings where Trent and Laura would have been frequent visitors for receptions and dinners, had made the sweat pour off her despite the clear, chill skies. And tomorrow was the anniversary of his death. Oh, God, she thought. What was she doing?

She had to get out of the soulless room. Glancing out of the window again, she reckoned she had a couple of hours of daylight left. A run would bring her back to herself before she tried to find the private investigator Alex Mavros at the café again. She hoped he had more going for him than the fat guy's dump but she wasn't too optimistic, despite the pitch she'd been given by the police commander the embassy had put her on to. Pulling on a sweatshirt, she caught sight of herself in the full-length mirror. Long legs that looked okay even in the loose jogging pants, tanned face with the cheekbones emphasised by the ponytail she'd made of her blonde hair. Yeah, Grace, she thought. You'll do.

Outside, the cars and taxis roared down the wide avenue in a blur; they only stopped reluctantly when the lights changed, the front vehicles blocking the pedestrian crossing. Grace Helmer gave the drivers a resigned smile as she strode over, her legs moving effortlessly on to the uneven paving stones. She had soon ascended the steepening street that led up the flank of Lykavittos, the largest hill in the centre of the city. Skirting pensioners with small dogs and noisy teenagers, she took off up the concrete pathway that led away from the highest point. She could see people around a small church and in a bar up there, and she wanted to find a more secluded place to do her exercises. As she loped along, she wondered if her parents had ever been up here. She felt sure they had, and that brought a sudden tightness to her chest.

The ground sloped away to the north beyond a theatre that had been erected against the hillside and she found herself alone. The light was fading and the sound of animated voices was suddenly fainter than the underlying rumble of the traffic from below. Now the path ran through trees, the scent of conifers strong. Traversing the ridge, she slowed her pace and stopped beside a dense thicket. She guessed she was on the north-west side, looking towards a high, snow-capped mountain. Her breath was still coming easily.

But someone else's wasn't. Turning quickly, Grace saw the dog and smiled in relief. It was a skinny mongrel, its dark hair scratched away in parts and its eyes wary.

'Come on, boy,' she said, registering its sex. 'I won't hurt you.' She knelt down on one knee and clapped her hands lightly. The dog approached slowly, his head moving ceaselessly from side to side as if at any second he expected an attack. 'There you are,' Grace said, smoothing her hand carefully over the pitted skin on the creature's head. 'Poor thing. Nobody's been looking after you, have they?'

Then the dog jerked his head round and let out a low growl. Before Grace could move, he hurtled away into the darkening undergrowth. She stood up quickly, her senses alert. She saw the man before he came out into the open.

He was tall and wiry, quite young, his face partially hidden by a thick black beard. He came towards her and stopped, seemingly aware of her alarm. 'German?' he asked, a loose smile on his lips. They were scabby, as were the hands that protruded from an ill-fitting and filthy denim jacket. 'You German?'

She rolled forward on to the balls of her feet and shook her head.

'Sveedish?' he asked, drawing out the first vowel. 'Here,' he said, stepping forward suddenly. 'I got something for you.' He held out a hand and laughed.

Grace took in the unwrapped pink condom that lay on the cracked skin. She was pretty sure

31

it had been used. 'No, thank you,' she said evenly. 'I have to go now.' But she didn't move her legs.

'No, no,' the man said, now less than a metre from her. He let out a harsher laugh. 'We fuck now. We fuck, yes?'

Grace had been weighing up what to do. Her training and experience had told her from the outset that the guy wasn't going to take no for an answer, but she was holding back. There had been an incident in Zaïre when she hurt a local who turned out to be a harmless simpleton. But it wasn't just that. Since she had turned thirty earlier in the year, she'd become more critical of herself, more inclined to give the other person a chance.

'We fuck, no,' she said, leaning forward at an angle to take the weight off one leg. 'Goodbye.' When she saw the man's eyes narrow, she knew her instincts hadn't betrayed her. They never did. Before he could raise a hand, she brought her right elbow up swiftly into his jaw then, as he dropped, she drove her knee hard against his chin.

She was away through the trees in a few seconds, the points where she had made contact with her assailant numb but moving freely.

So much for giving the other person a chance, she thought, as she ran. It seemed she'd learned nothing from the dispossessed people she'd encountered all over the world. She was still as much of a hard-nosed bitch as she'd ever been; it was just that she'd got better at hiding it beneath a caring exterior. Christ, she should never have got on the plane to the country she'd been avoiding for so long. Even if she found what she was looking for there could be nothing but bitterness and pain for her in Greece. But, like the gun-slingers in the movies, there were things you couldn't say no to, there were things you had to do.

She headed back to her single room, wishing someone was waiting for her there.

Mavros decided to go the long way round to his mother's. She had asked him to come to lunch and, although he'd seen her only a couple of days before, he wasn't playing hard to get. It wasn't as if he had any urgent business to detain him. Besides, he'd been wanting for years to meet the special guest she'd invited.

He slid between two ramshackle lorries stuffed with cartons of merchandise on Ermou and headed up Athinas. The pavements were filled with traders' goods, chainsaws and crates of padlocks sharing space with garish novelty toys and kitchen gadgets. The traffic noise was interspersed with the salesmen's raucous cries, their slick lines provoking laughter from the passers-by.

'Our prices are the best,' yelled one vendor. 'We sell for free.'

'We sell for free,' countered another, '*and* we throw in a pension.'

Unable to resist smiling, Mavros turned into the recently renovated Varvakeio, the hall containing the central market named after a sea captain who'd made good in the nineteenth century. He often came in here when his spirits needed a lift. The butchers in their bloody tunics diverted him, as did the fishmongers tossing prawns and whitebait into cones of paper. He wasn't the only one to fall under their spell. There was always a crush of price-conscious Athenians exchanging quips with the traders even though the place was the front room of a slaughterhouse, its walls hung with skinned animals, their innards heaped on open tables. But the market was a typical Greek paradox: it was full of life.

Cutting through the back, past restaurants with the most gruesome views in the city, Mavros found himself on Sofokleous. He walked towards the main avenue of Stadhiou on the opposite side of the road from the Stock Exchange. The grimy façade was even more forbidding than usual because of the presence of numerous policemen in Kevlar tunics carrying snub-nosed machine pistols. Security around business centres had been increased since the murder of a prominent investor at the beginning of December. The Greek government, already suffering the global economic effects of the terrorist attacks on New York and Washington, was now close to full-scale panic. Like everyone else, Mavros had been transfixed by the catastrophe at the time but more recently he'd begun to lose interest, even though it was the biggest law-and-order issue since he'd been an investigator. He'd been finding it hard to care about his profession. The high-profile case he'd been involved in on the island of Trigono in the early autumn had knocked him off-course and he'd only taken a

34

few bread-and-butter jobs since then. He'd even been struggling to keep on his brother Andonis's faint trail. What had once been an obsession that took up much of his free time was now becoming a nagging family duty. After years of failure on that case, Mavros was beginning to lose heart and the regular flashes of Andonis's smiling face were getting even harder to live with.

'Shift your arse.' The roughness of the voice was only slightly muffled by the black motorcycle helmet.

Mavros turned to see a guy in leathers trying to mount the pavement with his machine. Bikers, the bane of his life. And this one was as bad as it got – a courier. No doubt he was carrying urgent documents to some slob of a speculator in the Stock Exchange.

'Shift my what?' Mavros said, squaring up to the rider. Given that there was a team of policemen a few metres away, he wasn't taking too much of a risk.

The courier looked round and bowed his head. 'Go to the devil, wanker,' he muttered, as he busied himself with his pannier.

'Want to take that kiddie's protector off and look me in the eye?' Mavros asked. 'Wanker.' He repeated the term of abuse with more volume than the biker had given it, knowing that his ironic reference to the helmet that the country's hot-headed motorcyclists hugely resented would have stung him.

'Another time,' the courier said, moving across the street, 'I'll eat you alive.'

Mavros would have considered doing something

to the tyres if the policemen opposite hadn't been scrutinising him. It wouldn't have been the first time he'd taken revenge on the scumbags who rode like maniacs and parked as if they owned the pavements. He headed on, his mood suddenly lighter. There was nothing like a bit of brainless repartee to kick-start the day.

The feeling didn't last. He knew he needed to get a grip on himself. His apartment on the slopes of the Acropolis wasn't cheap and he was running short of cash, but he wasn't sure that he could face taking on a high-intensity, high-reward case yet. It was sometimes like that: his work depressed him till he came across a client who piqued his curiosity. That hadn't happened for some time now. Passing the neo-classical portico of the university with the incongruous statue of William Gladstone, representative of the Great Powers who'd controlled the country's destiny in the past, he turned right on to Solonos. There were numerous bookshops in the area but he resisted the temptation to browse. He could lose himself for hours and that would not impress his mother, even though she still ran her own successful publishing house. He considered asking her for money – she'd offered to help him often enough when he'd started his business ten years back – but he dismissed the thought immediately. He was too old for hand-outs from parents.

Climbing the lower slopes of Mount Lykavittos, Mavros felt the chill in the December air increase. As he turned on to his mother's street, the sea's bright blue caught his eye. He looked back between the apartment buildings towards the blurred flanks of the nearest islands, then shivered and walked on. A familiar figure was getting out of a Mercedes.

'*Ela*, Alex. *Ti kaneis?*'

'Hello, Anna.' Mavros leaned forward to kiss his sister's cheek. Although as kids they'd always spoken English at home in Athens on the insistence of their Scottish mother, Anna had got used to speaking Greek with her Cretan husband and their teenagers. 'You've been summoned too?'

'Mmm.' Anna slammed the car door and straightened her pale green designer skirt. 'Here, hold this for a second.' She handed her brother a bag bearing the logo of a well-known music store and took a small mirror from her purse.

'You haven't turned into a groupie, have you?'

Anna stared at him as she put away her lipstick. 'What? Oh, very funny. These are for the kids. They want the CDs autographed.'

Mavros laughed. 'Yeah, yeah, that's what they all say.' He took out his key and ushered her into the building.

'Well, it's true,' his sister said, over her shoulder. 'Though I must say I do like some of the lyrics.'

'Bit left-wing for you, aren't they?' he said, pressing the lift button.

Anna's expression darkened. 'Do you mind? I haven't completely forgotten that our father was a Communist.'

'Even if your husband supports the forces of conservatism?' Mavros smiled. His brother-in-law, Nondas Chaniotakis, was a bubble-gum-chewing

37

Cretan stockbroker who inevitably had links to the party of big business.

Anna jabbed her elbow into his side and took the bag from him. 'Lay off, Alex. I'm not rising to it.' She stepped out of the lift briskly when it reached the sixth floor.

Mavros watched her walk purposefully down the marble corridor, heels clicking and jet-black hair swaying from its clasp. She was forty-four, five years older than he was, but there was still no sign of grey. Obviously, working as a columnist for several high-circulation glossy magazines arrested the ageing process. Unlike pounding the streets as a private eye.

'Ah, there you both are.' Dorothy Cochrane-Mavrou came to the door as soon as the key was turned. 'I was beginning to wonder what–'

'We're early, Mother,' Anna said crisply. 'How are you?' She kissed her and moved into the main room without waiting for an answer.

'Alex.' His mother put her hands on his shoulders and ran her eyes over him. 'You look tired. Have you been eating properly?'

Mavros bent into the embrace, his nostrils filled with the scent of the talc and the understated perfume he'd known since he was a boy. 'I'm fine,' he said, stepping back and returning her gaze. 'Never mind me. You look radiant.' And she did. Although she was in her mid-seventies and her naturally wavy hair was pure white, Dorothy seemed to gain more vitality as she aged. Maybe that's the way it was, Mavros thought. On the female side of the family, at least – they go on for ever, while the men fall by the wayside.

'He's here,' his mother said, in a stage whisper.

'Right.' Mavros took her arm and steered her into the large *saloni* with the view to the Acropolis.

The figure at the glass balcony door turned slowly from Anna as they approached. He was dressed in an old grey corduroy suit, a red cravat round his neck. Mavros knew his profile from photographs, but in the flesh he was even more striking. The full mouth and perfectly straight nose were surmounted by unusually large eyes, the brows thick and dark, as was the hair. Like Anna's it was untouched by grey, though the man must have been almost eighty. Mavros wondered if he dyed it, but dismissed the thought as unworthy.

Anna had evidently introduced herself already. 'Mr Laskaris,' she said in Greek, her tone formal, 'this is my brother Alex.'

'Please,' the old man said, 'my name is Kostas.' He extended a hand that wavered slightly. The grip was weak and the skin clammy. Although the famous poet was standing straight his troubled expression suggested he had been acquainted with pain, mental or physical, for many years.

'How do you do?' Mavros said.

'I do as well as I can,' the old man said, with a restrained smile. 'So you're the investigator.' He ran his eye over Mavros's leather jacket and faded jeans. 'You look more like a revolutionary student with that outfit and all that hair.'

Mavros smiled back at him, remembering the reputation the poet had for forthright speaking. 'Revolutionary, no. I missed that gene. Student?

39

Well, I suppose in my business it pays to be a student of human nature.' He was expecting to be given a hard time by the former leading Communist for his choice of what many saw as a profession that gave support to the establishment, but Laskaris only nodded, his expression sombre.

'No doubt you follow your father and brother in your own way, young man.' He glanced over at the black-and-white photographs of Spyros and Andonis Mavros in the plain wooden frames that sat on one of Dorothy's many bookcases. Spyros had died in 1967, worn out before his time. 'You have your father's eyes,' the old man said, looking back at Mavros. 'Except...' He turned towards Dorothy, then nodded again. 'Ah, I see.' He gave a wider smile. 'How interesting. A poet less decrepit than I am could make much of the symbolism.'

There was a pause as the others considered that observation. Alex Mavros certainly had his male relatives' blue eyes, though they were not as brightly coloured as Spyros's or Andonis's. But he also had flecks of Dorothy's brown in the left iris, a flaw that threw some people and attracted others. Trust a poet to see it in metaphorical terms.

'Would you sign these recordings for my children?' Anna asked, fumbling in the bag and shooting Mavros a warning glance. 'They love the songs so much.'

'Ah, my dear Anna,' said Laskaris wistfully, 'how I wish I shared their enthusiasm for the music. But in truth this is hack work, no matter how many people it reaches.' He took one of the CDs. 'Really, my friend Randos should concen-

40

trate on composing symphonies. Here all he has done is steal the rhythms of folk tradition and the *rembetika.*'

Mavros inclined his head and took in the photograph on the cover of the wild-haired musician notorious for his left-wing views and, in the past, his associations with female singers of the bouzouki-driven music that had originated in the 1920s criminal underworld. 'Surely you don't dislike "The Voyage of the *Argo*",' Mavros said. 'That's a beautiful song.' He smiled. 'And not only because of your lyric.'

Kostas Laskaris shrugged. 'It's a pretty tune. The verses mean more than the musical composition suggests.'

Anna handed a pen to the old man and watched as he inscribed his name in a flowing script on the inner sleeves of the CDs. 'I loved that song when I was young,' she said. 'You must be so proud of it.'

The poet finished signing and looked up at her. 'What I feel about it doesn't matter, Anna,' he said apologetically. 'After the verses are written, they take on their own life. The meaning is what you, the listener or the reader, bring to them.'

Dorothy stepped forward and took the old man's arm. 'Come, Kosta,' she said. 'It's time to eat.' She led him to the dining-room.

The meal passed pleasantly enough. Dorothy had gone to the trouble of cooking several Greek specialities for her guest. Laskaris expressed delight at the vine-leaves stuffed with rice and dill, and the *psari plaki*, fish baked with tomatoes and onions, but it was noticeable that he didn't

41

eat much of any dish. Mavros had the impression that his mood had been affected by his question about the song that had inspired a generation of student activists in the sixties. Although, like Mavros's father, Laskaris had been a resistance fighter during the Axis occupation in the forties and a Communist official from the fifties after the Party had been driven underground, Mavros had the feeling that a rift had developed latterly between his father and the poet. Still, his mother was being friendly to him so things obviously hadn't come to a head. Dorothy started trying to talk Laskaris into agreeing to an English trans-ation of his selected works, one that her company would be happy to arrange. Mavros swallowed a laugh. His mother's business acumen, dormant for decades when she was married to a committed Marxist, never failed to impress him. It would be quite a coup if she succeeded. Kostas Laskaris might have spent part of his career writing popular song lyrics, but his more serious poetry had a European reputation and he had even been talked of as a Nobel candidate.

Laskaris stalled Dorothy effectively and looked across the table at Mavros. 'So, Alex,' he said seriously, 'you work for the forces of law and order.'

Mavros had thought earlier that he'd got away with it, but he should have known better. People on the Left never forgot the repressive police regimes that most governments had applied in Greece during the twentieth century. He opened his mouth to mount a half-hearted defence, but stopped when he saw the poet raise his hand.

42

'It's all right. Your mother told me that you look for missing people. Good for you. It's hardly the same as beating up students on peaceful demonstrations, is it? God knows, the authorities need all the help they can get.' He gave a smile of encouragement. 'What do you think about the shooting of that businessman earlier in the month? Can it really be that Iraklis is back after all this time?'

Mavros lowered his head, wishing he'd read the papers more carefully. Now he was going to look like a fool in front of his mother and sister, never mind one of the country's leading writers.

Fortunately Anna saved his skin. 'Iraklis?' she said scathingly. 'Anyone can pretend to be Iraklis. All they need to do is murder someone and drop a piece of carved olivewood on the body. There's been no sign of those terrorist lunatics for at least ten years and there was no proclamation claiming responsibility like there always used to be. No, the talk in the media is that the super-rich investor Vernardhakis was killed because he got in the way of the Russian Mafia bosses who are setting up in the country.' She put down the knife she'd been using to peel an apple. 'Nondas – my husband' she clarified to Laskaris '–Nondas told me he had some very dubious friends.'

'He certainly does,' Mavros put in.

Anna gave him a pained look. 'Vernardhakis, you idiot, not Nondas.'

The poet smiled at the domestic scene, then froze, his face white.

'Are you all right, Kosta?' Dorothy said anxiously, getting to her feet and moving round to the old man's side. 'Some water, Anna.'

Mavros was there first, the carafe in his hand. He watched as Laskaris drank deeply, his free hand gripping the table edge so tightly that the veins stood up like the lines of earth raised by a plough. Then the colour gradually came back into his face and he released his hold on the wooden surface.

'Ah,' he said. 'Excuse me. Sometimes I ... sometimes I have a pain.'

'Have you seen a doctor?' Anna asked. 'I know some very good ones.'

'And so do I, my dear,' the old man said, smiling weakly. 'And so do I.'

Soon afterwards the lunch party broke up.

The poet Kostas Laskaris, face gaunt and hands clenched, was lying on the bed in his hotel room above Syndagma Square. Until a few minutes ago, he'd been looking at the illuminated yellow walls of the former royal palace that now housed the Greek parliament, watching the soldiers in their ridiculous kilts and nailed boots adorned with pompoms mount guard in front of the memorial to the unknown soldier. Then the pain had knifed into his belly again and he'd been forced to lie flat. It had been coming more and more frequently in recent months. He'd consulted specialists. The results of the tests that morning hadn't surprised him; neither had they frightened him. He had gone to lunch as arranged with Spyros Mavros's widow after the hospital appointment, and he was sure no one there would have guessed the weight he was carrying if the cursed cancer hadn't decided to exert itself at the table. At least he'd managed to control it and make a respectable exit.

But he shouldn't have gone. It was bad enough being away from his beloved tower in the Mani at the country's southernmost extremity, it was bad enough looking down at the memorial – how many fighters had he known whose names were now forgotten? A hundred? Five hundred? The memory of his old comrades had been oppressing him recently. Was that why he had telephoned Spyros's widow after all the years that had passed? If he'd thought seeing his old friend's family would make him feel better, he'd been badly mistaken. Dorothy was as understanding as ever, despite her unwanted attempts to get hold of his poetry rights. But the children, Anna and that long-haired son with the blemish in his eye, they had brought back the guilt to him with the force of a glacier that had started to move after centuries of immobility. Anna and Alex. At least they were still alive, at least they had gained some pleasure from his writing, even if the full import of 'The Voyage of the *Argo*' was beyond them. They were the lucky ones. What about their brother Andonis?

Laskaris clenched his hands as another wrench of pain seized him. What about Andonis Mavros? And what about the murdered businessman Vernardhakis? The killings were starting again, the wheel of violence was turning like it had when he was young, crushing the country's children beneath its unrelenting edge. It shouldn't be happening. The struggle was over, the world had

45

moved on.

The old poet felt himself slip into another dimension, an underground realm where shadowy figures ran screaming before a monstrous form wearing a lion skin and wielding a huge club hewn from an olive tree. Then he recognised the face. It was one he had known from childhood.

It was Iraklis.

2

Mavros spent the early evening at a central cinema. The American cop movie was cliché-ridden and turgid, its constant action sequences a pain to eye and ear – his own fault for not bothering to read the reviews. Coming out with the depressingly enthusiastic crowd, many of whom seemed to be Albanian and Russian immigrants, he turned on his mobile phone to check for messages. There weren't any. It was eight thirty. If he jumped into a taxi he could make it to Niki's flat by nine. He stood at the edge of the bustling street for a few moments, then made up his mind. To hell with it. He'd take a chance on her temper. He switched off his phone and strode towards Omonia Square, ducking his head into the icy wind that was blasting up the wide avenue.

The shops and stalls in the city's main commercial area were bedecked with Christmas decorations, carols thundering out from speakers that had been stationed on the pavements. Even the *periptera*, the ubiquitous kiosks where Athenians bought newspapers, cigarettes and everything else they needed to sustain their daily lives, were strung with flashing lights and plastic holly. It was all a huge con, Mavros thought sourly. He remembered the decorations and lights in Edinburgh when he was a student. They were gross enough, but at least the seasonal celebrations had some claim to be traditional there. In Greece, New Year had been celebrated more than Christmas – until businessmen and shopkeepers realised what they were missing.

'*Kleftes kai malakes*,' Mavros mumbled – thieves and wankers. He reached the wide circular expanse that acted as a hub for several of the city's main streets. Vehicles were careering round as relentlessly as ever, the whistles of the traffic police in their tall white hats almost drowned by the crash of gears and the gratuitous sounding of horns. The central part of Omonia was obscured by building equipment; the underground railway was being upgraded in advance of the Olympic Games, reducing this and many other inter-sections in Athens to permanent construction sites.

There was a group of people arguing at the top of their voices next to a *periptero* that sold soft-core porn magazines openly and triple-X material if you winked at the trader. Mavros listened for a while, then moved on when he realised they were discussing the financial probity of a well-known tycoon who owned a major football club. He wasn't interested in the debate. You didn't have to be a Communist to know that people who bought football teams were ruthlessly on the make. The shouting was interspersed with virulent abuse. Mavros smiled. So much for Omonia, he thought – the square had been named in honour of 'concord', which presumably included harmony and reasoned agreement.

The shiny magazine covers with their empty-eyed, pneumatic blondes had given him an idea of what to do next. It didn't involve his genitalia. His professional pride had been stung when the old poet had asked him about the killing of the investor Vernardhakis. He intended to rectify that by picking the brains of the country's leading crime reporter. Lambis Bitsos had a weakness for three things: pornography, alcohol and food. Unless he was working a hot story, he'd have completed his round of the wank-mag suppliers by now and would be refuelling in his favourite ouzo-house.

Mavros pushed through the crowds of shoppers who were heading for the underground station weighed down by plastic bags. The rent-boys and hookers leaning against the walls regarded them with blatant disdain, resentful that wages were being spent on family and friends rather than the pleasures of the flesh. The odour of burnt meat from the *souvlaki*-joints was permeating the wind-blown side-streets, cut by exhaust fumes and the railway's unmistakable blend of sweat, sewage and electrical equipment worked to the limit. He opened the door of To Kazani, the Cauldron, with relief, letting the wave of warm, smoky air dash over him. He hadn't touched a cigarette for over a year, but other people's smoke was more acceptable than the poison gases that made up the *nefos*, the Athens pollution cloud.

'Lambis Bitsos?' Mavros said sternly. 'You're under arrest.'

The reporter's head shot up from the plate of *imam bayildi* he was devouring. In his shock, he dropped a piece of bread into the oil-drenched baked aubergines. 'Fuck it, Alex,' he said, with a

49

groan. 'You almost gave me a heart-attack.' He picked up the bread and stuffed it into his mouth.

'Got a guilty conscience, Lambi?' Mavros asked, as he sat down opposite the bald, middle-aged man. Bitsos was very thin, the skin on his face taut and sallow. If Mavros hadn't seen him eating so frequently and substantially, he'd have put him down as anorexic. 'What have you picked up tonight?' He stretched round and lifted a brown-paper bag from the seat at the side of the table. *'Asian Housewives Go to the Zoo?* Christ and the Holy Mother, you don't care, do you? What would your daughters think?'

The journalist was divorced, his three girls grown up. 'They'd probably show it to their boyfriends to spice up their sex-lives. The young of today...' Although Bitsos was a staff-writer on the country's most liberal daily, like most crime reporters he was a social conservative.

'Give it a rest, Lambi,' Mavros said, beckoning to a waiter. He ordered another carafe of ouzo and some courgette fritters. 'You're getting to be as bad as that idiot who runs the Justice Ministry.' He assumed a strait-laced tone. 'Strenuous action is needed if the traditional values of our society are not to be washed away in a torrent of filth and—'

'Very funny,' Bitsos interrupted. 'And how many kids have you got?'

Mavros raised his hands in surrender. 'All right, my friend, calm down. What's chewing your balls?'

The journalist pushed away his plate and tipped ouzo into his glass. 'Nothing in particular, Alex.

You know how it is. Sometimes you get sick of being called out to crime scenes in the middle of the night. You can only see so many scab-covered junkie corpses in one week.' Bitsos narrowed his eyes. 'What are you after, anyway?'

Mavros poured a dash of water into his ouzo and raised his glass. 'Our health,' he said, waiting for the reporter to repeat the toast. 'What am I after? That's nice. We've known each other for years and your first thought is that I've come to pump you for information.'

'Well, you have, haven't you?' Bitsos said, with a weary smile. 'Where have you been recently, Alex? On another sensational case in the islands?'

Mavros ignored the jibe. 'Keeping my head down. In fact, that's why I wanted to see you, Lambi.'

The journalist gave a hollow laugh, then speared a *kolokytho-keftedhaki* with his fork. 'I knew it. I hope you've got something to trade.'

'Screw you,' Mavros said, his eyes catching the other's. 'I gave you an exclusive on the Trigono case. You owe me for years after that.'

Bitsos nodded slowly. 'I owe you, true enough. But not for years, my friend.'

'Don't worry.' Mavros raised the carafe and refilled the reporter's glass. 'I don't want anything too sensitive. Like I said, I've been out of circulation over the last few weeks. I just wanted the low-down on the Vernardhakis murder.'

Bitsos waved to the waiter and asked for a portion of grilled prawns. 'That's a pity,' he said, with his hallmark hollow laugh.

'What do you mean?'

51

'Because there isn't a low-down on the Vernardhakis murder.'

Mavros raised an eyebrow. 'Pithy but incomprehensible, Lambi. Explain.'

The reporter took another sip of ouzo and let out a long sigh. Then he began to speak, his voice low and monotonous.

4 December 2001

Take them when they least expect it. Take them when their guard is down. That had been the experts' refrain at the training camp and the hit man had never forgotten it.

Sitting in the unit fore-cabin of the yacht in the small harbour of Tourkolimano on the eastern side of Piraeus, he kept his eyes on the restaurant across the asphalt. For most of the year tables were laid on the quayside, even during winter at lunchtime, but in the evening people had to dine inside. That suited Vernardhakis – it meant that he was safe from prying eyes and gave his bodyguard an easy job. The investor had taken over the Poseidon's Trident for the celebration of his latest financial coup. There was a line of Mercedes and BMWs down the curved coastal road, as well as a police car to reassure the VIPs that the forces of law and order were watching over them, a pair of bored cops periodically winding down their windows and dropping their cigarette butts on to the ground. It was far too cold to patrol on foot.

The countdown was well advanced. The man in the yacht had been there since early morning. He had checked out of the Athens Ledra Marriott at three a.m., having ordered a taxi for the airport. He changed the destination as they approached the columns of the old temple at the top of the avenue, giving the driver ten thousand drachmas to keep him sweet. Getting out at Omonia Square downtown, he had taken another cab, criss-crossing the city centre until he was sure there was no tail on him. Then he had changed again, directing the last taxi to the ferry-port of Piraeus, and walked through the back-streets to the picturesque harbour on the eastern edge of the peninsula where the rich men kept their toys. It was still dark when he slipped on to the yacht and fitted the key he'd been given into the lock on the main hatch, his hands sheathed in thin leather gloves. He entered the numerical code to disable the alarm system and settled down to wait.

In the old days he hadn't been troubled by nerves. Even in the beginning when he wasn't much more than a soft-faced kid he had always slept well before operations. And even during the act itself, the dispatch of the targets, he had been able to remain in control, his heartbeat regular and his senses unblurred. Nothing had changed with the passage of time. He had learned so well when he was young and he had kept himself in good condition.

The sounds from the maintenance workers on the neighbouring boats had died away in the afternoon, and as darkness fell again, the cold began to bite. He was unaffected by it, the thermal vest and leggings he wore under his blazer and slacks enabling him to avoid starting up the yacht's generator. Long experience meant that he didn't need much to keep himself together. He took only occasional sips of water from a bottle in his coat pocket and chewed carefully separated squares of chocolate to stop his stomach rumbling. He didn't intend to leave any trace of his presence, not a solitary crumb. That was what he'd been taught and that was the system he'd always followed. It had served him well.

Around nine o'clock the cars began to pull up, men in expensive suits and women in evening dresses getting out and entering the restaurant with distant nods to the white-shirted waiters. He watched through a pair of compact Zeiss binoculars, paying more attention to the security personnel than to the guests. As he'd expected, most of the businessmen, despite their wealth, employed drivers who doubled as bodyguards. None of the muscle-bound individuals gave him any cause for concern.

The host Vernardhakis arrived last, displaying the lack of respect for conventional modes of behaviour that was typical of him. The killer had put a cross next to that characteristic in the target's file the first time he read it. Greece's most successful investor of 2000 was the son of a tobacco farmer from the province of Macedonia rather than the scion of a wealthy family like most of his competitors. After school he had done five years' service in the élite Marines, leaving under a cloud when it was discovered that he had been running a gambling syndicate with funds obtained by threats from fellow squad members. In under a decade he had made a fortune on the newly deregulated Stock Exchange, treating leading businessmen like shop assistants, and regularly giving bankers and politicians the edge of his uncontrolled tongue in the newspaper he part-owned. He was openly gay and had provided the Athens gossip columnists with a succession of field days involving acne-pitted schoolboys and unrepentant sailors. There was no shortage of people who would be overjoyed when Vernardhakis got what was coming to him.

It was 21.36 – under five hours to go – when the investor's vintage bottle-green Bentley pulled up, the bodyguard hitting the pavement and checking out the vicinity with a practised eye before the wheels had stopped rolling. Then the rear door on the restaurant side opened and Vernardhakis stood up. In magnification the man on the yacht clearly saw the investor's green and yellow zigzag shirt – no sober suit for him – and his straggly dyed hair. The target turned to his muscleman for a moment, his fleshy, unshaven cheek and badly broken nose filling the lens in profile. It was said that Vernardhakis had successfully taken on the Marines' most vicious sergeant, and had left his nose unset after the fight as a statement of intent.

By two o'clock most of the guests had left. It was a Tuesday night and they wanted at least some sleep before making more money in the morning. The watcher knew that Vernardhakis wouldn't be on his way yet – he was famous for hitting the bottle till very late, then going straight to his office. But there was always the chance that a target might behave unpredictably, especially one like Vernardhakis.

It was time. The hit man took a deep breath, then picked up the mobile phone he had bought from a shifty street trader in the Flea Market the day before and pressed out the investor's private number. It was one that had been given only to a small circle of confidants, but it was always possible to find such information if you had the right contacts – and his people had all the contacts.

'Speak to me,' came Vernardhakis's rough tones. 'Fast.'

'I'll say this only once,' the man on the yacht replied quietly, in unaccented Greek, his voice deliberately unhurried. 'I work for Fyodor.'

There was a brief pause.

'He gave you my private number, I suppose,' the investor replied, suddenly compliant. 'I'm listening.'

'The Kangouro Burano deal is in jeopardy.'

'What? What's gone wrong?'

Through the binoculars the killer saw that Vernardhakis was on his feet in the restaurant, his head flung back in a dramatic pose. 'We think we can control it,' he said, 'but I need to go through the details with you immediately. In person and alone.'

The investor was nodding avidly. 'Yes, yes, of course. Where?'

'I know exactly where you are. Walk across the road to the quayside. You'll see a boat called the *Axione*. Come on board. And tell that gorilla of yours to keep his distance. I can't afford to be seen by anybody else. You know how much this business is worth to all of us.'

'No problem. Stand by.'

The hit man closed the connection and put the phone in his pocket. Soon it would be on its way to the bottom of Faliro Bay. Stand by. The idiot fancied himself as some kind of undercover agent. And he was coming like a dog after a bitch on heat. There had never been any doubt that greed was his weak point, as the file had pointed out frequently. The background to the hit had been researched immaculately. Mentioning the Russian gangster and the latest deal he was working on had been the boss's masterstroke.

He went to the hatch and slid it open, then re-armed the alarm system. Outside, after closing the padlock, he loosened the line on the Zodiac inflatable with the powerful outboard engine that was bobbing at the stern of the yacht. Everything was prepared for his exit. Now all he had to do was carry out the hit. He breathed in and let a loose smile spread across his lips.

Vernardhakis's figure appeared at the restaurant door. He put his hand on his bodyguard's chest. For a few seconds it looked like the heavily built man was going to make trouble, then he stepped back without argument, obviously used to following orders no matter how foolish they seemed. Vernardhakis came out and crossed the street with his arms round his chest. The fool hadn't brought a jacket and his patterned shirt was doing nothing to keep out the cold. When he reached the bow of the yacht he bent down to check the name, then clambered on, his patent leather shoes giving limited purchase on the fibreglass hull.

'Are you there?' came a loud whisper. 'Fyodor's man?'

'Back here. Keep quiet.'

The investor came towards the stern, his hands grasping the shrouds. 'What's going on?' he demanded, ignoring the instruction. 'Who the fuck are you, exactly?'

The killer waited until his target had stepped down into the seating area behind the wheel. His heart was beating no more rapidly than normal and his breathing was regular. 'Who the fuck am I?' he said, raising the silenced Glock. 'I'm Iraklis.' He squeezed the trigger.

A single bullet to the heart finished the investor, the spit of the shot and the almost contemporaneous slap of its impact no more audible than the traffic noise from the dual carriageway to the north.

After delicately placing the piece of whittled olivewood he'd taken from his pocket on the victim's blood-soaked chest, the hit man freed the hawser, stepped on to the Zodiac and activated the electric starter. Keeping the engine revs down, he motored towards the gap between the arms of the harbour walls, the lights from the far side shining brightly in the moonless night. He glanced back as he reached the open water. Vernardhakis's bodyguard was inside the restaurant, concentrating on a newspaper, and there was no sign that anyone else had noticed his departure. Ahead, the smooth carpet of the bay beckoned him home.

The first labour of the new cycle had been completed.

Mavros was shaking his head, as much in despair at the execrable singing that was coming from the *ouzeri's* sound system as from his companion's words.

The reporter Bitsos had been right: there wasn't much of a low-down to pass on. After more than two weeks the police had turned up no productive leads. Although a couple of waiters, as well as the disgraced bodyguard, had seen Vernardhakis board the yacht, no one had noticed the inflatable until it neared the outer harbour wall, its occupant or occupants indistinguishable. The Piraeus businessman who owned the *Axione* had been hauled in for extended questioning, but the alibi his associates gave him and his repeated protestations of ignorance eventually convinced the investigating officials. As for the Zodiac, it had never been located among the hundreds of similar craft that filled the marinas on the coast of Attiki. There were no fingerprints on the yacht and no sign of the murder weapon, nor had anyone been seen boarding the yacht in the twenty-four hours leading up to the killing. The relevant telecommunications company identified the number that had been used to call Vernardhakis, but the fact that the handset in question had been stolen and never used subsequently meant that that was a dead end too.

'So has the group led by the mysterious Iraklis started operations again after all this time?' Mavros asked Lambis Bitsos. 'Their trademark miniature olive club was found on the body, but there was no–'

'Proclamation,' completed the journalist. 'That's right. In the past, there were always interminable letters sent to newspapers claiming responsibility and justifying the murders in extreme Marxist-Leninist terms.'

Mavros had cast his mind back to the terrorist unit's early assassinations. 'They used to execute their victims with a knife, didn't they?'

'In the beginning, yes. I think the idea was a symbolic slaughtering of the class enemy, like sheep. Remember the atrocities on both sides back in the forties? But they gave that up after the first three murders. Too messy. A pair of terrorists on a motorbike were almost caught near the old Fix brewery when drivers saw blood all over their clothes.'

'That's right,' Mavros said, dredging his memory. He'd been a schoolboy in Athens and then at university in Scotland when the Iraklis group had carried out most of their attacks. 'They started using handguns and explosives, didn't they?'

'Mmm.' Bitsos took a sip of ouzo. 'And before you ask, there was no ballistic data linking the murder weapon to any previous shooting. It was a nine-millimetre Glock with a hollow-point bullet. Vernardhakis's heart was turned to mush.' He snorted. 'At least the thieving bastard didn't feel anything.'

'Steady, Lambi,' Mavros said, surprised by the reporter's vehemence. 'No one deserves to die like that. Even if he was up to his neck with the

60

Russians who are muscling into every dirty trade they can.' He refilled their glasses. 'That's what the word is, isn't it?' he asked, remembering what his sister had said earlier. 'That Vernardhakis was taken out by them for business reasons.'

Bitsos chewed his lip. 'And they left the piece of Iraklis olivewood as a blind? Pretty imaginative for a bunch of drug-pushers and whoremongers.'

'So you think this was another red death?' Mavros asked. The Greek press had given that name to the left-wing terrorist assassinations back in the seventies.

'Red death, black death, purple fucking death,' Bitsos said with a grunt. 'I don't suppose Vernardhakis cared what colour it was.'

Mavros nodded, the curiosity stimulated by the old poet's question about the murder satisfied for the time being – at least he knew more than his sister did now. Not long afterwards he said goodnight to the reporter and walked out into the icy air. He could have thought of more uplifting subjects to discuss over a carafe of ouzo, but at least his mind had been occupied for an hour or two. Now he was face to face with his own problems again, and the Christmas decorations weren't doing anything to raise his spirits. Neither would Niki when she caught up with him. He went home and discovered irate messages from her on the answering services of his mobile and his home phone. He called back to calm her down, but discovered that she had turned off her phones. He was forced to leave a stumbling apology, pleading pressure of work. He knew she wouldn't buy it. In frustration, he turned off his own phones and eventually passed out on the sofa.

Lying there in the early dawn, sleep now as distant as the mountains of Crete, Mavros thought about the terrorists who had operated under the collective name of their leader Iraklis. They had killed over twenty people between the end of the Colonels' junta in 1974 and the early 1990s. Although the majority of their victims were Greek citizens whom they regarded as class enemies and traitors – former security police commanders and torturers, right-wing newspaper owners, businessmen branded as profiteers – they had also achieved worldwide notoriety by assassinating an American diplomat and, ten years later, an off-duty British naval officer. Intense pressure had been applied to the Greek authorities to track down the terrorist cell but no member had ever been found, leading to speculation that senior politicians had engineered a cover-up. At least Iraklis had ceased operations years ago, to the relief of everyone in the Greek establishment; other groups were still at large.

Mavros sat up and swung his legs off the sofa. His eyes were heavy but his mind was racing. Iraklis. According to its voluminous proclamations, the group had come together during the dictatorship, its members galvanised by the Junta's harsh treatment of its opponents. But Iraklis predated many of its rivals, who had been inspired by the regime's brutal reaction to the occupation of the Polytechnic building in November 1973 that killed dozens of demonstrators. Mavros had been only eleven at the time, but he'd heard the screams and the shots from the family home in the inner-city area of Neapolis – his mother hadn't yet moved to the flat on the slopes of Lykavittos that she still occupied. His brother Andonis had been a leading light in the underground resistance movement, but he had disappeared the year before. The family was fearful that he might have come out of hiding to take part in the demonstration that signalled the beginning of the end of the Colonels' hold on power. But there had been no sign of him then, or in the decades since. That was why Mavros had never paid more than passing attention to the activities of Iraklis. Andonis had always opposed violent confrontation with the authorities because of the cost in human lives that it would entail. The terrorist group had no such scruples.

Mavros drew the curtains to let in the daylight and wrapped a towel round his waist. His flat was warm, the communal furnace that ran the central heating belching out its contribution to the Athenian pollution cloud. He'd like to have opted out on ecological grounds, but in the depths of winter he found it hard to manage without the heat. He went into his small kitchen and started cutting oranges. The season's harvest from the Peloponnese was in full swing and he had bought a ten-kilo bag from an itinerant vendor in the street. He had finished squeezing and was pouring the juice into a glass when the doorbell rang.

He glanced at his watch and let out a sigh of relief. It was before eight, so it couldn't be Niki – she was always in a rush to get to work in the morning.

'*Poios einai?*' he said, into the entryphone. Who is it?

'Alex Mavros?' came the reply. 'My name is Grace Helmer.'

Mavros was nonplussed, then the American accent prompted him. 'Ah, are you the one who was looking for me at the café?'

'Yeah. Can you let me in? It's freezing out here.'

Mavros pressed the button to open the street door and went towards his front door, cursing the Fat Man for giving out his address. As he opened it, he realised that he was still only wearing the towel.

'Hi. Is this too early for you?' The woman was tall and slim, her blonde hair drawn back in a ponytail, emphasising prominent cheekbones. She extended her right hand as she took in his appearance. 'Like I said, I'm Grace.'

Mavros took it and felt a firm grip on his own. 'Em, hi, Grace. I'm Alex. Sorry about the state of undress...' He stood back and let her walk past him, catching a hint of his mother's perfume from her denim-clad frame. She was a fine-looking woman, as Yiorgos had said.

'Doesn't bother me if it doesn't bother you,' she said, from the door of the sitting room. 'In here?'

Mavros grabbed his dressing-gown and quickly closed the door to the bedroom, aware that sheets and clothes were all over the place. 'Yes, in there. I've just made some fresh orange juice. Would you like some?' As he dragged on the dressing-gown, he felt the towel drop to the floor.

'Yeah, that would be great,' she said, with a

64

smile. The tanned skin around her blue eyes creased.

'Have a seat,' he said, trying to remember if he'd left anything embarrassing on the sofa or the table. No, he hadn't been perusing the volume of nude female photographs that the Fat Man had given him for his name day last year – as much to irritate Niki as for his own enjoyment.

When he came back with the juice, Mavros found his guest at the window.

'Thanks,' she said, taking the glass. 'What a view you have. And it's so quiet here.' She stepped back and sat down in the single armchair. 'I can see the Acropolis from my hotel room, but it's further away and lost in the smog. And the traffic noise...'

'It's a big city and everyone wants a car. But, yes, it is peaceful here. The narrow streets and the parking restrictions put drivers off. I like it.' He was being disingenuous. He didn't just like his flat, he loved it. He often struggled to pay the rent but it was definitely worth it – living in the calm, classical eye of the Athenian hurricane justified the hours he spent tracking people down on its noisy streets.

'I'm sorry I turned up unannounced,' Grace Helmer said, giving him a more tentative smile. 'It's just that I thought I was never going to find you at that café. I went back yesterday evening. The blinds were down but I could see a light on behind them. No one answered my knock.'

'No,' Mavros said. 'The Fat Man's only open in the mornings.' Yiorgos ran illicit card games in the evenings, taking a cut of the winnings. He

65

was very attached to earning black money: he claimed that ensuring the capitalist state didn't take a cut was every Communist's duty.

'The Fat Man?' Grace said, raising an eyebrow. 'That's not a very kind nickname.'

'Yiorgos doesn't mind,' he replied. 'In fact, he's proud of his bulk.'

'Is that right?' She didn't sound convinced. 'Anyway, I went back this morning – Jesus, there were some crusty old guys in there – and told him I couldn't wait for you any longer. He seemed to get the point and gave me your address. So here I am.'

'So here you are.' He'd be having words with the Fat Man, Mavros thought. When he'd told the café-owner to give the mystery woman his number, he'd meant that of his phone, not his flat. 'What can I do for you?'

'Right.' Grace Helmer put down her empty glass on a newspaper that was lying on the antique oak table. 'What can you do for me? Well, it's rather a long story.'

'I see,' he said, stretching over to his leather satchel and taking out a notebook and pen. 'Before you start, maybe you'd better tell me how you found out about me.'

The American crossed her legs and appraised him with a long look. 'All right, Alex. I went to the embassy and told them I needed a reliable private investigator. Initially the guy wasn't too keen. He told me I should go through official channels, that the embassy was responsible for US citizens' interests in Greece, et cetera, et cetera. But I made him see my point of view.' She gave him a brief smile. 'He put me on to a Greek policeman called Kria ... Kriaras?'

'Kriaras,' Mavros repeated, stressing the final syllable.

Grace Helmer blinked as the sun caught the corner of the window. 'Yeah, that was him. You've worked with the embassy before?'

Mavros nodded.

'How come they don't have your phone number or address?' There was a hint of suspicion in her voice.

'Nikos Kriaras acts as my unofficial clearing house when it comes to foreign nationals.' Mavros caught her eye and was immediately aware of a deep inner strength. 'I prefer to keep people like US embassy officials at arm's length.'

Grace Helmer laughed lightly. 'I can understand that, especially in this country.'

'It's true that many of my countrymen regard yours as imperialists who supported the repressive regimes that were in charge from the forties to the seventies. I don't think things are that simple.'

She frowned. 'You say "my countrymen". Are you Greek or what? Your English is perfect.'

He laughed. 'My Scottish mother will be glad to hear that. I have dual Greek and British nationality.'

'Well, good for you.' Grace smiled again. 'But you're based here full-time?'

'Yup. And I've been a private investigator for ten years, in case you were wondering.' He swallowed the last of his orange juice. 'So what about that long story you were going to tell me?'

'Okay.' She closed her eyes for a few moments as if she was steeling herself, then opened them, looking straight into his. There was a brief expression of puzzlement as she registered the brown mark in his left eye. Over the years Mavros had got used to women noticing it. Some found it alluring in a way that sometimes struck him as perverse, as if imperfection were a good thing. Grace didn't seem to be one of those: her gaze soon shifted to a bare patch of wall above his right shoulder.

'Okay. Where to begin? I was born in Khartoum, where my father had a posting–' She broke off and changed the position of her legs. Suddenly she seemed ill at ease. 'He was a diplomat.'

Mavros narrowed his eyes, a hazy recollection coming into focus.

'Anyway,' Grace continued, 'we moved to Athens when I was three. My dad–'

'Excuse me,' Mavros interrupted. 'Do you mind telling me how old you are now?'

She raised her shoulders. 'No. I was thirty last July.'

He finally made the connection. 'Helmer. Your father was murdered in 1976, wasn't he? By the terrorist group Iraklis.'

'That's right,' Grace replied, her voice level. 'My mother and I left Greece a few weeks later, and I haven't been back until now.'

Mavros was struck by the coincidence. He'd been talking to Lambis Bitsos about the Iraklis group's possible reappearance last night, and now the daughter of one of their first victims had shown up. Before he could start calculating the odds of that happening, he heard a key turn in his front door.

A few seconds later Niki was looking down at his bare legs. Then she turned her acid gaze on the American woman in the armchair. 'Who's this, then, Alex?' she asked in Greek.

Mavros got up and went over to her. 'She's a potential client.' He stretched out a hand, only to have it smacked away.

'Do you always meet clients in your dressing-gown?' Niki shouted, her eyes wide. They were bloodshot and surrounded by dark rings, suggesting she hadn't slept much. 'Fuck you, Alex! She's your latest tart.' She let out a great sob. 'Oh, God, I gave you that dressing-gown for your birthday last year.' She stepped up to him. 'Bastard! Where were you last night?'

Mavros glanced at Grace Helmer. She was sitting as she had been, her eyes on the wall. The conversation was in a language she probably couldn't understand, but Niki's raised voice hadn't provoked a reaction.

'I left you a message,' he said, trying to get close to his raging girlfriend. 'I had work ... I...' He let the excuse trail away: it would do him no good – Niki was out for his blood. 'In God's name grow up,' he said, resorting to the aggressive tactics she was using, 'you're making a fool of yourself.'

She laughed bitterly. '*I'm* making a fool of myself? Look at you, drinking orange juice with your latest pick-up in the dressing-gown I gave you.' She stepped up to him and punched him in the belly with enough force to double him up. 'Who's the fool now?'

Mavros stayed bent to catch his breath and to protect his abdomen from further blows. Niki took the opportunity to turn her fire on Grace Helmer. 'Eh, whore?' she yelled in Greek. 'Did you give him a good time? How much did you screw from him?'

'I told you, Niki,' Mavros said, straightening up partially. 'She's a potential client, or at least she was. She's American.'

That only increased Niki's antagonism. 'Oh, so you're an American hooker,' she said, in the English she'd perfected at college in London. 'Well, fuck off back to the land of the free, you—'

Mavros took her by the arms and pulled her away. 'Sorry,' he said to Grace, over Niki's writhing shoulder. 'Maybe we should postpone this meeting.'

The American's expression displayed mild amusement rather than alarm. 'See you around, Alex,' she said, moving to the door with unhurried strides.

Mavros watched her go, pretty sure that was the last glimpse he would have of Grace Helmer. Then he turned back to the emotional crime scene that was taking place in his sitting room.

3

The poet Kostas Laskaris made his way carefully down the steps from the plane and into the terminal. The airport was to the west of Kalamata in the flatlands of Messenia, fields of tobacco and lines of olive trees stretching out across a wide river delta. Further away, the mountains of the southern Peloponnese were snow-capped, the air much clearer than that of Athens two hundred kilometres to the north-east. But, despite the bright sunlight, there was a bitter wind blowing and the poet felt the breath catch in his lungs and a chill spread through his body. Inside, while he waited for his driver Savvas to collect his bag, he lit a cigarette and exhaled smoke against the plate-glass window. Although it was warm enough in the building, a shiver racked him as he looked towards the scarred flanks of Taygetos – the range of peaks cascaded down from its summit south of Sparta, over two thousand metres sinking to a few hundred above Cape Tainaron at the end of the land mass's middle finger. In that direction was the tower, the place he had made his home. And further on was the cave that in ancient myth led directly to the underworld. He drew hard on his cigarette and suppressed another shudder.

'Ready.' The swarthy young man peered at him. 'Are you all right, Kyrie Kosta? You look exhausted.'

Laskaris caught a glimpse of his drawn face and slumped shoulders in the window. 'You don't have to shout,' he said waspishly. 'People are allowed to have a cigarette in peace.' But in truth he was glad of the interruption. Left to himself, he would have been consumed by his thoughts, burned up in the flames of guilt that had been building in the last few weeks. There would be no escape later on when he was alone in the *pyrgos*, but at least Savvas would distract him with the latest village gossip on the two-hour drive south. He had only been away for a couple of weeks – the tests in Athens, a trip to Moscow for a literature festival, then the return to receive the diagnosis. He'd been given as little as a month if he didn't go under the knife, maybe a year if he did and then was lucky. But he had already decided that he wouldn't be leaving the treeless slopes and stone-ridden fields of his birthplace again. He had seen too many bodies cut open by the unforgiving steel.

'Listen to this, Kyrie Kosta,' Savvas said breathlessly, as he steered the poet's battered Japanese four-by-four out of the airport car park. He launched into a lengthy story about a young couple from the village of Kitta, a few kilometres from the tower. Laskaris tried to follow it, but found himself more captivated by the scenery. After Kalamata, the road left the coast, the mountain's rocky sides forming an impenetrable barrier to the left. The asphalt strip finally met the sea again at Kardhamyli and the poet felt his spirits soar as the rippled blue water filled his eyes. Although the stone of the upper ground was barren and bare, winter had brought a carpet of green to the lower slopes. The Mani, ancient fastness of the country's most violent families, was flaunting its finery; pretending it was a place fit for human beings to inhabit.

'...and then Myrsini's brother swore that he would avenge the family's honour,' Savvas was saying. 'You see, Kyrie Kosta, her fiancé Theodhoros hadn't just been caught in the cheese-making hut with the German woman. He was also seen with another foreigner in Porto Kayio last week and...'

Laskaris let the driver's words wash over him. Savvas meant well. He was the son of the woman who cleaned the tower and, despite the impression of dimness given by his close-set eyes and uncontrolled voice, he was quick-witted enough. At least he'd stayed in the village. Most of his contemporaries had moved to Kalamata or Athens as soon as they'd got the chance.

'I swear he'd have cut Theodhoros's balls off if the policeman hadn't arrived in time...'

Laskaris looked ahead, past the cultivated land south of Kardhamyli with its orchards and cypress trees to the wall of rock beyond Itylo. That area was the Deep Mani, the harshest and most blood-soaked land of all. As Savvas's story showed, the tradition of the vendetta, the blind defence of family honour, survived even now. In the old days, even not very long ago, the lascivious Theodhoros and his relations would have been besieged for months in their fortified tower, no mercy extended to the menfolk by their opponents with their ornate guns and razor-sharp

73

swords. At least there was a degree of restraint now, even though the luckless policemen drafted in to the Mani from distant, less savage areas, occasionally had to use force to get the locals to observe the law.

And then the poet's defences crumbled. He remembered the scenes he had witnessed as a young man; witnessed and taken part in. In his lifetime savagery hadn't only reigned in the Mani, it had taken over the whole of Greece. He knew it was time he described the terrors that had gripped the country, time he made a fitting memorial for his lost comrades.

'The wind took one of the shutters from the top of the *pyrgos*,' Savvas said, as they ground up the steep road beyond Limeni. 'From the top bedroom.' He glanced round. 'Don't worry, Kyrie Kosta. I fixed it.'

'Watch the road, Savva,' Laskaris shouted, grabbing the seat as a motorbike swerved round the corner and almost hit them. He felt the pain stab into his belly again. It would be beyond irony if he was killed in a traffic accident before the cancer did for him – before he had written his last poem.

They reached the ridge. Ahead lay Areopolis, main town of the Deep Mani. Originally called Tzimova, it had been renamed after the war god Ares because of the local men's bloodthirsty prowess in the fight for independence from the Turks. Laskaris gazed down the coast towards the promontory that lay beneath his tower, the sea moving around the base of the rock in an undulating petticoat. The war god Ares. He might have structured the poem around him since the horror was at its worst during times of conflict. But he had another protagonist in mind, the hero who had laboured in the Peloponnese and who symbolised all that was admirable and all that was awful about the region. He had been working on the ideas behind the poem for years, planning it and moulding it even though he had never written more than a few lines. And he had a title. 'The Fire Shirt'. Everything was ready for his last major work. But would he have time to complete it?

He took in the bleak hillsides and their thin layer of vegetation, the latter given a deceptively lush appearance by the light and by the blue of the water beyond. Soon the green would be burned away, soon he himself would be nothing more than the shadow of a departing cloud. His task, before he went, was to write a poem that would live for ever. Did he still have the power to accomplish that? He had to find it within himself. It was more than a duty, a task to be accomplished for the Party: it was an obligation of love.

He closed his eyes as the pain grew worse, forcing himself to think about the poem. There had been many heroes over the centuries and many in his own time whom he would celebrate. There had also been many, like poor Spyros Mavros's son Andonis, who disappeared into the limpid air.

And greatest of them all was Iraklis.

Mavros glared at the Fat Man across the chill

cabinet. 'Have you any idea what you did, you idiot?' he shouted. There was no one else in the café to witness the performance.

The café-owner was drying a glass in his thick-fingered hands. 'Gave you a pleasant surprise first thing in the morning?' he asked, with a tentative smile.

'Oh, yes, a very pleasant surprise. The Third World War in my sitting room, a fist in my guts, and that ringing noise in the ears you get when a relationship hits the ground without a parachute.'

The Fat Man picked up another glass and applied his off-white cloth to it. 'I was only trying to fix you up with some work,' he said, his cheeks reddening. 'You told me to give the American woman your number.'

'I meant my phone number, you bucket of lard, not my flat. She walked out when Niki started putting the knife into her. So much for getting me a job. You lost me one, as well as terminally screwing up my relationship with Niki.'

'Tragic,' said Yiorgos Pandazopoulos, under his breath. 'It's about time you sorted out your love life. You said so yourself.'

Mavros bent down and examined the contents of the cabinet. 'Yes, well, I'd prefer to choose the time and place myself to do that, if you don't mind.' He glanced up. 'Is that what I think it is?'

The Fat Man refused to catch his eye. 'How do I know what you think it is, you smartarse?'

Mavros raised his eyes to the ceiling. 'Christ and the Mother of God, Yiorgo, don't play the martyr. All right, I'm sorry I shouted at you. Now, is that a piece of your mother's delectable *baklava*?'

The Fat Man nodded solemnly, still playing hard to get.

'Can I have it?'

'Yes. But only if you promise never to be so rude to me again.' Yiorgos Pandazopoulos paused, then burst out laughing. 'I had you there, Alex. You really thought I was sulking.'

Mavros went over to a table to wait for the honey-drenched pastry. He wasn't sure about Niki – it was usually a good idea to let her cool down on her own for a few days after she'd blown her top – but he hadn't yet written off Grace Helmer. The fact that her father had been assassinated by the Iraklis group intrigued him. He wanted to hear the rest of her story, and he wanted to find out what she required of him. It was about time he got himself an interesting job.

After he'd finished the *baklava* and drunk a cup of the Fat Man's coffee, he checked the hotel section in the *Golden Guide*. Grace had said that she could see the Acropolis from her room, though it wasn't as close to the citadel as Mavros's flat. There were several hotels that had such a view and he knew which one he was going to try first. He decided to walk up to it and try to see the woman in person. She would be more likely to give him the benefit of the doubt after Niki's scene if he made the effort to meet her rather than telephone. And if she wasn't there, it wouldn't matter – he'd be in range of his mother's flat and he wanted to drop in.

'Go to the good, Yiorgo,' Mavros called, on his way out.

'You too,' the Fat Man responded from the

toilet, where he was carrying out the daily mopping-up operations that Kyra Fedhra had recently given up so she could devote more time to her baking. 'And remember, never trust a capitalist.'

Mavros laughed, and stepped into the cold sunlight.

Grace Helmer was in the bar on the ground floor, a martini on the table in front of her. She had changed into a patterned skirt that ended above the knee and showed off her long legs to good effect. Her yellow blouse was a vivid patch of colour among the sober-suited businessmen who comprised the majority of the customers, and her blonde hair, now loose and brushed out, made her look even more like an exotic creature.

'Hello,' Mavros said, approaching her table from the side. His worn leather jacket had led to a raised eyebrow from the security man at the door, but he'd been granted admission. The guy would have been used to the gilded youth of Athens arriving in similar garb to salute their parents before going off to race each other in their sports cars on the central avenues.

'Well, well,' said the American woman, raising her glass and beckoning to him to sit down. 'The intrepid private eye. How did you find me?'

'You said it. I'm intrepid and I'm a private eye.'

'No, really,' Grace persisted. 'Did you ring round all the hotels?'

'I took a gamble. You said you could see the Acropolis. I'll have a beer,' he said to the waiter, who had materialised in front of them. 'Amstel.

How about you? Another of those?'

'One's enough during the day.' She took a pack of Camels from her bag and offered him one.

'No, thanks. I gave up last year.' He took out his blue worry-beads. 'Now I amuse myself with these.'

Blowing smoke away from him, Grace smiled. 'If that was meant to be a demonstration of your skills, I'm impressed. I'm even more impressed that you had the nerve to show up after your girlfriend – I presume that's who she was? – came to say good morning.'

Mavros opened his hands. 'What can I say? I'm really sorry about that. Niki's ... well, Niki's got a Mediterranean temperament.'

Grace was looking at him with an amused expression. 'You could call it that. You know, I spend a lot of time in foreign parts and I'd say she wins the Oscar for most convincing tantrum anywhere in the world.' She put her hand on his arm. 'Are you all right? I mean, that was quite a hit you took down below.'

'I've had worse,' Mavros said, aware how dysfunctional that made his love life sound. 'Not from Niki. In the line of work.' He poured Amstel into his glass and drank half of it.

'Okay, okay, you've convinced me.' She stubbed out her cigarette. 'I take it you want to hear the rest of the story I began to tell you.'

'Very much. Though I can't promise that I'll be able to commit to whatever it is you want done.'

Grace Helmer nodded. 'That's all right, Alex. I take it we're on first-name terms if that's what the client wants.'

'Sure,' he replied, returning her smile. The American woman had an easy-going manner that was hard to resist.

She looked around the bar – the nearest people were six men speaking Arabic some tables away – took a sip from her glass and slipped an envelope from her bag. She held the cream-coloured paper tightly between the thumb and fingers of her right hand. Mavros couldn't see any writing on it.

'Okay,' she said, 'here we go. You already know about my father. I was five when he ... when he was killed, and I can't really remember much about him.' She paused, the fingers of her left hand moving back to the cigarette packet, but she didn't open it. 'My mother – Laura was her name – was much more important to me when I was small. She didn't go out to work, and although we had the usual domestic servants, she spent a lot of time with me.' Grace gave a sad smile. 'That soon changed. After the murder she went into herself and she was never the same again.' She shrugged. 'You see, she saw it happen. And they – they used a knife on him.'

Mavros could remember the outrage that had caused. He bowed his head. 'It was terrible,' he said haltingly. 'I'm very sorry.'

Grace looked at him and nodded slowly. 'Thanks.' This time she opened the cigarette packet and took one out, striking a match with a deft movement of her hand. 'Anyway, we moved back to the US not long afterwards, back to the small town my mother had grown up in – Lawson in upstate New York. I went to local schools, but all that time she was drifting away

80

into a world of her own. My grandmother mostly looked after me when I was younger. You see, my mother was an artist. Never a well-known one. She'd been to art college, but then she met my father and didn't paint so much when she was with him. But when she got back to Lawson she devoted all her waking hours to her paintings. They were big canvases, full of brutal colours and tortured human figures. I always hated them.' Grace smiled again. 'She was sweet, she never yelled at me even when I messed up her palette out of spite. But she was distant, her eyes always moving, and she'd let herself go. She was heavy and she never washed her hair. And then ... and then one day, when I was fifteen, she killed herself.'

Grace fell silent and Mavros looked at her. The skin on her face was taut but there was no sign of tears on her delicate eyelashes. He was struck by how little emotion she was showing, though he knew how some people could shield their grief and make it a personal possession – he had done that himself.

'Sorry. There are some things you can never get over, no matter how much you try.'

'Maybe it's better not to get over them,' he said. 'Maybe it's better to keep the memory alive.' He was thinking of Andonis. He had always tried to keep him close, but it grew harder with every year that passed.

'Maybe,' she said, looking at him thoughtfully. 'Sorry, Alex, I'm getting to the point, honest.'

'Don't worry, I'm in no hurry.'

'Thanks. Anyway, she did it when I was away

from home staying with a friend, so I never got to say goodbye to her properly. That's been very difficult for me to live with. Even when I'm abroad she'll come to me, often when I'm asleep.'

Mavros was struck by the similarity to his brother's frequent appearances in his thoughts and dreams. 'You seem to be abroad a lot,' he said, changing the subject. He was unwilling to get too close to a potential client's pain in case his judgement was clouded. 'What do you do?'

'I work for an aid agency,' Grace replied. 'Meliorate, World Humanitarian Relief. Last month I was in the Philippines, last year I was in Liberia.' She touched his arm again for a few seconds. 'Anyway, Alex, you'll need to know what I want from you. You see, my grandmother died back in October.'

Mavros swallowed beer and put down his glass. The meeting was turning into an emotional obstacle course. 'I'm sorry,' he began.

'Don't worry,' Grace said, raising a hand. 'She was old and she'd had enough pain – a cancer was eating into her colon. The thing was, after the funeral the lawyer handed me an envelope that she'd left for me.' She lifted up the one she'd been holding throughout her narrative and took a deep breath. 'It was from my mother, addressed to me and dated the day she killed herself – which was the tenth anniversary of my father's murder. And that's why I've come back to the country where it happened.'

Mavros looked at her uncomprehendingly, as hooked by a client's pitch as he'd ever been. Then he took the envelope Grace handed to him and slid out pages covered in a large, erratic script.

19 December 1986

My darling Grace,
This is the hardest thing I've ever done. You know
that words aren't my medium. Maybe painting isn't
either – I know that my work repulses you – but at
least I feel at home with oils. Writing has never been
comfortable for me. Too much self-analysis, too many
explanations. And, I suppose, too much opportunity
for emotion to slip through. I know, I know, my sweet.
I shut myself off from you, I didn't give you the love
you needed when you were growing. I did once. You
probably don't remember, but I loved you openly and
unconditionally when you were small. Until you were
five and your father was taken from us. But even then
I was betraying you both.
And now what can I say to you to make up for my
failure to raise you as I should have? I've been
thinking about this for a long time. As I've watched
you turn from a quiet little girl to a strong and
independent teenager, I've often thought you were
ready. You probably were. Ever since we came back
from Greece you were in control of yourself, you only
cried when you got hurt, and even then there weren't
many tears. When you took the skin off both your
knees that time, riding your bicycle off the road, your
Ganma cried more than you did, my little ice maiden.
I admired your nerve, but it didn't seem natural.
Though I know why you were like that. I made you
that way, it was my fault.
Yes, there were plenty of times, especially in the last
couple of years, when I thought you were ready and I

could take my leave. But I saw the look in your Ganma's eye, saw the way she watched over you, almost willing me not to do what she knew I was on the brink of doing. So I waited, thought long and hard about what legacy I should leave you. And now I have decided. I will tell you what happened in the months before your father's death. You are his daughter as well as mine. You have the right to know.

The truth is that your father and I weren't well matched. Sure, I fell for him the minute he walked into the restaurant in New York where I was waiting tables. I was almost finished at art school and I didn't have any firm plans. Suddenly I found myself in this whirlwind romance, flowers, champagne, the works. But he was about to be posted to Africa, his first embassy job, and I had to choose. The Bohemian grind – tips, scratching for the rent each month, never mind having enough for paint and canvas, cockroaches – or a pampered expatriate lifestyle with plenty of time for my work. It wasn't a tough call. Except it didn't turn out the way I thought. I didn't fit in with the other wives: I was seen as a loudmouth with unreliable views on the war in Vietnam. And I never did much painting. You came along – to my great joy, Grace, you must believe that – and I lost interest in art for a while. You were the centre of my life, my comfort in the long, hot days and the interminable nights when I used to stay awake listening to your gentle breathing. It was almost enough for me. And then we were sent to Athens.

Everything changed there. Soon you weren't an infant any more, you were a toddler and then a lively, sparkling little girl. We inherited a nanny from the previous resident. Youli was a friendly Filipina and

84

you loved her. Your father was much more occupied with his work than in the Sudan. Whole days passed when I never saw him. There had been major American involvement in Greece since the Second World War, and he spent most of his free time with army commanders and businessmen. Wives were not required at those gatherings.

I found things outside the apartment to fill my time. Even in the early seventies Athens was a big city, much bigger than Khartoum. Back then there was no need for caution. I used to walk around the dusty streets, staring up like a hick at the Acropolis when it suddenly sailed into view between the modern buildings. As for the museums, for an artist they were just inspiring. I found that I was beginning to get my touch back. I started sketching statues, those monumental figures of young men and women with their braided hair and arms by their sides. I was sitting in front of a kouros *in the National Museum when the man who destroyed my life walked up.*

Grace, I'm telling you this because I want you to understand why I became the obsessive, selfish person whom even your Ganma, my own mother, dislikes and distrusts. I'm not telling you my story because I want you to act on it. In fact, for what these words are worth, I expressly forbid you to pass this information to anyone in authority. I was too much of a coward to tell anyone when it mattered. Anyway, as you will see, there is little that they could do with it.

His name was Iason, Iason Kolettis. At least, that's what he said he was called. At the time I had no reason to doubt him. I heard his voice before I set eyes on him because I was bent over my pad, engrossed in the sketch I was making. He said something in

85

German. I suppose the blonde hair that you inherited from me made him think I was that nationality. I didn't understand but the softness, the gentleness of the way he addressed me, had an immediate effect. I looked up and was lost.

Iason – I must call him that even though I'm sure it wasn't his real name – was a stunning-looking man. He was tall and very slim. His hair was dark and down to his neck in the style of the mid-seventies and he had a heavy moustache. Most of the young Greeks did, I think it was some kind of macho thing. But he wasn't macho at all. His face was beautiful in a weird, female way, his features delicate and his skin, though it was sallow, was very soft. He was like a boy who had grown up only a minute before I met him, a boy on the threshold of manhood, even though I later found out that he was over thirty. Apart from his gentle, loving voice, what struck me most about him were his eyes. They were dark, almost black, and although the skin around them was often creased in laughter, he had an intense stare that reminded me of the Mona Lisa. She projects an air of innocence, but it's cut with an understanding of how much power over other people she has at her disposal. Iason was the same, but I only discovered the true nature of that power later.

My first thought was that he was a 'harpoonist' – that's what they were known as, the young men who preyed on unaccompanied foreign women. I'd been told about them by the other embassy wives. I'd also been advised to be polite but firm with them. In fact, earlier that day in one of the central squares I'd told another guy where to put his harpoon. But Iason was different. To start with, he didn't seem to want *anything at all from me. He told me all sorts of esoteric stuff about the statues – how there was Egyptian influence in their style, how the arms were by their sides because the sculptors hadn't worked out how to support outstretched limbs yet. He bought me coffee, hailed a taxi for me, said that he always came to the museum on Thursday mornings because he found the exhibits uplifting. But he didn't try anything, didn't even touch my hand. What he did, looking back, was cast a spell on me. I was a willing enough victim.*

I won't embarrass you by describing what we eventually did on numerous afternoons in various seedy hotels. I'm sure you'll discover the joys of unbridled passion for yourself soon enough. Maybe you already have. The fact was that it was glorious, full of joy and abandon, no guilt, no strings attached. I would return to the flat in the northern suburb, glowing, my appetite for life rekindled. And your father? He never noticed. He was so caught up in his work. The dictatorship had fallen a couple of years before and Americans were deeply resented because they had supported the Colonels. Trent saw it as his mission to rebuild ties between the US and the Greek people, though how he hoped to achieve that by carousing with sleazy businessmen and cynical generals, I don't know. Youli, the nanny, knew that I was up to something, but she didn't seem to disapprove. She would greet me with a wide smile when I came back and took you from her for a while. Women understand these things, I guess.

Believe me, Grace, being in love fills your life: it makes you feel that you are a goddess, capable of anything. But it blinds you too, it drives you to ignore the consequences of what you're doing. I loved Iason with all my being. I loved everything about him, from the peasant family in the southern Peloponnese that he told me he'd worked his way up from to his work – he was a printer and I used to wash the ink from his hands before he ran them over me; once I let him touch me without cleaning them and I had a terrible job to get the stains from my body – to the flat he sometimes took me to in Neapolis, a residential area near the museum; to the burning idealism he sometimes showed without realising (I should have grasped earlier that he was a devoted Marxist); to the Greek songs he sang to me, the strange, almost Eastern rhythms steeped in a bittersweet melancholy; to the way he spoke English, faltering but with a surprisingly good accent. Maybe he'd attached himself to a British diplomat's wife before me.

Yes, it will be obvious to you that Iason Kolettis was a manipulator, an undercover operator, a liar. I think that, deep down, I knew it too, but I was powerless to resist. Such is the hateful strength of love. But the worst of it is this: I am convinced, I am a hundred per cent sure that Iason loved me too. I refuse to accept that it is possible to dissemble so completely. When he was with me, Iason loved me as much as I loved him. It was just that he had another agenda when we were apart. I don't know what he expected to learn from me. I suppose he would have gathered details about our home, about Trent's routine and about the lack of any armed guard. People were naïve back then. There were plenty of left-wing terrorist groups in Greece that had survived the Colonels, but they weren't perceived to be a threat to Americans.

You know what I'm leading up to, don't you, Grace?

You suspect, but I want you to be sure. The man who killed your father, the man who drew that knife across Trent's throat, was my lover Iason Kolettis. He was wearing a Balaclava, but I recognised him from his eyes, the dark, dominating eyes that had run over every inch of my body, that had looked deep into my own when he said, 's'agapo, I love you,' at the moment of our climax. He slaughtered your father like an animal, then disappeared into the night. And still I love him, still I live in his arms, his voice whispering in my ears the 's'agapo'. I tried to hate him too, please believe me, and I never set eyes on him again after that last terrible night outside our home. Not that he ever tried to contact me. Obviously I had served my purpose. His political beliefs, his mission, were more important to him than I was.

Now I can't stand it any more. Not just the emptiness of the years since Iason betrayed me, and the guilt that I never admitted my relationship with Trent's killer. No, the worst thing of all is that I have never been able to summon up the courage to tell you about my part in your father's death.

I know you have no religion, my sweet, despite your Ganma's best efforts, so I will not ask you to pray for me. But think of me from time to time and do not condemn me. I let myself be beguiled and others suffered for my foolishness —Trent, your Ganma, perhaps you most of all, for you changed from a trusting child to a bitter and unforgiving young woman. I don't blame you for that, I blame myself. I know you won't believe it but I always loved you deeply, my darling.

Your mother Laura.

Mavros folded the letter carefully and put it back into the envelope.

Grace Helmer leaned across and took it from him, keeping it in her hand. 'Well?' she said. 'What do you think?'

Mavros looked around the hotel bar. It was quieter now, most of the businessmen having departed while he'd been reading. The afternoon sunlight was streaming in through the plate-glass windows, cars moving up the wide avenue in a blur of colours. 'What do I think?' he repeated, fumbling for an appropriate description of his feelings. The letter had struck him as tragic beyond words, but he didn't want to upset Grace. Besides, he needed to know more about its provenance. 'So your mother wrote this to you before she ... before she took her own life?' he said.

She nodded. 'But I only got it recently, after my Ganma died. She left a note for me, explaining that she'd read my mother's letter back in 'eighty-six before I came home and decided that I should be spared it. But she felt bad about that so she didn't destroy it.' Grace bit her lip. 'You have to realise that my grandmother was a principled woman, Alex. She disapproved of extramarital affairs and she regarded suicide as an offence against God and the family. She never spoke to me again about my mother.'

'I see.' Mavros ran a hand through his hair. He could see where this was heading and he wanted to be clear about Grace's motives. 'You want me to find this Iason Kolettis, don't you?'

She looked straight at him. 'Yes.'

90

'Why?'

Grace Helmer held his eye for a few moments, then stared out at the traffic. 'Look, this is difficult for me, Alex. I've been abroad for most of my adult life. I'm an independent woman. And I ... I don't handle emotion well.' She glanced back at him. 'Probably because of what happened to my father and how distant my mother was when I was a kid, I don't know. I've devoted myself to caring for people who have nothing – their families killed in civil wars or by disease, their homes destroyed by floods, that kind of thing. And now I've realised that I've ignored my own family for too long.' She took out a cigarette and lit it in the same practised movement. 'My Ganma dying on her own brought it home to me. I only saw her for a few days each year and I think she took that hard. And my mother, I hated her for years after she'd killed herself, hated her for her selfishness and her absorption in those horrible paintings.' She waved away the smoke between them. 'And I hated her even more when I read the letter. But now... I don't know... If I can get closer to her by meeting the man she loved and who loved her, I might be able to forgive her and finally get through this nightmare.' She smiled weakly. 'I might become more of a normal human being.'

Mavros glanced down at his notes. The fact that this was turning into a therapy session didn't make him feel at ease. 'Right. Well, I haven't got much to go on. Your father was murdered in 1976, wasn't he? Twenty-five years ago.'

'To the day,' Grace said, inhaling deeply from her cigarette.

'Really? What you might call a trail that's gone stone cold,' he said. 'We also have to assume that Iason Kolettis was a false name. What else have we got? He was a printer – that seems credible because of what your mother said about the ink. And he lived in Neapolis.'

Grace looked up from the butt she was crushing in the ashtray. 'Do you know that place?'

'Oh, yes,' he replied, and decided against mentioning that he'd once lived there himself. He wasn't sure he wanted the job yet, and he didn't want to get her hopes up. 'And he might have come from a village in the Peloponnese, unless he made that up too.' He shrugged. 'It's a large area.'

'Perhaps I can narrow it down a bit,' Grace volunteered. She held out a colour photograph. 'This is one of my mother's paintings. See the bottom?'

Mavros made out some writing in red beneath the sombre depiction of two writhing, blood-drenched human forms. 'What is that? "Lament for Kitta"?'

She nodded. 'I looked Kitta up in the atlas. It's on the middle prong of the Peloponnese, the one that's called the Mani.' She raised her voice at the end of the sentence. 'Is that how you pronounce it?'

'Maani,' Mavros said, stressing the first syllable. 'Interesting. You think your mother's lover came from there?'

Grace raised her shoulders. 'Seems a reasonable chance. There were no other names on the paintings.'

'I don't suppose your mother kept a photo of Iason Kolettis?'

'I didn't find any in her things. Apart from one of me as a kid.' Her eyes caught his. 'There wasn't a single one of my father.'

Mavros looked away awkwardly. 'Okay. Listen, can I think about this?'

Grace's face fell. 'You don't want the job. You think it's a waste of time.'

'I didn't say that. I'll make some calls, see what I can turn up.' At this stage he wasn't going to tell her that he was interested – the timing of her appearance a few weeks after the killing of the investor Vernardhakis with its putative link to the terrorist group that had murdered her father disturbed him. 'What did the people at the embassy say?'

Her eyes widened. 'I didn't give them any details. Don't you remember? My mother told me not to talk to anyone in authority.'

Mavros wasn't convinced that a self-confessed independent woman who hadn't been close to her mother would have followed those instructions. 'What did you say, then?'

'Oh, I asked how I would go about finding a childhood friend in Greece.' Grace's eyes were still on him, her expression guileless.

'Do they know who you are?'

'I had to show my passport. I don't know if anyone made the connection with my father.' She gave a bitter smile. 'I was told how to contact the policeman Kriaras and ushered out quickly enough.'

Mavros got to his feet. 'How long are you going

to stay in Athens?' he asked, putting down some banknotes to cover the drinks.

'Don't worry.' Grace handed back the money. 'I'll get these.' She caught his eye again as she stood up. 'I'm staying as long as it takes,' she said, in a determined voice.

'I'll call you,' Mavros said, shaking the hand she'd extended.

He'd only gone a couple of paces when he stopped and turned round. 'Sorry, there's something else I need to know.' He gave an apologetic shrug. 'How did your mother die?'

For a few moments Grace Helmer was silent. 'It was as if she wanted to copy what her lover did to my father. She took a carving knife and slashed her throat. When Ganma found her, she was covered in blood.'

Mavros walked slowly away. He didn't need to know how Laura Helmer committed suicide for investigative reasons alone. He'd wanted to see how her daughter reacted to the question. Grace hadn't shown any hint of emotion. He wasn't sure if he wanted to work for a person whose soul was colder than the permanent snow on the highest mountain-tops.

4

Mavros waited outside his mother's door before he inserted the key. He could hear voices and he wanted to work out whose they were. Some of Dorothy's friends were tedious elderly writers, who spent their lives complaining about their minimal pensions and the lack of respect they were afforded by succeeding generations of critics. After a few seconds he made out his sister's habitually impatient tone, moderated by her husband Nondas's more emollient baritone. He went in to join them.

'Honestly, Mother,' Anna was saying, 'I can't understand why you won't come with us to Argolidha for Christmas. The Palaiologi have invited you, and it's not as if you have anything pressing to do in Athens.'

Dorothy turned as her son came into the sitting room and smiled at him. 'Ah, there you are, Alex. Save me from this pair of seducers.'

Mavros grinned at his sister and brother-in-law. 'Interesting terminology. Have you ever been called one of those before, Nonda?'

Anna gave a disapproving sniff, but there was a flicker of a smile on her lips. Nondas and she had a famously solid marriage.

'Often, Alex,' the well-built Cretan replied, his mouth occupied with gum as usual, 'but by the people I do business with rather than my

95

relatives.' His English was fluent, with only the trace of an accent – the product of years at an expensive private school in Athens and university in the States. He beamed at his mother-in-law. 'But Anna is right, Dorothy. You really should come down with us to the Peloponnese. The kids would like it and the Palaiologi aren't so bad.'

'I'll be the judge of that, Nonda,' Dorothy replied sharply. She had a soft spot for the indulgent Greek who had done much to soften her daughter's domineering nature, but ingrained Scots reserve prevented her being open about that. 'Contrary to what the pair of you think, I have plenty to do here. Both socially and professionally.'

Nondas looked at Mavros in mock desperation. 'Help us out here, Alex,' he said. 'Tell her it'll do her good to leave the big city.'

Mavros stood between the warring factions, his arms outstretched in a gesture of appeasement. 'Why don't you go for a few days, Mother? Nafplion is a lovely town.'

'Don't try to persuade me, Alex. Besides, that awful woman's house is on the top of a hill miles from civilisation.'

Mavros stepped back, aware that his sister's temper was about to ignite.

'Veta is not an "awful woman",' Anna said. 'She's a senior opposition spokeswoman and a future leader of her party.' She shook Nondas's hand off her arm. 'For goodness' sake!'

Dorothy never allowed herself to lose control. Under attack she resorted to withering disdain. 'Veta Palaiologou is nothing more than a right-wing hardliner disguised as a populist. And as for her husband...' She deliberately left the sentence uncompleted.

'Oh, come on, Dorothy,' Nondas said, a trace of irritation in his voice, 'Nikitas is one of the country's major entrepreneurs.'

'One of the country's major sources of corruption, more like,' Dorothy said, turning away. Although she had never been a Communist like her late husband, she had little time for Greece's super-rich.

Mavros watched as his sister and brother-in-law exchanged meaningful glances.

'Time for us to go, I think,' Anna said. She went over to her mother and pecked her on the cheek. 'I'll send the children their grandmother's love, shall I?'

'Of course, dear,' Dorothy said, squeezing Anna's arm. 'You'll pick up their presents before you go, won't you?'

Anna nodded and headed for the door.

'Goodbye, Dorothy,' Nondas said, with a wry smile. 'I'll get her to call you later. When she's calmed down.'

Mavros watched as his brother-in-law followed Anna out, his bulky frame sheathed in a well-cut but crumpled Savile Row suit – the Cretan had little time for the clothes his business as a stockbroker required and would happily have gone to the office in cut-off jeans and flip-flops if he could have got away with it. 'Well, that was enjoyable,' he observed.

'Sit down, Alex,' his mother said, lowering herself cautiously into an armchair. She had fallen over a few times recently and Anna had read her the Riot Act about taking more care of herself. 'Well, what did you expect me to say? I don't want to spend time with those Palaiologi. Your father would never forgive me.'

Mavros looked beyond her to the framed photographs of Spyros and Andonis. 'Except,' he said, 'as you never stop reminding me, my father and brother are no longer here. What does it matter what one or other of them might think?'

Dorothy held her gaze on him. 'We have to let them go, Alex, but that doesn't mean we have to forget everything they stood for. What does Anna think she's doing, planning to eat at the table of a family like the Palaiologi?'

'Is that what you call letting things go, Mother?' Mavros countered. 'I thought there was supposed to be a spirit of reconciliation in this country now. So their fathers were notorious collaborators and anti-Communists during the Second World War. They're not responsible for what happened to supporters of the Left back then.'

Dorothy was looking out of the window towards the distant sea, her eyes moist. 'You're right, Alex,' she said. 'It's a long time ago and things have changed. Besides,' she added, with a sardonic smile, 'Anna's a very good journalist. Perhaps she's doing an in-depth story that will dish the dirt on the family.'

Mavros laughed. 'I rather doubt it, considering that the husband is one of Nondas's closest friends and business colleagues.'

'What are you planning for the festive season, Alex?' Dorothy asked. 'Are you and Niki doing

98

things together? Alex?'

Mavros came back to himself. He had been thinking about Grace Helmer and the mystery man who had been her mother's lover. 'What am I planning?' he repeated. 'Em, nothing special. Working, probably.'

'Oh, you've found something to investigate, have you?' his mother asked, with irony. 'I was beginning to think you'd given up being a detective after that dreadful case in the Cyclades. Though I couldn't blame you. Those awful murders in such a beautiful setting, the way the war is still remembered...'

'Mmm,' Mavros said, still distracted.

Dorothy leaned forward. 'I notice you're saying nothing about Niki. Are you two still having problems?'

'What?' he said. 'Well, yes, we are. She's not very happy with me at the moment.'

'If it's finished, you should tell her, Alex,' Dorothy said, her tone serious. 'It's only fair.'

Mavros got up. 'Yes, you're probably right. Except I don't know if it *is* finished.'

His mother shook her head. 'Honestly, men.' She had never been a great admirer of Niki Glezou, feeling that she was too possessive for Alex's self-sufficient nature, but she frequently stood up for the younger woman on the grounds of female solidarity.

'I'll try to drop in tomorrow.' Mavros bent over to kiss her. 'I might know more about my plans by then.' He moved away, then stopped. 'By the way, Mother, when we lived in Neapolis you never happened to hear of, or meet, a man called

Iason Kolettis, did you?'

The fact that he was more interested in a name from a case he hadn't even accepted than he was in his lover didn't escape him. It didn't make him feel proud of himself.

The face in the mirror made Iraklis swallow hard. For as long as he could remember he'd kept an iron grip on his emotions, but since he'd returned to Greece they had become unreliable. A wave of nostalgia was bursting over him and he fought to bring himself back to the surface, his lungs constricting.

'Who am I?' he asked, under his breath. For the last ten years he had used the identity he'd bought from a softly spoken Chinese in New York City, but that name had slipped away from him in recent days like old skin from a snake. So had the name he had grown up with and the aliases he had assumed in the sixties and seventies. The most useful had been Iason Kolettis, but the printer, the lover, was long gone – he was sure only he had any recollection of that name now. Now he was Iraklis again. But that was a cover too – Iraklis was a name that meant much more than the terrorist group. He blocked out the thought. He'd come back to uncover his family's buried secrets: he'd been offered the chance to find the piece in the jigsaw that had always escaped him. But things were no longer as simple as they had been during the armed struggle. He had to be careful, take one step at a time. Some people out there were playing a dangerous game.

He examined his features in the glass, trying to

keep a grip on himself. The skin on his face was lined, though there was little sagging of the flesh – the massages provided by his barber back in Queens had kept his complexion in good condition. And his hair was still thick and lustrous. But his eyes troubled him. The rings around them were heavy, the irises an intense, blackish brown that saw everything. They looked inwards to his pain and his most burning desires, but it was what they had seen when they looked outwards that was unbearable. Not the violence and bloodshed, not the horror, but the joy. Those were the eyes that had studied her, that had looked into her eyes when he said the 's'agapo' truthfully. It didn't matter that he had lied to her about everything else; it hardly seemed to matter that he had killed her husband. His eyes had looked into her eyes, into the eyes of the woman whose name he hadn't been able to say in his thoughts since the night he had ridden away into the darkness with her husband's blood on his hands. Although it was twenty-five years since he had seen her, he was still shaken whenever he remembered the times they'd spent together. And the agony was worse now that he was back in Athens. It was breaking him, making him doubt his mission. Would the training he'd been through all those years ago be sufficient?

Iraklis turned away from the mirror and went into the bedroom, a towel in his hands. As he dabbed his eyes with it, he focused on where he was and what he had to do. Menandhrou Street, a couple of hundred metres south-west of Omonia Square in central Athens; the Hotel

Romvi, chosen for its run-down insignificance. Despite his poverty-stricken childhood on the wind-ravaged slopes of the Mani, he felt uncomfortable in the grimy building – he had got used to the well-appointed attic apartment in Queens. Room 845 had a view over a dilapidated neo-classical building used by the city's Russian immigrants for illicit card games and sex. Mangy cats were prowling across the flat rooftops, torn plastic bags caught in the aerials and the air-conditioning vents. But this was his command centre. 'Focus on the mission,' he said, under his breath. 'Forget yourself. Forget her.'

He pulled on a white shirt and buttoned it, suddenly aware that the room was cold despite the clanking radiator. He slid his hand behind the thin plywood wardrobe and pulled out the diskette he had secreted. He hadn't expected that a thief would think of looking there when he was out and if they'd tried when he was in the room he was sure he'd have prevailed unless he'd been seriously outnumbered. But he had been trained to take every precaution and he couldn't break the old habits – even if he was dangerously close to losing his grip.

He concentrated on booting up his laptop. When it was ready, he slipped the diskette into the drive and entered the password he'd been given over the phone by his controller. And there it was. The story he'd never expected to read. The story of the war, the story that included his father, though it broke off before the end – the conclusion was what he had to discover. But that wasn't all. There was also a profile of the target.

Before he could restrain it, a shudder caught him. Did he have it in him? Could he undertake the final, most costly mission of all?

Then the old slogans came back to him, the ones he'd learned during the first months in the youth party and then spray-painted on the walls of government buildings and banks during the dictatorship. 'The Only Good Capitalist is a Dead Capitalist'; 'Their Wealth is our Blood'; 'Down with the Junta and the Americans who Pay their Wages'. He felt his lips form a smile. The old spirit was still there. After all this time it felt good to be back in the struggle, even if these labours were more personal than political.

It was finally time to extract payment from the people who'd destroyed his family.

Mavros went back to his flat and made himself a sandwich. The sun was in the west now, its pollution-filtered rays coming over the Pnyx and the ancient marketplace. He took his plate out on to the narrow balcony outside his front room. The street was quiet in the late afternoon. The foreign workers from the neighbouring building sites – old houses being renovated for wealthy Athenians – had gone and there were only a few tourists on their way down from the Acropolis in the winter air. But Mavros sat and let the ineffectual sun play over him all the same. The chill would sharpen his thinking.

He hadn't been surprised when his mother had declared ignorance of Iason Kolettis. He hadn't told her anything else about the man who had been involved with Grace Helmer's mother –

client confidentiality meant a lot to him, even though he hadn't yet accepted the job. If she'd shown any familiarity with the name, he might have opened up further, but it was a long shot and he knew it. Dorothy had never paid much attention to the intricacies of her husband's political activities and Spyros had been careful to protect her from anything that might bring her into conflict with the authorities. The Iraklis group that had murdered Trent Helmer and numerous others had proclaimed its Marxist-Leninist ideals often enough in the pronunciamentos it delivered after the assassinations but, as far as he knew, it never had any connection with official Communist organisations – though he intended to dig further in that area.

His mobile rang. It slipped between his legs as he tried to answer it and almost dropped on to the hard balcony floor. He scrabbled to rescue it.

'*Nai?*'

'You fucking bastard.' Niki Glezou often used English with him when she was on the attack. 'Why didn't you ring me?' she demanded, switching to Greek.

'I did ring you,' Mavros replied. 'You'd turned off all your phones. I left a–'

'Why didn't you come round to my place?'

He sighed. 'Because I didn't want a fist in the belly. Or worse.' Niki had perpetrated some humiliating punishments on him in the past, one involving honey smeared across the floor of the communal staircase. 'Anyway, I was–'

'Working. Yes, I know. The great detective's work always takes priority. What were you doing with that bitch in–'

'Niki,' Mavros said, interrupting in turn. 'Is this going anywhere?' He meant the conversation, but he realised too late how she would take the question.

There was a pause. 'No, it's going nowhere. Go to the good, wanker.' She broke the connection.

Mavros let the phone drop from his hand. His heart was thumping. It was always like this with Niki. She was a full-blown Mediterranean hothead and he came off worst in exchanges with her because of the less volatile side he had inherited from his mother. Sometimes he wished he were different, a hundred per cent Greek who was emotionally demonstrative. Perhaps he would have got out of his system the sense of loss he felt for his brother; perhaps he would have been able to function more effectively with women. But he couldn't change how he was, that much he had learned over the years. Maybe Niki had learned it too and was cutting her losses.

Mavros ran the fingers of his right hand through his hair, feeling the long strands slide across the skin, and thought about the background to Grace Helmer's story. The Iraklis group killings, the red deaths. Apart from the 17 November terrorists, with their long record of action against political and business targets, the Iraklis group had been Greece's most wanted criminal organisation – most wanted and most discussed, especially now, with its apparent return to the front line after years of absence. In the run-up to the 2004 Olympic Games, security concerns were dominating political debate both inside and outside the country. The Americans in particular were alarmed by what they saw as the ease with which assassins continued to evade capture. Not a single terrorist had been convicted in the twenty-seven years since the fall of the dictatorship, despite the increasing involvement of foreign police and secret-service personnel. In recent years, speculation had been mounting that Greek government figures who had been involved in the opposition to the Junta were protecting the assassins – even manipulating them, according to the most virulent right-wing newspapers. On the other hand, some journalists on the Left claimed that the CIA was pulling the strings.

All of which made the Grace Helmer case extremely sensitive. Mavros knew that he should already have told the authorities about the man who called himself Iason Kolettis – Grace's mother's links with the assassin were a new development, and it seemed likely that the terrorist's name and background were also unknown to them. But he had several reasons for hanging back. The years he had spent working for the Ministry of Justice after university had taught him to be cautious about the system. Volunteering information about a high-profile target such as Iraklis would lead to days, maybe even weeks of questioning for him and the rest of his family because of his father's Communist background and his brother's record of resistance during the dictatorship. He didn't want to land that on his mother at this stage in her life.

And then there was Grace herself. She was reserved, cold, but she needed to know the truth about her family and he could relate to that. She resembled him, still burning after all this time to find out what had happened to Andonis. He knew better than anyone how little use the authorities had been in that search. Why should they be any more effective with an assassination that had taken place twenty-five years ago, which they had signally failed to solve in the intervening period? There was also, he forced himself to acknowledge, his professional pride. Grace Helmer had come to him for help and he didn't want to turn her away. In the past the only cases he'd refused to accept were those in which the potential clients were not really interested in the outcome: parents who were going through the motions of looking for offspring they were secretly pleased to have seen the last of, rich men trying to track down trophy girlfriends who had found a better payer. Grace wasn't in any such category.

Still, he thought, as he fingered his phone, it was a close call. He would be taking a big risk concealing what Grace had told him about her father's killer. Maybe it would be better to talk to one of his contacts in the police. The commander Nikos Kriaras, who had steered Grace towards him, was a source of many clients – particularly foreigners – whom the police didn't want to handle officially. Kriaras was a long-serving officer who, behind the scenes, had gained the trust of politicians from several parties. But he was also secretive, restricting his contact with Mavros to brief telephone calls, never on mobiles, which could be intercepted by the newspapers.

Unless Kriaras's suspicions had already been raised by Grace's approach, it might be better to leave him in the dark, at least until the outline of the case and its potential consequences were clearer.

Mavros sat back in his chair and looked up at the Acropolis, the lower levels of the rock swathed in winter vegetation. On the tall pole at the western corner, the Greek flag was flapping in the breeze. If it goes limp in the next minute, he said to himself, I'll call Kriaras. If it doesn't, I'll go and talk to the Fat Man.

The flag's blue panels and white cross remained visible for much longer than a minute as it rode the relentless wind.

The mountains of the northern Peloponnese were snow-capped, buzzards hanging on the air currents above the slopes, but the plain of Argos below was warm in their stony embrace. The waters of the gulf were rippled gently by the breeze, and the cargo vessels bound to and from Nafplion had cut huge V-shapes in the blue. All around there was a faint hum from insects that had been woken by the sun's heat, the scent of oranges rising from the blanket of trees that spread across the wide expanse of cultivated land.

'Ach, how fine it is.' The woman at the table on the terrace stretched back in her chair, her weight making the wooden legs scrape on the tiles. 'How fine this country of ours is.' She looked across the array of plates and bowls, fruit and bread piled high around pots of yoghurt and honey. As was the custom, they had eaten a late lunch, served by the sombre butler she was beginning to wish she hadn't hired. 'Eh, Nikita?' Suddenly her voice had an edge to it. 'Isn't it?'

Her husband looked up from the sheaf of papers on which he had placed an electronic calculator, his fingers frozen over the keys. 'What, Veta? Oh, shit, I lost my place.' He bent lower, the bald patch on the top of his head glinting in the light. Although it was natural, it had the look of a monk's tonsure, even if the expensive styling and the thin line of moustache on his upper lip detracted from the ecclesiastical effect. If anything, he had more the appearance of a nightclub-owner, an impression fostered by the garish harlequin dressing-gown he affected. The juxtaposition of his lanky form with his wife's bulk was a source of illicit amusement in Athenian high society – their ill-advised appearance as Laurel and Hardy at a fancy-dress ball had brought the house down.

Veta Dhragoumi-Palaiologou, local Member of Parliament and shadow shipping minister for the conservative opposition, glanced at her husband with ill-disguised annoyance. 'Come on, Nikita, lunch here is one of the few times we spend together. Can't you do those figures when you go back to the office?' She looked beyond him to the factory chimneys on the coastline. The Palaiologos family had always been major landowners on the plain, but after the Second World War her father-in-law, God forgive his rapacious soul, had established orange-pulping and tomato-canning plants between Nafplion and Argos. Her own

109

father was a ship-owner who had made a fortune carrying fruit and other sensitive cargoes around the Mediterranean and the Black Sea. Her marriage to Nikitas had been a business deal made in heaven for the two old men, both long dead.

'Ah, to the devil!' her husband shouted, throwing down the calculator and his papers to the floor. 'The fools I employ, I'll fire the lot of them.'

Veta poured a glass of juice and handed it to him. 'In the name of God, calm down. Try some of your company's latest product. Actually, it isn't bad.'

Nikitas scowled at her. 'You think I haven't already tasted it?' He gulped the juice. 'Some idiot junior manager wanted to call it "Nectar of Iraklis",' he said. 'The last thing those bastard terrorists are going to get is free advertising from me.'

'I told you before,' Veta said, watching her husband's face turn red, 'calm down or you'll have a heart-attack.' She twitched her lips and her face suddenly looked more youthful. The prominent pair of moles on her right cheek gave it a curiously unbalanced look. She referred to them ironically as her 'beauty spots' and they were a gift to the country's political cartoonists. 'Come, Nikita, you're not really frightened of those madmen, are you?'

She looked around the fortress-like house that old man Palaiologos had renovated in the sixties when the Colonels' regime had indiscriminately handed out planning permits to its supporters. The main building was like a military blockhouse,

110

the heavy stone walls interspersed with small windows. When they were newlyweds, Veta had tried to get the windows enlarged, but Nikitas's tame architect had claimed that the structure would be fatally weakened. She had done her best to leaven the heavy atmosphere of the place, adding white pergolas and a swimming-pool to the terrace, but still it had the feel of a converted army base. During the Axis occupation and the civil war that ensued, this part of the Palaiologos estate had been used as a prison camp for members of the Communist resistance movement.

Nikitas stood up and went towards the house, his thin frame bent as if under a great weight. Veta watched him go. When she had first known him, he was a typical rich man's playboy son with a sports car and a speedboat. That side of him hadn't attracted her at all. After all, she was rich man's spawn herself and wouldn't have been seen in anything other than luxury vehicles. But she was also a blue stocking, the holder of a first-class degree in economics from Cambridge, and her knowledge of sex was limited. Nikitas had never been bright – he had struggled to finish a business-studies degree at a minor Italian university – but he was renowned as a sexual athlete of Olympic prowess. The first time he turned curious eyes on her in a nightclub near Glyfadha, she had felt her knees weaken. The fact that he had even noticed her would have been enough, but then he took her in his arms before he drove her home and she knew she was lost. It didn't even disturb her when she found out that he had gone after her on his father's orders.

Veta sipped her coffee and looked at the briefing notes her office had faxed from the big city. No, there was no need. She already knew what she was going to say to the journalist from the business broadsheet who was coming to interview her the next morning. In fact, she knew more about shipping than most tycoons, her father had made sure of that. Being an only child had been a great advantage to her. If only her own two offspring had shown the same single-mindedness to achieve, but her son was lazy, a fourteen-year-old who had mastered only computer games and self-abuse, and her eleven-year-old daughter showed interest in nothing more than ponies and her doll collection.

The politician sat back again and ran her eyes over the view beneath the house. Straight down the slope, rising up from the shimmering leaves of the orange groves, were the titanic walls of ancient Tiryns. The place had always fascinated her, even before she became mistress of the Palaiologos weekend retreat. Huge blocks of rough-hewn stone dragged into place by hordes of doomed slaves, spectacular triangular galleries and casemates, a secret stair and, on the top, the foundations of a royal palace. Compared with Athens or Mycenae, the acropolis was small and narrow, but on misty days it floated above the plantations like a looming grey battleship.

Vera stood up slowly, resting her hands on the table to support her bulk. Before she had the children she had watched her weight, but now she didn't care. Nikitas found younger flesh to satisfy his demands and she devoted herself to her work. Like the Bronze Age fortress below, her bulk was essential, a guarantee of her strength and probity.

Then she remembered the mythological figure who had been born in Tiryns and felt a shiver run up her spine beneath her silk gown – Iraklis, great hero-god of the Peloponnese, slayer of monsters and harrower of hell.

Could his modern counterpart really be back on the trail of the country's rich after a decade's absence?

Mavros pounded on the door of the café. The Fat Man always slept in the afternoon, his body suspended on the springs of an ancient, rusting bed-frame that he had wedged into the storeroom behind the counter. He had a normal-sized room and a substantially more comfortable bed in his mother's house in Neapolis, but he preferred to keep out of range of Kyra Fedhra's stinging tongue during the daytime.

'Come on, Yiorgo, let me in!' Mavros shouted. 'I'm not a tourist. Or a taxman.'

After a substantial delay – the Fat Man making clear his displeasure at being disturbed – there was the sound of bolts being drawn. Mavros pushed at the door when the figure behind the frosted glass turned away without opening it.

'Very welcoming,' he said. 'I'll have a *sketo* if you're making coffee.'

'You'll have nothing as I'm not,' the café-owner said, glowering over his shoulder. His eyes were puffy and the hair on the sides of his head was sticking out. 'What the hell do you want at this

113

time, Alex? I was in the middle of undressing Claudia Schiffer.'

'That's more than I need to know,' Mavros said, sitting down at an unwiped table and taking out his mobile. 'Go on, Yiorgo, make me one little coffee. I'll pay for it, honest.'

The Fat Man went behind the chill cabinet and lit the flame of his small gas burner. 'Oh, yes, you'll pay, all right, comrade,' he said firmly. 'I'll amend my earlier question,' he went on, his tone now that of the fastidious committee secretary. 'What the fuck do you want, Alex?'

Mavros was peering at his mobile. 'I'm trying to make up my mind. Should I call Bitsos and ask him for help or not?'

Yiorgos Pandazopoulos looked round. 'Bitsos? That rat-faced journalist?' The Fat Man had the Communist's traditional contempt for the drones of the capitalist press. Naturally, workers on the Party organ *Rizospastis* weren't subject to that sentiment.

'Lambis Bitsos isn't your average shit-raker with a laptop,' Mavros said.

The café-owner guffawed. 'No – from what you've told me, he's your average shit-raker with a dirty magazine.'

'Mmm.' Mavros sat thinking for a few moments. Behind the banter lay a serious issue. Bitsos the crime reporter was potentially his best source of information about the Iraklis group and the man known as Iason Kolettis. But anything he got from Bitsos would come at a price. As he'd discovered to his cost in the past, he needed an even longer spoon when dealing with journalists than he would to sup with the devil. They would sometimes part with useful nuggets, but in return they expected exclusive stories and full details; the fact that the latter were subject to client confidentiality rules led the gentlemen and women of the press to do little more than scratch their groins. So, was it worth it? Mavros decided to stall, at least until he had tapped another source that was substantially closer to hand.

The Fat Man came over with a tray containing two small cups and two glasses of water. 'You're paying for mine as well, in case you were wondering,' he said.

'My pleasure,' said Mavros, with a wide grin.

Immediately Yiorgos Pandazopoulos's face darkened. 'Oh, I get it. What do you want this time? I'm not lending you my *Godfather* videos again. Get your own, you Scottish skinflint.'

'No, no, nothing like that.'

'What then?' The café-owner looked as suspicious as a pedestrian accosted by a laughing beggar.

'Lighten up, Yiorgo. I want you to help me in an investigation.'

The Fat Man's face took on an exultant expression. 'Ach, Alex, now you're talking.' He sat down heavily and pushed a cup and glass towards his sole customer. 'What do you want me to do?' he asked, more enthusiastic than a boy who'd been dropped into the driving seat of a tank.

Mavros realised that what he was going to ask probably wouldn't be enough to satisfy his friend's appetite for intrigue, but he pressed on: 'You have to keep this to yourself, Yiorgo, eh?'

'Of course,' the café-owner said impatiently. 'I know how the system works. I've seen enough detective films.'

'Yes, well, this is the real world, not a gang of Californian playboys pretending to be tough.' Mavros ran his eye over the bulky figure across the table. 'Though, come to think of it, you do look a bit like Sidney Greenstreet.'

'Get on with it, Alex,' the Fat Man threatened, 'or I really will make you pay for the coffee.'

'Right.' Mavros had already decided to make no mention of Grace Helmer. Yiorgos Pandazopoulos had messed up the last time he'd dealt with her. He was going to stick to his friend's background. 'You grew up in Neapolis, you've lived there all your life.'

'Yes, yes. And?'

'And you knew everyone on the Left. The Moscow Communists, the EuroCommunists, the splinter groups and the ... and the loose cannons.'

The Fat Man was peering at him suspiciously now. 'Where's this heading, Alex?' He'd been hauled in by the Junta's security forces often enough to know when a sensitive subject was about to be broached.

Mavros gave up trying to sweet-talk his old friend. 'All right, here it is. Did you ever hear of a guy called Iason Kolettis back in the seventies?'

There was a long pause, during which the only sounds came from the motorbikes passing on the road outside and from the birds settling down for the night in the worm-infested pergola to the rear

116

of the café.

Eventually Yiorgos leaned over, his weight almost making the flimsy table buckle. 'Why do you want to know about him?' he asked, in a low voice.

'Can't tell you,' Mavros replied.

'Oh, I see. You can't tell me anything but you expect me to spill my guts?' The Fat Man sat back, his expression serious. 'This isn't a joke, Alex. Unlike you, I'm a member of the Party. By rights I should report your interest to the central committee.'

Mavros was trying to conceal his excitement. It looked like Yiorgos knew something about the mystery man. 'Why?' he asked. 'I'm not a policeman and you know I'm not going to do anything that would be bad for the Party. I might not be committed but my father was a leading light.'

The Fat Man puffed out his cheeks, then bit his lower lip. 'I know, Alex, I know. It's just ... there are some things that are still restricted. I'm going to have to talk to the comrades about this. I mean it.'

Mavros stretched out a hand and put it on his friend's forearm. 'Don't, Yiorgo. That would be a very bad idea. I only asked out of curiosity. The name came up in a line of enquiry I'm pursuing.' He felt guilty about putting Yiorgos in a difficult position, but he wanted to know more about Kolettis. 'What's the big deal? Who was the guy?'

The café-owner stood up and backed away. 'Lay off me on this, Alex,' he said, his face pale. 'I mean it. You'll get into all kinds of shit if you dig any further.' He started collecting the cups

117

and glasses, beads of sweat on his bald head.

'Shit?' Mavros said, realising that he wasn't going to continue. 'For God's sake, Yiorgo, I only wanted to know if you'd heard of him.'

The Fat Man bent forward and let the tray crash on to the table. 'Oh, yes, I've heard of him. In fact, I met him a couple of times. But I won't admit as much to anyone else, you understand?'

'Why not?' Mavros demanded, playing dumb about what Grace Helmer had told him. 'What's so special about Iason Kolettis?'

Yiorgos Pandazopoulos backed away. 'What's so special about him?' he repeated, in a hoarse whisper. 'He's the most dangerous bastard I've ever come across in my life.'

And that was all the Fat Man would say.

5

The poet Kostas Laskaris felt the familiar knifing pain in his belly as he got up from his bed. Until recently he had slept in the topmost room, three levels above the ground, but now the steep staircases were too much for him so he confined himself to the long living space, the tower rising out of it like the forefinger from a clenched fist. He staggered over to the nearest of the compact windows and unbolted the solid wooden shutter. It swung open easily enough, Savvas having oiled the hinges at the old man's request so that he didn't have to rely on anyone else to let in the daylight every morning.

He breathed in deeply and looked out over the rocks to the peninsula below. It was an overcast winter's day, the clouds low over the gulf that separated the Mani from the western prong of the Peloponnese. The air was damp, suffused with the scent of dew-soaked vegetation, and the clang of a goat-bell rang out across the water from the slopes to the south. Only one herdsman kept a few beasts now; the other families had given up livestock to direct their energies towards servicing the tourists.

Laskaris took in the rough circle-shape of the Tigani peninsula, which lay beneath the settlement of Ayia Kyriaki. The low acropolis was separated from the mainland by a handle of rough ground, giving it the look of the frying-pan that the Greek name indicated. He could just make out the crumbling walls of Castle Maïna, built by the Franks on more ancient foundations. It had been one of the three most important fortified strongpoints in the southern Peloponnese, and now it was nothing more than a shambolic array of collapsing cisterns and shattered tombs, some open to the elements. It was a tourist attraction if ever there was one, but few travellers made the difficult trek across the racks of sharp stone, past the salt pans where the locals used to scrape a paltry harvest every summer. He had seen a couple of men pick their way across it a few weeks earlier, stopping frequently as if the desolation of the place had disoriented them.

Tigani, the frying-pan. Laskaris preferred to see the peninsula as a mirror, another manifestation of the stone and metal objects from different periods that had been found in excavations all over Greece. That metaphor was multi-dimensional; as a craftsman of words, it appealed to him. The small mass of rock in the southern Peloponnese was a mirror of history, reflecting the glory and the violence that had marked this land, the bloodshed and waste, from ancient times, when the Spartans had ruled the region with a will of iron that extended no rights to its native people; to the Middle Ages, the Franks and the Venetians, their shiny leather jerkins and brightly coloured banners now rotten in the earth and leaving only dust motes in the confines of the ruined castle; to the savage

Maniates during the War of Independence in the 1820s who had cut the Turks to pieces with the honed blades of their yataghans; to the wars he himself had fought in – the Axis occupation and the desperate horror of the civil war that had followed between 1947 and 1949. The mirror of history.

The poet went over to the kitchen, which Savvas's mother kept gleaming, and made himself a cup of camomile tea. He eyed with distaste the packet of oatmeal that was supposed to form the major part of his diet and left it untouched. Better to work hungry, better to let his accursed gut wrench and clutch at his very being. That way he would re-create the horror more authentically; that way his poem would be imbued with the agony of the times he and his ancestors had lived through.

Yesterday he had made a good start. He had been surprised by how many pages of the leather-bound notebook he had filled with his spidery script. 'The Fire Shirt' was under way at last, the hero Iraklis having left his home fort of Tiryns to meet the cowardly King Eurystheus of Mycenae who would assign him his labours: the feeble king sending his strongest young man into battle against inhuman forces. It hadn't been difficult to expand the imagery with elements of his own century: the dictator Metaxas and the puppet King George despatching the youth of Greece to die against the Italians and the Germans in 1940–1: Stalin and Tito using the Greek Com-munists as standard-bearers of the revolution, then abandoning them in the final stages of the

121

civil war – though it had taken him many years to accept that reading of history. There was no shortage of relevance in the old myth.

Suddenly Kostas Laskaris felt the years slip away from him. His mind seemed to float away from the present day in the tower and he found himself on the other side of the Mani as he had been in 1943, his face turning towards the sun, which was rising in a blast of crimson over the eastern mountains beyond Sparta. His legs were strong again, the muscles under the torn battledress trousers knotted after months of clambering up the slopes with heavy loads. He was twenty-one, his beard shiny and long, his hands scarred and pitted by frontal attacks and close exchanges. He'd been a volunteer in the snows of Albania when the Greeks had defeated the Italians by raw passion; he had stood against the German tanks near Thermopylae and only retreated when the rifle was blown from his hands; and now he was a soldier of ELAS, the army of the liberation movement EAM, which had captured the hearts of the Greek people.

'The world is ours to win, comrade,' said the man with the burning eyes beside him, his unwashed face split by a broad smile. 'We will clear the forces of oppression from our mountains and from the rest of Greece. Then we will establish a government that respects all citizens.'

Laskaris had heard the speech often enough before, but he never tired of hearing it from this man. He was the band's leader, the most resourceful of the guerrilla fighters, their inspiration, as well as his friend from childhood.

122

He nodded, feeling the pack lighten on his shoulders. 'Yes, we will do that,' he said, as he reached the spine of the ridge. 'And you will show us the way.'

Kapetan Iraklis nodded and stepped quickly ahead.

The old poet Kostas Laskaris came back to himself in the tower above the windswept peninsula of Tigani, his body racked with the cancer's assault. The clock told him he had been lost in the past for hours. But now he was being nagged by another thought: who would the terrorist group set up by the son of his wartime leader target next? He shivered and gripped the table as another wave of stabbing pain washed over him.

Mavros had rung Grace Helmer at her hotel and told her he wanted to see her. She didn't sound too surprised when he declined her invitation to meet in her room, saying that he preferred another location nearby. He didn't want to be seen at the hotel with her again.

As he headed up towards Syndagma Square on foot, he tried to make sense of what he was doing. This looked like a seriously dubious proposition. Not only would the authorities regard his involvement in a terrorist case with extreme prejudice, but the party that had been his father's spiritual home was shaping up to be equally antagonistic. After the Fat Man had clammed up about Iason Kolettis, Mavros decided against making any further enquiries about him among other Communist sources. He reckoned that Yiorgos Pandazopoulos would keep his enquiry to himself if only for reasons of self-protection – Greek Communists had as much of a record for turning against their own as their comrades in other countries. But what was it about Kolettis that had spooked him? Could there have been links between some members of the Party and the Iraklis group?

After beating the traffic across the road outside the Grand Bretagne Hotel and gaining an approving wink from the policewoman on point duty, Mavros walked up Vasilissis Sofias Avenue with his head humming. The easy option was to reject Grace Helmer's job offer. That way he would keep himself in the security establishment's good books and avoid any angst from the Communists. He might also escape the notice of the killer who had done for the investor Vernard-hakis, if there turned out to be a connection between him and the man who had assassinated Grace's father. So what was he doing striding avidly towards the White Hart pub? He could easily have turned her down by phone. No, he had already decided he was going to take the job. It was too tempting to resist. Maybe the case he had cracked in the Cyclades last October had given him a taste for living dangerously.

The White Hart had been in the street near the Hilton since the seventies, a counterfeit English pub that served lager from the barrel, provided a tattered dartboard, and played soft rock to junior diplomats and nostalgic expatriates. Mavros wasn't a regular but he sometimes used it for meetings – the booths gave a degree of privacy and the drinkers, aware that they had committed a sin against good taste just by entering the establishment, kept themselves to themselves. When he got there, he discovered that Grace Helmer had already taken up residence in the far corner. She was smoking a cigarette with an air of abstraction, her loose white blouse setting off the deep tan of her arms and neck even in the subdued lighting of the pub. She had left her blonde hair loose. It gave her face a soft, lustrous frame.

'Hi,' Mavros said, indicating the half-full wine glass in front of her. 'Another?'

She shook her head. 'No, thanks. This came from the business end of a horse. I'll have a beer.'

He gave the order to the waiter who had appeared at his side – self-service, English-pub style was not an option – and sat down opposite her in the booth. 'Sorry I'm late.'

Grace Helmer glanced at her watch. 'Don't worry, I've been on my own in worse places.'

Not for the first time, Mavros caught a glimpse of the steely layer that lay beneath her easy-going urbanity. He wondered if she had been born like that or if her experiences as a child had made her that way.

'Cheers,' she said, raising the frosted glass that had been placed in front of her.

Mavros followed suit, feeling the cold beer clear the traffic fumes from his throat. 'That's better.' He drank again and saw her watching him with an expectant smile.

'So,' she said, her voice suddenly throatier, 'are you going to help me?'

It didn't escape him that she was making an

appeal rather than simply asking him if he wanted the job. But her words didn't make him feel that he was being manipulated. On the contrary, they encouraged him. He found it hard to handle cases that didn't engage him and he'd been concerned that she was too dispassionate.

'I think so,' he said, pausing to see how she reacted. Although her smile widened, her eyes were still giving off cold glints. 'But it isn't going to be easy.' He'd been considering how much to tell her about the case's sensitivity. 'You understand that the authorities, both Greek and American, would be reluctant to countenance a private investigator digging around in a terrorist assassination, even if it is twenty-five years old.'

Grace gave a brief laugh. 'Countenance?' she said, repeating his word ironically. 'What are you? A poet?'

'Think of Raymond Chandler's Marlowe,' Mavros said, with a smile. 'Private investigators soon become poets of the human condition.' He looked into her eyes. 'But do you understand, Grace? Do you understand how dirty and how dangerous this could get?'

The smile had disappeared from her lips. 'Sure I do, Alex,' she said. 'I've lived with the consequences of my father's death for most of my life. You imagine I haven't thought this through?'

He looked down at the cigarette-scarred table-top. 'I'm not suggesting that. It's just that in this country things are more complicated than you might imagine. For a start, there's a chance that the Iraklis group has recommenced operations. A rich investor was–'

126

'I know about him. I read the international papers.'

'But that isn't why you're here.'

Grace stared at him with what seemed to be incomprehension. 'No, of course not. I told you. I came because I got my mother's letter after my Ganma died. And because it's a quarter of a century since–' She reached for her cigarettes.

'Okay. I'm sorry. But you have to be aware that the assassin and his friends might realise that I'm digging up things from the past.' He decided to leave out the Communist angle for the time being.

Grace blew out a plume of smoke and threw back her head. 'I don't care. It's about time the ice cracked.' She looked at him. 'Are you scared by any chance, Alex?' she asked, with a mocking smile.

'Yes, of course I am,' he replied, without hesitation. 'I specialise in finding people, not taking on professional killers.'

She reached for her glass. 'Good. Fear is the key. Without it, you give your opponent the upper hand.'

Mavros thought about that as he sipped his beer. It sounded like the gnomic utterance of some eastern philosopher. Or a bullet point from an operational training manual.

An old Eagles number came over the speakers and Grace Helmer groaned. 'Shit, I hate this song.' She ground out her cigarette. '"Witchy Woman", my ass.'

Mavros grinned. 'Seems pretty appropriate to me.'

'Back off,' Grace said. She smiled and waved to the waiter for more drinks. 'Let's get down to business. What are your rates?'

He told her. She didn't seem too concerned and he almost wished he'd pitched them higher. Then he remembered that she was an aid-agency worker. This trip would be costing a large part of her annual savings.

'And how do you intend to go about finding–'

Mavros raised his hand swiftly and looked around. 'No names,' he said. 'Well, I've got various contacts whose chains I can pull – journalists, Justice and Public Order Ministry staff, policemen.' He stopped when he saw Grace's expression. 'What's the matter?'

'You just told me that we had to keep a low profile on this. Can you trust those guys?'

Mavros was impressed by her grip of the situation. He was about to launch into the list of secondary sources he'd been compiling, people he could approach in a more oblique fashion to minimise suspicion, when she leaned closer and beckoned him to do the same.

'Never mind,' she said, her breath fanning his ear. 'I've got another lead I didn't tell you about.'

'What?' he said, unable to keep his voice down. 'Sorry.' He waited for her to bring her head close again. 'What do you mean another lead?'

'I was waiting to see if you would take the case. Security is essential, don't you agree?'

'Yeah, yeah,' he said, registering the echo of his earlier warnings. 'What is it?'

'Do you really think I'm a witchy woman?' she asked, putting on a sultry voice.

'Give me a break, Grace. What's the lead?'

She leaned even closer, this time briefly touching the upper part of his cheek with her own. He breathed in her scent, something restrained cut with cigarette smoke. The proximity to her made the hairs on his neck rise. 'Actually, it's to do with music. After my mother died, my Ganma collected up all her things and put them in crates in the loft. She didn't want me to be unduly influenced. You can see why, I suppose. Anyway, a couple of years ago I was going through the boxes when I was back on leave. And I found this Greek record, a single. I didn't play it, but I copied down the writing on the label. You see, it was the only Greek disc my mother had and I figured it must have meant something to her.' She sat back, took a piece of paper from the pocket of her jeans and slid it across the table.

Mavros glanced over his shoulder, then unfolded the note. On it were several lines of Greek that had clearly been transcribed by someone unfamiliar with the language. '"The Voyage of the *Argo*",' he translated, suppressing the quiver of surprise that had run through him. 'I know this song. Everyone in Greece knows this song. It was one of the composer Randos's first big hits.'

He thought of the poet Kostas Laskaris, whom he'd met at his mother's. He had written the words to what had subsequently become one of the most popular songs of resistance to the Colonels' regime in the late sixties. What was it the gaunt old man had said? That the lyrics

129

meant more than the music suggested?

'We had this in my home when I was a kid, even though it was banned by the dictatorship. My brother Andonis used to play it in the evenings, at a volume that was much higher than was sensible until my mother intervened.'

Grace was watching him thoughtfully. 'So is it any help?'

Mavros blinked and came back to himself. 'What? Is it any help?' He raised his shoulders. 'I don't know. The song was generally taken as a metaphor for political change. The voyage of Jason and the Argonauts and their quest for the Golden Fleece was an exhortation to Greeks to strive for a more just government.' He smacked a hand to his forehead. 'Shit. Jason and the Argonauts.' He leaned close again. 'Jason is Iason in Greek. As in Iason—'

'Kolettis,' Grace murmured. 'You think the song was written about the man who killed my father?'

Mavros stared at the transcription. 'But this record was first released in the mid-sixties.'

'More than ten years before my father was killed.'

Mavros's expression was troubled. 'And Kolettis was in his early thirties when your mother knew him, so he would have been a very young man back then.' He ran his fingers through his hair. 'There's something else. It's a long time since I studied Greek mythology, but I can remember some of the crew members of the *Argo*. Jason chose the bravest, most skilled men he could find.' He looked across at Grace. 'One

130

of whom was the greatest hero of his time.'

She returned his gaze blankly.

'Whose name was Hercules,' Mavros said. 'Or in this country, Iraklis.' He wondered if Kostas Laskaris, former leading Communist, knew more about the terrorists than he'd ever publicly admitted.

Neither Mavros nor Grace noticed that the music in the Red Lion had changed. Now The Who were playing 'Won't Get Fooled Again'.

The beggar had been opposite the Megaro Mousikis all afternoon. Although there were often policemen around the nation's major concert hall, not least because the American embassy was the next building down the broad avenue, they didn't pay him much attention. He had taken care to work the grime well into his face, hands and lower legs in the hotel room. He had put on the ragged clothes he had picked up from the barrows in the back-streets around Omonia and slipped out of the building when no one was around. As soon as he took up his position on the pavement, he had rolled up his trousers and twisted his feet into unsightly angles, the toenails uneven and discoloured with earth from a park picked up on his way. He had spent hours in the pose over the last week and knew he could keep it up without getting cramp – his regime of physical training was almost as rigorous now as it had been all those years ago in the training camps. And the pose had been convincing. He had been given several thousand drachmas' worth of coins throughout the afternoon by sympathetic passers-by, most of them elderly women.

The sun had made him sweat earlier on, but now it had gone and there was a chill wind blowing down Vasilissis Sophias. He wasn't concerned. He had grown up in the country and nothing Athens could throw at him caused any problems. The straggly beard he had obtained from a theatrical outfitter was irritating the skin of his face and neck, and the rough workman's shirt was also a penance, but there wasn't long to go now. He wasn't wearing his watch, considering that no self-respecting beggar would make the mistake of displaying such a possession, but he had it in his pocket and cast surreptitious glances at it from time to time. Three-quarters of an hour to go – the VIPs' cars would soon be arriving. Less exalted ticket-holders were already streaming into the rectangular concrete and glass box that had been erected on a piece of parkland a few years before. Fur coats and evening suits were in evidence, though many of the audience were in casual clothes. The production they were to see was of Verdi's *Macbeth*, in modern dress. 'Death to all tyrants,' the beggar muttered to himself, with a cracked smile.

He stayed on the opposite side of the road, biding his time. He knew from the briefing he had memorised that the target always arrived close to curtain-up, leaving his office as late as possible. No rest for the tycoon, at least not until tonight. He would have eternal rest soon enough. He touched the thin object in his breast pocket, hoping that the metal casing and the timing device he had set earlier was as infallible as he'd been assured. It was the best on the global market. Who said capitalism was a worthless system? It produced weapons you could rely on – if you had the funds to obtain them.

There was a constant stream of cars pulling up, armoured Mercedes with smoked-glass windows dropping off politicians, even a Rolls-Royce with the British flag depositing a harassed-looking ambassador with his wan, pearl-bedecked wife and granite-faced bodyguard at the foot of the steps. Soon the target would be here.

Then there was a flash of headlights and bodywork to his right. That was it – a silver Jaguar with an old-style radiator grille. The beggar cut across the traffic with unexpected speed, arriving on the opposite pavement before the police had caught sight of him. As the Jaguar's nearside doors opened, the security man out first to usher his employer into the building, the dishevelled man started up his incantation in a high, cracked voice.

'Sir, spare a few coins for an invalid.' He pointed to his twisted legs. 'I cannot work, I have a sick wife and three helpless children. Sir, spare a few coins...' He broke off as the bodyguard raised a fist, then let out an ear-piercing shriek. 'Don't hurt an invalid. I'm incapable, I'm weak...' He was making his voice as heart-rending as possible, blinking tears on to his filthy cheeks. That way the target would be shamed into approaching him, fearful that if he didn't the watching police and late-arriving ticket-holders would comment on his stinginess.

The tactic worked. The rich man tapped his bodyguard's shoulder and stepped close to the beggar, a sheaf of thousand-drachma notes extended.

'Oh, sir,' the beggar said, 'thank you, sir, you are a good man, may God bless you, sir.' And he stumbled towards the target, his hand slipping the narrow metal tube into the inside pocket of the silk-lined tuxedo before the gorilla manhandled him away.

The beggar limped away down the street, an expression of beatific joy on his face. As he got further away, he let the smile fade but kept up the awkward gait. The target was doomed. Even if he discovered the extra pen in his pocket and removed it, the motion sensor would detonate the concentrated explosive. The amount had been reduced as much as was feasible so that people in the close vicinity wouldn't suffer serious injury. The man playing the beggar had suggested slipping the weapon into the target's pocket after the performance so that the explosion would take place in the car, but his boss had been adamant: the death had to occur in the concert hall for maximum public effect. That was why he had to risk a close encounter. And the piece of olivewood was to be dropped into a leading newspaper's mailbox later that night along with the statement claiming responsibility.

The second labour had been designed to raise the stakes considerably.

In her hotel room Grace Helmer lay back on the

wide bed and blew smoke into the temperature-controlled air. Glancing around at the character-less furniture and the neutral reproductions on the pale yellow walls, she felt that she could be anywhere. She should have booked herself into a smaller, family-run hotel, maybe on the slopes of the Acropolis, rather than this soulless dump – there, she might have been able to shut herself off from the past, if only for a few moments each day. Her work had taken her to so many of the world's hellholes, the nights spent in plush hotels in big cities framing tours of duty on the front line where nobody had any luxuries, free time, or even a single breath that wasn't tainted by the stink of physical corruption. She wondered why she had let her career rule her life, wondered if there really was a chance that her work could unlock the emotions she had kept in check for so long.

She stretched across to the bedside table and emptied the miniature of whisky that she'd taken from the mini-bar. Why was she tormenting herself with pointless questions? She knew why her work was so important to her. Ever since she'd left home at eighteen, she'd felt the need to make her own life: her father was long dead, her mother had floated in her own distant dimension, her grandmother was strong-willed and restrictive. She'd also wanted to put as much space as she could between herself and the world in which she'd been raised. Service abroad was perfect, and she was good at it. The only reason she hadn't been promoted further was that she refused to give up foreign postings: otherwise she'd have been sitting in some air-conditioned block in the US, her spirit shrinking as her prospects improved. To hell with that.

And now Greece, after a quarter of a century. Was she up to it? The decision to return hadn't been difficult to take when the time had come at last – she'd been turning it over in her mind ever since she'd become an adult – but she was still uncertain. Could she handle being back in the country where she'd seen her father murdered?

A vision flashed before her of her father's head being pulled back by the hair, the blade slicing across his throat to release a fine spray of crimson. And in that instant, as so often before, everything she had achieved in her life was nullified, turned to insubstantial shadow and smoke. However much she tried to get beyond it, his death continued to haunt her, to define her life. The only salvation was to find the man who had killed him. Not for anything as simplistic as revenge, though she sometimes wanted to wreak some awful physical retribution on the butcher. No, what she needed was the sense of an ending, the tying of a knot, a steel cap over the damped-down fires of her early life – and that would only be attained by hearing the man's explanation of his actions; then she might at least have a chance of moving on.

And then, maybe, she might finally be free to find a man, she thought, spreading her arms and legs across the king-size bed, a man who meant something. The only ones she'd ever known fell into two categories. There were the one-hour stands, the pick-ups who gave her brief moments of hungry fumbling and stifled release – there had been plenty of those over the years – but she was tired of the routine, the farewell fuck that tipped her into an abyss of dreamless sleep at the end of each tour in the jungle or the desert. And there were the carers, the guys who tried to bring her out of herself, apparently inspired only by the desire to help her. One was on her case now. She was sick of the pattern her emotional life had fallen into. There must be something more.

Grace got up and went to the window. The multicoloured lights of the city were spread out all around like those of competing stalls in a vast fairground, the sound of the traffic – accelerating engines, brakes and horns, the angry shouts of drivers and pedestrians – carried up on the caustic air. The place was a madhouse, she thought. What was she doing here? There were over three million people in this conurbation alone. How was she going to find a guy with a false name who'd disappeared into the night twenty-five years ago?

At least she had enlisted someone to help her. Alex Mavros's slim figure in leather jacket and jeans appeared before her. He was as Greek as any Athenian male, but his dual heritage gave him something else, a hint of the alien north in the Mediterranean city. With his long hair and unshaven face, he didn't look like an investigator. But there was something about him that reassured her, a reservoir of calm beneath the driven exterior. He gave the impression that he knew what he was doing, and his caution about how to proceed with the case struck her as pretty smart.

Then there were his eyes. She'd noticed them the first time they met, in his apartment when the crazy woman had laid into him with her fists. The right one blue and perfect, the left one drizzled with flecks of brown. She'd never seen such a thing before, apart from rock stars who affected contact lenses that didn't match. For some reason, Alex's eyes had provoked a kindred feeling in her. Maybe it was because she had recognised him subconsciously as an outsider like herself, a pariah living on the margins of conventional society. She smiled. Or maybe she just had the hots for him.

The telephone on the glass-covered table rang. She looked at her watch. The prearranged call was never missed. But before she could put the receiver to her ear, an over-amplified orchestra of sirens began to play along the street below.

When Grace looked down, it took her a couple of seconds to work out that the bright red patch that had suddenly appeared on her free hand was a rose petal. It must have dropped from the single rose she'd been given with the hotel's compliments.

Welcome to Athens.

Mavros had left Grace Helmer outside her hotel, having promised to call her in the morning with a detailed plan of action. She'd insisted on accompanying him everywhere he went on the case, which he wasn't keen on but was prepared to go along with at least temporarily. After all, she was paying. Usually clients who clung like limpets let go after a day or two, finding the

138

legwork and the repeated questions that made up the investigator's day more tedious than filling out a tax return. Right now he was still on the job, even though he'd told Grace he was going home. The lead she'd given him about the song 'The Voyage of the *Argo*' had made him want to find out more about the poet who'd written the lyrics, and he knew who could give him a detailed character sketch of the old man.

'Mother?' he called, after he had turned the key in the lock and found his progress barred. He was relieved to find that she'd followed his advice to apply the security chain in the evening, though the downside was that it was harder to get to her if anything happened inside the flat.

He heard tentative footsteps and waved his hand through the gap.

'Alex,' said Dorothy, as she opened up. 'How nice.' She kissed his cheek. 'If unexpected.'

Mavros caught the hint of disapproval. Although she spent her life trying to get him to call round, she liked to manage her timetable. 'Sorry. I'm not disturbing you, am I?'

'Of course not, dear,' she said, linking her arm in his as she led him into the *saloni*. Her desk was heaped with open volumes, a typescript in two uneven piles in the centre. The radio was playing softly in the background – Dorothy always had the classical channel on when she was working. 'I'm just starting to read a book I was given by a man I first met in the sixties. Do you remember Geoffrey Dearfield? I wish he'd bought himself a computer. He must have used the same typewriter he had when he was a young man.'

'Dearfield?' Mavros said. 'The English guy who was in the mountains during the war?'

Dorothy sat down on the sofa and beckoned to him to join her. 'That's right. He was in the Special Operations Executive, fighting the Germans and Italians, and then he was some kind of military adviser to the government forces during the civil war.'

Mavros had a dim recollection of the man. 'Wasn't he an MP in the UK?'

His mother nodded. 'In the fifties, yes. But he came back here permanently after that. His wife's Greek. He's written what he calls a "polemical memoir". If it lives up to that description the lawyers will have to read every line, even though most of the protagonists will be dead now.' She shook her head. 'You know how sensitive people are about their family name in this country.'

Mavros raised an eyebrow. 'What would the old man think of you publishing a book by an ex-British officer? Those liaison guys weren't exactly friendly towards the Left.'

Dorothy gave him a sharp glance. 'Your father was many things, but he wasn't a bigot. If Geoff's book adds to our knowledge about those terrible times, I'll bring it out without a trace of guilt.'

Mavros opened his hands in submission. 'All right, all right. I'm no fan of censorship.' He sat back and ran his fingers across his forehead. 'God, those bloody wars. Everything seems to lead back to them. The Colonels all fought in them, didn't they?'

Dorothy turned to look at him, her own brow furrowed. 'What are you talking about?'

140

He told her about 'The Voyage of the *Argo*', how the song had cropped up in a case, without mentioning Grace and her father. 'Remember how Andonis used to play it during the dictatorship and you used to turn down the volume?'

His mother looked stricken. 'Yes, I remember. But what's that song got to do with the occupation and the civil war? Oh, I see. Kostas Laskaris wrote the lyric.'

'He was in the resistance. And in the Democratic Army during the civil war in the late forties.'

'He was,' Dorothy agreed. 'Poor man. He suffered terribly. Your father knew him, of course. They were in the concentration camp on Makronisos together after the final defeat.'

Mavros had a flash of the narrow island off the coast of Attiki, one of several used to confine left-wing prisoners. Many had died on its arid slopes. 'You knew Laskaris too, didn't you? After they were released.'

'Yes, your father and I saw him occasionally when he came up from that old tower he was renovating in the Mani. They fell out about the Party's policies in the sixties, I think.' She sighed. 'And now he's dying, I'm sure of it. His eyes were restless and he's losing the fight. I'd like to–' She broke off as Mavros made a movement with his hand and went closer to the radio.

'...normal programming to bring our listeners an emergency news report,' came the excited tones of the announcer. 'There has been an explosion inside the Megaro Mousikis during this evening's performance of Verdi's *Macbeth*. It is not yet known how many people have been

141

injured. Police and fire-fighters are...'

'Oh, my God,' Dorothy said. 'Oh, my God.' She was staring at her son, her features twisted in horror. 'Anna and Nondas – they were going to the opera tonight. Oh, my God, Alex.'

Mavros was already pressing buttons on his mobile phone.

6

The Fat Man had been in his bedroom listening to a football match on the radio. The illicit card table he held every evening in the café had finished early because the players had run out of cash. He didn't care – he'd already taken his cut and they'd be back tomorrow. That would be their last chance until after Christmas as he was leaving for a week in the Peloponnese with his mother. Maybe it would do his soul good to stop making money for a while. If the comrades found out how much he had in his bank account, they'd want most of it for Party funds. No chance. Karl Marx would have understood, he knew how the market worked, though Lenin and the megalomaniac Stalin wouldn't have been so forgiving. So what? He was a Greek first and then a Communist. And Greeks were born individualists, weren't they? They'd never taken well to authority.

'Yiorgo?' his mother called from downstairs. 'Come and help me. Now.'

He raised his eyes to the ceiling. Although Greeks might think they were individualists, they had to operate within the close confines of family, Communists included. He'd tried to shake off the coils, but after his father had died on the prison island in the sixties, he had known he was stuck with the old woman for life. Kyra Fedhra was now in her eighties. All day she'd been working in the kitchen of the two-storey apartment prior to their departure for the south. The Pandazopoulos family had moved to the central district of Neapolis from their mountain village before the war. He had grown up in the streets around the hill of Strephi, an overweight lump even during the famine years of the occupation because of his mother's devotion. His father Vladhimiros was a hardliner who had been a commissar during the war and had paid for it, then and afterwards. Yiorgos had run errands for the Party as an adolescent, had worked in the lower echelons of the banned organisation until the dictatorship fell, but in the last decade he had begun to drift away. The comrades had almost given up on him, regarding his café as a capitalist tourist trap, which showed how infrequently any of them visited it.

Yiorgos got up from his bed and lumbered downstairs.

'Ah, there you are,' his mother said. 'I've been waiting for hours. Fetch me down those oven pans. I'm going to make a *baklava* for our relatives in the village.'

'Now?' the Fat Man said, looking at his watch. 'Didn't the doctor say you should be in bed by ten?'

'Never mind him,' Kyra Fedhra said dismissively. 'What does he know? Besides, I've been so busy with other things that I haven't made your *galaktoboureko* yet.' She gave her son a sharp look. 'And where would your customers be without their morning treat?'

Yiorgos handed her the pans and rapidly

withdrew. As usual, the old woman was right. He'd have a riot on his hands if he didn't have a pastry for his regulars – Kyra Fedhra's delicacies were renowned among the market traders and the Flea Market con-men who drank their coffee in his place every morning. Alex Mavros wouldn't be impressed either.

As he heaved his bulk back upstairs, the café-owner thought about his friend. What the devil was the madman doing? No one talked about Iason Kolettis – no one spoke that name if they had a brain in their head. There were some things that the Party had always managed to keep secret and he was sure that had remained one of them. Otherwise the authorities and the press would have been on Kolettis's trail years ago. But Alex wasn't to know. He'd only been a kid when the name was first used, and even when the Iraklis group was operating at full throttle, he had been little more than a pimply student. But, Christ and the Mother of God, where had he picked it up? The only people who knew about the butcher were the comrades, and not many of them were in on the secret. After the madman had split from the Party, security had been as tight as a cat's arse. Alex had better keep his head down.

The Fat Man pricked up an ear as another goal went in. He wasn't particularly interested in the game, but the noise kept his mother at bay – she hated football with a passion. He felt worms of unease twisting in his gut. One related to his decision not to report Alex's use of the name to the Party, despite the unwritten but firm order issued years ago about that. Leaving aside his years of friendship with Alex, he had too much respect for the memory of Spyros Mavros to bring down the wrath of the comrades on his son's head. But that wasn't all. A bigger worm was squirming around, a worm of guilt. He should have told Alex: he was entitled to know. Every day of his life his friend was haunted by the unburied shade of his brother. But that evening Yiorgos had remembered a rumour that Andonis Mavros had once had dealings with the man who called himself Iason Kolettis. What would that do to Alex? What would the consequences be if he started to dig out that filthy pit?

There was a break in the radio transmission, the gabbled commentary suddenly replaced by a more officious voice. Marx and the martyrs, what next? Some crazy fool had tried to blow up the opera.

Mavros got the messaging service on both Anna and Nondas's mobiles. He called their home number and heard the voice of their usual teenage babysitter, one of his brother-in-law's nieces. As far as she knew, they had gone to the opera as planned. She clearly hadn't heard the emergency news bulletins, so Mavros left her in the dark to avoid panic. He cut the connection and turned to his mother. Her face was pale and her eyes wide.

'Look, I'm going down to the concert hall,' he said, touching her arm. 'The emergency number will be jammed and my contacts in the police won't be much use so soon after the event. I need to be on the spot.' He squeezed briefly, feeling bone beneath the slack muscles. 'Don't worry. The chances are they're fine. I'll ring as soon as I can.' He ran to the door.

And ran all the way down the flank of Lykavittos to the wide avenue, his ears filled with the wail of sirens and the burgeoning hubbub of traumatised people. As he approached the concert hall, the mass of humanity on the pavements increased, off-duty police personnel vying with curious onlookers. Turning on to Vasilissis Sophias, he saw a dense crowd outside the building, the road on that side blocked to traffic by fire engines and other emergency vehicles.

'What happened?' a middle-aged man asked.

His companion shrugged, striding ahead with an avid expression. 'I heard it was a bomb. Lunatic terrorists.'

'It's Iraklis, you can be sure of that,' put in a raddled woman, with mascara-laden eyelashes.

Mavros pushed on through the press of humanity. Greeks were not known for their reticence when it came to accidents and crime scenes. He was struck that people were already assuming that the long-extinct terrorist group was responsible. If nothing else, that showed how easy it was to manipulate opinion; a piece of olivewood left on the victim in Piraeus and there you were – resurrection.

The police had erected barriers on the pavement, bulky operatives in riot gear lined up behind. Since the incident had happened in the middle of the embassy district, it hadn't taken the much-despised MAT riot-control units long to appear. Mavros considered flashing his private investigator's licence, but dismissed the idea. All that would do was draw attention. Better to see if he could spot someone he knew in authority.

'Alex!' came a male voice to his right.

He peered through the crush of bodies and made out the tall figure of Lambis Bitsos. He thrust himself into the mêlée.

'They won't let me in,' the crime reporter complained, when Mavros reached him. 'Arseholes! Even the press has to wait on this side while they clear the building.' He stared into the eyes of the riot-control officer in front of him. 'This is a free country, isn't it? There is freedom of the press here, isn't there?'

Mavros watched as the policeman's eyes narrowed behind the wire face-guard of his helmet. In the old days those questions would have earned Bitsos a truncheon in the belly, but the MAT were more circumspect now. There were several camera crews in the vicinity.

He stood on tiptoe, trying to pinpoint Anna and Nondas. There was a large huddle of people on the road in front of the Megaro, their clothes rumpled and their faces slack with shock. None seemed to be injured, though they were being tended by paramedics, who were handing out blankets. The flow of the audience coming out of the building was weakening and it struck Mavros that there would be several emergency exits. His sister and brother-in-law could be anywhere around the large concrete box.

Then, above the scream of the sirens and the shouts of the onlookers, he heard his mobile ring. Fumbling to receive the call, he heard a voice he knew. 'Alex?'

'Nonda? Are you all right?'

'Yes, don't worry.' There was a jumble of sounds in the background. 'We're both fine. We got out the back way. Anna called your mother and discovered that you were coming down. Where are you?'

'At the front.'

'Let's get clear of this fucking chaos,' Nondas said, with an uncharacteristically nervous laugh. 'There's a bar called Pineapple on–'

'I know it,' Mavros interrupted. 'I'm on my way.'

Bitsos was staring at him. 'What's going on?' he asked, his journalist's nose picking up the scent of a story.

Mavros told him, not mentioning Anna's name. The crime reporter had no time for what he'd once called flatter-the-rich journalism.

'Christ, you had relatives in there?' Bitsos chewed his lower lip. 'I'd better stay here in the hope that they eventually let me through, but can I ring them later? Get their story?'

'I'll give them your number,' Mavros said, certain that Anna would be writing her own story about the evening's main event and that Nondas would be under orders to keep quiet until it was published.

'I'll hold you to that.'

'Lambi?' Mavros said, looking round and drawing closer. This wasn't the time or the place to consult the reporter about Iason Kolettis, but he wanted to put down a marker for the future. 'I might have something hot for you,' he said.

'Stand by for my call.'

'Yeah, yeah,' Bitsos said, his eyes fixed on the scene behind the riot policeman. 'I've heard that one before.'

Mavros turned to go, then stopped abruptly. He had caught sight of two people he knew. The first was the Greek police commander Nikos Kriaras, his expression even more guarded than usual, stepping out of an unmarked car with a tall man in a well-cut dark blue suit. His appearance at the concert hall struck Mavros as strange – Kriaras was a senior administrator, not an operational unit leader. He watched as the policeman went up the steps to meet the uniformed officer in charge. Mavros struggled to identify Kriaras's companion and finally put a name to the impassive face. His name was Peter Jaeger and he worked at the American embassy. It was the fair hair plastered down over the scalp that did it – when they'd been introduced to each other at a Christmas party, Mavros had immediately got the impression that the guy was trying hard to make himself look like a diplomat. He joined the police commanders and immediately fell into animated conversation.

Lambis Bitsos was watching the men avidly. 'So much for progress,' he said, in a low voice, nodding towards the high fence that surrounded the US embassy further down the road. 'Who says their influence receded after the end of the dictatorship?'

Mavros shrugged. 'You can't blame them for being concerned about the security implications.' Then he focused on the crowd behind the car that Kriaras and Jaeger had arrived in, having caught a glimpse of another person he recognised behind the barrier. Her eyes were fixed on the tableau before her, upper body sheathed in her denim jacket and hair now tied back, but Grace Helmer was as striking as ever. Why was she rubbernecking outside the concert hall with what looked like great interest?

Mavros's face was creased in thought as he went to meet the survivors.

In the house above the plain of Argos in the north-eastern Peloponnese, Veta Palaiologou had been watching a TV debate in which one of her party's more right-wing spokesmen was relentlessly mauled by a young presenter out to make his mark. She was about to turn it off and go to bed with the shipping newspapers when the emergency bulletin cut in. She watched it with her heart in her mouth, certain that many people she knew would have been at the opening night of the opera. She would have been there herself if she hadn't decided to take a few days away from the city in advance of the Christmas break.

Her husband appeared at the door of the expensively decorated *saloni* with a scowl on his face. He had been to dinner in the nearby town of Nafplion with a delegation of Ukrainian fruit importers. 'Christ and the Holy Mother,' he said, with a groan. 'Those people only know one thing and that's how to drink.' He noticed that his wife was pressing buttons on the phone, her face tense. 'What's the matter?'

She raised a fleshy arm to the TV, the volume lowered so that she could make her calls. As she

151

tried and failed to get in touch with people in Athens, Nikitas Palaiologos stared at the screen with his mouth open. He was still standing in the same position in the middle of the room when she put the phone down.

'They're all engaged,' Veta said, wiping the sweat from her forehead. 'Family and other friends trying to find out if they're all right, I suppose.'

'Bastard terrorists!' Nikitas shouted. 'Why can't the useless wankers in the police catch them? Why do I pay my fucking taxes?'

Veta gave him a cold stare. 'I'd be grateful if you didn't use that language. Besides, you employ a team of tax consultants to minimise the tax you pay.'

'The tax *we* pay,' her husband corrected. 'What's mine is yours, dearest.' He finally snapped out of his frozen pose and stepped over to the drinks cabinet. 'My God, this country is going to hell faster than a lift with a broken cable.'

Veta looked away from him. 'I suppose we shouldn't jump to conclusions. It might not have been a bomb.' She raised the volume and followed what the TV was showing. Over a sea of heads, people were coming out of the Megaro Mousikis, their arms supporting each other, their eyes jerking around nervously. 'There's Kostas and that wife of his. And there's Ioanna. She looks all right.'

'Is that a good thing?' Nikitas said snidely, then emptied his glass.

'Stop drinking,' his wife ordered. 'You're no better than those Ukrainians you were complaining about.'

Nikitas Palaiologos went back to the well-stocked bar and lifted a bottle, then had second thoughts. 'What am I supposed to do, Veta? The worst terrorists of all are back in action again, I'm sure of it.' He started walking up and down the wide room, rubbing his hands together distractedly. 'Don't you remember what they did to their first victims? They cut their throats.'

'Sit down, Nikita,' Veta snapped. 'I'm trying to watch the TV. Anyway, why are you so convinced that Iraklis is involved? Because your friend Vernardhakis was found with a piece of olivewood on his body?'

'That,' her husband said, running a hand over his bald patch, 'and the fact that tycoons like him were exactly the targets the animals used to hit – money-making machines with all the trappings of capitalism.' He gave her an anxious glance. 'Don't forget that I did a lot of business with him.'

'So you think they'll be after you next, do you?' Veta asked scornfully. 'When all's said and done, you're only a fruit and vegetable wholesaler, Nikita. Why would anyone bother to assassinate you?'

Nikitas's look turned vicious. 'I'm also married to a senior conservative politician who comes from one of the country's leading shipping families. Fruit and vegetable wholesaler be damned. We make a tempting double target. You'd better remember that, Veta. If they come looking for me, they'll take you out as well.'

Veta looked away from the screen. 'And vice versa.' Then she let her shoulders slacken. 'All

153

right, I'm sorry I said that about you. We have to stick together, don't we?' She gave her husband an encouraging smile.

'I suppose so.' He always came out on the losing side when his wife played tough because his bluster wasn't backed up by any real strength of character. He knew well enough that she was the major player in their relationship.

Veta continued to follow the TV pictures, marking the appearance of friends and colleagues, as well as several opponents. She kept her eyes off her husband. He was weak, fearful at the first hint of trouble. What did he have to worry about? He had much less to lose than she did if the Iraklis group really was back on the scene.

And then she remembered the guests she was expecting in a couple of days. 'Oh, my God,' she said, 'Anna and Nondas. They were going to *Macbeth* tonight, I'm sure she said so.' She glanced back at Nikitas. 'Have you seen them?' she asked. 'Have you seen them come out?'

Her husband was pulled out of his self-concern by her words. Nondas Chaniotakis was one of his financial advisers as well as a friend. The fears he and his colleagues, the businessmen of Greece, had buried for years were resurfacing. His father's generation had saved the country from the threat of Communist-led mob rule, but now it seemed their bitterest enemy was back. Could it be that the grinding horror of the old wars had been in vain after all?

The Pineapple Bar in the back-street on the slope above the concert hall acted as a magnet

154

for people who had been forced to leave by the rear emergency exit. Its restricted inside space was full and the small terrace to the left was crowded despite the chill night air. Mavros fought his way to the bar and ordered a half-bottle of Metaxas. When he saw that the waiters had their hands full, he took it and three glasses to the corner that his sister and brother-in-law had occupied outside under a bougainvillaea.

'Thanks, Alex,' Anna said, after she'd drained her glass. Her eyes were damp, but her makeup and her expensive outfit were largely unscathed. 'I needed that.'

Nondas nodded to Mavros for a refill. 'Well, that was a novel way to spend an evening.' He put his arm round his wife's waist.

Mavros wanted to find out what they'd seen, but there were family matters to finalise first. 'You spoke to Mother?' he asked.

'She's fine,' his sister replied. 'And so's the babysitter. She told the kids not to worry.'

Nondas laughed. 'Just as well you didn't let her know what was going on, Alex. My niece is as skittish as it comes.'

'It runs in your family,' Mavros said drily. The Chaniotakis family was about as laid-back as it was possible to be in Greece.

'Thanks for coming down, little brother,' Anna said, blinking two or three times. 'It was good to see a friendly face.'

'No problem,' Mavros said, feeling uncom-fortable. It was rare for his sister to let the mask slip. 'So what happened in there?'

Anna glanced around the covered terrace,

lights from it shining on to the thick foliage of the small park's evergreens, and shivered. 'God, it's good to be outside. That auditorium is a big enough space, but I felt like I couldn't breathe as soon as the alarm went off.'

Mavros turned to Nondas. It seemed that his sister's journalistic objectivity was still absent without leave. 'Did you hear anything before the alarm?' he asked his brother-in-law.

'That was the funny thing,' Nondas said. 'We were in seats in the middle with some of my investment colleagues. I don't know if you've been to the Megaro, the Friends of Music concert hall?'

'Once, to see Theodhorakis, but I couldn't afford the good seats.'

Nondas nodded. 'The company paid for ours. From where we were I could see a lot of well-known people close by. Including Paschalis Stasinopoulos.'

'The property mogul?'

'Among other things,' Anna put in. 'Stock Exchange player, conservative party supporter, arms dealer–'

'And all-round-shit,' concluded Nondas.

'He has a reputation for being dirty but untouchable because of his political contacts and his lawyers,' said Mavros.

'*Had* such a reputation,' his brother-in-law corrected.

Mavros pricked up his ears. 'What happened to him? Was he near the explosion?'

'Oh, yes,' Nondas said. 'I happened to look in that direction a few moments before the bomb went off – I'm not much of an opera fan and the

156

production wasn't exactly captivating, all soldiers in pinstripe suits and witches in bikinis – and I saw Stasinopoulos put his hand in his inside jacket pocket. I don't know, perhaps he was worried he'd dropped his wallet. Suddenly it looked like his upper body was too big for his clothes. Then there was a blast – Christ, you could hear it above the orchestra.'

'It was a relatively quiet moment,' Anna said. 'Lady Macbeth trying to convince her man to do the deed.'

Mavros looked at each of them. Neither seemed keen to continue the story. 'And then what? What did you see next?'

Anna raised her bony shoulders. 'Me, nothing. Thank God. The people around Stasinopoulos leaped to their feet.'

'Yes, you were lucky, all right,' Nondas said ruefully. 'I ... I saw blood and pieces of him spray out. Then the alarms kicked in and people moved with amazing self-control towards the exits.'

'Shit,' Mavros said. 'You're sure it was a bomb rather than a gunshot? You didn't see anyone with a weapon?'

Nondas shook his head.

'I think the police will be wanting to talk to you,' Mavros warned him.

'I'll call them tomorrow,' Nondas said. 'I can't face them to–' He broke off as his wife's mobile went off.

'Oh, yes, hello, Veta,' Anna said. 'No, don't worry, we're both fine.' She looked at her husband, then at Mavros. 'No, I don't know what happened exactly. Look, can I call you tomor-

157

row?... What?... Oh, I don't know... Yes, I imagine we'll still be coming down. I'll let you know... Yes, all right, Veta.' She twitched her head in annoyance. "Bye.'

'Madame Dhragoumi-Palaiologou?' Nondas said. 'Worried that her Christmas plans are in jeopardy?'

Anna grimaced. 'Honestly, she could have waited. You know what Veta's like. Everything arranged to the last detail, no deviations allowed.'

Her husband squeezed her waist. 'Don't worry, my love. You'll feel better in the morning.' He laughed. 'After you've filed your eyewitness report with the highest-paying newspaper.'

Anna jammed her elbow into his gut.

Mavros swallowed the last of the brandy. 'I think it's time for bed, children.'

The hit man waited in a darkened doorway down the street from the newspaper's offices, his dark jacket, polo-neck sweater and jeans making him almost invisible. As planned, his return to the hotel had passed unnoticed, the beggar's clothes dumped in a back-street waste-bin after he had left again. There were plenty of people around Omonia and he had merged into the crowds, though he had made sure no one saw him get rid of the unwanted garments. Now, in the deserted street west of the old parliament building, he was ready to make the drop. The sirens had faded into the night and he reckoned that things would have quietened down at the concert hall. It was time to tighten the screw again.

He raised his collar and wrapped a tartan scarf

round the lower part of his face, then stepped noiselessly on to the pavement. There was a night-watchman in a booth inside the entrance to the country's leading independent paper, but he was engrossed in a black-and-white film on a miniature TV. The envelope was in the post-box before the watchman was aware of any noise, the killer stepping out on his way to the next side-street. He kept walking quickly for five minutes, his head bowed, then turned without warning into another doorway. Apart from a pair of entwined lovers weaving up the pavement and the blur of taxis taking advantage of the sparser late-night traffic to speed up the central avenues, he was on his own. The mission had been accomplished without any hitches.

The woman he picked up in a bar off Omonia Square was Russian, that much he could tell from her accent. She was surprised when he answered in her own language. It was years since he'd spoken it, though he'd heard it in the street markets in New York. He was a young man when he had learned the alphabet and taken his first stumbling steps in the tongue of the Party's wise men. By the time he'd finished the training course and been given his first posting, he was able to strike up conversation with a pretty girl on the bus in Moscow; and able to talk his way into her narrow bed in the tiny apartment in the frozen suburb. The girl's face swam up before him for a few seconds, then was replaced by the haggard features of the woman next to him now, her platinum hair dark at the roots and her lips bruised.

'Turn round,' he ordered, unable to look at her any longer. He glanced around the shabby room she'd taken him to, the walls peeling and undecorated apart from a single faded photograph of a featureless town. The woman's life was even emptier than his, he realised, his erection gone.

'Forget it,' he said, stepping back.

The woman stood up, keeping her back to him. 'You don't like me?' she asked, in a defeated tone.

He extended a hand but withdrew it before he made contact with her ashen skin. In the past he'd always needed a woman after a job. He needed to lose himself, even if only for a few seconds. But he had failed with the Filipina he'd gone with after the Vernardhakis hit and now he'd failed again. He gave her a wad of notes and waved away her smile of gratitude, but it was too late. The woman whose name he couldn't say was suddenly in front of him, blocking out the Russian. He blinked hard and left the room quickly, sweat on his forehead. She was haunting him, had done so ever since he'd first laid eyes on her at the embassy reception over a quarter of a century ago. She would have his soul before he could finish the labours.

Back in the hotel room, he stripped off his clothes and stood under the shower, having opened the cold tap as far as it would go. Then he towelled himself down, turned on the television and emptied the single miniature of good whisky that he was allowing himself. The channels were full of garbled news reports, most showing harassed-looking reporters outside the police line at the concert hall – harassed because they had little to report, he soon gathered. The authorities had made no statement beyond confirming that an explosion had occurred in the buildings and that there had been a single unnamed fatal casualty. Either the target had found the extra pen in his pocket or the much-vaunted device had exploded early.

The killer lay down on the uncomfortable bed. He could break cover and head back to the flat, but the boss wouldn't be pleased. Better to stick to the plan. Christ, the plan. What kind of chance were they taking? The government might fall, the country might be torn apart. Then he clenched his fists and got a grip on himself. No, the plan was good, even if his motivation was a lot more personal than the others'. The woman. It all came back to her. Trent Helmer's beautiful, faithless wife. She had destroyed people's lives without realising it; she was still destroying them years after her death. Christ, the power of the woman. It made his own power seem feeble and insignificant, even though he had wielded it mercilessly over his many victims.

He closed his eyes and willed himself to sleep. The thundering city with its twenty-four-hour rush and babbling crowds, its guns and explosive devices, its shattered bodies, wasn't the real world, even though it had been his life for decades. The real world was in his dreams, where the woman he'd never even kissed lived, unchanged despite the ravages of time and the knife she'd put to her own throat.

161

The hit man went there with a smile on his face.

Mavros got a call from Lambis Bitsos not long after he got back to his flat.

'I don't know why I'm doing this,' he said, the noise of other voices in the background.

'Because you enjoy waking people from their well-earned slumbers?' Mavros could tell that Bitsos had something he was burning to pass on, but he knew that rushing things would only put him more in the journalist's grip. 'Because you've run out of dirty magazines and want to confess your sins to someone responsible and understanding?'

'If I give you this, I want something good from you in return, okay?'

'Mmm,' Mavros responded noncommittally. 'Won't I be able to read it in tomorrow's paper?'

'I don't think so. The paper's already gone to press and, besides, this is so hot that the government will have to approve publication.'

Now Bitsos had Mavros's full attention. 'All right, Lambi,' he said. 'I'll play ball.'

'You'd better, Alex,' the journalist said threateningly. 'And you'd better keep this to yourself. Or should I say, you'd better keep *these* to yourself.'

'These?' This was getting better by the second. 'You mean you're going to give me leads plural?'

Bitsos groaned. 'I must be out of my mind. All right, get this. Preliminary investigation shows that the explosion took place in the auditorium's most expensive seats. The victim was the property developer Paschalis Stasinopoulos. It seems he was blown apart by a small explosive device, bits of him ending up over a lot of horrified politicians and Athenian society figures. What do you think of that, Mr Detective?'

'Interesting, Lambi,' Mavros said, concealing the fact that he'd already heard all of that from Nondas and Anna. 'What else?'

'Christ and the Holy Mother, there's no satisfying you,' the journalist complained. 'All right, how about this? The experts reckon it was a sophisticated anti-personnel device.' He paused. 'The kind used by only the most skilled terrorists.'

'Don't tell me,' Mavros said, registering the tension in the reporter's voice. 'There's a link with the Vernardhakis killing.'

'Exactly. My paper just received a statement from Iraklis claiming responsibility.' Bitsos paused for dramatic effect. 'And there was a piece of olivewood in the envelope.'

Mavros kept his mounting excitement under wraps. 'Well, well. Are the authorities impressed?'

'Changing their underwear, more like,' the journalist said. 'They've taken the statement away, but we managed to copy it first. I've been comparing it with some of the old ones, especially those that weren't made public. I reckon it's genuine.'

Mavros whistled but didn't speak. These developments made the Grace Helmer job even more risky. And what had she been doing in the crowd outside the concert hall, which was only a stone's throw from her country's embassy?

163

'Hello, is anybody there?' Bitsos asked caustically.

'What? Oh, sorry, Lambi. Just thinking.'

'That's what I was worried about. Make sure you tell me the results of your thought processes, eh?'

'Okay. Thanks for the intelligence.'

'I hope I haven't made a career-threatening mistake,' Bitsos said, sounding unsure. 'And, Alex? Tell me you gave my number to your relatives.'

'Sure I did,' Mavros replied. 'Well, I will do. Sweet dreams.' He cut the connection before the reporter could protest then turned off his phone.

Sweet dreams. He had the feeling he wouldn't be having too many of those.

7

November 1943

The sun was bright over the stone skin of the mountains, but the air was cold, carrying the smell of winter, which had already mounted the wind's back far to the north. The Soviet winter, the young poet thought, the power that would blast across the old world and cleanse it of the exploiters' legacy. He glanced ahead at the long line of his comrades, men and women crushed under great loads, a few bony mules interspersed. They were the tools of the revolution, the corrosive acid of justice, the saviours of the people. His family had been unlucky, his parents and grandparents taken by disease when their bodies were weakened by malnutrition, his brother run down by an Italian Army truck in Kalamata. But he and his fellow fighters would build a new Greece on the bones of their ancestors.

'Slow down, Comrade Kosta,' panted the boy behind. 'I can't keep up with you.'

'You must,' Kostas Laskaris replied. 'The Germans and the collaborationist jackals have our scent.' He looked round and gave the fresh-faced volunteer a death's-head grin. 'Besides, ELAS commanders shoot malingerers.'

The boy's face blanched and he marched on

with renewed vigour. 'Comrade Kosta?' he said, after five more minutes of battling with the uneven stones on the steep trail. 'What's a jackal?'

The poet didn't answer. He was staring ahead, taking in the twin cliffs that hung down from the peaks of Taygetos like the adamantine walls of a cruel king's castle. Beneath them was a small piece of flat ground, a lower ridge of exposed rock circling it. He felt the snake writhe in his belly. The years he had borne arms had taught him to recognise terrain suitable for an ambush. Kapetan Iraklis had led them to the perfect killing ground.

There wasn't time for an extended speech from the band's leader or for any more indoctrination by its political commissar Vladhimiros. Iraklis, his fatigues as torn and filthy as anyone's, roused his troops for battle. As he spoke, his black beard glistened in the sunlight, his eyes flashing splinters of passion.

'Comrades, brave fighters of ELAS Lakonia, the hour has come. The occupiers have been massacring our old people, our women and our children.' He looked around the faces of the unit – wrinkled men with long beards, women with grimy faces, youths with wispy eyelashes. 'They have allowed the so-called Security Battalions to be formed, led by Greek officers whose love of the king and hatred of the people has turned them into traitors, and manned by common criminals. Now they think they have caught us in their trap.' He raised an arm and indicated the curtains of rock to his rear. 'But everyone knows

166

that true Greeks fight hardest when their backs are to the wall. Victory for our fatherland and our people!'

The comrades cheered wildly, paying no heed to the enemy that was on their heels. Then they listened to their section commanders as the dispositions were handed down. In under fifteen minutes the plateau was cleared, the single tripod-mounted machine-gun they had captured in a skirmish outside Sparta hidden behind the rocks on the western flank. Fighters were arrayed round the low ridge, their rifles laid out on the stone in front of them, the precious clasps of ammunition removed from bandoliers in readiness.

Kostas Laskaris found himself in the centre, the young peasant boy on his right and a hard-faced woman from Kitta on his left. She had lost her husband to the Italians in Albania and her two brothers during the German armoured advance through the Peloponnese. More recently her sister had been raped and murdered by a squad of gendarmes because she was suspected of Communist sympathies.

'Aim steady and true, Comrade Stamatina,' came a soft voice from behind her. She gave a harsh smile and tightened her grip on her rifle.

Kapetan Iraklis turned to the boy. 'And you, Comrade Dino. Today your family in Alika will have you to be proud of as well as your brother who died on the Albanian front. You will become a hero of the people.'

Kostas glanced at the youth beside him; his eyes were moving constantly and he was licking his lips. He was amazed that Iraklis remembered

167

the background of everyone in the band – he himself hadn't known where the boy came from.

Then Iraklis looked into his eyes and he felt his heart swell, the blood course through his veins like liquid fire. 'And you, my Kosta, be as merciless as ever.' The *kapetanios* squeezed his calf briefly and moved away. The area he had touched throbbed like a wide but pleasurable bruise. For a few minutes the fighter lost himself in a morass of indulgent thoughts – of how long nights around meagre fires in mountain caves and in ruined goatherds' huts had made him realise that the feeling he had for the man who'd named himself after the ancient hero, the man he had known from childhood, was the deepest love; of how that love was returned, he was sure of it, even though it was impossible for any open acknowledgement to be made in wartime; of how in the future, when victory was assured and a more tolerant world established, he and Iraklis would no longer have to conceal their emotions.

Kostas gazed up into the sky and watched the birds of prey circling, their cries coming down to him like a bitter benediction. Like them, the fighters had nothing except their weapons and their unbreakable will to keep them alive. Until then he never had any doubt that they would prevail. But now the guerrilla band had to fight Greeks as well as Germans.

In a rising cacophony of heavy boots and clipped commands, the enemy, foreign and native, approached the place of slaughter.

Mavros was woken by the sound of the telephone.

168

It seemed only a few minutes since he'd been talking to Bitsos, but a glance at the clock told him that it was seven in the morning.

'You do provide a twenty-four-hour service, don't you?'

He recognised Grace Helmer's voice through the fog of sleep. 'Did I say that?' he asked, his mouth sticky.

'The customer's always right, huh?' She sounded like she'd been awake for hours.

'Of course.' Mavros had a flash of his client behind the police line at the concert hall, her eyes wide. Maybe her desire to stick to him during the investigation was just as well – that way he'd be able to carry out covert surveillance on her. There was something about Grace Helmer that made his antennae quiver, and it wasn't just that she was a seriously attractive woman. 'I suppose you want to know what we're going to do today.'

'Got it in one, Marlowe.'

'Have breakfast, for a start.'

'Second breakfast in my case. All right, where? Oh, I know. That charming little dump you frequent, the one with the waiter who doesn't like Americans.'

'You noticed?' Mavros wasn't sure that it was a good idea to have Grace and the Fat Man under the same roof, but he was still wondering about his friend's reaction when he'd tossed the name Iason Kolettis at him. There might be something to be said for playing off the two against each other. 'All right. I'll see you there in an hour.'

'Don't be late.' Grace cut the connection.

'There's a challenge,' Mavros muttered, into the

169

buzzing receiver. Then he headed for the shower, but stopped mid-stride in the doorway. Before he went any further with the case, he needed to check his client's background. He booted up his computer, logged on to the Internet and ran a search for Meliorate, the Washington-based charity Grace had said she worked for. Up came a flash-looking home page with a menu. He clicked on the Key-Personnel button and there she was, photographed in worn green top and trousers against a backdrop of jungle, a tired smile on her lips and a group of children around her – 'Field supervisor Grace Helmer at our resettlement camp in Burundi', the caption said. Case proved, he thought. Maybe he shouldn't be so suspicious of people. He flicked around the site, learning that the charity was funded by donations and operated independently of the US and all other governments. He logged off and went for his shower.

At the Fat Man's there was relative calm. A pair of elderly shop-owners in the far corner nodded when Mavros arrived, their voices low. They were probably planning the next season's assault on unsuspecting tourists. At least that meant that Yiorgos Pandazopoulos didn't have to pay attention to his female customer. He was hovering around the two men's table, his face split by a grin – anything to do with extracting cash from the foreign bourgeoisie went down well with him.

'I thought we said an hour,' Grace Helmer said, her tone accusing.

Mavros sat down opposite her. 'We don't work

170

on English timing here. Besides, I had to make myself look respectable.'

Grace raised an eyebrow. 'You blew it. Anyway, you don't have to impress me. I hired you for your mind, not your body.'

Mavros let that go and watched as the Fat Man lumbered over. 'Morning, Yiorgo,' he said, in Greek. 'This is your last day, isn't it?'

The café-owner nodded, giving Grace a sceptical look. 'That's right. What's she doing here?'

'Taking in the local colour.' He glanced at the table. 'Would you like anything else?' he asked, indicating her half-drunk coffee. 'I'm having whatever pastry he's got.'

'I'm not a big fan of pastries.'

'No, I don't suppose you are,' he said, glancing at her lithe form. He turned to Yiorgos. 'What have you got today?'

'*Galaktoboureko*,' the Fat Man replied. 'You're in luck.'

'What? You haven't eaten it all?'

'No,' Yiorgos said irritably. 'The old woman only got round to baking in the middle of the night so it's even fresher than usual. I'm telling you, she's more excited about going back to the village than a teenager on her first date.'

'It'll be cold down there at this time of year, won't it?' Mavros said, with a sardonic smile. 'You'll be able to do some mountaineering.'

'On Taygetos?' Yiorgos moved away to make Mavros's coffee. 'You must be joking,' he said, over his shoulder. 'It's a man-eater.'

Grace Helmer was staring at Mavros. 'What

171

was all that about?'

'Nothing much. He's going down to the Peloponnese with his mother for Christmas and he's not looking forward to it.' He wondered if there was any chance that she understood Greek and was feigning ignorance of the language; then told himself not to be so paranoid. She'd left the country when she was five and had probably only picked up a word or two in the English-speaking house – the nanny was foreign too, he remembered. It was hardly likely that she'd spend her minimal time off in the jungle with a textbook and a cassette-player learning Greek.

'The Peloponnese,' Grace repeated, lowering her voice. 'He's not from the Mani, is he? Remember that painting my mother did?'

Mavros took out his notebook and found the entry he'd made after their meeting in Grace's hotel. '*Lament for Kitta?* No, Yiorgos's village is on the other side of the mountain.' He was thinking about how the Fat Man had characterised it – 'man-eater'. Was that a standard Lakonian epithet or had he a personal reason to hate Taygetos?

Grace sat back. 'Right, Alex. How are we going to get on the-man-whose-name-I'm-not-going-to-mention-in-public's trail?'

Mavros was studying her. Her hair was pulled back again, emphasising the prominent features of her tanned face. She was wearing the same jean jacket that she'd had on outside the concert hall. 'I've been thinking about that,' he said, turning as he heard Pandazopoulos's heavy tread behind him. He got up quickly and led his friend

172

back to the chill cabinet. 'Tell me, Fat Man,' he said, turning the screw on the Communist, 'do you remember that song "The Voyage of the *Argo*"?'

'How would I not remember it, Alex?' said the café-owner. 'We all sang it under our breath for years during the dictatorship.'

'And do you remember who wrote it?'

'Of course. It was one of Randos's first big hits.'

Mavros glanced back at Grace. The conversation was in Greek and she didn't appear to be following it. 'With words by Kostas Laskaris, yes?'

The Fat Man nodded, his expression wary.

'Who was the captain of the *Argo*, Yiorgo?' Mavros demanded, his eyes meeting the other's.

His friend stiffened. 'Fuck you, Alex,' he whispered hoarsely. 'I told you not to talk about him.' He went behind the chill cabinet with surprising speed.

Mavros wasn't proud of himself for hinting at the name of Iason Kolettis via the name of the ancient hero who led the Argonauts, but he'd wanted to see if Yiorgos would crack. 'Don't worry,' he persisted. 'I'm going to question Randos himself about it.'

The Fat Man kept his head bowed.

'And then I'm going to question the poet Kostas Laskaris.'

'You're out of your mind,' Yiorgos shouted, losing control. 'They won't talk to you about him. They're the last people who'll talk about him. Now, take your American woman away and leave me in peace.'

Mavros bit his lip, guilty that he'd provoked his

173

friend but at the same time disappointed that he hadn't got anything more out of him. He picked up the tray and took it over to the table – he didn't intend to miss out on his breakfast.

'Was he talking about me?' Grace asked. 'Am I *Amerikanidha?*'

'Mmm,' he mumbled, his mouth full of custard-filled pastry. It seemed clear that she'd registered the café-owner's scathing tone, but not the meaning of his words. He drank his coffee in haste and stood up, dropping notes on to the table. 'We'd better get going.' He turned as he went. 'Merry Christmas when it comes, Yiorgo.'

There was no reply – only a hurt glance and a melancholy shake of the Fat Man's head.

Geoffrey Dearfield eased himself into the front seat of the old Rover and looked ahead across the isthmus to the mountains of the northern Peloponnese. The sun was high over the barren peaks, Acrocorinth with its wavy line of battlements standing firm in the near distance like a medieval challenge to the destructive power of time. Over these walls the Byzantine commander Leon Sgouros had ridden to his death in 1208, he and his doomed charger crashing to the rocks in a gesture of crazed defiance against the besieging Franks. The merciless rocks of this artificial island, Dearfield thought, his eyes now on the bridges that spanned the narrow cut separating the Peloponnese from mainland Greece. How many fighters braver than Sgouros had fallen to rot on the fields of stone in his own time? They were countless, forgotten by history. For decades he had

174

seen their deaths as necessary, as a sacrifice for political stability and economic prosperity. Recently he had become much less sure of that and his return to the region where he'd spent years as a young man was hard to bear.

'Come on, Flora,' he said irritably. 'It's time we were on the move again. Veta and Nikitas will be wondering what's happened to us.'

His wife checked his seat-belt, her smooth-skinned face as neutral as ever, and started the engine. Since Geoffrey's second heart scare in the spring she'd taken over the driving, much to his disgust. The Rover was his obsession; that and his precious 'polemical memoir'. Flora Petraki-Dearfield was in her mid-sixties, fifteen years younger than her husband, and the burden of caring for him was getting heavier every year. She edged out of the parking area outside the restaurant where they'd stopped so that Geoffrey could empty his bladder, only accelerating when there was a large gap between the thundering lorries.

'Come on, woman,' the old man complained. 'We want to arrive *before* Christmas.'

Flora ignored him and drove across the bridge. The December light was bright, but the sunglasses she was wearing filtered it effectively. She was wearing an elegant trouser-suit that she knew made her look younger than her years, while her husband was in the heavy tweed that he wore from October to April whatever the weather – the habits he had grown up with in the damp of England had never left him despite the years he had spent in Greece.

'Isn't this interesting?' she said, as they followed the motorway to Tripolis. 'Soon we'll be passing Nemea, where the lion was slain by Iraklis in his first labour.'

'Hercules,' corrected Dearfield. 'You're speaking English, so you should call him by his English name.'

'But classical scholars call him Heracles,' Flora countered, unwilling to let him have his own way. She was the one who had lectured in Greek history at the university in Athens, not Geoffrey.

'Use that name, then,' he replied, blinking his rheumy eyes behind the heavy frames of his glasses. 'Not the modern version those blood-thirsty terrorists took.'

Flora glanced at her husband. His heavily lined face, the thick white moustache stained yellow by the cigarettes he was now forbidden, was reddening. 'Don't let yourself be disturbed, Geoff,' she said softly. 'The authorities haven't said that the explosion at the Megaro Mousikis was anything to do with the Iraklis group.' They had friends who'd been at the production, one of whom had seen the blast that had killed the property developer Stasinopoulos.

'It's them, all right,' Dearfield said, his hands, knotted with dark blue veins, limp on his thighs. 'I feel it in my water. Old campaigner's premonition.'

They drove on past the ravine at Dhervenakia where the Turks had been slaughtered by the Greeks in 1822, four thousand Muslim corpses left unburied for the carrion birds and the blowflies. Geoffrey Dearfield knew every corner

176

of the peninsula, having criss-crossed it on foot as a British liaison officer in the Second World War and in a variety of military vehicles during the ensuing civil conflict. When he was young he had found the violent history of the place fascinating and was forever regaling his colleagues with tales of the Greek War of Independence and the Byzantine, Frankish, Venetian and Ottoman atrocities that preceded it. But now, in his dotage, he found the faint but unmistakable tang of blood that he caught in the air difficult to take. He hadn't admitted as much to anyone, but he was sure he wasn't the only person to be oppressed by the Peloponnese's savage atmosphere. His wife had never been affected by that weakness. He could remember Flora standing on the acropolis of Mycenae and beneath the titanic walls of Tiryns, her face burning with enthusiasm. She was inspired by mythical heroes like Agamemnon and Hercules. So much for the professional historian's objectivity.

Flora followed the road towards Argos, progress slower now they were off the motorway. Ahead, the orange groves spread out to the shores of the gulf, a shimmering lake of green beneath the grey arms of the encircling mountains. They would soon be at the Palaiologos house on the hill above the plain and her husband would feel more at ease. He had known Veta and Nikitas's fathers in the war, and they had spent many nights there in the years since the younger generation had taken over the old family retreat. She knew Geoff was worried by the apparent reappearance of the

177

Iraklis group. In the seventies and eighties he had lived on a knife edge, forcing her to move to a high-security apartment block and never going out without careful planning. He had made enemies on the Left because of his involvement with the government side during the civil war and the consultancy work that he never specified with the Americans during the dictatorship. When the terrorists had faded from the scene ten years ago, he had relaxed, though more recently he had been driving himself to finish his book – the memoir he had refused to let her see.

Flora had shown no interest in his writing, concentrating on her own study of the Peloponnese from prehistoric times to the present. Looking through the windshield at the peaceful plain, she knew her ideas were well founded. The ancient myths had so many points of connection to later history. Many of the former inhabitants of this area, Argolidha, had been brutal tyrants – Pelops, Atreus the child-murderer, Thyestes, who unwittingly ate his own offspring, Agamemnon, slaughtered in the bath by his wife and her lover. Such viciousness had been repeated often by rulers both foreign and Greek, from the Byzantines in medieval times to the German and Italian occupiers in the 1940s. And what about Iraklis? Slave to a brutal master, he had laboured against terrible odds till he prevailed. No wonder so many of the wartime resistance commanders, let alone the terrorist group, had taken his name. He was an example of unflinching courage, an inspiration to all freedom-loving people.

'Flora?' Geoffrey Dearfield's voice was

tentative. 'You'll be sure not to mention my memoir to Veta and Nikitas, won't you?'

His wife took her eyes from the tail of the decrepit truck that was crawling down the road ahead of them. 'Yes, you've already made that clear, Geoff,' she replied, screwing up her eyes behind her sunglasses, 'though I don't understand why you're being so reticent.'

Dearfield looked away. 'I told you. I want to wait until Dorothy Cochrane-Mavrou takes the book on before I tell people about it.'

'Surely she will,' Flora said, checking in the mirror and accelerating past the lorry. 'You've spent so much time and energy on it.'

'I'm not sure at all,' he said, his voice low. 'It may be too polemical for my own good.'

Geoffrey Dearfield closed his eyes for a few seconds, but that was a mistake. In a flash they were before him, making him start and arresting the passage of air in his windpipe: the faces he had confined for years to the darkness, but which had recently come back to ambush him at every turn – faces that were dirt-stained but soft, the faces of young men and women with pleading eyes and broken teeth; faces on heads that had been detached from bodies and were floating unsupported in the air. And the blood – oh, God, so much blood, rivers in spate that never ran dry – that was pouring from the roughly severed necks. But worst of all was the man on the X-shaped cross, his eyes staring in bulging agony before his head fell like a stone on to his shattered chest.

Would he never be free of the horror?

179

'You want to do what?' Grace Helmer had stopped in the crush of humanity outside Monastiraki station, her eyes wide.

Mavros took her arm and led her past the building site that made access difficult to Ploutonos, the street that ran towards Syndagma Square. Although it was only mid-morning, the waiters from the *souvlaki* restaurants were already touting for custom and the air was filled with the smell of grilled meat.

'I want to talk to the composer Randos about the song your mother kept. What's so surprising about that?'

Grace pulled her arm out of his grip. 'It's about as oblique an approach as I can think of,' she replied. 'What about all those contacts you mentioned? Shouldn't we be asking them about—'

Mavros raised a finger to his mouth before she said the mystery man's name. 'Remember what I said about this case? How sensitive it is? If I use any of my contacts, the authorities or the Communists will hear about our interest soon enough. Then they'll blunder in and you'll never find the guy you're looking for.' He started walking up the street towards a small shaded square and decided to play his ace. 'You were in the crowd outside the concert hall last night, Grace.' He turned to her quickly and saw that her face was expressionless. 'What were you doing there?'

She raised her shoulders. 'I heard the sirens and went to check it out. Anything wrong with that?'

180

'No,' he said, keeping his eyes on her. 'Do you know what happened there?'

'There was an explosion, from what I saw on the news afterwards.' She was looking at him now. 'They didn't say what it was. Oh, God.' Her tone was suddenly tense. 'It wasn't Iraklis again, was it?'

'It's possible,' he said, keeping Bitsos's information to himself. 'But even if it wasn't, the government and the police will be even more jumpy. Now do you see why an oblique approach, as you call it, is a good idea?'

'Yeah, you're right,' Grace conceded. 'But what makes you think this composer will see us? Surely you can't just walk into such a big shot's house off the street.'

'I called him this morning and told him I was a devoted fan of thirty years' standing.'

She stopped abruptly, making a pair of tourists in dirty clothes swerve around her. 'Are you kidding? He's an international star, isn't he? That was enough to make him agree to see you?'

'That and the fact that he was in the Communist Party with my father. He knew my brother too.' Mavros smiled. 'It's all about personal contacts in this country.'

Grace walked on, her eyes turned to him. 'The brother who went missing?'

He didn't reply.

When they walked into the open space in front of the cathedral, Grace tried again. 'You're still trying to find him, aren't you?'

Mavros nodded slowly. 'I'll never stop looking for Andonis,' he said, glancing at the statue of a former archbishop. 'The rest of my family think it's a curse. Maybe it is. But it's also a duty, a debt that runs in my blood.' He glanced at her. 'You can understand that, can't you?'

She looked away.

'It would probably be easier for me to talk to Randos alone,' Mavros continued. 'Are you sure—'

'I told you,' Grace interrupted, 'I want to be in on everything.'

'You're the boss.' He wondered why she was so insistent about being present throughout the investigation. Was the need to find her father's assassin so overwhelming?

'So where does he live, this musical paragon?' Grace asked. 'In some villa surrounded by fences and security guards?'

'I think you're going to be disappointed.' Mavros beckoned to a passing lottery salesman. He chose a ticket from the old man's pole. 'Here,' he said, handing it to Grace. 'Maybe it'll bring us luck on our quest.'

She accepted it, peering at the lettering. 'Thank you, kind sir, but you shouldn't have. Gambling is the opium of the people.'

'Well said,' he replied, starting to walk. 'Randos would no doubt agree with you. He's a Communist of the old school.'

Grace caught up with him. 'Where is it that he lives?'

'Wait and see.'

She gave him a long-suffering look, then followed him into Syndagma Square.

The air in the well-appointed room in the basement of the American embassy was cool and highly filtered, but the atmosphere was heavy. Three men and a woman were sitting around the dark brown conference table, files open in front of them and mobile phones close to their hands.

'Status report, Ms Forster,' the man at the head of the table said in an inert voice, his fair hair plastered close to his scalp.

'The subjects are in Syndagma Square right now, apparently waiting for a trolley-bus.' The woman's voice was slow and deep, the drawl indicating that she was from a southern state. Her pale blue eyes were wide and fixed on the man who had spoken. She was dressed in a well-cut grey trouser suit, her auburn hair pulled back in a tight bunch. 'We have three operatives on them.'

'Let us hope they are not noticed,' said the man opposite her. His English was cultured, though it was clearly not his mother tongue. 'Mavros is not an amateur.'

'Neither is Grace Helmer,' said the fair-haired man. 'None of your people are involved, Niko?'

The police commander Kriaras jerked his head back once. 'The instruction from my minister was clear. As the woman is a US citizen, you are to take the lead in this operation.' His manner suggested that he was not in agreement with his superior. 'He has complete confidence in your capabilities.' He looked across the table. 'But you, Peter Jaeger, do you have such confidence?'

The American met his gaze and then stood up. He was tall, well over six feet, the lines of his suit

183

failing to mask the well-developed layers of muscle. He glanced at the third man in the room, then nodded slowly. 'I have absolute confidence in my team, Niko. You can be sure of that.'

Kriaras gave a tight smile. 'Good. We will hold you to that.' He turned to the woman. 'Jane ... I mean, Ms Forster, can you make sure that nothing untoward happens to the subject Mavros? He has proved useful to us in the past without always being aware of it.'

She looked at Jaeger. 'Our operatives will follow orders at all times,' she said mechanically.

Kriaras shifted his gaze to the third man. 'And you, Mr Milroy?' he said, taking in the older figure at the far end of the table. The man was wearing a loose sports jacket, his shirt unbuttoned at the neck. His hair was almost pure white, cut short at the back and sides with the forelock hanging over his lined forehead, but it was his face that struck the policeman. It was inexpressive, almost featureless – the nose unremarkable, the cheeks smooth and the eyes an indeterminate hue – as if it were the template for a person yet to be created. 'Will you do as you are told in this particular case?' Kriaras asked.

The man remained silent for a while. 'Sure I will,' he said, his voice level and unaccented. 'I'll do better than that. I'll follow my conscience.' He gave a slack smile.

The police commander laughed, then realised that none of the others had joined him. He felt a chill run up his spine as he realised that he was meddling where he shouldn't.

'Let's review the incident at the opera,' Jaeger

said, striding over to a display board and lifting the cover sheet. 'Niko, what's the present state of your people's knowledge?'

Kriaras looked down at his file, trying to keep Lance Milroy in the corner of his eye, and marshalled his thoughts. Not for the first time in his career, he had the distinct feeling that he was in the grip of forces he couldn't comprehend, never mind control.

In Syndagma they caught one of the city's gleaming new yellow trolley-buses, Mavros cancelling the tickets he'd taken from his wallet in the machine inside.

'What is this?' Grace Helmer demanded. 'A magical mystery tour?'

Mavros smiled. 'Lighten up. Take in the sights while you're here.'

The trolley passed the National Garden then swung past Hadrian's Gate and the thirteen columns of the Temple of Olympian Zeus, both monuments sheathed in scaffolding.

'They're busy cleaning everything ancient in the city in advance of the Olympics in 2004,' Mavros said. 'That temple was the largest in Greece and, as far as my memory goes, it took seven hundred years to complete.'

Grace Helmer looked out at the immense marble shafts. 'Impressive,' she said. 'But I'm not giving you a tip.'

The sun had disappeared under a layer of grey-white clouds by the time they got off.

'This used to be a working-class area,' Mavros said, looking up towards the apartment blocks on

185

the slopes of Philopappos. 'Now it's being bought up by developers and yuppies.'

Grace took in the discoloured buildings. 'I suppose it's fairly central,' she said. 'And there's a park nearby.' She pointed up to the tree-covered ground higher up.

'Mmm,' Mavros said, with a wry smile. 'It was from Philopappos that Morosini bombarded the Acropolis in 1687, when the Parthenon was almost blown to pieces. And there were troops stationed there in 1967 when the Colonels secured the city during the coup.'

'Thanks for the history lesson,' she said, buttoning her jacket against the chill that had suddenly set in, 'but I'm still not giving you a tip.'

Mavros led her along a narrow street to the uppermost row of apartment blocks. 'This is it,' he said, consulting his notebook. 'Number eighteen.' He looked at the buzzer panel. Most of the name cards were faded, a couple covered in garish colours. The one bearing the name Randos was almost illegible. He pressed the button next to it.

'*Ela!*' came a bellow that was loud even through the dubious electrics of the mechanism. Before Mavros could identify himself, the buzzer went. '*Ektos orofos!*'

'Sixth floor,' he translated, taking in Grace's blank look as he pushed open the street-door.

They entered a small, decrepit lift and came out on a dusty landing, the walls covered with graffiti. Looking closer, Mavros realised that much of the scrawl consisted of lines from the composer's songs. 'Done by your fans?' he asked

186

the bearded, bull-like figure who opened the door in front of them.

'Done by me,' the man said, scratching his groin beneath a loose fisherman's jersey, 'to irritate the assholes who moved in next door. A pair of stockbrokers, would you believe?' He stared at Grace, screwing up his eyes. 'You didn't say you were bringing your squeeze.' He turned back to Mavros. 'You are who I think you are, aren't you?'

'I'm Alex Mavros,' he said. 'This is my friend Grace. Do you speak English, Comrade Rando?'

The composer glared at him. 'You invite yourself to my home and expect me to speak the language of oppression and global capitalism?'

Mavros raised his shoulders. 'How often do you get the chance to converse with a beautiful American woman?'

Randos thought about that and smiled. 'Since you put it that way...' He beckoned Grace in with exaggerated courtesy. 'Good morning, pretty lady,' he said, in heavily accented English. 'My house is your house.'

She favoured him with a quizzical smile, then pulled Mavros in after her by the arm. 'Is this guy for real?' she whispered.

The composer had the look of a man who hadn't seen the light of day, let alone experienced polite company, for a very long time. His apartment was dim, the blinds all drawn and the only light coming from a small Anglepoise on the lid of the grand piano that took up most of the *saloni*. There was a strong smell of cats and hand-rolled cigarettes. Looking around in the gloom,

187

Mavros made out a cardboard box on the floor. It contained a cat nursing a tangle of black-and-white kittens.

'Ah, you see Psipsina?' Randos said, running his hand through the grizzled stubble on his chin. He nudged Grace towards the box. 'She had five little bastards last week. Now they suck all day and all night. This teach her not to make sex, no?'

'I like cats,' she said, kneeling down by the box and stroking the queen gently.

The composer went over to the window and pulled up a blind half-way. The trunks of the trees on the hill's lower slopes were visible beyond. 'I keep it dark for Psipsina. She is not liking the sun.' He took a half-smoked cigarette from an ashtray and lit it.

'She is not liking the smoke either,' Grace said, standing up and staring pointedly at the cigarette.

There was a pause, then Randos let out a roar of laughter. 'She is not liking the smoke! Very good!' But he kept the roll-up alight. He turned to Mavros. 'So you are Spyros's son, Andonis's brother,' he said, in Greek, his expression clouded. 'Great tragedy,' he said. 'Andonis was a hero.' He nodded vigorously. 'A hero. And Spyros too. He was a great man.'

The composer seemed nervous, whether because he was uncomfortable with an American woman in his home or for some other reason, Mavros couldn't tell. 'Thank you,' he replied. 'And you, too, are a great man.' Experience had taught him that artists of all kinds were susceptible to flattery, those on the Left more than most. 'We grew up singing your songs. The country was sustained by them during the difficult years.'

Randos looked suitably gratified. 'Thank you.' He gestured to them to sit down on the sofa, which was covered with cat hairs. 'You like wine?' he said, switching back to English. 'I do not make coffee – it is stolen by the big companies from the peasants. My woman is in the shops again. She is spending my money so that I stay a poor man.'

Mavros and Grace exchanged glances and declined the offer.

'In fact,' Mavros said, 'it's about one of your songs that we came.'

'Oh, yes?' The barrel-chested composer looked interested. 'What song?'

'"The Voyage of the *Argo*",' Grace said, taking the lead and ignoring Mavros's glare.

'You hear this song in United States too?' Randos asked, in surprise.

'Em, yes,' she replied. 'It's known all over the world, isn't it?'

'But it is understood best in Greece,' Mavros put in, trying to control the questioning.

Grace ignored him. 'We wanted to ask you about the lyric, Mr Randos.'

'Don't call me "Mr",' the composer said irritably. 'Title of the bourgeoisie, no?'

'Comrade Rando?' Mavros tried.

The big man jerked his head back in denial. 'Too late for comrades now, comrade,' he said, with a weak laugh. 'Communist Party fucked all over the world,' he said, giving Grace a meaningful look, 'thanks to very democratic America. No,

189

you call me Randos only. No shit first name approved by shit-eating church.' He looked more closely at them. 'You want to ask about the *stichous*, the lyric? Why?'

Mavros realised that caution was necessary – the composer was already suspicious. 'The voyage of the ship filled with heroes, it was a metaphor for Greece, wasn't it?' He made his initial question as general as he could.

'*Metaphora?*' Randos said, his face slackening. 'Yes, but not only for Greece, for every country in the world. They must look for and fight for the – how you say? – sheepskin of gold that–' He broke off when he saw the involuntary smile on Grace's lips.

'Golden fleece,' Mavros corrected.

'Yes, golden fleece,' the composer said hurriedly, embarrassed by his mistake. 'Golden fleece is symbol for better world, truth, freedom, justice. But many heroes die on the voyage and the ones who return are never the same again.'

'"You, Iasona, are fated to lose your darling sons. You, Irakli, will soon endure the flames of the pyre,"' Mavros intoned in a low voice.

'Yes, yes,' Randos said, grinning widely. 'You cannot sing, young Mavros, but you know the lines.' His expression turned serious. 'Iason–'

'We call him Jason,' Grace put in.

'Iason,' persisted the composer. 'You remember the myth, *Amerikanidha?*'

'Sure,' she said. 'He returned home with the Princess Medea and took her as his wife, but she grew jealous of him and slaughtered their children.'

190

Mavros couldn't put off the question any longer. If Randos passed on what was about to be said to the comrades, too bad. 'Iraklis,' he said, catching the composer's eye. 'Iason. They were the same, weren't they?'

The bulky Greek went as pale as a sheet, drops of sweat sprouting on his face. 'What you mean?' he blustered. 'Iason and Iraklis very different heroes.'

'I'm talking about Iason Kolettis,' Mavros said, stepping closer. 'I'm talking about the terrorist group Iraklis. Iason Kolettis was an Iraklis member, wasn't he?'

Randos opened his mouth to protest, but no sound came.

'He killed my father,' Grace said, her eyes burning into the composer's. 'I have to find him.'

Mavros put a hand on her arm to restrain her. 'You knew him, didn't you, Rando? You knew him in the sixties.'

The country's most popular songwriter looked distractedly at them both. Then he began to weep uncontrollably.

8

Kostas Laskaris lifted his head from the pages of manuscript that were strewn across the dining-table in the tower. He looked at his watch and was surprised to see that it was late afternoon. He had been writing all day, his thoughts with Iraklis as he battled the writhing Hydra at Lerna in Argolidha; each of the heads severed by the hero represented one of the evils that had beset Greece in the poet's own time – collaboration with the Axis occupiers, black-market profit-eering, treason, rape. Most difficult of all had been the depiction of Iraklis. In the earlier parts of the poem, he had restricted himself to a standard heroic formula – impulsive, strong of limb, indomitable will – but now he wanted to be more specific, more human. Inevitably the template had been that of his own hero, the *kapetanios* who called himself Iraklis during the mountain years of the Second World War – the warm voice, the hair that shone even though it went unwashed for months, the one who had inspired his band of Lakonian freedom fighters and who had disappeared when victory was in sight.

Now the poet was also faced with the need to put himself in the work. Later in the war he had been known as Iolaos, after Iraklis's faithful friend in the fight against the Hydra and subsequent mythical labours. He decided that that was how he would appear in the poem.

Dragging himself to his feet, he surveyed the scattered sheets of paper. It would be a struggle to put them in order. Often he had been encouraged by friends in the big city to use a computer, but he'd resisted. Computers meant sharing his thoughts with another intelligence. They also meant being in touch with the rest of the world. In the sixties when he had returned to the Mani to restore the old tower, he wanted to keep at bay the world that had ruined his life and the lives of those he had loved. So he had no telephone – land-line or mobile – no electronic mail, no television. Even the radio he used sparingly, and never for the news. He took the Communist paper *Rizospastis* once a week and that sufficed. The modern world, with its technical sophistication and its glittering, empty heart, was not for him.

Laskaris put on his coat and opened the heavy door. The sun was low over the western peninsula, its rays turning the sea into a morass of seething purple cut with white now that the wind had got up. He took a stick, which he had whittled clean from a length of driftwood, and walked slowly down the path that led to Tigani. The headland stretched out before him, the crown of its ramparts standing proudly against the last of the light. Soon he had to stop, the pain in his abdomen jabbing regularly and the breath rasping in his throat. 'That's enough, old man,' he muttered. 'You can't go any further.'

And yet he knew he must, in mind if not in

body. The thought that had been torturing him since he'd been in Athens had to be confronted, and Tigani was the place to do it. Even if he had to content himself with looking down on the jutting rocks rather than trace his way across them as the two young men had done nearly thirty years ago; one of them the bright-faced, blue-eyed elder son of Spyros Mavros, who had vanished soon afterwards.

Andonis Mavros had arrived at the tower in the middle of a rough November night in 1972, knocking on the door twice, then three times, then twice again in the prearranged signal. Laskaris had made his way down from the top bedroom, his legs moving much more quickly than they could now.

'Come in, my boy,' the poet said, raising a hand to silence his visitor. There was no need of the password. He had met the young man occasionally in Athens despite the rift that had opened up with Spyros before his untimely death. 'Did anyone see you in the village?'

Andonis Mavros shook his head. 'No, Comrade Kosta. I was careful.'

'Just as well.' The poet took the soaked duffel coat the young man had removed and spread it on a chair near the roaring fire. 'There are some who retain the Mani's traditional love of extremist patriotism.'

'And hatred of the Left?' Andonis Mavros accepted the glass of rough brandy he was offered.

'Oh, yes,' Laskaris replied. 'They sometimes try to break my windows.' He shrugged. 'These old

194

towers were built to repulse far worse attacks.'

'So I see,' the young man said, taking in the roughly hewn stone walls and the small shutters. 'I haven't been down here before.' He sat by the fire and started to unlace his boots. 'Do your people still get involved in vendettas?'

The poet brought him a plate containing the heel of a loaf, some olives and a slice of *siglino*, the local smoked pork. 'Some of the more hot-headed ones. The vendetta survives more as a threat, an invisible skein supporting their world, rather than actual violence.' He gave a tight smile. 'Unless you assault their wives or daughters.'

'Not my style,' Andonis Mavros said, with an assurance that, despite his age, suggested he was familiar with the close attention of women.

'Your mother?' Laskaris asked. 'Your siblings? They are all well?'

Andonis's jaw jutted forward. 'As well as anyone can be in these times of misfortune.' His face relaxed. 'Anna is fifteen and ... wilful is the word that springs to mind. And Alex, little Alex, he is ten.' He sighed. 'I don't think he has much idea of what is going on around him. My mother tries to keep him wrapped in a cocoon. She remembers how much my father paid for his beliefs.'

'She must be worried about you, then, young man,' Laskaris observed. 'It is not necessary for you to make the same sacrifices as Spyros. He achieved enough for all of you.'

Andonis Mavros smiled sadly. 'Except the world does not work that way, Comrade Poet – as you know only too well. Without the dedication

195

of the young, society will never change.' His voice hardened. 'This government of thugs and their American backers will never be overthrown unless we unite to act. Let's hope the meeting you've arranged with Iason Kolettis ends in a new unity.'

Kostas Laskaris's ears rang with the resistance leader's words. He was right, there could be no argument about that. More than that, he was magnificent: a young god whose powers were immeasurable. What glory could he achieve with a band of willing helpers? How much good could he bring into the world?

And then the poet had remembered what had happened to his own generation of idealists; what had happened to Iraklis and Stamatina and poor deluded Dinos. Their labours ended ingloriously; they had brought no benefit to suffering humanity. Everything was shrouded in a mist of illusion, but he could not tell the young man opposite him that. It was his duty to struggle and go under, the same as had been that of the resistance fighters in the occupation and the starving remnants of the Democratic Army during the civil war. Life was an uneven struggle, and the struggle had no end but death.

Laskaris shivered as the sun finally disappeared beyond the fortresses of Koroni and Methoni on the distant headland. Andonis Mavros had come back to haunt him, his shade hovering in the wolf light of evening like an avenger. But did he have the courage to admit what he knew about the young man to his family, especially now that the Iraklis group seemed to have started operations

196

again? His brother Alex was an investigator, an independent one rather than a lackey of the authorities. Maybe he would listen without passing judgement.

The realisation that he had one more duty to discharge before the disease prevailed over him almost crushed the old poet's spirit.

Grace Helmer took the composer Randos's arm. 'Come,' she said softly. 'Sit down and tell us what you know about Iason Kolettis. You'll feel better after that.' She dabbed tears from the stubble-covered face after they had settled on the tattered sofa.

Mavros squatted down in front of them. 'I know this is difficult,' he said. 'Dangerous, even – though only if you let anyone know that you spoke to us.'

The stricken man took a deep breath and gently pushed Grace's hand away from his face. 'You do not know what you are asking,' he said, lowering his eyes. 'There are some things that cannot be spoken. Like the ancient *mysteria* they must remain secret.' His voice was hoarse and almost inaudible.

'No,' Grace objected. 'This isn't sacred, this isn't a mystery that only initiates can know.' She put her hand under the composer's chin and forced his head up. 'I was five years old when my father was murdered.' She glanced briefly at Mavros, then turned her gaze back on Randos. 'I saw the knife slit his throat, I saw his blood spray out across the paving stones.'

'You – you saw–' The composer fell silent.

197

'Yes, I was watching from my bedroom window,' Grace continued. 'And you know what else? The murderer looked up and saw me, before he used the knife.' She moved her face to within a finger-length of Randos's. 'I only want one thing in my life, but I want it so badly. I want the man who called himself Iason Kolettis to look me in the eye and explain why he did that, why he destroyed my family.'

Mavros watched as Randos tried to fashion a reply, the musician's heavy body trembling under the woman's relentless stare. Grace hadn't told him that she had witnessed her father's killing. It went a long way to explaining her motivation, but it also showed how skilled she was at concealing things. He wondered what else she might have omitted to mention.

'It hurts, doesn't it?' Grace was saying. 'The pain of what you know has been crushing you for years.' She touched the back of Randos's hand. 'That pain is in your music, isn't it?'

The composer nodded. 'It is true,' he said. 'The pain is in–' He stopped, tears flowering in his eyes again. 'Lady, there is little I can tell you, but you are right. It is time I open my mouth.' He wiped a heavy hand across his face. 'Iason Kolettis, he was ... he was nobody.'

Mavros and Grace looked at each other.

'What does that mean?' she asked.

Randos shook his finger slowly at them, as if they were children. 'It means that he was a secret person, an undercover man with many names, a ... what you call it? Animal that changes colour of skin, kind of *savra?*'

'A kind of lizard,' Mavros said. 'A chameleon?'

'Yes, chameleon.' The musician pronounced the word in its Greek form, stressing the second 'e'. 'He changed his appearance, he moved among us and among the enemy like a ghost.'

'Yes, but what was he?' Grace persisted. 'Some kind of agent? Who controlled him?'

Randos looked across to the cat with her clutch of squeaking little ones. 'An agent?' he repeated. 'If you like that word. He killed people. I heard he was trained by the Soviets. The comrades here at first used him for the dangerous operations, the ones they were not sure about. But they didn't control him. I don't know if anyone controlled him. He made Iraklis himself, with a few people he took from the Party. There were rumours that someone else was involved, someone who wasn't a comrade, but I never heard who that was.' He sat back panting, as if confessing the secret knowledge had drained him of energy.

'And you never knew Kolettis's real name?' Mavros asked.

The composer raised his chin in a negative gesture. 'No one did. Not even his own people. He lived in different places, sometimes in Neapolis, I heard. But most of the local comrades didn't know him.'

'And what did Kolettis look like?' Grace Helmer's voice was encouraging.

'I didn't meet him very often. Each time he looked different. I told you, he was a chameleon.'

Mavros moved closer. 'How can we find him?'

The composer shivered. 'You are crazy. You do not want to find such a man.' He shifted his eyes between them and seemed to realise how serious they were. 'I don't know. He has not been active for many years. I thought, I hoped he was dead. But now, with the killing of that investor Vernardhakis, I don't know.'

'They found a piece of olivewood on him like the ones Iraklis used to leave,' Mavros said. 'And last night there was another suspicious killing.'

'Crazy bastards,' Randos gasped. 'They were all crazy bastards, but he was the worst of all.'

'If they were all crazy, why did you write a song about Jason – I mean, Iason – and the *Argo?*' Grace asked, her brow furrowed.

'That was early, when Iason was a figure of hope.' The composer raised his head. 'And Laskaris wrote the lyrics, not me. You should ask him about – about the chameleon.'

'We will,' Mavros said. 'But in the meantime we need more from you. If you know nothing about him, you must know something about his colleagues in the Iraklis group.'

Randos grunted. 'Two of them are dead,' he said blankly. 'The ones who called themselves Markos and Thyella. We thought he killed them.'

Mavros was staring at him. 'He killed his own comrades?'

'We thought so. We found out from one of our people that they were identified by the new anti-terrorist squad about ten years ago. They tried a – how do you say? Double-game?'

'Double-cross,' Mavros supplied.

'Yes, double-cross. Used the group members to plot against their leader. When they were both hit by cars, we thought he had done it. But maybe they refused to play that game and the bastard security forces killed them, I don't know.'

Grace leaned closer again. 'You said two of them were dead. Are others still alive?'

'Ah, no,' the composer said, forcing himself back into the sofa. 'No, I cannot.'

'Yes, you can,' Mavros said, smiling at him coldly. 'Or the comrades will find out that you've been opening your mouth to us.'

There was a long pause, then Randos gave in. 'All right. But you keep my name out of this, yes? There was one man, used to drive the killer on motorbike or car. Took the name Odhysseas, after the ancient hero. His real name was ... real name was Dhimitrakos. I remember, it came up in a secret committee meeting once. Babis Dhimitrakos. I never met him. I think he was from some village in the Mani. That is all I know.' The overweight man in the fisherman's sweater summoned his strength and levered himself up from the sofa. 'Now go. My wife will soon come. You not be seen here.'

Mavros beckoned to Grace. The visit had been more enlightening than he had expected. As they approached the door, the composer called out in Greek: 'Young Mavros?'

He turned and saw the big man cradling a pair of mewling kittens in his arms. 'There is pain everywhere in this story, pain for you too.' Randos let out a long sigh. 'Your brother Andonis.'

Mavros felt the floor shift as if an earthquake had struck.

'Andonis,' continued the musician. 'He knew Iason ... the chameleon. He met him once,

201

outside Athens. Ask Laskaris.' His eyes opened wide. 'Ask the old poet, you hear.' Then he turned away and closed the door.

Outside on the graffiti-bedecked landing, they waited for the lift.

'Are you all right?' Grace asked. 'You've gone very pale. What did he say at the end? Was that your brother he was talking about?'

Mavros fended off her questions, saying that he needed fresh air after the suffocating atmosphere of the smoky apartment.

'Yeah, it certainly wasn't the kind of home I imagined for Greece's most famous living composer,' Grace said, as they reached the main door. 'He must be serious about his beliefs.'

'Oh, yes,' Mavros said, glancing down the street. 'He's a Communist through and through. But that never stopped him owning a beach-side estate and a skiing lodge.'

Grace laughed, then caught the direction of his gaze. 'So she's still watching us,' she said, taking in the smartly dressed woman who was reading a newspaper in a doorway about fifty metres away.

'You spotted her before?' There was surprise in Mavros's voice.

'Sure,' Grace replied, as they started walking. 'She was on the trolley, pretending to be interested in the ancient monuments.'

'Where did you learn counter-surveillance techniques?'

'I didn't,' she countered evenly. 'I just got used to looking out for myself in some of the world's most dangerous cities.'

Mavros was impressed by the smoothness of the

202

reply; impressed, but not completely convinced. Right now he had more pressing things to worry about than his client's credibility, such as who had put the tail on them. The Greek authorities, the comrades, some foreign agency? Or, worst of all, the terrorist group that seemed once more to be active on the streets of Athens?

Iraklis lay in the dark and tried to reconstitute the woman he still loved, her smooth, freckled skin and her perfect body. But she was staying away from him, taunting him with her absence, daring him to speak her name, to call her back from the void. He couldn't do it. He closed his eyes and tried to join her, but he seemed to have become insubstantial himself, an empty space, a shade. All he had achieved by returning to Greece had been to put even more distance between them. If only he could forget her and find peace. But he didn't want to let her go...

He woke with a start in the early afternoon. After shaving and dressing in a badly cut working-man's suit, he pulled a scuffed cap down over his eyes. He walked out of the cheap hotel into the watery winter light that was emanating from a layer of cloud. His peasant bones told him there would be rain before long. He headed for the harbour front, anxious to stretch his legs. Later he would punish himself with his usual exercise regime, but for now a stroll would suffice.

Below the red-and-white striped chimney of the power station that was Lavrion's main landmark, the town clustered in a mass of grimy buildings. Only the yacht harbour hinted at wealth, most of it belonging to Athenians who appeared only at the weekends. Raising his eyes, he looked beyond the cape to the neighbouring island, feeling the blood rush in his veins. Yes, he still felt the fire that had been burning in him since he was a child. There lay Makronisos, the breaking ground of the Greek Left; the prison island where many had left their faith and their bones. That was why he had come out here, to rekindle his faith. The woman he loved was nothing here: she was consumed in the flames of the legitimate struggle.

For this was his real life, this was the world he had belonged to from birth. He had grown up in stony poverty, the sacrifices made by his family as real to him as the collapsing farm buildings and the sheep with their protruding ribs and glassy eyes. As soon as he could he had joined the party that despised the affectations of the rich, those bought with the sweat and blood of the workers. But in the last ten years he had compromised himself. None of his old comrades would be able to recognise him now, and not just physically. Thinking about that was painful, but he made himself go over what had happened in the early nineties to keep his mind from the woman.

The Iraklis group had been caught because someone had talked. The bastards in the Greek secret service, originally set up by the CIA in the fifties, and in the new anti-terrorist police unit had finally made one of his comrades into an informer. And they were smart – whatever you thought about their soulless ideology, they knew

204

what they were doing. Otherwise they'd have executed him on the spot that night in Koropi when they surrounded the disused glue factory that the group used for its irregular meetings. They were clinical, no doubt because of the Americans operating behind the scenes. They worked on the others first, but he was the big prize. They wanted him to testify in court that the Iraklis group had links to leading politicians in the socialist party, which had ruled the country for most of the eighties and which was threatening to replace the weakened conservative government.

But he had resisted them. The comrades he had trusted – Odhysseas, Thyella, Markos – were beaten by the enemy, but the controller, still at liberty, had stood by him. Money had been handed over and one night he had found that the door in the safe-house where he was being kept was unlocked. A few seconds were all he needed to get out, the car waiting for him where it was meant to be. In under twelve hours he was on the yacht, clearing the southern Peloponnese, Cape Matapan the last glimpse he had of his homeland. He knew he couldn't come back for a long time, but he had surprised even the controller by disappearing in Portugal and eventually making his way to the US – no one would have expected him to go there. The Iraklis group's capture and his subsequent escape were never made public, presumably to save the government's face. So he had lost himself in the back-streets of New York and spent years working hundreds of metres above the ground for a construction company. He managed to forget the past, but he never forgot the woman whose husband he had assassinated, even though she had killed herself five years before he reached her country.

Iraklis stood on the quayside, clenching and unclenching his fists. When he had found out she was dead, he had considered following her to the other side. He could easily have jumped from the topmost spars of the skyscraper he was working on at the time, or slit his wrists in a hot bath, like a Roman senator, back in the attic apartment in Queens; or he could have bought some drugs and drifted away in a painless dream. But the thought that he might one day go home kept him from suicide, the thought that one day he might find the people who had destroyed his father and consigned his mother to a lifetime of hate. Then, a few weeks ago, the controller had finally uncovered the information he needed, though it wasn't yet all in place. The killing of the investor Vernardhakis had made their job harder and he was sure that the explosion in the concert hall was tied to it, even though the newspapers had confined themselves to hinting that was the case. Someone was posing as Iraklis and that individual or group would pay the price when the controller identified them – it was only a matter of time.

Iraklis looked out towards the barren island, remembering the traditions of vengeance he had grown up with – honour, the prestige of the family, had been one of the few traditions of his homeland that stayed with him, but it was more than that. It was a question of staying alive to perform the act that would free him and those who had preceded him into the darkness from the pain of the past; from the pain that was etched into the faces of everyone he had ever held precious, including the woman whose name he could no longer say.

But had he the right to continue the cycle of violence? He was no longer sure that he did. The years of studying history and politics at night school in New York City had made him doubt that – and the men who had trained him as an underground fighter always said that doubt was the most lethal of enemies.

He closed his eyes and suddenly found himself back on the scarred slopes of the mountain, a boy of fourteen whose step was long and whose eyes were clear. Ahead of him was the poet, his brow furrowed, a stick in his right hand as he navigated the narrow, winding path to the ridge that split the Mani in two. Behind them the land dropped silently into the blue glass of the sea, the rounded peninsula with its delicate handle picked out by the sun. A harsh croak made him look up. Ravens were circling on the wind, the feathers ruffled at the tips of their outstretched wings.

It was the day he had visited the place for the first time, the confined plateau between the rain-scoured peaks. The place where, in the ice-cold Alpine atmosphere, his childhood dreams had turned with the poet's words into the nightmare that had underpinned his adult life. The place of slaughter.

'We'll split up,' Mavros said, in a low voice, as the trolley-bus swerved to avoid a motorcyclist on Amalias Avenue, making him bump into Grace. Her slender frame was surprisingly soft in parts.

'Okay,' she said. 'I guess you're the expert at this.'

'I guess I am.' He smiled tightly. 'Get off at the next stop. All you need to do is take the first right and walk for ten minutes to your hotel.'

'I think I can manage that. What about you?'

'I want to see if the tail stays on me. If she does, I'll shake her off and see if she has any support. Don't worry if she sticks to you – ignore her.' He nudged his client as the trolley slowed. 'Stay in your room. I'll be in touch.'

'This isn't the deal,' Grace complained. 'I want to go wherever the case takes you.'

'No time,' Mavros said, pushing her towards the open door. 'Trust me on this.'

'All right,' she said reluctantly. 'But call me within the hour or else.' She stepped lightly from the vehicle.

Mavros kept his eyes to the front until the trolley moved off again, then nonchalantly flicked them round his fellow passengers. The smartly dressed woman was in a seat to his rear, nose in her book. He could make out the title. It was a volume of the Nobel-winner Elytis's poems in Greek. As he prepared to make his move, he considered whether her choice of reading indicated who she was working for.

The trolley stopped beyond the neo-classical buildings on Panepistimiou and disgorged a crowd of passengers. Mavros bided his time until the mass of boarders clambered on, then stepped forward to help an old woman with a couple of blue plastic bags. An instant before the doors closed, he stepped off, catching a glimpse of the tail's shocked face. Before she could get to her feet to press the emergency button, he ran across the road, provoking a horn blast from a taxi-driver, and cut into a back-street. There were enough people around to cover his passing. He had made it. Now all he had to do was work out a plan of action.

That didn't take long. He knew that, given the surveillance, he had limited time to make progress in the case. There was only one option and that was to get out of Athens and follow up the leads he had – Kostas Laskaris and the Iraklis driver Babis Dhimitrakos, the one who had been known as Odhysseas. He rang his mother.

'Hello, Alex,' she said brightly. 'How nice to hear your voice.'

'Hello, Mother. Listen, I'm a bit pressed for time.' He jammed himself up against the window of a leather-goods shop as people bustled past. 'Have you got Kostas Laskaris's phone number down in the Peloponnese?'

'Kostas Laskaris?' Dorothy said, a hint of surprise in her voice. 'Why do you want to talk to him?'

'Never mind.'

'Oh.' His mother sounded put out. 'Well, he hasn't got a telephone.'

'What? How did you get in touch about the lunch you gave him?'

'He wrote me a letter and I replied in the same

209

way.' Dorothy was waspish now. 'There are people who still use that mode of communication, you know. Kostas doesn't like to be easily contactable in his tower.'

'All right, Mother, I'm sorry. Where is it that he lives exactly?'

'The tower is outside a small village called Ayia Kyriaki. Near Kitta, I think, in the western Mani. Why? You're not planning on going there, are you?'

'Maybe,' Mavros said, thinking about the painting Grace Helmer's mother had done with the nearby village's name in the title.

'Only I'm going to be in the Peloponnese for Christmas after all,' Dorothy said, her tone softening. 'What happened at the opera, Anna and Nondas being so close to that dreadful killing, made me want to be with them and the children.'

'So you're going to stay at the Palaiologos place?' Mavros tried to keep the disapproval out of his voice.

'Oh, I know you don't like Veta and Nikitas,' his mother said. 'But family is what counts, now more than ever.'

Mavros thought about that for a few moments. Randos's mention of his brother Andonis was rattling around in his head. 'Yes, you're right, Mother,' he said. 'Maybe I'll pass by their house at some stage. 'Bye for now.'

'Goodbye, dear. And be careful.'

His mother often said that. Mavros usually ignored the words but this time they made him shiver. He had the distinct impression that he

210

was swimming with the big fish, and some of them had razor-sharp teeth.

It was time to conjure up a dual disappearance.

Randos was at the piano, his eyes firmly closed, trying to lose himself in the crashing chords. His wife had returned not long after his visitors had left, seen the state he was in, and gone out again. She had learned when to keep clear of him, though he imagined he didn't often look so disturbed when he was composing. The cat didn't have any option. Psipsina had draped herself over her kittens, their tiny bodies almost smothered by her loose flank. She opened her eyes from time to time, giving her master pained glances, but the sound from the piano didn't stop.

The composer's thoughts were jumping between scenes of his old life, the years he thought he'd exorcised in his music. That bastard who called himself Iason Kolettis, how could they have been so blind? He was a madman, they should have seen that from the beginning. Old Spyros Mavros had never wanted anything to do with him, he had seen the empty glint in the killer's eyes even before he started his murderous activities. But the others had wanted to use him for the good of the Party. The fools. He had used them, he had sucked them dry and then left them in disarray to set up his private gang of assassins. Even young Mavros, the lost hero Andonis, had failed to see the dangers of working with Iraklis. And it seemed he had paid the heaviest price of all for that misjudgement. But he was young, innocent of the world's harsh ways. The others, himself, Laskaris – they should have warned him. Instead, they had left him to be consumed by the killer's fire. Randos cursed himself for a coward. The one time he had tried to reason with Kolettis, the killer had smiled viciously, his hand on the haft of a heavy knife, and told him that he would take no interference from comrades who spent their time arguing with each other rather than fighting for the cause. God, he had been so frightened. The thought of the assassin's eyes still made him quiver.

And now he had sent the younger Mavros brother into the same cauldron. Christ and the Mother of God, what had he been thinking of? Laskaris would sacrifice him just as he had Andonis, sacrifice him to save himself, the old queer. And what of the woman, the American? Did she have any idea what she was letting herself in for by trying to find her father's assassin? There was a hardness about her, a calculating inner core that reminded him of the most ruthless comrades. Was she taking Alex Mavros for a ride, planning to ditch him too when the time came? The legacy of hatred was still as powerful as ever, whatever side people were on.

Randos slammed his hands down in a final apocalyptic chord and slumped over the keys, his breath catching in his throat. Then he heard the buzz of the doorbell, brash and insistent. He tried to ignore it, but it wouldn't stop. Cursing, he staggered to the entryphone and pressed the button, not interested in who was there. Maybe his wife had forgotten her key. He opened the

212

apartment door and went back into the *saloni*, listening to the kittens' high-pitched cries.

'So, comrade,' said a soft voice, 'I hope you will share with me what you told your visitors. Word for word.'

He looked up to see a figure loom over him and knew instantly that his time had come. The phone calls he had made after Mavros and the woman left, he had known they were a risk. Perhaps, deep down, he had wanted to take that risk. At least someone would pay for what had happened to Andonis Mavros and to all the other victims of Iraklis.

The composer rose unsteadily to his feet. He was ready to join the army of shades, the fighters who had given everything for their dreams even if those dreams had never been fulfilled. And he didn't intend to say a word to the bastard in front of him.

'Guess who,' Mavros said, as soon as Grace Helmer answered her phone. He knew that other ears might be listening. 'Wait for me outside.'

In under ten minutes he was at the hotel in a taxi. Grace Helmer was at the head of the hotel driveway, wearing a fleece jacket and carrying her dark brown shoulder-bag.

'What gives, Alex?' she asked, as the taxi-driver, a fresh-faced young man with the look of a moonlighting student, accelerated away in the direction of the Megaro Mousikis.

'Let's see,' said Mavros, looking over his shoulder. The sun was in the west but the street-lights were not yet on. In the fume-filled gloom he

213

made out a sleek, dark blue Citroën about fifty metres behind them. 'Don't turn round. I think we've got company again.' He leaned forward and spoke to the driver in rapid Greek. The conversation ended in mutual laughter.

'I asked you a question,' Grace said. 'What the hell gives?'

Mavros smiled. 'I just told him that your husband's on our tail.' He put his hand on her thigh. 'Darling.'

She raised an eyebrow but allowed the hand to remain. 'And Tom Cruise here is going to shake him off, is he?'

The taxi swerved in front of a bus and took an unsignalled left turn into the back-streets. Although the traffic was heavy, the driver managed to avoid the numerous blockages caused by cars pulling in and lorries making deliveries.

'All right,' Mavros said to the grinning young man, 'well done. Stick to the back-streets and get us to the KTEL at Kifissou.' He glanced at Grace and changed to English. 'We're going to catch the bus to the island of Pelops.'

'How quaint,' she said drily. 'Thanks for giving me advance warning. I'd have brought a change of clothes.'

'They have shops down there,' Mavros countered. 'I think.'

Grace looked out of the window at the neighbourhood supermarkets and restaurants. 'It's not bad in this quarter. There's more character than in the rich people's streets around my hotel.'

'I grew up in this area,' Mavros said. 'Our mystery man spent some time here too.'

'Oh, so this is Neapolis, is it?' She peered out with even more interest. 'There are some fine old houses.'

'Lawyers and merchants built them in the old days. My father's family owned one.' He had flashes of summer evenings kicking a ball around in the narrow streets, and chill winter mornings on the way to school, his breath pluming into the air like a thought bubble in a comic.

'What did your father do?' Grace said, clutching the back of the seat in front as the driver screeched to a halt. 'Jesus.' She watched as a skinny black cat scuttled under a car.

'He was a lawyer,' Mavros said. He decided to open up a bit: perhaps that would encourage her to do the same. 'Because of his politics he was in various prisons and concentration camps during the forties and fifties. After that he had to keep his activities secret because the Party was banned.'

'Must have made for an interesting childhood.' Grace turned to him. 'You realise that my father was working for the other side.'

'Of course. But that's all in the past now.'

She registered his sceptical tone. 'Yeah, it seems that the past is still pretty much in evidence in this country.'

'In all countries, I'd say.'

'Well, if you want to jack the case in, I'll understand.' She looked out again as the cab passed the National Museum. 'We seem to have attracted people's interest. Have we shaken them off?'

'I think so.' Mavros realised suddenly that his

215

hand was still on her thigh. As he removed it he said, 'No, I want to stick with it. I'm in need of stimulation.'

Grace Helmer frowned, as if he wasn't taking things seriously enough.

The taxi-driver set them down in a back-street off Leoforos Kifissou. 'Go to the good,' he said. 'I hope the wanker never finds you.'

Mavros tipped him well after asking him to erase them from his memory. He was pretty sure that would happen. The driver's complicity suggested that he might be carrying on an illicit relationship himself.

In the vast hall of the bus station, the atmosphere heavy with diesel fumes, Mavros went to buy tickets. He left Grace in a secluded corner with instructions to stay put. She greeted those with a mocking smile but squatted down obediently.

'Right,' he said, on his return, brandishing the tickets. 'I've got us on the Patras bus.'

Grace stood up and shook the pins and needles from her legs. 'Patras? That's the port for Italy, isn't it?'

'In the north-west of the Peloponnese, yes. Don't worry, we're getting off before that. But just in case anyone asks questions...'

The turquoise and cream bus pulled out at exactly six p.m., the majority of its seats taken. Mavros and Grace sank down, keeping their heads bowed. Soon the vehicle was surrounded by traffic on the main exit road to the west, the refineries and metal works beyond the ridge pumping gas-clouds and flames into the darkness.

'Are you going to tell me what we're doing now?' Grace asked.

'Need to know is the standing order in this kind of situation, isn't it?'

'What?' she asked, looking puzzled.

'Don't you watch spy movies?'

'There aren't many cinemas in the jungle.'

'Right. Well, we're going to talk to Kostas Laskaris, aren't we? Find out what he knows about the man we're after. I met the old poet recently – he was a friend of my father – so he should grant us an interview. Even though he's much more of a recluse than Randos.'

'And you're going to try and trace that other guy, the driver?'

Mavros nodded. 'Everything seems to lead to the Mani, and one small part of it.'

'Maybe our man came from there.'

'Maybe.' Mavros was hoping so, remembering again Laura Helmer's painting *Lament for Kitta*. Maybe they'd be lucky – though unexpected breaks in cases often proved to be more trouble than they were worth.

They fell silent, unwilling to draw attention to themselves by speaking English outside the tourist season. The bus sped along the motorway through tunnels bored into the rock of precipitous cliffs. When another array of flames marking the refinery east of Corinth came into view, Mavros gave Grace a nudge. 'Prepare for disembarkation,' he whispered. 'The bus will stop for a quarter of an hour at a café. Wait until everyone else has got off, then follow me.'

The bus pulled up outside a line of brightly lit

217

establishments selling *souvlakia*, burgers and other refreshments. As the last of the passengers headed for those attractions, Mavros and Grace stepped down and walked away into the darkness beyond, keeping their pace steady.

The scent of the Peloponnese came across the isthmus on the wind, its orange and pine breath carrying a promise of spring in the heart of winter.

9

November 1943

The resistance fighters stood around the survivors of the battle in an uneven circle. Above them the buzzards were circling, wings spread wide as the gusts from the peaks of Taygetos buffeted them. Outside the ring of rifle-bearers bodies were scattered, some in the tattered clothes worn by ELAS members, but the majority in German field grey and Greek service uniforms. There were also several in the skirts and woollen stockings traditionally worn by the élite *evzones*. To Kostas Laskaris the plateau smelled of fresh blood and he was having trouble keeping control of his stomach now that the haze of battle had passed from his eyes. He tried to shut out the things he had seen and done – bullets tearing into unprotected flesh, his rifle butt smashing into the face of a youthful blond soldier.

A pair of scouts came back up the narrow track.

'The rest of them have gone, *kapetanie*,' the older man said to Iraklis. 'The cowards will not be back.'

'I shot one,' said his young companion, eyes wide and expression joyous. 'I saw him fall.'

'Bravo, Comrade Dino,' Iraklis said, from the centre of the circle. 'Didn't I tell you that you would become a hero of the people today?'

There was a murmur of approval from the fighters. The men in the ring, six of them, lay flat, their tunics torn and blood-spattered. Only the movement of their backs, their desperate breathing, revealed that they were alive.

'You are all heroes,' Iraklis shouted. 'And heroines,' he added, glancing at the woman Stamatina. Her face was bruised and the bayonet on her rifle was dark-stained. She gave her leader a broad smile.

'What about these pigs?' asked a wizened old guerrilla.

'I'm coming to them, Comrade Mano,' Kapetan Iraklis said, looking down at the Greek prisoners – the German who surrendered had already been despatched. 'I haven't forgotten them.' His voice was less certain now.

The men on the ground let out a muffled collective groan, their bodies pressing harder to the stony soil. They knew what lay in store for them.

The iron-willed political commissar Vladhimiros pushed his way to the front. 'Comrade combatants of ELAS,' he proclaimed, 'there can be only one fate for those who conspire with the occupier to exterminate the people's fighters and their families.' He ran his eyes around the ring of grim-faced guerrillas. Most had lost relatives to the merciless violence of the occupiers and, more recently, to the collaborationist Security Battalions; and most were from the Mani, where vengeance to restore family honour was bred in the bone.

'I volunteer,' came a firm female voice.

All eyes, including those of the prisoners, turned to the woman with the bayonet on her rifle. Kapetan Iraklis shook his head at her, his eyes wide.

'Volunteers are not required,' Comrade Vladhimiros said dismissively. During the dictatorship of Metaxas before the war he had served time in the prison of Akronafplia, the so-called university of Greek Communism. 'Execution duty should operate on a rotating basis. Every member of the revolutionary band has the duty to take part when his or her name comes up.' He gave a cold smile. 'I believe Comrade Stamatina has already accounted for at least two collaborators.'

One of the prone soldiers, a young man whose face was pocked with the marks of smallpox, let out a thin squeal of terror.

Kapetan Iraklis looked at the commissar with distaste. 'I am in command here, comrade,' he said. 'Consult your list for the next four names.' He nodded to the stony-faced woman. 'Comrade Stamatina and I will go first.' He looked around the circle again. 'There is no glory in such acts, my friends, no cause for exultation. But our country must be purged of traitors such as these.'

Vladhimiros was consulting a dog-eared sheet he had taken from his briefcase. He read out four names. Kostas Laskaris was relieved that his turn had not come again – he had served as executioner more than once in the past. Staring across the ring of fighters, he saw young Dinos's expression of disappointment. Already the boy was becoming a killer. In these conditions it

221

didn't take long.

Iraklis bent over the nearest prisoner, the blade of a cut-throat razor glinting in the sun; no bullets were to be wasted. He looked up, his eyes dark as night, and caught Kostas's gaze, then gave a melancholy smile and whipped the well-honed steel across the traitor's throat.

A few seconds later Stamatina's victim was twitching out his last throes, the earth of the mountain plateau soaking up the crimson flood that had been loosed by her saw-edged bayonet.

Kostas Laskaris was thinking of the six mothers who had been deprived of their sons, measuring the implacable hatred of the revolutionary fighters that would be stored up for generations despite the justness of their struggle. In the past, prisoners had been taken. But that was before the Security Battalions started their campaign of ferocity against EAM/ELAS members and their families. He shook away his concerns. Such thoughts were nothing less than treason, and comrades guilty of harbouring them would be treated in the same way as the battalionists. Besides, winter was biting and there was hardly enough food for the fighters themselves. But he knew that Iraklis was pained by what he had to do. That only made Kostas admire and love him more. The true hero cared nothing for his own feelings – he sacrificed them for the cause.

Not long afterwards the band made its way from the place of slaughter and disappeared into the twilight that was rapidly gathering around them. The corpses of their pursuers – foreign and Greek – were left unburied for the carrion creatures of the night.

Mavros found a seedy-looking car-rental office on the outskirts of Corinth. He and Grace had set off on foot from the cafés by the bridge over the isthmus, but a garishly painted pick-up soon stopped. The driver, a dark-skinned gypsy with long hair, had cheerfully pointed them to the empty cargo space, the front seats taken up by a trio of grinning children. Mavros didn't think anyone who was on their trail would catch up with the guy, but he took the precaution of signalling him to let them off well away from the car-rental premises.

Leaving Grace in the shadows down the potholed street, Mavros concluded the deal. In exchange for a wad of cash, a shifty old man wrote down a false name and address on the hire agreement. He took a note of Mavros's real name and credit-card details, pointing out to him that he had several male relatives well versed in the arts of extracting money from defaulters. Mavros got the message. He would return the car no later than a week from now or he'd be in need of a surgeon.

He went down the street to the car bearing the registration number that was on the key.

'You didn't fancy the executive selection, then?' Grace said, as she stepped out from an alcove.

'Nah,' Mavros replied, opening a door that was less than pristine. 'I reckoned you wouldn't want to pay any more than you had to.' He was still unsure how well-off his client was – aid organisations were hardly noted for generosity to their employees.

'Is this thing roadworthy?' Grace said, as she got in at the far side of the bottom-of-the-range Fiat Panda. It was red, but the paint beneath the scratches on the bodywork suggested that it had originally been another colour. 'Is it stolen?'

'Don't know, don't care,' Mavros said. 'It's insured, it's safe to drive – supposedly – and it's cost you rather less than renting from one of the big companies.'

'I presume you've taken steps to keep us anonymous,' Grace said, struggling with her seat-belt.

Now he was in the car, Mavros wasn't so confident about driving it. Although he had passed his test when he was in his teens, he would rather drink hemlock than drive in Athens so he hadn't been behind a wheel for some time. He turned the key and managed to engage first gear.

'Check your mirror,' Grace said, as he pulled out.

'We're in Greece, not upstate New York,' he said, his cheeks reddening as a passing car hooted.

'Just as a matter of interest,' Grace asked, 'when did you last drive?' She leaned towards him. 'Have you ever driven?'

'Very funny.' Mavros saw the sign to Tripolis and headed for the motorway. 'I last drove ... well, I suppose it's a couple of years ago now. My brother-in-law's Jeep was stuck in a beach in northern Attiki and I got it out for him.' He wasn't telling the whole story: Nondas Chaniotakis had lost patience with Mavros's slow progress digging out the rear wheels and had insisted on swapping roles. It was a mistake he wouldn't make again. Mavros's heavy foot on the accelerator had almost deposited the vehicle in a deep well he hadn't noticed behind a line of bushes.

'I last drove a week ago back home,' Grace said. 'How about I take over?'

'Later,' Mavros said stubbornly. 'You can direct me.' He handed her the map of the Peloponnese that the rental man had added to the bill.

'You're right, I can. Where are we going, exactly? Kitta in the Mani?'

'That's a bit of a long haul for tonight,' he replied. 'I think we should burn down the motorway to Tripolis. As far as I remember, the road from there to Sparta is pretty fast too.'

'Yeah, it looks okay on here.'

'Right. We can spend the night in Sparta and head on to the Mani in the morning.'

'What? In a hotel? Shit!' she exclaimed, as a car came out of the night behind them and swerved past with inches to spare. 'Jesus, there are some boy racers in this country.'

'Most of them middle-aged boys.' Mavros laughed softly. 'I, on the other hand, am a careful and considerate driver.'

'Yeah, well, you haven't got much choice, have you? This heap can hardly hold ninety kilometres an hour.' Grace glanced at him. 'Anyway, this business of staying in Sparta, what are you thinking? A hotel? Is that safe?'

'I'm wondering about that. If we stay in a hotel, there'll be a record of our presence in the

225

register. Guest-houses are less formal. But at this time of year there won't be many places renting rooms.'

'Let's have a look.' Grace pulled a paperback book and a micro-torch from her bag.

'You came prepared.' Mavros took in a sign that gave the distance to the Nemea junction.

'I always come prepared. Right, there are plenty of hotels open all year round in Sparta and...' she brought the book closer to her eyes '...one establishment that rents rooms. Kyra Froso, Vrettakou twenty-three. "Clean, comfortable and welcoming", it says here.'

'Let's aim for that, then.'

'And let's swap drivers at Tripolis,' Grace said, her tone making it clear that she, the client, was laying down the law.

They drove past the darkened slopes of the northern mountains of the Peloponnese, the motorway bisecting them with sinuous curves. There was a sign to Argos and Nafplion. That made Mavros think of his mother and sister – soon they would be on the same road, heading for the Palaiologos house. At least he hadn't been invited, though if he'd expressed an interest in accompanying his family no doubt he would have been. Hobnobbing with politicians and tycoons wasn't for him; even a quick stop on the way back wasn't enticing. Maybe Grace would be his get-out clause.

They changed over in a lay-by outside Tripolis. The air around Arkadhia's main city was bitterly cold, the height of seven hundred metres plus above sea level giving the street-lamps frosty haloes. The traffic shooting around the bypass faded quickly after they took the road south and Mavros sat back in the uncomfortable seat as Grace handled the car smoothly. They climbed to an even higher plateau, then descended through a long defile towards Sparta, a slab of roughly hewn rock caught in the headlights marking one of the many memorials to wartime massacres in the area.

'Why didn't you tell me that you witnessed your father's killing?' Mavros asked, as they wound down the final hill. The vast wall of Mount Taygetos rose behind the cupola of light that marked the capital of Lakonia, the mountain's crown of snow glinting in the moonlight.

Grace didn't answer immediately. She manoeuvred the car dextrously round a petrol tanker that had been parked at the roadside, then glanced at him. 'Sorry about that. It's something I find difficult to talk about.'

'Except when you need to tighten the screw on someone who's holding out on you, like Randos was.'

She raised her shoulders. 'Sometimes you have to be brutal.' Her face hardened. 'Grow up, Alex. You're angry that I didn't tell you about it, but you're even more angry that I was the one who got the composer to talk.'

Mavros felt the sting of the words. He turned to her. 'No, I'm not, Grace,' he said untruthfully. 'But you need to be careful. Randos saw how driven you are. He might have passed that on to people who are less guilt-scarred than he is.'

'You're right. I'll watch my tongue in future.'

227

She looked ahead. 'We're almost there. How do we find the guest-house?'

'Simple,' he said. 'Pull up at that *periptero* over there.'

'That what?'

'Sorry, the kiosk that's covered in newspapers.' He got out when she stopped, and returned almost immediately. 'First left, third right.'

Grace followed the directions without speaking, parking in a tight space beyond number twenty-three.

'Well done,' he said. 'Did you used to work as a chauffeur?'

'Wise guy. Why shouldn't women be able to drive better than men?'

They got out and walked towards a detached two-storey house, the balconies swathed in plants. There were lights on inside.

Mavros rang the bell. 'I'll do the talking, all right? It'll be better for our profile if you don't come across as a foreigner. Just nod if I address you in Greek.'

Grace seemed unfazed by the instruction.

The door was opened by a plump middle-aged woman dressed in black, her sombre appearance immediately lightened by a wide smile. 'Good evening, good evening,' she said, gazing at them both warmly. 'You want a room?'

'Two rooms, please,' Mavros said. 'You're Kyra Froso?'

The woman nodded in assent, the smile fading. 'But I have only one room, my boy. There's a big meeting in the town, a lot of politicians and businessmen pretending to work, so I am almost

228

full. Not that they have returned from the tavernas yet.'

Mavros kept his eyes off Grace. 'You have only one room? How many beds?'

Kyra Froso gave him an encouraging look. 'One double.' Then she laughed. 'But there is a single one as well, if you need two.' She stepped closer. 'The lady is your sister?'

'One room will be all right, won't it?' he said to Grace in Greek.

She nodded, giving him a suspicious look.

Kyra Froso watched them with undisguised curiosity. 'Well, then, I will give you the room and may you have joy of it.' She ushered them in, nudging Mavros as he passed. 'My husband died last year, my boy. We used to sleep in that room. It saw many happy times.' She pointed to the end of the corridor and handed him a key-ring. 'The right-hand door. You'll find the bathroom straight ahead. The other key is to the front door. Eight thousand drachmas is my price. One night?'

'One night,' he confirmed.

'May it be a good one,' Kyra Froso said, her smile now tinged with melancholy.

Mavros led Grace to the room.

'I take it this is all she had,' she said, as he closed the door behind them. 'Because if I find out you set me up you'll be sorry, Alex.'

Mavros raised his hands in mock surrender. 'Honestly, this was her only free room. You'll hear a bunch of drunken conference delegates roll in later.'

Grace was looking around the large bedroom,

taking in the two beds and the surprisingly tasteful décor. 'Since you've been making all the decisions, now it's my turn. I'll have the small bed. Just to make sure you aren't tempted to join me.'

'Are you hungry?' Mavros asked, suddenly uncomfortable. 'There are probably still some places open.'

'Are you sure it's a good idea for us to be seen on the streets?'

'As sure as I feel like being. I'm starving.'

'Okay. Show me the hot spots.' She leaned forward and examined the embroidered panel on the wall above the single bed. 'Who's she?'

Mavros read the inscription. '*"I oraia Eleni"*. *La belle Hélène.*'

'Isn't that a dessert?'

'You're thinking of Poire Belle Hélène.'

'Right. And she is?'

'The fair Helen, wife of King Menelaus of Sparta, mistress of Trojan Paris – the face that launched a thousand ships.'

Grace took a lipstick from her bag. 'Oh, her. Just the person to have above my bed.' She added a layer of colour to her lips. 'Let's go, lover-boy.'

They walked out into the city beneath the snow-capped mountain.

The politician Veta Palaiologou beckoned to Loudhovikos, her butler. 'Some more brandy, Geoff?' Her English was fluent and unaccented, although her voice was slightly higher than it was when she spoke Greek. 'Flora?'

The white-jacketed servant went round with

230

the decanter, his face impassive. Flora Petraki-Dearfield declined with a murmur, but her husband allowed his glass to be refilled. Nikitas Palaiologos was drinking whisky, the beads of sweat on his bald pate attesting to the amount he had put away, while Veta was confining herself to water on doctor's orders.

'That was an excellent dinner,' the old soldier Dearfield said, raising his glass to the hostess. Although he had studied ancient Greek at school and university before the war, he had never made the transition to idiomatic modern Greek and felt uncomfortable in the language. 'In the tradition of this house.'

'My father always employed the best chefs.' Nikitas glanced at his wife. 'As did yours. We have maintained the traditions of our families.' He gave a nervous laugh. 'We are conservatives, after all.'

Veta was unimpressed by his flippancy.

'You have done wonders with this old place,' Flora said, trying to lighten the atmosphere. It had been oppressive all evening, her three companions tense and conversation forced. 'I can remember when it seemed like a spartan blockhouse, more of an army base than a family home.'

'That's exactly what it was,' Nikitas muttered, in Greek.

Veta gave him a frosty look, then turned to Flora. 'It certainly needed a lot of work. Central heating, interior improvements, the annexes. And the garden, well, it was nothing more than a wasteland of trampled earth.'

231

Geoffrey Dearfield emptied his glass and signalled for another refill, his face pale.

'It was a prison camp, for God's sake,' Nikitas said, keeping his eyes off his wife. 'It was a place of–'

'Be quiet!' Veta said, with the assertiveness she had acquired in Parliament. She pulled herself to her feet and moved towards Nikitas's armchair. 'People aren't interested in the war any more.' He raised his hands in surrender and concentrated on his whisky.

'I would like to tour around Argolidha now we are here,' Flora said. 'That's the curse of being a historian. Trips away from home always turn into research projects.' She looked across at her husband and blinked. 'Geoff has been so caught up in his book.'

Nikitas shot the old man in the tweed suit a glance, but remained silent.

'Yes, what is this great work you have been devoting yourself to, Geoff?' Veta asked, lifting a finger to keep the butler away from the clearly maudlin Englishman.

Dearfield remained silent for a while, swallowing the anger provoked by his wife's mention of the book – sometimes she was like that, sometimes she did what she wanted without regard to his wishes. He looked up at her, his eyes rheumy and opaque, then turned to the others. 'I ... I have decided to tell the truth about what happened in the Peloponnese during the Second World War.'

'The truth?' Veta repeated, a nervous smile flitting across her lips. 'I presume you mean the truth as we understand it, we who love freedom and justice.'

'Indeed,' said Dearfield weakly. But the élite families loved enriching themselves more than freedom and justice, he thought. Although all the friends he had made in Greece throughout his long association with the country were on the right politically, he sometimes found himself repulsed by their full-blooded commitment to personal gain – or, rather, familial gain. As a serving politician Veta Palaiologou was less involved in financial pursuits than most, but her husband? Nikitas was a former playboy whose only consolation now he was too old for that role was the acquisition of even more wealth than his grasping father had left him. And the two fathers? Prokopis Palaiologos and Sokratis Dhragoumis had been among his closest friends since the night he first parachuted into the Peloponnese in 1942. Until that terrible day outside this very house. He should have cut off all contact with them after that, but he hadn't the stomach to do it. His memoir would set the record straight, even though it went no further than 1945. His activities behind the scenes with the Americans from the late forties to the early seventies needed another book. He doubted he had the strength for it.

'Well?' Veta was saying. 'I do hope you are not – what is the expression? – dishing the dirt?'

Dearfield didn't answer. He had suddenly found himself back in this building, as it had been during the last year of the Nazi occupation – the rooms bare, the windows barricaded, the doors guarded by gendarmes and members of the local Security Battalions. Hard faces surrounded him, burning eyes and mouths that issued clipped commands in harsh tones; commands that consigned the men held in cages outside to torture or summary execution. He'd had no doubt about the rectitude of his complicity in those deeds. His superiors had given him clear instructions to restrict Communist influence by any and all means in his power. But events had got out of hand and, though he had blocked them out for decades, the truncated cries of defiance, the contempt and determination in the eyes of the prisoners had come back to him in recent years. That was why he had written the memoir, his own words leaping up from the page to clutch at him every day. The man on the cross, the unconscious woman who was dragged away – when would they leave him in peace?

'...often drops off in the evenings,' Flora was saying, in Greek. 'He's into his eighties now and he tires easily.'

'Have you seen what he has written?' Nikitas asked, his brow furrowed. 'Do you think there's any chance of it being published?'

Flora looked at him, concealing her emotions. She had never liked the Palaiologos son, though he had become less irritating in recent years. He'd made a pass at her that she had instantly rejected in the seventies and she hadn't forgotten it. 'No, he has not shown it to me,' she replied coolly. 'Why should he? As for publication, you will be able to ask the person who is considering

234

it tomorrow.'

Veta glanced at her husband. 'So he has sent the book to Dorothy Cochrane-Mavrou, has he?' She had told the Dearfields earlier that Dorothy and her family would be joining the party. 'An odd choice, considering her dead husband's politics.'

'Shit,' Nikitas exclaimed. 'What the hell's Geoff playing at? There are things that our families don't want in the public domain.'

Veta raised her hand. 'That's enough. I don't imagine our families will be to the fore of the narrative.'

Later, her husband snoring by her side, Flora went over the conversation. Nikitas Palaiologos had seemed concerned about the memoir and that interested her. What she had said about Geoff's book was true – he had never shown it to her. He had been secretive with the text that he had pounded out on his old Olivetti typewriter. His desk was often covered with photocopied documents that he had obtained from the Imperial War Museum and other archives.

She turned over and took in the lines of light from the enclosed garden that were shining through the slats of the shutters. She had been a child during the war, spending the occupation comfortably in her father's well-stocked house in the northern suburbs of Athens. Until that blood-soaked day when her family life had changed irrevocably. She had met her husband when she was still a student and he had provided a way out – as well as other advantages he had never suspected. But he had never given her

235

children. If he had, perhaps she would not have gone so far down the path she had been on since her early twenties. And Geoffrey had also allowed her to pursue her academic career. Greek history, from the ancient heroes to the turmoil of her own century, had always engaged her imagination.

The ancient heroes, they had stayed with her – especially one of them. Flora found herself thinking about Iraklis. He was the beating heart of the Peloponnese, the country of her early childhood. He had slain the lion of Nemea and the Lernaean Hydra, he had cleansed the Augean stables, he had captured the Ceryneian hind and the Erymanthian boar – all creatures and locations of the peninsula. She looked into the lines of light. Below the Palaiologos house were the great walls of Tiryns, the hero's birthplace. But the southern tip of the Peloponnese was the scene of his greatest labour. From Tainaron at the end of the middle finger, the hero had descended to the underworld – and conquered death by dragging Hades' hound Cerberus to the surface of the earth.

Sleep finally washed over Flora Petraki-Dearfield as she thought of the barren headland and the old church that lay above the shaded entrance to hell. It was in the Mani, land of her birth and forefathers. The long struggle to make history of her own life had started there.

Mavros woke to the sound of voices outside the room. He opened his eyes and saw the light streaming in at the edges of Kyra Froso's lace-trimmed curtains. His watch told him it was a

236

little after nine. As the conversation in the hall continued, a gruff male voice followed by the soothing tones of a woman, he glanced across and saw that Grace's bed was empty. Sitting up, he listened to the voices and recognised the landlady's. She was assuring the man that the bathroom would soon be free – as soon as the foreign lady had finished. So much for the scam to keep his client's nationality under wraps. It was fair to say that she didn't look much like a Greek.

Mavros sat on the edge of the double bed and scratched the stubble on his face. He hadn't slept well, the mattress uneven after the efforts of Kyra Froso and her dear departed. Last night, after visiting an unimpressive taverna and a bar that had delusions of grandeur regarding its prices, they had walked back through the streets with their lines of orange trees, the provincial town's citizens long since tucked up in bed. In their shared room, Grace had whipped off her sweatshirt and trousers without giving Mavros a second glance, and got into her bed. As far as he could tell, she had fallen straight into a deep, silent sleep. The glimpse he had caught of her lithe body and matching black underwear had kept him awake for a time.

The door opened and she came in, fully dressed with a towel round her head. 'Good morning,' she said, casting an eye over him. 'You've missed your turn in the bathroom. There was a sour-looking guy waiting for me to finish.'

'I'll survive.'

'Slow in the morning, are we?' Grace said, with

a smile. 'I've already been out to buy the essentials.' She went over to her bag and tossed him a brown-paper bag. 'Cleanliness is next to godliness, or so my Ganma always said.'

He opened it to find two pairs of boxer shorts. 'How much do I owe you?'

'Forget it. I'm the one who owes you, remember?' He hadn't insisted on her paying an advance.

Shortly afterwards they left the room and settled up with Kyra Froso. She gave Mavros a knowing glance that turned to a wince of consolation when he didn't respond in kind.

'*Sto kalo na pate, paidhia mou,*' she called after them.

'What was that she said?' Grace asked, as they got to the car. She had the key in her hand.

'She sent us to the good,' Mavros replied. 'And she called us her children.'

'That was sweet of her,' she said, as she slid behind the driving-wheel. 'Even if she didn't exactly have my virtue as her number-one priority.' She gave him a tight smile. 'Right, no cheating by asking at kiosks this time. Get map-reading.' She started the engine. 'And don't tell me that's not a man's job. While you were in the shower, I read about ancient Sparta in the guide-book. Girls and boys went through the same strict training regime. They were surprisingly modern about gender issues.'

'I don't remember Leonidas going into battle at Thermopylae with an army consisting of fifty per cent women,' Mavros muttered, as he found the town plan in her book.

Grace laughed. 'Maybe he'd have won if he had. Where to?'

He directed her to the main street. A left turn took them on to the road that led to the port of Yithion. It headed almost due south from Sparta, the imposing mass of Mount Taygetos to the right running all the way to the coast fifty kilometres ahead. Although it was only single lane in each direction, the road was reasonably fast, cultivated land interspersing with narrow defiles thick with trees. There was little traffic.

'This is schizophrenic country,' Grace said, as she overtook a tractor laden with branches lopped from the ubiquitous orange trees. 'Serious mountains on both sides' – she glanced at the more distant and rolling mass of Mount Parnon to the east – 'and fertile flat land in the plain.'

Mavros nodded. 'Although this area is fairly rich by rural Greek standards, you don't have to go far off the main road to find villages that are dying on their feet. The locals have been moving to Athens for years because of the harshness of life in the uplands. There was a lot of trouble here during the Second World War and after – massacres, reprisals, bad blood in spades. The southern Peloponnese was always very pro-monarchist, which meant that the Right's stand-off with republicans and Communists in the late forties was even more extreme than elsewhere.'

Grace took that on board without comment and Mavros wondered if mention of the Communists had made her think about the group that had executed her father. He kept

239

silent until they had passed through the last defile and reached the outskirts of Yithion, the port of Sparta in ancient and modern times.

'Not a bad-looking little town,' he said, taking in the long promenade, hotels and shops lining the shore.

'You haven't been here before?'

'Nope. My father's family was from the mountains to the north of Delphi and we went there for visits in the summer when I was a kid. Lakonia is the back of beyond for me.' Mavros caught sight of a small pine-covered island joined to the coast by a causeway. 'According to your guidebook, that's where Helen and Paris passed their first night together on their flight to Troy.'

'There's no escaping that woman around here,' Grace said. 'I'm following signs to Areopolis, yeah?'

'Yeah,' Mavros repeated.

Only a few kilometres beyond the port, the tourist installations – campsites and restaurants, rooms for rent and boarded-up souvenir shops – petered out. The countryside became more rugged. First there was a series of heavily wooded valleys, with medieval watchtowers and castles poking their crumbling ramparts through the dense foliage. Then the road started to climb and the trees thinned, finally disappearing altogether as they moved higher up the flanks of a grim, grey mountain. The sun had passed its zenith and the sky was covered in a layer of lowering cloud that made the atmosphere even more leaden. Mavros thought of the vendettas that had been fought out on this unforgiving land, then shivered – what the hell was he doing on the trail of a multiple murderer? If Iraklis was as good as his reputation suggested, perhaps he had turned the tables already and was following him and Grace. Somebody had certainly been interested enough in them back in the big city.

'God, this is a fearful place,' Grace said, glancing around. 'Are those vultures?'

Mavros followed the direction of her gaze and picked out a pair of birds circling high above the slopes. 'I doubt it. There aren't many in Greece. Not the avian kind, at least.'

She laughed. 'Politicians? Businessmen? Why do I get the impression you don't like your fellow citizens very much?'

'I don't like *some* of my fellow Greeks very much, it's true. Maybe it's because I'm only half Greek. I can be more objective.'

'Have your cake and eat it, you mean,' Grace said, moving the wheel to avoid a rabbit that darted across the asphalt.

'Do I?' he asked.

'I think so. You can claim all the virtues of this country – the history, the culture, the *joie de vivre* – and at the same time dismiss its failings.'

The observation struck Mavros as painfully accurate, so he let it pass unanswered. More and more, he was finding Grace Helmer to be an alluring woman – sharp, funnier than most and, like himself, driven – but he had to be careful. Getting too close to clients was never a good idea.

They came round the side of Mount Kouskouni and the road began to drop towards

241

Areopolis, the chief town of the inner or Deep Mani. The western coast of the peninsula stretched away to the south, the lower slopes green with the winter's vegetation but the summits as forbidding as the higher peaks near Sparta. Grace was right: this was a fearful place, spectacular and crushing at the same time. Somewhere down the coast was the old poet Laskaris's tower. Would he be willing or able to cast any light on the mysterious Iason Kolettis? And what had Randos meant about Mavros's brother? Could Andonis have been tied up in the activities of the Iraklis group? The thought made his stomach clench.

'Areopolis, two kilometres,' Grace announced. 'We'll change places there.' She gave him a mocking smile. 'I reckon the map-reading's about to get trickier so I'll take over.'

'You do that,' Mavros said, looking at the guidebook. 'Apparently the town used to be called Tzimova, but they changed the name after the War of Independence because of the region's fighting prowess.'

'Changed the name,' Grace repeated.

'Ares, god of war?' Mavros said. 'This is War Town.'

'Oh, great,' she murmured, as they approached the grey stone walls of the first buildings.

Oh, great, indeed, Mavros thought, looking around at the barren fields and crags. Being a warrior in this hard country must have been hell, no matter which enemy you had the misfortune to be fighting.

By six a.m. the Fat Man had managed to load his mother and her myriad possessions into the ancient Lada Samara he'd borrowed from a friend. Despite the early hour, the streets of Athens were already busy, the inhabitants keen to get to work as early as possible to finish their main employment and go on to their supplementary jobs. The Christmas exodus wasn't due to start for another few days, so by the time they got to the motorway the traffic was bearable. Yiorgos felt the tension in his limbs slacken. He didn't drive often and every time he got behind the wheel he found that his fellow Greeks had learned new ways to dice with death on the roads.

'Yiorgo?' his mother said from the back – she refused to sit in the front of the car on the grounds that her son didn't drive with sufficient care. 'You are not to go above ninety kilometres, do you hear me?'

The Fat Man looked in the mirror, most of the view filled by wicker baskets and plastic bags containing the offerings his mother was taking to the family, then raised his eyes to the low roof. 'You think this wreck can do ninety, Mother?'

'Of course it can,' she replied sharply. 'I have been watching the speedometer and it has already touched ninety several times.' She snorted. 'I thought you called yourself a good Communist. This is a Soviet wreck, is it not?'

Yiorgos bit his tongue and drove on past the laid-up ships in the Bay of Elefsis. His mother had distracted him for a few moments, but the thought that had kept him awake most of the

243

night came back with a vengeance as soon as she stopped talking. The thought, the fear. Why did it have to be him? The comrades must have lost their collective mind. He had no field training. All he knew about that, he had learned on the streets during the dark years of repression. Why had they given him this job? They were no doubt testing his loyalty – they had probably heard about the card games he ran. But why that subject?

He pressed his fleshy lips together to stop himself shouting from frustration. It was bad enough going back to Anavryti with the old woman, bad enough going back to Lakonia with its *kafeneia* full of crazy fascists and monarchists who had been in the bastard Security Battalions and were proud of it. But being ordered to carry out surveillance on an old comrade was worse than all of that. Whichever way he looked at it, the conclusion was the same. He was about to become the worst of all creatures, a traitor – either to the Party, if he failed to carry out the orders to the best of his ability, or to a man he had always admired.

Looking ahead, the Fat Man made out the jagged pyramids of the Peloponnese's mountains. Returning to the region of his birth had never filled his mouth with such a bitter taste.

10

'Are you sure this is right?' Mavros demanded, pulling up at the start of a narrow unpaved track. The branches of untended olive trees were hanging down on both sides, almost obscuring the way.

'I reckon,' Grace replied, squinting at the map. 'This thing was supposedly produced with the co-operation of the Hellenic Army Geographical Service, but it doesn't seem to show all the roads. I'm guessing Ayia Kyriaki is this way.'

'We must have missed a turn-off earlier on.' Mavros looked in the Fiat's rear-view mirror. A huddle of stone houses was grouped around a junction, a dilapidated tower standing above a tiny chapel. 'I could go and ask in that village back there, but I'd rather not attract attention.'

Grace was looking ahead. 'The sea's that way,' she said. 'Isn't the poet's tower meant to have a view over a headland?'

Mavros had called his mother half an hour earlier and asked her if she knew anything that could help him locate the place. He hadn't been surprised when she'd started to give him an exegesis of one of Kostas Laskaris's poems that described his home in symbolic terms. The gist was that the building he had spent years renovating was above a promontory called Tigani. 'Let's hope the road doesn't get any

245

rougher,' he said. 'This heap rides pretty close to the ground.'

'Want me to drive?' Grace said, with an ironic smile.

Mavros engaged first gear and moved off. 'I can manage, thanks.' He swung round a blind corner. 'Shit!' Slamming on the brakes, he managed to stop a few centimetres in front of a somnolent black cow that was standing in the middle of the track. Before he knew it, Grace was out of the car. He watched as she manoeuvred herself down its flank then gave it a slap. The animal performed a surprisingly dextrous *volte-face* and trundled off down the lane.

Grace beckoned him forward. When the cow turned into a field, she got back into the car.

'Where did you learn to handle livestock?' Mavros asked, as he started to move again.

'I have many talents you don't know about.' Grace laughed softly. 'In Africa, if you must know. Cows have a tendency to colonise the roads there.'

'Makes a change from my Scottish ancestors.'

'Don't tell me, Alex,' she said, with a groan. 'You have a hang-up about colonialism.'

'Why not? Powerful states take over weak ones, make use of whatever assets they have – minerals, crops, manpower – and then bugger off, leaving them in the lurch.'

'Jesus, that is so misguided,' Grace said, her eyes wide. 'Didn't the British build roads, set up schools and welfare systems, provide jobs all around the world?'

Mavros saw a gate across the track. Beyond it the

grey-blue surface of the sea stretched away to the southern extent of Messenia across the bay. 'Yes, they did,' he conceded, seeing that he'd touched a nerve. 'I suppose what your organisation does is put something back into those countries.'

'Yeah, it is,' she said. 'And we weren't even the former colonial power in most of the places I've worked.' She looked to the right. 'There are some buildings over there. Do you think this is it?'

Mavros cut the engine after pulling into the side where the track widened. 'Could be.' He made out the upper part of a tall tower, the silver-brown stone and the shutters on the small windows in good condition. He got out and shivered. 'Christ, the temperature's taken another dive.' He reached over to the back seat for his jacket.

Grace joined him on the track, seemingly unaffected by the chill air. The fleece she was wearing was obviously a high-quality one. 'Some house,' she said, gazing up at the imposing building. The tower grew like an outsize factory chimney out of a solid two-storey block with a red-tiled roof. 'I hope we can talk our way in.'

Mavros was wondering how to approach Laskaris. The old poet had been friendly enough at his mother's lunch, but he was clearly unwell, buckling under the weight of a long life. How prepared would he be to open up old wounds in front of an American? For most long-standing Party members that would be almost as bad as selling Lenin's tomb to the Disney Corporation.

'Are we going?' Grace asked, with a questioning look.

He started walking from the car, taking in the path that led away from the gate. In the distance he could see a broad extension of land like a causeway. It led to a raised acropolis, the summit as flat as the surface of the water beyond. The desolation of the place made him flinch even more than the cold. 'Look, Grace, Laskaris isn't like Randos. He's older and prouder. It might be better if I talk to him on my own.'

She glanced at him. 'No chance, Alex. That's not the deal. I'm in on everything or I'm not paying.' She opened her hand. 'I've also got the car keys. If you go up there on your own, you'll have a long walk back to civilisation.'

'You've got all the moves, haven't you?' Mavros said, looking up to the heavy clouds. They were getting lower by the minute, rolling down the pyramid-shaped hills to the east like an invading army. There was a metallic smell in the air that presaged rain.

'Yeah, I have,' she said. 'So are we going?'

Mavros set off up the sloping path to the tower without replying. If he was lucky, Laskaris wouldn't be able to speak much English – all the conversation at his mother's had been in Greek. But he didn't feel lucky. Rather, he had a sourness in his belly, a feeling of apprehension at what the composer Randos had said about Andonis. Did the old poet really know something about his brother? More than once Mavros had found himself at the point where he thought he'd finally cracked the case that had remained unsolved since he'd started out as an investigator, but his hopes had always been dashed.

248

'Cheer up,' Grace said, overtaking him. 'It may never happen.'

'That's what I'm afraid of,' he said, in a low voice.

They reached the heavy wooden door. It was studded with the heads of large nails and in the centre was a spy-hole like the ones on the doors of prison cells. Beneath it was a knocker in the shape of a human hand. Grace lifted it and let it fall three times.

For a time there was no sound apart from the chirping of the birds in the lentisk bushes that ringed the building. Mavros stepped back and glanced around. The tower was on its own on the spine of a low ridge, a few stone outhouses to the rear. Further inland there was a small group of houses, all of one storey. The undulating ground between them and the poet's home was rocky and uncultivated while the land beyond had been split up into small fields, only a few showing signs of recent cultivation.

'Nobody at home?' Grace said, moving her hand to the knocker again.

Then they heard the sound of bolts being drawn and keys being turned. Mavros went back to the door, nudging Grace gently aside. He wanted the old man to be confronted by someone he knew. The heavy panel swung aside and there he was, blinking in the dull light like a mole whose subterranean chamber had suddenly been revealed.

'Is it you, Alex Mavros?' Laskaris said, in Greek. 'Is it you?' His eyes were wide with surprise.

'It's me,' Mavros replied, extending a hand. He

was concerned that the poet might need physical support – he looked unsteady. 'Are you all right, Kyrie Kosta?'

Laskaris gave a crooked smile. 'No titles, Alex. I told you. First names only.' He gave Grace an appraising look. 'And what is your friend's first name?'

'This is–' Mavros broke off. 'How is your English, Kosta?'

'Ah, I was thinking you were foreign,' Laskaris replied, in smooth but accented English. 'Are you American, miss?' His expression was unreadable.

Grace nodded. 'How did you guess?'

The poet raised his shoulders. 'Know your enemy,' he said. 'The wholesome smile, the healthy body, the sensible clothes.' He smiled again, this time more openly. 'But we are no longer enemies, are we? The war is over and you are the victors.' He extended a shaky hand. 'Kostas Laskaris.'

'Grace Helmer,' she said, taking the hand in a gentle grip.

'Come in, both of you,' Laskaris said, looking beyond them. 'You brought no other unexpected visitors?'

Mavros shook his head and followed Grace into the long hall that took up the ground floor. 'I'm sorry. I would have telephoned, but my mother told me you prefer to live without one.'

The poet ushered them towards the fireplace at the far end of the room. Although there was a log fire burning in the grate, the house felt cold. Mavros noticed papers spread across the table on the right. He wondered how the old man could work in such a temperature.

'I hate telephones and computers, fax machines and televisions,' Laskaris said. 'All they do is distract people from the important things.'

'And what are they?' Grace asked, her eyes running around the undecorated walls.

'The injustices of life,' the old man said, indicating a sofa spread with a traditional rag cover. 'The shallowness of contemporary culture. The need to change.'

'The revolution, in other words,' Grace said. 'I thought you said you'd lost that war.'

'We can still hope that people will see reason,' Laskaris said, his face tightening. He sat down heavily in a leather armchair.

Mavros leaned forward. 'Are you all right?'

The poet raised a hand. 'It will pass. I ... I have taken my pills.'

Grace got up, went to the kitchen area and returned with a glass of water she'd poured from an earthenware jug.

Laskaris drank gratefully. 'Thank you, thank you,' he said, dabbing his lips with a handkerchief. Then he looked at each of them. 'What is it that brings you here, so far from the real world? I hope your mother is well, Alex. I know it is only a few days since I saw her, but at our age...' His words trailed away.

'She's well,' Mavros confirmed.

'She didn't send you down here on some errand? Something about the edition she wants to do of my work?' The poet smiled. 'Her business has been very successful. Even Spyros would have been impressed.'

Mavros returned the smile. His father had never approved of his mother working. Like many male Greek Communists, he had never come to terms with the idea of wives working despite his lifelong commitment to social change.

'So ... so what is the reason for your trip to the Deep Mani?' Laskaris's eyes shone out from the pallid contours of his face. He glanced at Grace. 'Helmer. The name means something to me.'

'My father Trent was in the Athens embassy.' Grace's voice was level. 'He was murdered by the Iraklis group in 1976.'

The old man was silent for a while. Then he said, 'Of course. I remember that ... that tragedy.' He met her gaze. 'Those people were traitors to the cause, you know. The Party had disowned them.'

Grace said nothing but her face visibly hardened.

Mavros intervened before she did something to antagonise Laskaris. 'Iason Kolettis,' he said, resorting to shock tactics. 'We know he was behind Iraklis. We want to trace him.'

The poet's expression didn't change. 'So does the anti-terrorist squad. I shouldn't tell you this, but the Party would like to catch the killer too. Some of the comrades still feel guilty that the group was formed by people whose roots were in the struggle.' He shrugged. 'It's foolish, like so much the comrades do now. I am not in contact with them any more.'

'You think Iason Kolettis is responsible for the killings of the businessmen?' Mavros asked, encouraged by the old man's frankness. Perhaps

252

Laskaris trusted him because of his father, or perhaps Grace's presence had loosened his tongue. That had worked with Randos.

'He may be,' Laskaris replied. 'Be sure, there will be a statement claiming responsibility. There may have been one for the first murder. It wouldn't surprise me if the government kept quiet about it. It must be in a state of panic.'

Grace stood up and approached the armchair. 'Do you have any idea how we can find him?' she asked, her voice tense.

Mavros raised a hand and waited till she had sat down again. 'I think we should tell our host what we heard from Randos before we ask him for help.' He ran through what the composer had said about Iason Kolettis and the reference to him in the lyric that the poet had written.

Laskaris studied him as he spoke. 'What are you saying, Alex?' he asked, when he had finished. 'You think that "The Voyage of the *Argo*" is some kind of code? I wrote many song verses using ancient myth. I had to because otherwise the fools who governed the country would have sent me back to prison or had me killed in a so-called accident. But that doesn't mean I knew Iason Kolettis's real identity.' He let out a long sigh. 'No one did. That was his skill, his greatest achievement. He was better than any actor. He changed appearance, he disappeared every few months and returned with another identity.'

'But you met him, didn't you?' Grace said. 'You must know something about his background.'

The poet looked at her as if she were a child. 'I

253

sympathise with your pain. God knows, I have lost enough dear ones myself. But this is a hopeless thing you are doing. The Party was an underground organisation for decades. We were experts in protecting ourselves. People knew only the bare minimum about each other, even people who were much less cunning than Kolettis. That was the case even for political officials like me.' He blanched, taking several deep breaths before speaking again. 'For field operatives like him, the precautions were even more elaborate.' He gulped down the last of the water from his glass and licked his lips. 'Besides, Iraklis was a proscribed organisation. We lost contact with the madman as soon as he was expelled from the Party.' He sank lower into his chair. 'I'm sorry, I cannot help you.'

Mavros looked at Grace. He wasn't sure what she was thinking, but he had the distinct feeling that the old poet knew more than he was saying. The question was, how could they break through the walls he had built around himself?

Iraklis drove the hire car he'd picked up in Athens across the Isthmus and into the Peloponnese. The traffic wasn't heavy, the truck drivers eating their midday meals and most Christmas revellers not yet on the roads. He gunned the big Citroën's engine and headed down the motorway towards Tripolis in the fast lane.

Yesterday he had spoken to his controller and discovered that people had been asking questions about him in his old persona of Iason Kolettis. There was time before the confrontation that was planned, time that he could use to clear up some unresolved issues, personal as well as professional – though, since his return to Greece, the two had been getting harder and harder to separate.

For years he had blocked out the end of the Iraklis group, spending the time in New York City when he wasn't working on educating himself. The apartment in Queens was filled with books on politics and history. Often he put on his headphones when the noises of the throbbing city kept him awake, listening to the English phrases and repeating them till his accent was good. But since he'd been back in Greece, the need to see the surviving member of the group, the only survivor of his former comrades who had been captured, had been growing. There were things he had to say, things he had to hear. What action he then took would depend on the man who had been known as Odhysseas. Babis Dhimitrakos had been reliable until the enemy had taken him, but he hadn't known much about Iason Kolettis – the assassin had kept everything to himself, even within the small terrorist cell. Apart from that one night – the night he had killed the American – when he'd lost control after the operation and drunk himself into a stupor. Had he talked? Had he blurted out something that might still give him away in the hours after he had killed the husband of the only woman he had ever loved? The splinter of doubt had turned into a sharpened spike, like those the Turks had used to impale their prisoners. Babis Dhimitrakos. He had to make sure of his old brother-in-arms.

By mid-afternoon he was past Sparta and on

the road to Yithion. It was then that Iraklis began to feel anxious about another old comrade. He hadn't been in the western Mani for decades – not since he had visited Kostas Laskaris during the dictatorship. The poet. Should he be fearful of him as well? He had followed his work in the New York Greek community's newspapers: the international awards and nominations, popular songs, the reputation he had acquired for mordant criticism of the contemporary Left. No, Kostas was old now, near death. He could do nothing, he would do nothing to harm Iraklis. But it would be a good idea to see him again – he owed the former resistance fighter much.

South-west of Yithion, the clouds tumbling down the stone flanks of the peaks, he had felt the weight of his early years crush him more than it had since he was a teenager. When he returned during the Colonels' regime, he'd been on fire with the struggle and hadn't given a thought to the bitter pain he had suffered as a child on the Mani's barren soil. But now it came back to him, leaped on him like an assailant in an ambush to squeeze the breath from his lungs. He pulled in to the side of the road, provoking a horn blast from the van that had suddenly appeared behind him. It swerved past, the youthful driver mouthing obscenities.

Ach, this place, he said to himself. Great dams of stone shutting it off from the rest of the world, only the sea offering any respite, and that a chill one without profit except for the most dedicated fisherman; the men intemperate and fierce. Why had he come back?

Iraklis closed his eyes and remembered the tall figure of his mother, her face shrouded by the hood of a tattered coat, the first time he had met her. Before that he had never even seen a photograph of her. His grandmother had beckoned him into the low stone house he shared with her outside Kitta when he came back from locking up the goats for the night. The movements of her hand were so quick that he thought she had been taken by a fit. And then he saw there was another woman behind her.

'Here he is,' his grandmother had said. 'Only six years old, but he looks older. Like a young fighter already.' When she pronounced the word *palikari*, the sadness in her voice seemed infinite, as if his fate, a terrible one, had already been written.

'Come, Michali,' the woman behind said. 'We have things to discuss.' Her tone was businesslike, grown-up to grown-up, like the men he'd heard bargaining in the *kafeneion*. Although he didn't know her, he understood she was his mother. The deep scar on her cheek didn't frighten him. It made her look as noble as a warrior woman in the old stories.

'Mama,' he began, opening his arms to embrace her and feeling her bony body beneath them. She didn't make any movement to circle her own arms around him.

'My son,' she said simply, her voice still level, 'sit down and listen to me. There isn't much time.' She motioned to her mother to close the door.

'Where have you been, Mama?' the boy asked, taking in the woman's ragged blouse and skirt,

257

and the dark-ringed eyes in her drawn face. He blinked at the scar on her cheek and looked away, tears now filling his eyes.

'I have been on an island,' she replied. 'Locked up like a dog. I have been freed, but soon they will want to catch me again.' She frowned at him. 'So listen, Michali, you are the man of the house now that my father is dead.'

He blinked back tears for the old man who had been the only one to smile at him and who had died in the winter, worn out by a lifetime of toil.

'You must look after your grandmother,' she continued. 'And you must stay at school as long as you can.' She looked away. 'Even though what they teach you is nothing more than lies, stinking nationalist and monarchist poison.' She stared back at him and he felt the power of her eyes. 'You must learn to read and write, you must study. And then...' she gave a smile that lit her face with an unexpected expression of joy, '...and then you must join the struggle.'

'Yes, Mama,' he replied avidly. 'But what is the struggle?'

'The people's struggle, my son,' she said, her expression stern again. 'The struggle for a better world.'

The boy had sat there, not understanding the meaning of her words but convinced by their force. He had remembered them every day and had joined the Party's underground youth organisation as soon as he could.

Throughout the exchange his grandmother had stood motionless, but her expression was disapproving. When her daughter rose to leave,

258

she shook her head. 'What good will he do?' she asked, her voice cracking. 'He's only one and they are many.'

His mother had smiled once more. 'He will do much good, I am sure of that.' She pulled the hood back over her head and moved to the door, limping heavily.

'Don't go, Mama,' he cried, clutching at her. 'When are you coming back?'

'I must carry on the fight.' She squared her shoulders. 'I will return when I can, Michali.' She stepped away from him.

'And my father?' he asked. 'Where is my father? When will he come?'

She looked at him but didn't speak.

The fifty-seven-year-old Iraklis sat up in the driver's seat and looked out over the sides of the Pendadhaktilos, grey stone running down the great ridge beyond Itylo into a layer of fresh green growth. His homeland looked fertile, and for a few moments he was fooled into believing that it wasn't the quarry of violence and death it had been throughout history.

But how could he be fooled? He was more in tune with the blood-drenched landscape of the Peloponnese than anyone alive. He was a descendant of the region's heroic line, a warrior defending his family name to the last.

Kostas Laskaris gave Mavros and Grace a meal – coarse bread, *feta*, a salad of tomatoes, olives, onions and capers, with a heavy local wine – after he had cleared his papers from the heavy antique table. He willingly answered their questions

259

about the region and his work, but refused to talk any more about Iason Kolettis. When a local woman, dressed from head to toe in black, came into the house and collected their plates, the poet went with her to the kitchen area. Mavros took the opportunity to speak to his client.

'This isn't getting us very far, Grace,' he said, his voice low. 'You have to let me speak to him on my own.' He opened his eyes wide at her. 'It's the only way.'

The American pursed her lips. 'Okay. But you're going to tell me everything he says.'

He agreed even though he didn't intend to divulge anything Laskaris said about Andonis if he succeeded in getting the old man to explain the composer Randos's reference to his brother – that was family business.

'I usually take a walk outside at this time,' the poet said, when he returned to the table. 'You are welcome to join me.' He was respecting the traditions of hospitality even though it was clear he would have preferred them to leave.

Mavros stood up. 'I'll come with you.' He glanced at his client. 'Grace will help with the dishes.' He smiled, as she shot him a ferocious look.

'There is no need,' Laskaris said to her emolliently. 'Take your ease in front of the fire, my dear. The weather is fit only for dogs, old Communists and the sons of old Communists.'

It wasn't raining yet but the clouds had come down further, obscuring all but the lowest slopes of the hills. Mavros shivered in his thin leather jacket.

'You will need more than that if you stay in the Mani at this time of year, Alex,' Laskaris said, in Greek. He smiled, but there was an undercurrent of tension in his voice. 'Are you planning to stay?'

Mavros was unsure how to initiate the conversation about his brother.

'I would invite you both to sleep in the tower,' the old man said, glancing round at his home, 'but it isn't very comfortable for people used to life in the city.'

'It's very fine,' Mavros said, taking in the stone walls then turning towards the headland and the sea that lapped around it. 'I can see why you wanted to live here. Don't worry, we aren't staying. There is someone else we have to see.' He considered asking Laskaris about the Iraklis band member Babis Dhimitrakos, whose name the composer Randos had given them, but decided against it – if the old man didn't want to talk about the terrorists' leader, why would he say anything about a lesser member of the group?

'You will not find the man who was Kolettis,' the poet said, moving forward awkwardly and looking down over Tigani. Then he took a deep breath. 'Nor will you find your brother here.'

Mavros felt steel fingers grip his heart, taken aback that the old man was volunteering to talk about Andonis. Even though he had been preparing himself to broach the subject, he now found that he could hardly speak. 'Andonis?' he gasped. 'What do you know about Andonis?'

Kostas Laskaris took his arm and squeezed it weakly. 'You see the promontory? The sharp rocks, the old walls?' He turned to look at

Mavros. 'That is believed by many experts to be Castle Maïna, the most impregnable fortress in the area in the Middle Ages.' He gazed across the causeway with its pattern of salt pans and sharp boulders. 'Your brother went down there with Iason Kolettis.'

The breath stopped in Mavros's windpipe and he had to force himself to breathe, the raucous cry of a gull over the headland bringing him back to himself. 'What?' he stammered. 'Andonis was here? Andonis met Kolettis?'

'He did.' Then the poet let Mavros's arm go. 'But I don't know what they discussed or what resulted from their conversation.'

'When was this?' Mavros asked, trying to slow down the thoughts that were cascading through his mind.

'November 1972, if my memory is correct,' Laskaris said, poking the bush in front of them with his stick. 'Yes, I think that is right.'

'The month before Andonis disappeared,' Mavros said, staring at the old man. 'Why didn't you tell us? Why didn't you tell my mother years ago?'

Laskaris's eyes were lowered. 'What would have been the point? As I said, I don't know what they discussed. I only facilitated the meeting, gave them somewhere safe to stay for a night.'

'But ... but what could Andonis have been doing with Kolettis?' Mavros asked, directing the question at himself as much as at the old man. 'None of his colleagues ever said anything about a contact with the Iraklis group.'

'They wouldn't have known,' Laskaris said

262

gently. 'Andonis might have been young but he knew how to take precautions. He grew up with your father as an example.'

Mavros faced him. 'You knew what Iason Kolettis was like, though. You knew that he was capable of anything. Why did you let Andonis have contact with him?' He stepped closer, then restrained himself. The poet was ailing, his strength gone. It wasn't right to berate him, even though he couldn't understand why Laskaris had suddenly admitted this long-held secret. Did he want some kind of absolution?

'I'm sorry, my boy,' the old man said, his rheumy eyes lowered.

Mavros touched his shoulder, feeling the bone through the jacket. 'Won't you tell me what you know about the assassin?' he said softly. 'The American woman Grace is suffering because of what he did to her father.'

'I cannot, Alex,' Laskaris replied. 'It's a question of honour.'

'What honour?' Mavros said, fighting to keep his tone even. 'There's nothing left for you to protect now. The Party's finished, the struggle is lost, your life's work has failed.'

The poet looked at him, his face racked by a terrible sadness. 'Maybe that's all true,' he said. 'But every man still has the right to act as honour requires. Your father and your brother understood that.'

Mavros caught his eye, then nodded slowly before walking back to the tower.

Grace was standing in the doorway, her jacket on. 'Get anywhere?' she asked, peering at him through the gloom. 'What's the matter?'

'Nothing,' Mavros mumbled, walking past. 'Nothing I can do anything about.'

Grace caught up with him. 'What is it, Alex?' She glanced over her shoulder and saw Kostas Laskaris leaning on his stick, his eyes on them.

Mavros stuck out his hand for the car keys. He got into the Fiat and started the engine.

Grace turned round and raised her arm in a wave. The old man was framed by the heavy walls of his home, the war tower rising up behind him. He returned the gesture, then walked back to the building, his head bowed.

'Want to tell me what you talked about?' she asked, when she got in.

'Family matters,' Mavros replied, reversing the car and turning with excessive pressure on the accelerator.

'Is that right?' Grace said. 'Very appropriate for the Mani.' She picked up her guidebook. 'It says in here that vendettas–'

'Never mind what it says in there,' Mavros interrupted. 'Just concentrate on finding the road to Kitta.'

'All right, all right.' Grace glanced at the map and let it drop to her lap. 'Back the way you came and keep going until we hit the main road. Kitta's on the other side. We saw the towers on the way here, remember?'

Mavros headed up the track, this time without interference from the cow. After weaving his way down a couple of narrow, stone-walled roads, he reached the highway that led from Areopolis to the Mani's southernmost settlements. The extended village of Kitta was spread out across the hillside beyond, the upper parts of its towers lost in the mist.

'How are we going to find this Babis Dhimitrakos?' Grace asked.

Mavros extended his chin in a gesture of uncertainty. 'Don't know. He may not even call himself that any more. But Kitta is as good a place to start as any. I checked in the phone book in the guest-house back in Sparta. There are more people with that name than in any other village in the Mani. Including one whose first name is Haralambos – Babis, for short.'

Grace was looking at him sceptically. 'And you think he'll open up to a pair of strangers about the Iraklis group?'

Mavros took his eyes off the road for a second. 'Not if you tell him who you are. It might have been him driving the motorbike the night your father was murdered. You aren't going to be the person he most wants to meet.'

Grace watched as they passed the first stone buildings and wound up the narrow road to the village square. It was deserted, the shops closed and the run-down *kafeneion* empty. 'Welcome to Deadsville, Lakonia,' she murmured.

'If you get a welcome you'll be doing well,' Mavros said. An old woman had pulled her head back round a corner the moment his eye landed on her. He took out his notebook and looked at the list of names and telephone numbers he'd copied down, then checked his mobile phone. He'd forgotten to charge it and the battery was almost gone. There was a public phone on the other side of the square.

As he got out of the Fiat, the rain started to come down at last. He was cold, dispirited and about to get soaked. He could see why, for centuries, the Mani's inhabitants had been getting out as soon as they could.

Kostas Laskaris waited until the cleaning woman had finished in the kitchen area of the tower, then spread out his papers across the table again. He wanted to work, he needed to work, to shut out the agonised face of Alex Mavros. The American woman's expression had been troubling enough – years of pain and incomprehension etched into what were still fine features. But she was different: she was foreign, the daughter of an enemy. And there was something about her, a burning will that tempered the sympathy he felt for a child who had lost her father. From Alex he had no hiding-place – son of one of the Party's most heroic members, a man who had been his own friend for decades; and brother of the young resistance leader who could have achieved great things against the dictators. If only he had never encountered the man who called himself Iason Kolettis. Laskaris had always suspected that Andonis Mavros's still unexplained disappearance was in some way connected with the Iraklis group. Shortly after their meeting down on Tigani, shortly after Andonis went into the dark, Iraklis had started to murder policemen and Junta sympathisers.

The poet tried to write, to move his work on to the blood-soaked final year of the German occupation, when the resistance had been driven to execute collaborators and Security Battalion-ists. The story was oppressive and the mythical parallel of Iraklis cleansing the Augean stables hard to make fresh. But that wasn't what was holding him back. No, it was the guilt he felt, the remorse that was gnawing at him. He should have told Alex Mavros and the woman more about the man who called himself Iason Kolettis. It wasn't as if he had anything to fear. The pain in his gut was worsening by the day, the pills he took having little effect. Even if the assassin had returned to Greece and was behind the latest killings, he might not find out if Laskaris put Alex Mavros on his trail, and even if he did, it would be a mercy. It was time that the cycle of death ended. But no. The chains of the past, the chains that tied him to his comrades, the woman, and the one he had loved more than any other were still secure. Even though what he'd said to Alex about honour was a lie: there could be no honour among murderers, he had finally come to understand that.

The old man slammed his hand down on the table and felt the shock course through his body. Coward, he mouthed. Traitor. You owed it to the Party to inform on the proscribed group. You still owe that, even though you despise the present leadership. He blinked and felt tears course down his cheeks. Iraklis was a precious link with the past. He hadn't seen him since that day in 1972 with Andonis Mavros, but he couldn't betray him. He couldn't...

There was a pounding on the door and, before he could get up, the handle turned and it was pushed open. He had forgotten to lock it after the cleaner had left.

'Kyrie Kosta?' His driver Savvas looked shocked, his eyes staring. 'I just heard on the radio. The composer Randos ... Randos is dead. They found him on the ground beneath his apartment. It seems ... it seems he fell.'

Laskaris slumped forward, his mind in turmoil and a foul taste in the back of his throat. Dhimitris Randos dead? An accident? He had visited the flat and seen how tightly closed the shutters were kept. And his old comrade would never have committed suicide, that was impossible – the life force that inspired his music was too great. But who would have killed him? The authorities had hunted him in the past, but not since the end of the dictatorship in the seventies.

And then a terrible thought struck the poet. Could Iraklis have acted against the old Communist? Randos had sent Mavros and the woman down to the Mani. Was it possible that the assassin had discovered that and seen it as a betrayal? If that was the case, what was in store for him, the writer of the lyrics to the composer's best-known songs?

Kostas Laskaris felt the shadows gathering around what remained of his life, and he was glad.

11

The air-conditioning fans gave off a low hum in the meeting room beneath the American embassy. There were three people sitting at the oval table, none showing any sign of the Christmas spirit.

Peter Jaeger, his striped tie knotted tight at the neck of his white shirt, looked across the table at his subordinate. 'So let's be clear about this, Ms Forster,' he said, his voice clipped. 'Your team lost Mavros and Grace Helmer in Athens yesterday afternoon. And you haven't managed to locate them since.'

There were points of red on the woman's cheeks. 'That's correct, sir.' Her southern accent was hard to pick up as she was swallowing her words.

'Fortunately, we came to your rescue, Jane,' the police commander Nikos Kriaras said, with a brief smile. He tried to control the shivering that had seized him after Jaeger turned down the heating on their arrival. 'We have confirmed a sighting of them at the Peloponnese bus station in the evening. They got on the bus to Patra.'

'But you don't have any idea where they are now,' Jaeger said, looking at the open file. His tone was neutral, but he managed to imply that, despite his own operatives' failure, the Greek authorities were out of their depth.

'We are checking in Patra and in Corinth,' Kriaras said, frowning at the American. 'They may have got off the bus at the Isthmus. The driver doesn't remember them being on board after the stop there.'

Jaeger stood up and strode over to the large map of Greece on the wall behind him. 'They could be anywhere, for Christ's sake.' He turned and glared at the woman until she raised her eyes to his. 'What are you doing to find them, Ms Forster? I hope you haven't done anything as foolish as to call his cellphone.'

'No, sir,' Jane Forster replied hurriedly. She glanced down at her yellow pad. 'Our contacts in all the main towns are on the look-out, especially those in the Peloponnese. And–' She broke off and looked at Jaeger, making a sideways movement of her head towards the Greek.

'We're all friends here, aren't we?' her superior said, smiling coldly at Kriaras.

Jane Forster turned to Kriaras, her bunched auburn hair flicking like a horse's tail, and took in a smile that was meant to be encouraging but made her feel like a little girl. 'And we're expecting a report from our own field operative any minute now.'

The police commander stiffened, remembering the man with the vacant stare who had been sitting across the table from him at their last meeting. 'You think we can rely on that individual, do you?' he said, staring at Jaeger. 'Lance Milroy should not be involved in this operation. He is compromised by his past.'

Jaeger smoothed a hand over his already flattened blond hair. 'I decide on the personnel, Niko,' he said. 'If you have any complaints, take

270

them to your minister.'

'I already have,' Kriaras said dispiritedly. 'He has been told by his superiors that you are to have full authority and that's all that matters to him.'

Jaeger smiled. 'He's worried that he will lose his job if the terrorist isn't caught.'

'We will all lose our jobs,' Kriaras countered. 'Or worse.'

Jane Forster's head was moving like that of a spectator at a tennis match as she followed the exchange.

'Keep calm, Niko,' Jaeger said, sitting down at the table. 'I know what I'm doing. Besides, Lance Milroy's past is relevant here. He knew Trent Helmer and he was involved in the operation that led to the dissolution of the Iraklis group.'

Kriaras nodded. 'It was unfortunate that the safe-house he chose turned out to be particularly unsafe.'

'You can't blame Milroy for the fact that Greek security personnel accepted bribes and allowed the prisoner to escape.' Jaeger glanced at Jane Forster, whose eyes were wide. 'Not all of what you're hearing is in the files,' he said sharply. 'Make sure you keep it to yourself.' He gave her a look that made her blink, then turned back to Kriaras. 'I understand that your people found several witnesses who have described the beggar outside the Megaro Mousikis.'

The policeman nodded. 'We got him on closed-circuit television too, but the images are blurred. The beard obscured his features.'

'But it could be the assassin Iraklis,' Jaeger said.

271

Kriaras raised his shoulders. 'It could be anyone. The olivewood and the proclamation that appeared at the newspaper office suggest that it is.' His head dropped. 'This is a nightmare. We have to catch him before the text is leaked, despite the minister's heavy pressure on the editor it was addressed to. If that happens we'll have a full-scale panic on our hands. God knows who's the next target on the list.'

Jaeger closed his file. 'In my experience God is no help in this kind of operation. I would advise that your government comes clean and releases the terrorist statement.' He gave a dry laugh. 'But what do I know? I'm just a humble embassy official.'

The meeting broke up shortly after Kriaras asked that he be advised immediately if Mavros and Grace Helmer were located – his bitter expression suggesting he had little hope that the Americans would keep him in the loop.

Peter Jaeger strode to his office, Jane Forster almost running to keep up with him.

'You didn't mention our operative Tiresias, sir,' she said, her southern drawl extending the vowels and making the name almost incomprehensible.

'Ti-re-si-as,' her superior said, mocking her pronunciation. 'Did you think I was going to tell the Greeks about our most precious resource, Ms Forster? You've got a lot to learn.'

The auburn-haired woman bit her lip and headed for the communications room.

Mavros got back into the car, having dashed across the square in Kitta through drizzle that was getting colder and denser by the minute. 'Shit!' he gasped. 'Don't you want the heating on?'

Grace had moved into the driver's seat while he used the public phone, but the engine wasn't running. 'This is nothing,' she said. 'You won't believe how cold it gets back home at this time of year. Ice, snow, frozen car locks...'

'Yeah, yeah,' Mavros said, wringing water from his hair. 'Everything including the winters is bigger and better over there.'

Grace looked at him. 'I don't think this is the time or the place for a debate about American supremacy.' She gave him a frosty smile. 'Ideological, strategic or meteorological.'

'No, it isn't,' Mavros agreed. 'Sorry.' He wiped raindrops off the cover of his notebook.

'So, what did you find out about Babis Dhimitrakos?'

'His phone's been cut off.' He glanced at her. 'And he isn't here.'

'Is that it?'

Mavros nodded. 'Just about. Most people called Dhimitrakos wouldn't talk about him, even when I said I was trying to find him because he'd won a holiday to the Seychelles.'

'Very smart.' Her eyes narrowed. 'You said "just about" and "most people", Alex. Do I have to squeeze what you discovered out of you with my bare hands?' She grabbed his wrist and exerted pressure.

'Ow!' he yelled. 'Let go, will you? Christ, how often do you work out?'

'Often enough, apparently,' she replied, loosening her grip. 'Talk to your client like a good little

273

private eye, huh?'

Mavros looked out of the windshield. Through the thick sheen of rain he could just make out an old man in a hooded cape leading a bedraggled donkey across the paving stones. The beast was weighed down with a load of firewood that would need a lot of drying before it could be used. 'Okay,' he said. 'I spoke to one of the guy's cousins. She told me he's been very ill. He had a heart-attack a couple of months ago. He came back from hospital in Kalamata last week and the old fool – her words – insisted on going back to his house in a village up in the hills to the south. Apparently he's very independent, won't accept help from any of his relatives. He doesn't have a phone any more. The number in the directory is years out of date.'

'And you have the name of this village?' Grace said, reaching for the map.

'Of course. I'm a professional.'

'I'm waiting, Alex.'

'Yeah, well, anyway. The place is called Kainourgia Chora, that is "New Village". Apparently it's about fifteen kilometres to the south.'

Grace ran her finger down the map. 'Here it is. The road weaves all over the place to get to it.'

Mavros peered through the windscreen again. 'It's getting pretty late in the day. By the time we've got down there and talked to the guy, it'll be hard to find a place to stay. There aren't many hotels at the end of the peninsula.'

'What are you saying?' she asked suspiciously. 'You want to put it off till the morning? This

274

wouldn't be your way of adding an extra day to the job, would it? How professional is that?'

'Jesus, Grace,' he said, raising his hands in surrender. 'Give me a break. The roads in the mountains probably aren't up to much, especially not in this weather.'

She kept looking at him and then relented, her face creasing into a smile. 'All right. Let's call it a day. I could do with a decent room after last night's shared bliss.'

'What does your guide say? Areopolis seems to me to be the best bet.'

She turned on the ignition and switched on the interior light, smiling as Mavros immediately ratcheted up the temperature. 'Yeah, let's see. There are four places open all year, a couple of them restored tower houses. They sound interesting. Let's go.' She doused the light and turned the car round, then headed back down towards the main road.

'Pity the weather's so shitty,' Mavros said. 'Kitta looked like an interesting place.'

Grace glanced at him. 'Why did my mother do that painting of it? Do you think...' She left the question uncompleted.

'Do I think Iason Kolettis had a connection with the place?' Mavros looked ahead: another old man with a donkey was coming out of the gloom, like a ghost, with his head lowered. 'Who knows? It was hard enough getting the locals to talk about Dhimitrakos.'

'Maybe that's what Laskaris was keeping from us,' she said, indicating right to turn on to the Areopolis road. 'That the killer came from here.'

'There was nobody called Kolettis in the phone book, not that there would be if it was a false name. But you're right. Laskaris is holding things back. I suppose we could try again with him tomorrow.' Mavros didn't feel optimistic about getting the old poet to open up any further.

Grace made no comment, concentrating on the driving.

There was little traffic, but several of the vehicles they passed were lacking tail- or headlights, as if the notoriously well-armed locals had taken pleasure in shooting them out. To Mavros the region seemed strikingly alien. There was none of the rural charm of other areas – the walls around the fields were crumbling and there were few animals to be seen. The sparse olive trees were low and stunted, as if the wind had sucked the sap from them. Stray dogs with protruding ribs darted across the road in the headlights, their eyes flashing dementedly. Even the churches were sinister, none of the whitewashed walls and bright red tiles that were common elsewhere in the Peloponnese – the Mani's places of worship were shrunken like mummified corpses, with walls of grey and brown stone that had absorbed centuries of rain and dust, and roofs that were caving in. Fortunately it was under twenty kilometres to the main town. They were there not long after six o'clock.

'Keep your eyes open for those towers that have been turned into guest-houses,' Grace said, as they turned off the main road and entered a wide square with an imposing bronze statue.

'This is the Plateia Athanaton, the Square of the Immortals,' Mavros said, looking up from the guide. 'And that's Mavromichalis, one of the old warriors who defeated the Turks in the War of Independence.'

'Good for him,' Grace said, slowing down as they passed a *periptero*, the usual display of newspapers hanging from wires. 'Where to now?'

Mavros glanced at the kiosk and blinked. 'Stop!' he shouted, opening the car door before she complied. He ran across the sodden paving stones and stared up at the national daily that was moving to and fro in the wind.

Grace appeared by his side. 'What is it, Alex?'

Mavros pointed at the photograph beneath the banner headline. 'The composer Randos,' he said, feeling an icy stab in his gut. 'He's dead.'

The Fat Man had reached his ancestral village of Anavryti in the early afternoon, his mother having forced him to keep his speed down even on the fast sections of the road. He had hoped to be able to drop her off and make a start on the mission he'd been given, but Kyra Fedhra had refused to let him leave.

'But, Mother,' he complained, 'it's Party business.' Although Kyra Fedhra had mixed feelings about the Communists, not least because her committed husband had spent much of his life in prison, she understood that her son had certain responsibilities and normally allowed them to take precedence. Not this time.

'Rubbish,' she said, as she tore about the old building, opening shutters that had been sealed since the previous summer. 'And you'd better be back in time for the dinner I'm planning for the

277

family on Christmas Eve.'

Yiorgos Pandazopoulos raised his shoulders. 'I don't know–' he began.

'Well, I do,' Kyra Fedhra interrupted. 'Now, get those bags in from the car. When you've done that, go and buy bread before the bakery closes.' She gave him a humourless smile. 'Then you can help me clean the house.'

He had gone out into the freezing streets to unload the Lada, feeling the eyes of the passers-by on him. There were only a few who acknowledged him, his father's leftist past causing the majority of the villagers to despise the family. Anavryti had been a typical Peloponnesian monarchist strong-hold and even now there were many who hadn't forgotten the old days. Shivering in the mountain air, which was now clogged with mist, the Fat Man cursed his mother for bringing him down here. He managed to avoid the trip she made every summer by claiming pressure of business in the café – not that many tourists ventured through the filthy door – and in recent years she had preferred to stay in the big city for Christmas. What had possessed her to come down this winter? Maybe she thought it was the last chance she'd get to see the village where she and her husband had grown up.

At last Kyra Fedhra was satisfied with the house, the diesel stove that Yiorgos had finally managed to light pumping some heat out into the damp kitchen.

'You will be back as soon as you can, my boy?' his mother said, peering at him and handing him a blue plastic bag filled with provisions. Now he was about to leave, she was suddenly solicitous.

The Fat Man nodded as he accepted it. 'I'll telephone you when I'm on my way,' he said, realising his mistake when she gave him a sardonic look. The phone had been cut off years ago when they had been short of cash. 'I mean I'll telephone Aunt Malamo.'

Kyra Fedhra gave him a sharp smile. 'And don't imagine that you will escape her *kreatopita.*'

Yiorgos groaned. Despite his fondness for food of all kinds, his aunt's cooking had been the bane of his childhood; her meat pies contained material that few other housewives would use even in times of hardship, such as chopped udder.

He drove the Lada down the winding road towards the highway that led to the port of Yithion and the Mani beyond. It was only then that the full import of the news he had heard on the radio earlier in the day struck him. For reasons he couldn't fathom, the comrades had sent him to keep an eye on Kostas Laskaris and report on all his visitors. The dead composer Randos had been one of the old poet's closest friends in the Party. What kind of filthy game was he being drawn into by the big players, the ones who could crush him like a fly?

Mavros punched numbers on the phone in the hotel bedroom. He and Grace had given up any idea of looking for a picturesque place to stay when they saw the newspaper, settling instead for the box-like Hotel Mani in the main square. At least it had plenty of vacant rooms – one for each of them – and, although the marble corridors

279

were freezing, the bedrooms were equipped with electric heating units that fanned out waves of warmth.

He started speaking in Greek to the journalist Bitsos in Athens, feeling Grace's eyes on him. The suspicion that she could understand the language flitted across his mind. He returned her gaze and spoke even more rapidly. Her expression remained the same and he let the thought go.

When Mavros put down the phone, she sat on the bed beside him. 'Well?'

'Bitsos didn't have much to say. Neither do the police. They reckon it was either an accident or suicide. There was no sign of a struggle.' He ran his hand through his hair. 'I don't believe it was an accident. You saw how he kept the shutters down when he was on his own.'

She was looking at him. 'So, was it suicide? Do you think what we ... what I said could have affected him so much?'

Mavros chewed his lip. 'I doubt it, Grace. Randos wasn't a depressive, like a lot of musicians and artists. He was famous for shooting his mouth off and getting outrageously drunk at parties, not sitting on his own and thinking how futile his life was.' He glanced at her. 'Besides, there's something else.'

'What is it?' she said, when he didn't go on.

'Bitsos said that the kittens were on the ground next to him.'

'What?' she said. 'You mean they'd been put out of the window?'

His lower lip was between his teeth again.

'Jesus Christ, he must have–' She gazed at him.

280

'Oh, no, I see what you mean. He loved those little creatures. He'd never have harmed them. You think someone murdered him?'

'I reckon so. Fortunately we're not in the shit. His wife came back after we were there – one of the neighbours saw her and noticed the time – so even if the people who were on our tail wanted to frame us, they'd have a job.' He shook his head. 'Not that it would be beyond them to produce a false witness if they wanted to.'

'They?' she said. 'Who do you think they are?'

'You tell me,' Mavros replied.

She looked away, feeling the hostility that was radiating from him. 'What do you mean?' she asked.

'Just this,' he said, standing up and leaning over her. 'Ever since we hooked up, things have started to happen. We get followed to Randos's place and from your hotel, the composer ends up dead, and Kostas Laskaris clams up tighter than a dead man when we visit him.' He moved his face close to hers. 'Is there anything you want to tell me, Grace? Remember, I can walk away from this any time I want.'

She was silent for a few moments, and then she pushed him back gently, the fingers of her right hand splayed on his chest. 'Stop it, Alex,' she said. 'I didn't ask for any of this to happen. I ... I just want to find the guy who killed my father. Why are you giving me a hard time, for God's sake?'

He held her gaze briefly, then moved towards the window. 'I'm sorry,' he said. 'I shouldn't have taken it out on you.' He was still struggling with

281

what the old poet had told him about his brother Andonis, and felt the urge to tell Grace about him. He managed to resist that. He had taken on the case to find her father's killer – Andonis was his own issue.

'That old Mediterranean temperament of yours coming out?' she said, with a smile. 'I could do with a drink.'

They left the hotel and found an under-patronised café where they could talk without the shouting that was a standard feature of *kafeneia*.

'I don't think you'll get a cocktail here,' Mavros said.

Grace laughed. 'I want a beer, not a Screw-driver.'

A young man appeared at their table, his shaven head proving that bad haircuts weren't confined to the capital city.

Mavros ordered a couple of Amstels and they took some hits. He began to relax. Then a piece of music started to play on the radio and he tensed again.

'What is it?' she asked.

'"O Erotas Kaiei",' he replied, his voice low. '"Love Burns". One of Randos's recent hits.' The waiter and a couple of other young men began to sing along. '"The world makes us suffer, but love burns away the pain." Laskaris wrote the lyrics.'

They listened to the lilting rhythms of the song and its naked emotion. It concluded to cries of 'Bravo' from the young men in the overheated room. A pair of old men who had looked sullen were clapping.

'That was beautiful,' Grace said.

'You see how popular Randos was? Even down here, in the most right-wing corner of Greece.'

She nodded. 'It's hard to think of an American composer who would provoke a reaction like that in a bar in the Midwest, let alone one with a major poet as his lyricist. I wonder if my father ever saw that side of Greece.'

They ate dinner in an adjacent restaurant, amazed to discover that what looked at first glance to be a quiet kitchen offered literally dozens of dishes.

'What on earth are they going to do with all that food?' Grace asked, as she finished a plate of veal in tomato sauce.

'Who knows? Feed all the old people in the Deep Mani?'

'An unofficial welfare service?'

'Why not? People look after their own in this country.'

After a brandy on the house, presented by the waiter with a flourish, they headed back to the hotel.

Mavros stopped outside her door; his own was further down the corridor. 'What time do you want to get going in the morning, Grace? If we're planning to stop in at Laskaris's tower after we talk to Dhimitrakos, we'd better not hang about.'

'Eight?' she said, then put her key into the lock. 'Good night, Alex.' She went in without looking at him.

It was only a few minutes later that Mavros heard a light tap on the door. He opened it. His eyes widened as she pushed him inside and her mouth met his. She had swathes of his hair in her

283

hands to keep him where she wanted him.

'Surprise,' she said, when they broke off for air. 'I thought you might need some company tonight.' She looked at him. 'What's the matter?'

He was studying her face. 'This is a bit unexpected.'

'That's in the nature of surprises, Alex.' Grace kissed him again, this time more urgently. She nudged him towards the bed, her hands running down his back then coming forward to his belt buckle.

'Look,' Mavros stammered, 'I'm not sure if this is a good–' He felt her hands on his groin.

'Sure it's a good idea,' she said.

'No,' he said, pushing her away gently. 'Remember Niki?'

Grace was still smiling. 'The one who landed a good low punch? How could I forget her?'

Mavros picked up her harsher tone. 'Well, I can't forget her either,' he said. 'We're a couple. I don't cheat on her.'

Grace's expression was blank now. 'Very noble, Alex. Very politically correct.'

'Besides,' he continued, 'it isn't a good idea for us to get involved. We need to concentrate on the case.'

'Involved as in emotionally involved, you mean?' Grace asked. 'I wasn't planning on getting emotionally involved, for Christ's sake. I got the hots for you, that's all.' She turned towards the door. 'Good night again.'

Mavros watched the door close behind her, then locked it and sat on his bed. That was a development he could have lived without.

The old soldier Geoffrey Dearfield lay in the first-floor bedroom in the Palaiologos house and listened to his wife's gentle snoring. He could see the hands of his watch in the light that was coming through the shutter slats from the garden, armed men patrolling outside the fence as they had done during the war. Three o'clock. He'd drunk too much the previous evening; he knew it would keep him awake, but he had needed the numbing effect of alcohol to damp down the fear that was increasing by the day. These murders – which he was sure were by the Iraklis group – and now the sudden death of the Communist composer Randos were swamping him. Something terrible was happening in his adopted country and the guilt he'd suppressed for years had at last begun to get the better of him. The guilt and the fear – they had their roots in the enclosed plateau on Taygetos, the frightful scene he had come upon too late. Kapetan Iraklis had been in command, the guerrilla fighter's face rising up before him again. Oh, God, he thought, why were the scenes from the Second World War so vivid, as if they had happened yesterday? Suddenly he was back there, watching himself as a young man.

'Hurry,' he said, over his shoulder. 'The gunfire came from beyond that ridge.' Captain Geoff Dearfield, Royal Engineers, but now seconded to the Special Operations Executive and acting as a liaison officer with the Greek resistance, was striding up the scree-ridden slope in the southern Peloponnese.

'We must be careful,' his guide Fivos called. He was trying to keep up, the stitching of his Greek Army-issue boots coming apart. 'The enemy column was long and heavily armed.'

The Englishman looked up at the bare peaks, the spine of Taygetos less high than it was above Sparta but still eagle-haunted and forbidding as it ran down to the sea at Cape Matapan, or Tainaron as the Greeks called it. His breathing was regular, the training he had undertaken in Egypt standing him in good stead.

'Why would the guerrillas have engaged them?' he asked bitterly. 'We've been developing a strategy of pinning the Germans down in the plains, not inciting them to run all over the place.' Although the Italians had initially been the occupying force in this area, their surrender the previous September had left the Germans in control – and they were now supplemented by the Security Battalions made up of anti-Communist Greeks.

Fivos raised his chin. 'I don't know. The ELAS unit may not have had any choice. There are many impassable places where it could have been trapped.' He had been a student at Oxford before the war and his English was good. When the brass hats discovered he had grown up in Lakonia, he was immediately transferred from the Greek Army of the Near East to Special Operations. The fact that he was staunchly monarchist had increased his appeal.

Dearfield slowed his pace as he approached the ridge. It had been some minutes since the gunfire had ceased. He glanced at Fivos and dropped to

286

his knees, then crawled towards the edge. When he got there, he moved his head forward carefully, having removed his beret.

'What are they doing?' he whispered, his heart pounding as he took in the scene a couple of hundred feet below. 'My God, what are they doing?'

Fivos swallowed hard. 'The butchers,' he gasped. 'They are – they are executing the survivors.'

Dearfield watched as a woman in torn combat gear squatted down by a man wearing the kilt of a battalionist and pulled his head back, then slit his throat with a bayonet. 'But that man's a Greek,' he said, aghast. 'They're killing their own people.'

Fivos's face was ashen, his eyes damp. 'This is what they do to traitors,' he said. 'But they are the real traitors to their country. EAM and ELAS are made up of Communist brigands. They will give Greece to the Slavs and the Russians.' He pulled his service revolver from its holster.

'No,' Dearfield said, putting a hand on the Greek's arm. 'If they have the nerve to execute Greek prisoners, they will not hesitate to kill you and me if we fire on them. We are heavily outnumbered. But I will go down there and remonstrate with their leader.'

'He will not listen. I have heard about the *kapetanios* who calls himself Iraklis. He is an ideologue as well as a common murderer. He has trained his men – and women like that bitch – to follow orders blindly. Besides, they view the British as imperialist oppressors who are no better than the Germans.'

'Nevertheless, my orders are to make contact with him.' Dearfield moved back from the edge. 'There is no way to the north from the plateau. If we head south, we will meet them.'

Fivos looked nervous but he complied. In a couple of hours the Englishman encountered Kapetan Iraklis for the first time and set out on the long road that ended on the cross.

Geoffrey Dearfield came back to himself with a start and moved his head, trying to fathom where he was. When he saw his wife's supine form in the neighbouring bed, he managed to get his breathing under control. He had not been good for her, he thought. He had loved her well enough when she was not much more than a girl after the war. He had taken her away from her studies when they went back to England, but she had kept at them when he was working. He'd admired her for that, but her ability to lose herself in her own world made her a less than ideal wife for an MP. And after they came back to Greece, Flora had managed to break into academia, no small achievement for a woman in the early sixties. Of course, she had her relatives and her contacts, the network of patrons and clients that everyone in Greece had to use if they were to make progress in their chosen field – even though she had never shown any affection for the surviving members of her family. She had always kept herself to herself, staying in her study late into the night.

Dearfield found himself thinking about his father-in-law. Petros Petrakis had been a banker with roots in the western Mani, a rich man who cared nothing for anyone outside his own class. During the war he had stayed in Athens, trying to keep what remained of the Greek banking system in operation. There had been rumours that he was too close to the Germans and the Greek collaborationist governments, that he had been involved in black-market activities, but nothing had ever stuck. That hadn't stopped a Communist youth-organisation member blowing his brains out on a street corner soon after the war. He didn't know what effect that had had on Flora. She'd never spoken of it or of her family life before the murder. Dearfield had the impression that she had had little love for her father.

Ah, Flora, he thought, you've been studying the myths and the history of this area since I knew you. But you never knew what happened here during the war, the brutality and the horror. You never knew the part your own husband played in the violence. Now, if my book is ever published, you will find out. But what will that do to us?

Dearfield felt himself slipping down a stony slope, his eyes rolling. Only when he was past the point of no return did he realise that a band of resistance fighters in ill-matching uniforms was waiting for him at the bottom, bayonets in hand. And this time there was no bearded leader to control them.

Mavros woke up with a jerk, one side of his body freezing. It was a little after four a.m. He got up and turned the heater back on. After Grace left he'd dispensed with it, but that obviously hadn't been a good idea. He went to the small bathroom.

When he got back into bed, he found that sleep had deserted him.

He lay there wondering what he was getting into. Grace Helmer was a stunning woman and she had pressed herself on him. There was no denying that he'd fancied her from the moment he opened his door to her in Athens. So what was he doing rejecting her? It wasn't as if his relationship with Niki was exactly flourishing – she'd made clear what she thought of him when she'd belted him in the gut and it wasn't as if she'd ever find out that he'd turned Grace down. But it wasn't just a question of sex, no matter how much mutual attraction there was between him and the American woman. The basic problem was a professional one. Not just on the level he'd expressed to Grace, that investigators should stand back from their clients to keep their minds on the case. No, the underlying concern that held him back was that he didn't fully trust her.

He pulled the rough blanket up to his chin and went over Grace's moves. She'd gone into her room without giving him a second glance, then had appeared a few minutes later and come on to him. Why? Was she just trying to surprise him, as she'd said, or was she playing a more devious game? Sex without emotion didn't seem to be a problem for her – maybe she'd got used to that because of her work in dangerous places, and besides, there was no shortage of women, these days, who fucked you and hit the road, as the journalist Bitsos had once stated in characteristically crude fashion. Men had been doing that for centuries, so why shouldn't women? But Grace had come on to him in a way that was too calculating. It was almost as if she'd gone to her room and found an instruction saying, 'Get back there and make him screw you.' But why? What did she want from him?

Mavros rolled on to his side and forced himself to close his eyes. He found himself back in the family house in Athens as a little kid, his brother Andonis whittling a boat for him out of a piece of firewood. It was a skill he had learned from their father – Spyros Mavros had sharpened the handle of a spoon into a blade when he was on the prison island of Makronisos and made driftwood figures with it when he couldn't sleep; he could have used it against the guards, but violence had always been anathema to him. Andonis's bright blue eyes were fixed on the blade of the knife as he moved it deftly across the surface of the wood, forming a curved hull. Then he raised his head and smiled at Alex.

Shaking his head to dispel the vision, Mavros tried to concentrate. He would soon have to decide on his priorities. Was he involved in this case for his client or for what he might discover about his brother? One thing he'd learned over the years was that working without a clear aim could be dangerous, even fatal. And that was without the presence of a master assassin in the wings.

12

Iraklis had left the car a kilometre from the village of Kainourgia Chora not long after five in the morning. The road was unmetalled and the Citroën's tyres had left tracks in the muddy surface. There was nothing he could do about that. Curious locals might notice the unfamiliar vehicle if he hadn't finished by daylight, but he had hired it using one of his false identities – that of a bookseller from Des Moines – so he wasn't too concerned. Trudging up the sodden track in a dark blue raincoat and waterproof boots, he breathed in the clean air, colder here on the southern heights of Taygetos. At least it had stopped raining. The moon and stars were obscured by clouds and there were only a few lights visible from the small harbour far below. Up to his right the wind was rustling through the bushes, the harsh croak of a nocturnal bird of prey shutting off like a tap as he inadvertently kicked a stone. Although he had a torch, he preferred not to use it. His night vision had always been good and was unaffected by years in the bright lights of New York City.

The walls of the village appeared round a bend in the road, illuminated by a couple of dim street-lamps. Crouching down, he took out the plan he had drawn and shone the torch on it. The woman he'd telephoned, the cousin of his former comrade Babis Dhimitrakos, had been surprised when he'd asked how to find the house. She had shouted to her husband for help, explaining that they had only been there a few times. Fortunately he was the type who enjoyed giving directions and rattled off a detailed description of the small, underpopulated village. Dhimitrakos's cousin had taken the phone back and asked who he was, openly curious. Iraklis mumbled that he was an old friend, then held the receiver closer to his ear. Apparently he wasn't the first person to ask for her relative that day, though all she could tell him about the other caller was that he was male and spoke with what she described as a 'city accent'. He'd been wondering who that could have been ever since he'd cut the connection. As he approached the first buildings, he put his hand on the silenced automatic in his coat pocket.

He found his old comrade's house without difficulty, slipping through the deserted lanes to the far side of the village. His destination turned out to be a hovel rather than a house, the shutters dangling from the windows of the small single-storey building. It was relatively new, not built in stone in the traditional style but of cement blocks, the external layer of plaster coming off in several places. The blue paint on the wooden door was faded and cracked, a light with a broken shade above it. The assassin looked around to check that no one was observing him and tried the handle. It turned, but the door wouldn't move. He slid his hand into his trouser pocket and took out a hooked steel rod. It took him under a minute to engage the lock. The hinges creaked as he pushed the panel so he slowed his movement and gradually inched it open far enough for him to squeeze in. He needn't have bothered – the sound of heavy snoring was audible from a back room.

The house reeked of cigarettes and sewage, the cesspit clearly in need of emptying. Stepping forward silently, the shapes of the room's meagre furniture easy to pick out in the light that was coming through the glass above the door, he entered the room at the rear. By the side of the single bed he made out a chair piled with clothing. Sweeping off the garments, he sat down. He brought the automatic forward in his right hand and turned on the torch, shining it into the sleeping man's face.

Babis Dhimitrakos jerked forward with a start, blinking like a mole. 'What–' He fell silent when he felt the end of the silencer on his temple.

'Keep the noise down, Odhyssea,' Iraklis said, using the other man's old terrorist code-name. 'Keep the noise down and I'll turn on the light. Understood?'

Dhimitrakos's eyes were wide, the dark rings on the skin around them and the bloodshot pupils standing out in the torch's beam. His head fell forward and he raised his hand in a weak gesture of assent.

The intruder felt for the bedside light and switched it on. A dim yellow glow illuminated the evil-smelling room and the blankets that the occupant had heaped over himself. 'My God, you look terrible, Babi. And you stink.'

'You!' Dhimitrakos gasped. 'I thought you were

294

dead.' His face was covered in grey stubble, the skin beneath it sallow. His hair was greasy and unkempt, standing up in patches like the feathers of a carrion crow that had been run over. 'What are you doing here?'

'I was told you've been in hospital,' the terrorist said, ignoring the question. 'Problems with your heart?' He pressed the muzzle harder into the skin. 'Is the guilt finally getting to you?' He leaned closer. 'I know you betrayed me, Babi.'

The man in the bed was panting now, the breath catching in his throat. 'No, it wasn't me. It was the others, it was Thyella and Markos.'

Iraklis smiled but his eyes were steely. 'Really? Well, they paid for their sins, didn't they?'

Dhimitrakos was swallowing repeatedly. 'So ... so it was you who did for them.'

The man on the chair shrugged. 'They were both killed by hit-and-run drivers who were never traced, weren't they?' Then he shook his head. 'I had other things on my mind.' He recounted his escape from the security forces. 'There were Americans involved,' he said. 'Did you talk to them? Have you seen them since?'

Dhimitrakos shuddered. 'No ... I – I was told you were the one who sold us out.' His eyes bulged as Iraklis stood up and moved the pistol nearer his mouth. 'Don't – please don't.'

'Admit you betrayed me and I'll take the gun away.' Iraklis leaned closer. 'Admit it.'

'Yes, all right,' Dhimitrakos whispered. 'I did it. I told them where to find you, I told them.' He let out a sob. 'They ... they hurt me.'

'What about the others?' The assassin had a

flash of the other two members of the Iraklis group, the young man with the wispy beard and the dark-eyed girl, whose father had lived in exile in Yugoslavia since 1949. 'Did they open up too?'

The man in the bed turned away. 'I don't know. We were kept separate.' He looked back, his eyes damp. 'Don't kill me,' he pleaded. 'I'm going to die soon – the doctors only give me a couple of years at most. Please. Let me tend my goats in peace.' The stench of his fear seeped out from the bed.

'Tend your goats?' the assassin said ruefully. 'Is this what the struggle has come to? What happened to your commitment to the Party? Why did you take part in all those murders? You coward, you're worse than the comrades who went into coalition with the Right in eighty-nine. You've been working for them, haven't you, you louse?'

Babis Dhimitrakos was staring at him. 'You've started again, haven't you? You're behind those killings in Athens. Why, after all these years?'

'You think so?' Iraklis said, sitting down. 'Have you not considered that maybe your friends are playing a game? That brings me to the reason for my visit to this hideaway of yours.' He gave a sad smile. 'I need to make sure you don't open your mouth about me again. You're not still in contact with the enemy, are you?' He watched as the man in the bed quivered. 'No, you're too sick to do their dirty work any more. Have you had any visitors from the big city recently?'

Dhimitrakos shook his head.

'Well, given the Iraklis group's apparent

296

reappearance, it won't be long before someone remembers you.' He ran his left hand down the silencer. 'How can I be sure you won't betray me again?' He moved the automatic away. 'There's only one way. But first I want you to tell me every little thing you let slip to the bastards when they grilled you.'

The former getaway driver pulled the blankets around him and started to talk in a breathless voice.

Mavros met Grace outside her room at eight. She smiled at him. 'Don't worry about last night, Alex,' she said. 'Business as usual.'

They drank a quick and unpleasant coffee in the hotel's deserted dining-room and settled the bill. Before getting into the Fiat, Mavros picked up a loaf of bread and a couple of *tiropites* from a nearby bakery.

'Cheese pie for breakfast?' Grace asked, wrinkling her nose.

'Suit yourself.' He'd have preferred one of the Fat Man's sweet pastries, but he hadn't liked the look of the Areopolis equivalent.

While Mavros ate, Grace drove down the main road to the south, the wheels spraying water from the puddles that had formed at the side. The morning was grey and overcast, the summits of the hills shrouded again, but the rain was keeping off. As they passed Kitta, Mavros glanced to his right. Tigani promontory wasn't visible, because of the contours of the land, but the top of Kostas Laskaris's tower was. He couldn't stop thinking of the conversation he'd had with the old poet about his brother. The fact that Andonis had been down here, at the tower and on the rugged peninsula, had made a deep impression on him. He felt the need to go down to the ruined walls of the castle and touch the stones to see if he could establish some connection with his long-lost sibling. Maybe there would be time for that later.

At Alika they took a left turn and the road narrowed immediately as it started to wind up the hillside. After passing through a windswept village and a desolate valley, they reached a junction.

'According to the map, that's our road to the right,' Mavros said. 'It's supposed to be unmetalled.'

They followed the sign to Korogonianika down a strip of asphalt that looked like it had been laid recently.

'They've been doing this all over the country,' he said. 'Using European Union money to improve the infrastructure. You can be sure the local council members and the construction companies take their cuts.'

'How cynical,' Grace said.

'How true.' Mavros looked ahead. 'Ah, this is more like it.'

The asphalt suddenly ran out, but the road ahead was a surprisingly firm mixture of gravel and mud. Soon they saw a huddle of houses and towers to their left marking the village that had been signposted.

'Another couple of kilometres,' Mavros said.

They passed a junction with a road that twisted

down the hillside in a series of hairpins and Grace stopped.

'Will you look at that view?' she said, getting out of the car.

Mavros joined her and took in the panorama of sea, indented bays and rolling hills to the south. Narrow promontories ran out into the grey-blue water like the snouts of huge amphibian creatures and, far out, a line of clouds marked the horizon.

'The way to hell,' Mavros said.

'What?'

'Cape Tainaron is beyond the last hill,' he explained. 'Also known as Matapan. The most southerly point on mainland Greece. It was there that Iraklis descended to the underworld to capture Cerberus.'

She looked at him thoughtfully. 'Iraklis the mythical figure rather than Iraklis the terrorist group, you mean?'

'Yes.' Mavros registered her tone and stared back at her. 'Look, Grace, if you're going to check out every place that the ancient hero went because of potential links to the modern-day Iraklis, forget it. He performed labours all over the Peloponnese, let alone the rest of Greece and the Mediterranean.'

'Okay, Alex. Calm down.' She took a final look at the view and got back into the car.

A few minutes later they drove up to the dead-end village of Kainourgia Chora, the approach road clear of moving and stationary vehicles. The small collection of houses seemed uninhabited and Mavros wondered if he was going to have to

299

phone Babis Dhimitrakos's cousin for directions after all – he'd presumed someone on the spot would help. Then there was a clatter of heavy boots and an old man came round the corner between two rundown houses. Mavros asked him where Dhimitrakos lived.

'Down the road towards the cemetery. Second-last house on the left.' The villager peered at them with sticky eyes. 'It stinks,' he added, before he trudged off.

Mavros led the way to a house that was more dilapidated than the rest of the buildings. 'I think this is it.' There was a short unpaved path leading from the track, several footprints visible in the mud. He went up to the door. Before knocking he squatted down in front of it and looked at the lock as he pulled on a pair of leather gloves. 'Either Mr Dhimitrakos has a very shaky hand or someone's jemmied the lock recently.' He pointed to the scores in the metal round the keyhole then thumped on the faded panelling. 'Kyrie Dhimitrako?'

'Gone to work?' Grace suggested, looking around at the overgrown fields and the walled cemetery with its marble crosses further down the track.

Mavros followed the line of her gaze. There was a small flock of goats up on the hill. Screwing up his eyes, he made out a couple of human figures above the animals – they were about ten metres apart, the rear one walking quicker than the man in the lead. Herdsmen or hunters, he presumed. 'I don't think there's much work to be done here. Everyone except the old people has moved to the big city.' He inhaled through his mouth. 'The guy back there said the house stank and he was right. A cesspit emptier could clean up around here.'

'Very funny. Are you going to try the handle?'

Mavros called out the occupant's name again. 'Might as well.' He turned the handle, pushed the door wide and took a step forward, one hand to his nose. The house was damp and sparsely furnished, no pictures or photographs on walls that hadn't been whitewashed for years.

'No one at home?' asked Grace, coming forward to join him.

He put a hand on her forearm. 'Wait here,' he said, in a low voice. 'And don't touch anything.'

He bent down and unlaced his boots, leaving them by the door. Stepping lightly into the front room, he felt the hairs rise on the back of his neck. Where was Babis Dhimitrakos? He glanced into a chaotic kitchen on the right to establish that no one was there. The smell got worse as he approached the open door to the back room. He looked round to check that Grace hadn't moved. She gave him a firm nod to urge him on.

Mavros moved forward, breathing only through his mouth. The room contained nothing more than a bed, a chair and a cheap wooden chest of drawers. There was a heap of clothes on the floor. But it was the bed that drew his attention. There was a mound topped by blankets on it, and the stench emanated from there. He could almost taste it.

'What is it?' Grace called.

'Wait!' he shouted, his voice taut.

Mavros gripped the top of the blankets with his

301

right hand and prepared himself for what lay beneath. Then he pulled them back swiftly, keeping his eyes directed towards the top of the bed. He had learned over the years that the first glance at a potential crime victim needed to be a controlled one if it was to remain in his mind.

But there was no one, only a pair of filthy pyjamas beneath an ancient bolster. Mavros swallowed hard and blinked. That would teach him to lose control of his imagination. He dropped to a squat to check beneath the bed and gagged as he found the source of the stench – an over-full saucepan that had been used as a bed pan.

'Jesus,' he said, under his breath, standing up and stepping back. Then he saw a foil strip on the mildewed dresser, three empty spaces where pills had been pushed out. He picked them up and read the brand name without recognising it. Was Dhimitrakos taking these for his heart condition? If so, would he have left them behind? Then he remembered the pair of figures he'd seen above the goats that were grazing beyond the village. Had the former terrorist left the house in a hurry, with someone else in close pursuit?

Mavros moved quickly back to the door.

'What's going on?' Grace said when she saw his face. 'Is he–'

'I think that might have been Dhimitrakos up on the hill,' he said, as he pulled on his boots. He looked up. 'There was a second man behind.'

'Iraklis?' she said, her eyes wide.

'Don't jump to conclusions,' he replied. 'But I'm not taking any chances. Go back to the car and wait for me there.'

'No.' She gripped his forearm. 'You know that's not the deal. I'm sticking with you.' There was no warmth in her smile. 'If you send me back, I'll just wait a while and then follow you. That could put me in even more danger.'

'For God's sake. All right, come with me. But do exactly what I tell you.'

'I thought it was the client who gave the orders,' Grace said, following him outside.

There was now no sign of the two human figures, the goats moving slowly upwards in formation.

'They must have gone over that ridge,' Mavros said. He set off down the rough path at a quick pace, glancing at Grace as she caught him up. 'Why did you assume that Iraklis was up there? It could have been another villager.'

'Oh, come on, Alex,' she replied, her breathing steady as they started up the slope. 'You look like a bloodhound that's picked up a very strong scent.'

'I wish I hadn't picked up any scent in that bedroom,' he said, his trouser legs already soaked from the heavy dew on the scrub and grass. 'Dhimitrakos obviously only empties his chamber pot once a week.' He peered ahead. 'Where could they be going? There wasn't any other settlement on the map, was there?'

'Not as far as I remember.'

They concentrated on the ascent. Mavros felt his throat tighten as his breathing quickened. At their approach, the goats looked up from their grazing, their black eyes shiny and wide. Then the animals broke away, keeping close together, their bells clanking.

'Shit,' Mavros said. 'We just let our guys know we're after them.'

Grace strode past him, her eyes fixed on the line of rock. As she neared the saddle, she lowered her upper body and slowed her pace.

Mavros watched her, remembering how she'd spotted the tail in Athens. She gave the impression of someone who could handle situations that most people knew nothing about. He kept his head down and joined her at a rocky outcrop, moving his eyes across the broken terrain ahead. There was a steep downward slope immediately beyond the ridge, its surface scattered with boulders and chutes of scree. Then, across a narrow watercourse, there rose a series of three sheer cliffs, interspersed with narrow plateaux, leading to a barren summit. High above, a buzzard circled on the air currents, its rough-edged wing tips fluttering.

'There's one of them,' Grace said, nodding towards a wide crack in the lowest cliff face.

Mavros looked down and made out a figure in a dark-coloured, knee-length coat. The man had a cap pulled low over his eyes and his legs were spread wide as he raised his head to take in the rock face.

'And there's the other.' Grace pointed to a hollow in the cliff, about ten metres above the man in the coat. A short, heavy man wearing ragged clothes was crouching in the small space, his arms outstretched for grip.

'I reckon that's Dhimitrakos,' Mavros said. 'He

304

looks like he's in his late fifties and in pretty bad physical condition. How did he manage to get up there?'

'God knows. I'd say he's terrified.' Grace cocked an ear. 'The man below is shouting at him. Can you make anything out?'

Mavros could hear echoing cries, but the wind was blowing down the watercourse and obscuring the words. He watched as the man up the cliff slowly raised himself to his full height. Then he toppled forward and fell to the stony ground below, his body horizontal as it took the impact. There was no more movement from him.

'Shit,' Grace said, pulling herself up. 'What's going on down there?'

Before Mavros could stop her, she was over the saddle and running down the slope. He followed as fast as he could, his eyes on the man in the long coat. He was now beside the body, bending down. Then he heard the rattle of the stones that Grace's boots were dislodging and his hand moved quickly to his pocket.

'Stop, Grace!' Mavros shouted. 'Stop! He's got a gun.'

They managed to control their descent about thirty metres above the man, who was now pointing a black pistol at Grace. His face was in the shadow of the peak of his cap. All Mavros could be sure of was that he had no beard.

'Fuck you, Iraklis!' Grace yelled, the arteries in her throat blue and contorted. 'You don't scare me.'

Mavros put a hand on her shoulder and pushed her into a crouch to reduce the target size. 'Shut

305

up, for fuck's sake,' he hissed.

The man in the coat held his weapon on Grace's midriff without wavering. Then he gave what sounded like a mocking laugh and started to walk in a measured stride up the slope towards them.

'Jesus Christ,' Mavros said, under his breath, trying to push Grace on to the ground and put his body between her and their assailant. His eyes were fixed on the approaching figure, his heart pounding and his throat dry.

Then there was an explosion of gravel and dust from the ground immediately in front of the armed man's leading leg. The crack from an unsilenced weapon followed immediately and the three of them – Grace, Mavros, and the man below them – looked away up the slope towards the source of the report.

Mavros made out a tall figure on a boulder half-way down the scree to their rear. He was also wearing a dark coat, a scarf pulled up to his nose. His hair was dark, the eyes beneath it heavily ringed. Before he could say or do anything, another shot was fired, this one kicking up stones a few centimetres in front of the man in the cap's other foot. He heard another laugh, this one less confident, then the man below backed away up the watercourse.

Grace's eyes were flicking between the two men, her brow furrowed. 'What's going on?' she said.

'God knows,' Mavros replied. 'Just keep still.' He glared at her and wrapped his arms round her legs to impede any movement. 'I mean it.'

The two of them watched as the man in the cap continued to move away, his pistol now lowered. After a few minutes he reached the end of the narrow valley and walked more quickly up the opposite slope, his head down.

When Mavros looked round again at the man who had saved them, there was no sign of him on the boulder or on the rocky incline above. He had disappeared like a ghost into the grey morning, and the spreadeagled body below was their only company.

Grace pushed him away, her eyes moving round the deserted landscape. She got to her feet quickly and went down to the watercourse.

'Wait,' Mavros said, running to catch her up. His heart was still beating hard and his hands inside the leather gloves were damp. 'Don't touch–' He stopped when he saw that she, too, was wearing gloves.

'Let's see if we can confirm his identity,' Grace said, stooping over the prone figure.

'Maybe we should check for a pulse first,' he said. 'Jesus, where are your feelings? This poor guy took a dive in front of our eyes. And then we almost got ourselves killed, in case you hadn't noticed.'

'Calm down, Alex,' she replied, without meeting his eyes. 'This should all be in a day's work for you.' She pulled off a glove and touched the man's throat. 'No pulse.'

Mavros watched as she located a tattered wallet in a trouser pocket. He took it from her and pulled out the ID card issued by the Greek police to all citizens, comparing the photo with the dead

307

man. 'Yes, this is Babis Dhimitrakos all right.'

'Why did he let himself fall?'

'Maybe his heart gave out.'

'Do you think the man with the gun was threatening him?'

'Could be. He wasn't exactly pleased that we witnessed the scene.'

Grace stood up. 'He was Iraklis, I'm sure of it.'

'Did you see anything of his face?'

She shook her head.

'And what about the other guy, the one who saved us? Who was he? And why did he disappear so quickly?'

Grace was looking around the rocky valley. 'How would I know? I think it might be a good idea if we got out of here without delay.'

Mavros was looking at Dhimitrakos. 'We can't just leave him.' He glanced up at the sky. 'There are birds of prey...'

'We'll tell someone in the village that we saw him fall,' Grace said, starting up the slope.

He gave Dhimitrakos a last look and followed her. 'Have you done this kind of thing before, Grace?'

'It's not the first time I've encountered the dead. We often come across them in the bush.' Her head dropped. 'I've been to a massacre site in Bosnia too.'

They reached the saddle. The village looked like a cluster of sheds for animals, the walls discoloured by the winter rains and by neglect.

'Look, Grace, we need to be careful,' Mavros said. 'Even if we only tell the villagers that we saw Dhimitrakos fall, they'll expect us to wait for the doctor and the police. If we don't stay, we'll be remembered and the authorities will want to talk to us.'

Grace gazed around again, searching for any sign of the armed men. 'No,' she said, her voice unwavering. 'We were close to Iraklis. He'll be after us now to stop us talking. If we go to the police, we'll scare him off.' She moved closer to him. 'So we walk away as if nothing happened and you make an anonymous call from the next village.'

'By which time the body will have attracted every carrion creature in the vicinity. Christ, this isn't right, Grace. We can't just leave him out here.'

She glared at him. 'He was a fucking terrorist, Alex. He was involved in my father's death. Who cares if the birds get him?'

Mavros had taken a step back, her words ringing in his ears. Until now he hadn't seen how much she wanted to find her father's murderer. She hadn't been scared by their assailant or by the gunfire, and that lack of emotion made him wonder even more about his client and her motives. He considered giving up the case, but dismissed the idea quickly. Grace would be at even greater risk if he wasn't with her and, besides, he wanted to find out about the terrorist's links with his brother Andonis.

'How do we get back to the car without being spotted?' Grace said, moving away down the hill.

'We'll have to take our chances.'

When they got to the village they walked at a pace that was brisk, but not hurried enough to attract attention. They were lucky. They reached the Fiat without encountering anyone in the narrow streets. Grace got in and started the engine, reversing and turning before he could open his door.

'Come on,' she said impatiently, and set off before he was fully in.

Mavros pulled his door shut and a wave of relief burst over him. At least they'd got clear of the dead man's village without running into either of the armed men.

Then he saw the state of the road that Grace had turned on to and his heart began to hammer again.

Kostas Laskaris looked out over Tigani through the small window by the front door. The raised brow of the headland with its ruined fortifications was floating above the grey water like a crown shorn of its jewels and decorative carvings; the crown of a king overwhelmed in a final desperate battle. As Kapetan Iraklis had been.

He twitched his head to dispel the scenes from his early life, but it seemed he had no defence against them. He was back with the man he had loved, the brown eyes solemn but a fearless smile beneath the jet-black beard – Kapetan Iraklis as he had been in the early days of the resistance campaign, before he had had to give the orders that set the band of fighters on the road to the underworld: the orders to execute their fellow Greeks. Could he have made his leader understand the cost of those orders? He had tried often enough, when the fighters were asleep and the bastard commissar Vladhimiros wasn't listening. There had been one particular time, a night around the embers of a fire in a cave high on Taygetos...

'We must be united,' Iraklis had said to him, when he finished his gloomy prediction. 'There can be no room for doubt, my comrade.' He laughed. 'You must be true to me, you must help me, as Iolaos helped Iraklis in the myths. He held the flame to the stumps of the Hydra after the hero had sliced off its lethal heads to prevent new ones appearing.' He touched his arm. 'That will be your task when the difficult times begin and we are assaulted from every side.'

Kostas nodded, momentarily disarmed by the subtle strength of his captain's voice. He had always known that few of the band would survive the war, known that the country would be in turmoil for many years to come. His father had fought in the Balkan Wars, then in the doomed Asia Minor campaign that had ended in the burning of Greek Smyrna by the Turks and the exchange of populations in 1922. 'War eats men,' the veteran had said. 'Those who die in battle are consumed quickly, but the survivors are condemned to a lifetime of torment. Because men are weak, and fighting for the nation is easier than making the nation fit for its people.'

'We will all become victims of the struggle,' Kostas said, as the force of his captain's words faded.

Iraklis leaned against him. 'We are already victims,' he said softly, 'but if we support each other through the worst times, there is nothing

311

that can hurt us.' He nudged his friend. 'Remember when we were kids, climbing into the rich man's estate? We stuck together then, didn't we?'

Suddenly the poet found himself on top of a high wall, the August sun beating down on his head. He was ten, his hair shaved close to his scalp to discourage nits. A summer on the rocks and in the sea near Kitta had burned his skin deep brown. His companion was only a few months older but he was already a leader. His wiry body was first into the banker's forbidden grounds.

'Come on, Kosta,' he called. 'There's no one here.'

Laskaris took a deep breath and jumped down, wincing as his bare feet landed on the stony soil. 'How do you know?' he whispered. 'The gardeners might be beyond the trees.'

'They're sleeping.' The other boy gave a wide grin. 'Anyway, we can run faster than anyone. We can beat the wind.' He turned and padded away through the olive trees, heading for the building at the far end of the grounds.

'Where are you going?' Kostas hissed, as he caught up. 'They'll catch us and beat us if we go near the house.'

His friend ignored him, running on towards the grey stone walls of the tower. It had been there for centuries, but only in the last two years had it been inhabited again. A rich man called Petrakis, not a local but a Maniate all the same, had bought and renovated the old building, adding a more comfortable modern extension. This

Petrakis was a banker in Athens who came down in the summer for a month. The rest of the year the house was closed up, the gardens tended by men from the village. They usually paid little attention to the boys when they climbed the wall, but when the owner was in residence they were fierce.

The pair ducked down behind a mimosa, then set off round the walls of the house. It was mid-afternoon and the shutters were half closed to keep out the sun and allow what little breeze there was to cool the interior. Kostas stopped by the corner and watched as his friend slowly raised his head to look inside, a mischievous smile on his lips.

'Little pigs!' came a harsh voice.

Before he could move, Kostas's arm was caught in a tight grip. He looked up to see a red-faced man in white trousers, braces curved over his belly. There was a thin line of moustache over his twisted mouth.

'What are you doing?' he shouted. 'This is private property.' He squeezed harder, making Kostas yelp. 'And you? How dare you look in the window? My wife is in there.' He stepped forward, dragging Kostas with him in an attempt to collar the other boy.

'Let him go.' The words were piped out in a high voice but the authority in them was unmistakable. 'You have no right.'

The heavily built man laughed. 'What do you know about rights, you little ruffian?' He moved forward again.

The boy pressed his lips together. Kostas

watched in astonishment as his friend swung his foot round in a blur, making solid contact with the banker's groin. He felt the grip loosen from his arm and leaped away. They ran a few paces, then stopped to look round. Petrakis was on the ground, his face even redder than it had been. He was gasping and trying to shout at the same time. They laughed and headed for the wall...

Back in the cave during the war Iraklis was nodding at him, the firelight making his eyes glint. 'You see? If we look out for each other, we'll be all right.'

'Yes, but the banker's men caught up with us outside the estate and beat us mercilessly,' Kostas replied.

'I know,' his captain said. 'And now that snake Petrakis is working with the Germans in the big city.'

'At least you reduced the chances of him having any children.'

They leaned together and swallowed their laughter, fearful of waking the fighters who were stretched out on the floor of the cave. Outside the wind was howling, but in their place of refuge Kostas felt as secure as he had ever done in his life.

It was an illusion, the old poet thought, turning from the window in his tower and going to the table that was strewn with his papers. Before the pain in his gut stopped him for good, his task was to describe the labours that Iraklis and his band undertook after the battle at the place of slaughter – when the Englishman who was to dog their footsteps to the end had appeared.

314

He didn't know if he could face it.

Mavros's eyes were closed for most of the drive down from Kainourgia Chora. Grace handled the Fiat skilfully, but the road surface was treacherous, deep mud on the crowns of the hairpin bends and slippery patches elsewhere that more than once threatened to send the car over the unfenced edges. On the few occasions that he looked, the stark beauty of the Peloponnese's last hills rolling into the still water took away what little remained of his breath. He saw from the map that the clutch of towers and houses round a sharply curved bay to their left was Porto Kayio, the Harbour of Quails. According to the guidebook, Venetians had trapped the birds in multitudes on the annual migration; and Allied soldiers had been taken off after the unstoppable German advance in 1941.

'That was fun,' Grace said, as she pulled on to the metalled highway at the foot of the slope. The testing descent didn't seem to have affected her.

'Where did you learn to drive on roads like that?' Mavros asked.

'Take your pick,' she replied, turning right and accelerating away. 'Upstate New York when I was a kid, Indonesia, Rwanda, the Philippines...'

'Very impressive,' he muttered.

'Where now?'

Mavros had been thinking about that. 'The old poet Laskaris. Maybe he'll open up about Iraklis when he hears how we were nearly killed.'

'I hope so,' Grace said, looking around the bleak hills. The clouds were still grey and

315

lowering over the summits, screening the sun and making it seem like late afternoon rather the middle of the day. 'I'd prefer to meet the terrorist in a less isolated place next time.'

Mavros wondered about that as he stared at the sinuous strip of asphalt leading north. Did Grace have a clear idea of what she was going to say to the man who had killed her father? Of what she was going to do?

'My God, will you look at that place?' Grace nodded to a line of towers on the spine of rock ahead. 'It's like Dracula's castle.'

Mavros took in the fortified buildings, some in good condition but most dilapidated and uninhabited. The place was bleak and forbidding in the restricted light, a collective monument to centuries of feuding and neighbourly hate. Grace was right. It had the atmosphere of a hill town whose inhabitants had been overwhelmed by vampires, empty by day but full of pallid hunters as soon as the sun set.

'Stop here,' he said, as they were cutting through what passed for a central square.

Grace raised an eyebrow. 'Do we have to?'

'I have a call to make, remember?' Mavros went over to a pay-phone by a shuttered shop. He rang the emergency number and asked for the police, giving them the location of Dhimitrakos's body but cutting the connection when the officer asked for his name. Then he took out his notebook and found the number of the dead man's cousin he'd spoken to yesterday. The police would track her down, but he didn't want her to find out that way.

'You must go to your cousin Babis's village,' he

316

said, when the woman answered. 'He needs help.' He had intended to leave it at that, but he couldn't. What he was doing wasn't fair to her. Family bonds were to be respected, especially in a traditional area like the Mani. Even a city-dwelling half-caste like him knew that.

'What do you mean?' she said, her voice rising. 'Has something happened to Babis?'

'He ... he's not well.' Mavros was trying to weaken the blow. 'His heart...'

'Who is this?' the woman asked. 'You're one of those who called yesterday, aren't you?'

He held the receiver closer to his ear. 'Yes, I am. A friend ... a friend of Babis. One of those who called? Who else did you speak to?'

'Another man, he said he was an old friend too.' Her voice grew louder. 'What has happened to Babis? Is he dead?'

'Who was the man?' Mavros insisted, his own voice rising. 'It's very important.'

'He didn't say, but he asked for directions to the house in Kainourgia Chora. You, tell me who you are!'

'I'm sorry,' Mavros said feebly, and hung up.

Grace watched him get back into the Fiat. 'What happened?'

'Shit,' he said, under his breath. 'Apparently a man asked how to get to Dhimitrakos's place yesterday.'

She took a deep breath as they passed the last of Vatheia's run-down buildings, the uneven coastline of the western Mani laid out ahead and below them. 'The guy in the cap.'

'Or the one who sent him packing.' Mavros

317

glanced over his shoulder at the clear road behind. He was wondering where the mystery men were now. Was one or other of them on their trail? Were they both after the Fiat?

Suddenly he wished he was back in the polluted streets of Athens. At least there he knew how to look after himself.

'Are you all right, Mother?' Anna Mavrou-Chaniotaki glanced at the limp figure in the front seat next to her.

'Yes, dear,' Dorothy said, in a long-suffering voice. She looked out at the scrub-covered hills lining both sides of the motorway. As soon as they had crossed into the Peloponnese, snowflakes had started to fall. Now they were thicker, floating down from dense clouds that were low over the peaks. 'I just wish you had a more comfortable car.'

Anna gave an irritated twitch of her head. 'Well, you should have gone in the Mercedes with Nondas and the kids.' She peered ahead through the gloom. The lights of her husband's new car were still visible, though she knew he would have preferred to go much faster. That was why Dorothy had insisted on going in the Lancia, even though there wasn't enough leg room for her. At least her daughter acceded to her requests not to speed. 'Anyway, it isn't long till the Argos exit.'

'I'm not a child, you know,' the older woman said. 'I'm sorry, dear,' she relented. 'I'm a bit on edge about this trip. It's the first time I've been out of Athens for the winter holiday since your

318

father was alive.'

'I know. I remember those times in the village.' Anna chuckled. 'All the Mavros adults behaving like children.'

Dorothy smiled. 'Of course, New Year was the big celebration then,' she said, 'as it was in Scotland when I was a girl. Now Christmas seems to have taken over everywhere. It's nothing more than an excuse for shopping and showing off.'

'The children like it.' Anna went along with her mother about the commercialisation of Christmas, but she didn't want to show it – agreeing with each other openly had never been a feature of their relationship. She flicked the indicator as the first Argos sign flashed past. Nondas had already disappeared down the slip-road.

Dorothy was rubbing the swollen veins on the back of her hand. 'The Palaiologi are a strange pair,' she said.

'Oh, don't start, Mother,' Anna moaned. 'We get on well enough with them. Nondas and Nikitas are close and Veta ... well, Veta's a major player in the country now and she likes people to be remember that. Otherwise she's all right.'

'For a conservative,' Dorothy said, her tone sharper. 'What would your father say?'

Anna kept her eyes on the road. 'That's all in the past and you know it. Anyway, your friends the Dearfields are going to be there.'

'I wouldn't say Geoff and Flora are exactly friends of mine. They're both pretty unusual too.' She squeezed her hands together. 'I'm half-way through a memoir he's given me and it's ... well,

319

it's very honest. Brutally so. It's making me wonder what kind of man he really is.'

'For goodness' sake,' Anna said, in exasperation. 'Is there no one you get on with?'

'The children,' Dorothy said quietly, after a pause. 'Alex. You, sometimes.'

Anna glanced at her mother, realising she was upset. In the past Dorothy had rarely shown weakness. 'I'm sorry,' she said, touching the older woman's knee. 'It'll be fine, you'll see.'

'Have you heard from Alex?' Dorothy asked, directing her gaze over the mist-covered plain.

Anna shook her head. 'What's he up to?'

Dorothy didn't reply, keeping her son's last call to herself and wondering whether he'd already gone down to the Mani to see Kostas Laskaris. The old poet was ailing. She'd have liked to see him one more time – he and Spyros had been through a lot together. The passing of her husband's friends and comrades distressed her, but in a strange way it also brought her dear one back from the darkness for a while. She'd have liked to ask Kostas about Andonis. Her elder son had said he was going to see Laskaris the month before he disappeared, though he'd told her never to mention the trip to anyone. She had followed his instruction, even keeping it from Alex when he grew up and started looking for his brother. She had never felt happy about that. There was something about Andonis when he returned, a strange emptiness in his eyes, that had worried her.

She looked out across the orange groves, suddenly feeling curiously light-headed. Now that her younger son was apparently making the same journey, maybe it was time to break that promise. If Alex appeared at the Palaiologos house, she'd find the opportunity to tell him. That way Christmas away from home might be worthwhile after all.

13

Grace drove down the rutted track towards the sea. Kostas Laskaris's renovated war tower stood out on the low ridge like a solitary cypress pointing the way to heaven. She stopped where they'd parked the last time.

'Probably someone out hunting,' Mavros said, nodding at the decrepit red Lada down near the gate that separated them from the Tigani peninsula.

'Hunting?' Grace asked, as she pulled on her fleece. 'What for?'

'Anything that moves.' Mavros had never been keen on the way rural Greeks treated wildlife. Even tiny songbirds were slaughtered, although down here the land gave its people so little that any supplement to the sparse diet was understandable, at least in the past.

'Goats?' Grace said, as she locked her door.

'Sure,' he replied. 'If they belong to someone else. What do you think the feuds were about in the old days?'

They walked up the slope to the poet's house. The clouds were even denser on the mountains now, the air fresh and still. Mavros sniffed. 'I reckon there's snow on the way,' he said. 'That'll make the roads even more of a joy.'

'Don't worry,' Grace said. 'I can handle them if you can't.'

He ignored the irony in her voice and rattled the hand-shaped knocker on the solid wooden door.

'Who is it?' the poet called, after a long pause. His voice sounded weaker than it had on their previous visit.

Mavros identified himself.

'I'm working,' Laskaris said, not opening the door. 'This is not a good time.'

Mavros and Grace exchanged looks. He translated the old man's words for her.

'I must talk to you urgently, Kosta,' Mavros said. 'It's about Babis Dhimitrakos.'

There was silence.

'Babis Dhimitrakos, also known as Odhysseas.'

This time there was a reaction, the bolts being drawn and the key turning. The old man stood in the doorway, his face ashen. 'Who did you say?' he asked, still speaking Greek. His rheumy eyes were fixed on Mavros's face.

'You know who I'm talking about,' Mavros said, switching to English for Grace's benefit. 'Can we come in? It's bitter out here.'

Laskaris admitted them reluctantly. 'I – I don't know any Babis ... what was it? Dhimitrakos?'

Mavros eyed him. 'Don't you? How about Odhysseas? You know who he was, don't you? He was a member of the original Iraklis band.'

'He's dead,' Grace said, moving closer to the old man. 'And the man who chased him up a cliff would have killed us too.'

'Ah.' Laskaris stepped back and Mavros just managed to grab hold of him before he fell against the paper-strewn table. He was panting for breath, his face flushed. Between them, they manoeuvred him on to a chair. Grace fetched a glass of water that the poet gulped down. After a few minutes he had regained his composure, but he didn't speak.

'Listen,' Mavros said, with a warning glance at Grace to keep her quiet. He described what had happened before and after Dhimitrakos's death. 'Randos is dead too,' he added, racking up the pressure.

'I know.' Laskaris swallowed a sob. 'I'll never accept that he killed himself. It must have been an accident.'

Mavros sat down opposite him. 'You don't think Iraklis could have killed him?'

'Why would he?' the old man demanded, his expression suddenly animated. 'My friend the composer was a loyal Party member. He knew nothing about terrorist operations. He was a cultural Communist, not a fighter on the street or an organiser.'

'But you were an organiser, Kosta, weren't you?' Mavros said quietly. 'You knew Dhimitrakos, didn't you?'

After a while Laskaris nodded. 'Of course I knew him. But before he joined the Iraklis group. I recruited him. His family was from Kitta.'

'We know that,' Grace said. 'What about Kolettis, the man who became Iraklis?'

The poet shook his head at her.

'When did you last see Dhimitrakos?' Mavros asked.

'Decades ago.' The poet's eyes were down again. 'He was expelled from the Party along with everyone else in the group in the early seventies. I heard he was broken by the other side, that he betrayed his leader.' He looked up. 'You think Iraklis tracked him down? Well, he had good reason. But who was the man who saved you?' He seemed confused.

Mavros looked at Grace. 'Do you not think the terrorist might come looking for you too, Kosta?'

'Me?' Laskaris's eyes were wide. 'Why would he come looking for me?'

'Maybe he's afraid that someone will reveal his identity.'

'I told you. I know nothing about that. He was Iason Kolettis when I first encountered him in Athens. That was an assumed name, of course. No, he has no reason to visit me.' The words were definite enough, but there was a hint of doubt in his tone. 'Besides, you said it yourself – Dhimitrakos could have died of a heart-attack before he fell. He had a history of them, did he not?'

Mavros wondered how he knew that. Local gossip, or had he seen the ex-terrorist more recently than he'd admitted?

'The man who was after him would have killed us if he hadn't been scared off,' Grace said. 'And we didn't even know Dhimitrakos. What makes you safe from him?'

Laskaris looked at her, his lips apart, then moved his head back in a negative gesture. 'I think you are just trying to frighten me,' he said, glancing at Mavros. 'Both of you. I've already told you, I know nothing that can lead you to Iraklis.'

'He slaughtered my father in front of me,' Grace said, bending over the old man. 'You were in the war. Did you never lose anyone you loved?' He grimaced. 'Yes, you know how it feels. Help me, please. I only want to understand why my father had to die the way he did.'

Kostas Laskaris blinked, then coughed. 'You're right,' he said, his voice almost inaudible. 'I know how it feels.' He looked into her eyes. 'Yes, it's too late for lies. There is ... there is something I can tell you.'

Mavros was studying him, trying to work out whether the poet was being straight with them. His limbs were slack, as if the tension resulting from years of self-imposed silence had finally been loosed.

'I do know something that might help you.' He met Mavros's eyes without wavering. 'I ... I didn't want to mention it before because the person concerned is very old.' He gave a thin smile. 'Even older than me.'

Grace took the old man's scrawny wrist. 'Tell us,' she said, her voice hard. 'Tell us what you know.'

Laskaris froze, then swallowed. 'I will, young woman. As soon as you release me.' He looked at her ruefully. 'You are very strong.'

'Yeah. I'm also very impatient.'

Mavros twitched his head at her and she sat back.

'Very well,' Laskaris said. 'There is a woman, a long-standing Party member who the man known as Iason Kolettis was linked to in the past.'

'Was linked to,' Grace repeated. 'What does that mean?'

The old man stared at her, then dropped his gaze. 'I think ... I mean, I know ... that she was his mother.'

'What?' Grace jumped to her feet, knocking over her chair.

Mavros raised his hand. 'Hold it,' he said, inclining his head towards the poet. 'What's her name?' he asked quietly. 'Where can we find her?'

Laskaris took a deep breath. 'Stamatina Kastania,' he said. 'That is her husband's surname. Even though we fought in the same ELAS band, I never knew her family name. She lives in Nafplion in Argolidha now.'

Mavros stared at him, still unsure how much to believe. 'When was the last time you were in contact with her, Kosta?'

The old man held his gaze. 'A week ago. I called her from Athens.'

'A week ago?' Grace said, her voice taut. 'I don't suppose you asked her if she had heard from her son recently?'

'Actually, I did. And she had. She said she was expecting to see him before Christmas.'

Mavros caught Grace's eye. He was wondering whether to believe the old Communist. The admission concerning the most wanted man in the country was so unexpected that he was almost convinced by it. 'Kosta, why should we believe you now?' he asked, trying to drive out his remaining doubts. 'You kept things from us the last time we were here. You said you didn't know anything about Kolettis.'

Grace was still standing. 'For all we know you might be expecting him to show up here any minute. You might be sending us on a wild-goose chase.'

The poet frowned, unsure what she meant. 'You are welcome to stay,' he said, 'though you will be wasting your time and I will not be good company. I must keep working on my poem, I must finish it before the pain finishes me. It is like a good Party member – it never gives up the struggle.'

'Is there anything we can do?' Mavros asked.

Laskaris shook his head. 'I advise you to go to Kyra Stamatina without delay. She too is unwell. And it is only three days until the proto-Marxist Jesus Christ's birthday, is it not?'

Mavros remembered that his mother and sister would be in Argolidha by now. The Palaiologos house was only a few kilometres from Nafplion. 'I hope we can trust you, Kosta,' he said. 'This is very important for Grace.'

'It is very important for you too, my boy,' Laskaris said, switching to Greek. 'You see, your brother stayed with Stamatina after he met Iason Kolettis here in November 1972.'

Mavros's heart pounded. Andonis had forced his way into the case again and he didn't know if he could handle it. At least he had no choice about what to do next. 'I presume Stamatina Kastania's number is in the phone book,' he said in English, standing up and taking in the poet's affirmative head movement. 'Come on, Grace.'

'What?' she said, glancing at the old man. 'What did he say to you? Do you trust him?'

328

Mavros looked at Laskaris once more, then beckoned to her. 'I trust him.' He turned to the door. 'Good luck with the poem, Kosta,' he said, over his shoulder. He didn't expect to see the old man again, and that hurt – he had been a comrade of his father, even though they had fallen out in the sixties. There wasn't time to ask what had caused their disagreement. Andonis was the priority now, Andonis and the man he had met down here nearly thirty years ago.

Grace caught up with him outside. The first snowflakes were floating down, obscuring the ruined walls at the end of the peninsula.

'Are you buying this?' she demanded. 'Don't you think we should wait here for Iraklis? He's probably close behind us.'

'That's what I'm worried about,' Mavros said, walking down the slope to the car. 'You said it yourself. It'll be better to meet the terrorist in a less out-of-the-way place. His mother lives in a large town.' He glanced at her. 'And he's hardly likely to use his weapon on us in front of her.'

'Maybe he's already here,' she said, looking down the track. 'Maybe that's his car.' She pointed. 'Where's it gone?'

The red Lada was no longer where it had been in front of the gate.

Mavros held out his hand for the keys to the Fiat. 'If that was him – and I don't think it's too likely that he goes around in a clapped-out heap, even a Soviet one – he's gone now. Anyway, you stay if you want. I'm going to Nafplion.'

'What did Laskaris say to you at the end, Alex?' Grace asked, keeping hold of the keys.

He told her about Andonis.

'Is this my case or yours?' she asked.

Mavros shrugged. 'I'll quit if you want. I believe the old man. He's dying. All he cares about is his poem. He's not going to tell us anything else, even if he knows more about Kolettis. But the terrorist's mother, she's a different story. Especially if he's going to visit her.'

'And especially if she knows something about your brother.' Grace handed him the keys. 'All right, we'll stick together. But you'd better be right. And I hope you can handle the car in this weather.'

'Of course I can.' Mavros glanced around the bushes, listening out for shotgun fire to confirm that the driver of the Lada really was a hunter who had moved elsewhere. There was none. After a few moments he got into the Fiat.

It was time to head north, into the storm.

'That was a very good lunch, Veta,' Dorothy Cochrane-Mavrou said, folding up her napkin.

The hostess smiled. 'Thank you. My chef used to work on one of my father's cruise ships. He's been with us for years.'

'Costs us a fortune,' her husband muttered, provoking a smile from Nondas Chaniotakis.

'Stop complaining, Nikita,' Veta said sharply. 'Who would like coffee?'

'I'm sure the kids have things they want to do,' Anna said, shooing her two away from the table with rapid movements of her fingers. 'They seem to have been adversely affected by the journey down.' Her children had been stifling giggles all

330

through the meal, egged on by Veta's pair, who were painfully spoiled, their manners already the subject of muted comments from Dorothy. 'I'd love some coffee.'

'Please excuse me, Veta,' Dorothy said. 'I'm going to lie down for an hour.'

Geoffrey Dearfield pulled himself to his feet. 'I will, too, if you don't mind. I didn't have a good night.'

The others watched them follow the whooping children from the dining-room, Flora giving her husband a curious look.

'I don't know what's got into Geoff recently,' she said, her hands spread wide. 'Most of the time he's in another world.'

'Senility,' said Nikitas Palaiologos. 'My old man was the same and so was my father-in-law.'

'Don't be so disloyal,' Veta said sternly. 'Both our fathers went through times in their lives that haunted them to the end.'

'How do you mean?' Anna asked, picking up the scent of a story but trying to disguise her interest. 'Oh, the Axis occupation, I suppose.' She knew that the Dhragoumis and Palaiologos families had begun to build up their wealth during the war.

'The occupation and the civil war,' Nikitas said, ignoring his wife's disapproving expression. She didn't like harking back to what she called 'the savage years'. 'They taught those Communist bastards a lesson they didn't forget.'

'Nikita,' Nondas murmured, the chewing-gum that he'd opened as soon as the meal was over lodged in his cheek. 'Anna's father.'

Their bald-headed host's eyes sprang open. 'Oh, sorry. I forgot that some of us come from left-wing families.' He didn't sound contrite. 'They took my uncle and aunt hostage in Athens, the ELAS butchers – after the fighting in December 'forty-four. And do you know what they did? They marched them through the snow for days, then cut their throats.'

Anna watched as Veta glared at him. 'Really?' she said quietly. 'That's terrible. But I don't follow my father's beliefs.' She looked across the table at him. 'Tell me, Nikita, is it true that your father sold produce that he confiscated from the families of EAM/ELAS members to the Germans and Italians at high profit?'

There was an icy silence as the sepulchral butler filled their coffee cups.

'For God's sake, Anna,' Nondas said, when the servant had gone.

Nikitas laughed. 'Don't worry, my friend. I'm not ashamed of what the old man did.' He looked at his wife. 'Veta's father worked the market too, but she doesn't like talking about it.'

The Member of Parliament got up. 'Let's take our coffee into the lounge, ladies,' she said. 'The men will no doubt welcome an opportunity to talk about important affairs.' She moved away without waiting.

Anna raised an eyebrow at her husband and followed, Flora bringing up the rear.

'Sorry about that, Nikita,' Nondas said, 'but you did ask for it. Anna's pretty easy-going about politics, but sometimes she has to stick up for the side her father was on.'

'Anna's all right,' Nikitas said, filling a brandy glass and shoving the decanter towards the Cretan, 'unlike that brother of hers. What's his name? Alex? I only met him once, at that party you gave a couple of years back, but he struck me as a long-haired layabout. Didn't he kill someone on that island?'

'No, he didn't,' Nondas replied. 'That was a massive case, the one on Trigono, and Alex cracked it on his own.' He helped himself to brandy. 'Be careful if you ever find him on your tail.'

Nikitas wasn't paying attention. 'I don't regret what the old men did,' he said, his fingers gripping the glass tightly. 'I admire them. They were monarchists, true patriots. They knew that the mob only understands one thing and that's violence. I wish the fools in Veta's party could get that into their heads.'

Nondas looked at his friend. 'It wasn't only the Right that followed that line in the past. What about the terrorists who were operating at the end of the dictatorship? Take the Iraklis group. All they wanted to do was kill their enemy. Now it seems they're back, but they're not interested in politicians any more. They're choosing targets from the business community. How does that make you feel? I can tell you, I'm shitting myself. I've got a wife I love, kids...'

Nikitas Palaiologos looked out of the windows to the wire fence beyond the garden. A security man in a Kevlar vest was on patrol. 'How does that make me feel? Not very happy. But at least we can afford to pay for protection.'

Nondas swallowed the vintage Cognac. Given that he'd brought his family to stay in the Palaiologos house, he hoped the fruit and canning magnate was right.

Above them, in the sumptuously furnished bedroom she'd been given, Dorothy Cochrane-Mavrou was sitting at the dressing-table, her hand resting on a thick typescript. 'This is not a good time, Geoff,' she said. 'I still have the last section of your memoir to read. Can't we talk about it tomorrow? In the morning, when the others go on Flora's tour of Tiryns?'

Dearfield was pacing up and down the broad room, his worn brogues sinking into the pile of a fine Persian carpet. 'All right, Dorothy. I'm sorry, but I have to know what you think. I have to know that you'll publish my memoir.'

She looked at him thoughtfully. 'And I have to read the full script.' She gave him a brief smile. 'Anyway, I don't usually respond in person. I wait until I am ready and then I send the author a letter.'

'But, Dorothy,' Dearfield said, desperation in his voice, 'you've had it for nearly a month. For God's sake, you must know whether it's of interest.' He came over to her and looked at her beseechingly. 'You're my only hope. No one in the UK will take on such a challenging book.'

'It's certainly written in a very ... how can I describe it? A very intemperate style, Geoff. For goodness' sake, stop marching up and down like a guardsman and leave me to finish it.'

Dearfield gave her a last look, his face

contorted, then went out of the bedroom. Dorothy took her page-marker from the script.

Mavros drove back past Areopolis, the lights of the town glowing in the premature gloom that the snowclouds had brought. Grace checked the distance and told him that they should be in Nafplion by early evening – if the roads weren't affected too much by the weather. As they went up the road that had been cut into the steep slope of Kouskouni, the peak's summit lost in a blur of grey and white, he realised how vulnerable they were to the elements.

'Are you all right with this? We could hole up in Yithion and wait for the blizzard to pass.'

Grace's eyes were on the road. 'This is no problem so far. I want to get to the terrorist's mother before he gets to us.'

He glanced at her. 'There's a lot of high ground between Sparta and Tripoli. Maybe we should buy snow chains when we stop for petrol.'

'They sell snow chains around here?'

'Taygetos is over seven thousand feet. You think snow is unusual?'

She smiled. 'No, I suppose not. It's just that I have this childhood vision of Greece as a land of burning sunlight.'

'Yet another only partially correct myth.'

Grace tensed as Mavros slowed behind a lorry showing no lights, then accelerated round it. 'Here's another,' she said. 'The US is a wicked imperialist state that tells smaller ones what to do.'

Mavros laughed. 'That's a myth, is it?' When

she stiffened he raised his hand to placate her. 'Anyway, why don't we talk about a figure from ancient myth?'

'Let me guess. You wouldn't by any chance be referring to Hercules, would you? I mean Iraklis. Why can't you guys call people by their real names?'

'Good question.' He looked out into the snow. The flakes were almost overwhelming the Fiat's feeble wipers. 'What's the assassin's real name? It's not Kolettis and it's not Kastanias, you can be sure of that. He's been covering his identity very successfully for decades. So how do we get beneath the layers of deception?'

'By asking his mother?'

'I think you can assume that, since the secret's been kept for decades, the old woman Stamatina is well versed in the arts of deception. The old poet said she was in ELAS. Maybe she taught her son all he knows.'

Grace was staring at him. 'We should have kept on at Laskaris. He knows who the killer is, I'm sure of it.'

'Shit!' Mavros jerked back in his seat as a dark form swooped down in front of the windscreen.

'What the hell was that?' Grace gasped.

'Bird of prey, I think,' he replied, trying to get his breathing under control. 'A buzzard, probably. When the visibility drops they come looking for prey.'

'As in a wing and a prayer?' Grace quipped.

'Very funny.' He looked at her, her face given a weird hue by the dashboard light. 'Forget Laskaris. He's said all he's going to say. We were lucky to get this much out of him.' He peered out into the flurries of snow, which were thickening. 'There are more people than Iraklis involved in this, Grace. Who was on our tail in Athens? I suppose it could have been the terrorist group, but there are other more likely suspects.'

'The Greek equivalent of the FBI?'

'There's a high-profile anti-terrorist squad,' Mavros agreed. 'That's what I thought initially. But why?' He turned his eyes on her again. 'It all comes back to you, Grace. We first spotted a tail when we went to see Randos. Why were they following us then?' He hadn't forgotten the points he found suspicious about her: her presence at the concert hall after the explosion, her extreme physical fitness, her attempted seduction of him, and her familiarity with investigative and undercover techniques – in the valley where Dhimitrakos died, she hadn't been disturbed by their assailant and the subsequent gunfire.

She held her gaze on the road. 'The embassy could have put them on to me via that police commander Kriaras.'

'Exactly,' he agreed. 'Because of your father, supposedly.'

This time she turned to him. 'Yes.' She looked puzzled. 'Why else, Alex?'

'You wouldn't by any chance be working for a certain secretive government agency based in Langley, Virginia, would you?'

Grace was silent for a few seconds, then she laughed. 'Are you serious? Me, work for the CIA? They've spent years getting exactly nowhere in the hunt for the man who killed my father. You're crazy if you think I'm one of them.'

Mavros was still looking at her. 'So they haven't assigned you to hire me and make use of my contacts?'

'No, they haven't,' she said, her voice rising. 'For God's sake, Alex, what kind of a guy are you? I've shown you my mother's last letter, I've shared everything with you. Christ, I even began to fall for you, though that was a big mistake.' She shook off the hand he'd put on her arm and swivelled round, clutching for her bag. 'Here,' she said, taking a card from her wallet. 'Call my employers and ask them about me.'

He glanced at the embossed rectangle of paper she was holding up and shook his head. 'I've already seen your picture on the organisation's web-site. But that doesn't mean you aren't an undercover operative.'

'Call them,' she repeated. 'Ask them what I've been doing for the last five years. You'll find that there hasn't been much time for playing James frigging Bond.' She looked away into the snow.

'If your cover's any good, all I'll hear will be well-rehearsed lies,' Mavros said, keeping the pressure on her.

Her shoulder was turned away from him. 'I suppose you think that what I did last night was part of my orders too,' she said. 'Jesus, you–'

'Maybe the guy who saved us was one of yours,' he interrupted, eyes on the road.

Grace shifted round towards him. 'Christ, you've been reading too many bullshit thrillers, Alex. You really think I've got a guardian angel looking out for my ass? Anyway, if he was one of ours, why didn't he take Iraklis out when he had the chance?'

Mavros couldn't think of an answer to that.

Soon afterwards they came down into the wooded plain under the old castle of Passava, the road surface clearing as they approached sea level.

'Anyway,' Mavros said, picking up his train of thought, 'let's say the Greeks and maybe the Americans are after us. Why? Because they expect us to lead them to the assassin?'

'Maybe it's more complicated than that,' Grace said. 'Maybe there are other people involved.'

'What do you mean?'

'I don't know,' she said, rubbing her forehead in irritation. 'Maybe things are out of control and nobody really knows what's going on.'

'That's a reassuring thought,' Mavros said. Then his face darkened as he looked into the mirror. 'Whoever they are, it's a fair assumption that at least one of them is on our tail. We haven't got much chance of evading them in this car. Maybe it's time for me to call Nikos Kriaras and tell him what we know.'

'No!' Grace grabbed his upper arm. 'No, Alex. Not yet.' She loosened her grip. 'At least wait till we speak to the terrorist's mother.'

He nodded slowly, still unsure of her motives.

Mavros filled up with petrol and picked up snow chains in a garage on the outskirts of Yithion. While he was paying he caught the weather forecast on the television. It would be touch and go. Some mountain villages in the northern Peloponnese were already cut off. He considered looking for a place to hire a four-by-four, but reckoned he'd be lucky to find any such establishment open in the winter. Besides, leaving the Fiat down here would get him into trouble with the dubious operator in Corinth who had rented it to him.

They swapped drivers. The road from Yithion to Sparta wasn't too difficult as it traversed a low plain, but north of the Lakonian capital things got trickier. The highway traversing the Kleisoura Pass had recently been upgraded, its bends and ascents well engineered. That was just as well because the snow had been falling heavily on the stony heights and driving conditions were worsening. Grace coped without complaint, only shaking her head when fools in fast cars overtook the Fiat. As they approached Tripolis, Mavros tried to persuade her that staying the night there would be sensible.

'Forget it,' she said firmly. 'You said these conditions are expected to prevail for the next couple of days. I want to get there tonight.'

'Okay, but I'm going to drive for a bit.'

'Are you sure you're up to it?' Grace asked, with a hint of a smile.

'As soon as I have any doubt, I'll give you back the wheel,' he replied, unamused.

They exchanged seats on the Tripolis bypass. The small Fiat was handling surprisingly well on the mushy surface and they made reasonable time up the snaking road that led into Argolidha. He had considered going the long way round, following the motorway to the north, but had

340

decided it wasn't a better option – it climbed to a tunnel high on Mount Artemision and there was even more danger of disruption.

They progressed slowly but surely towards the Gulf of Argos, following the tail-lights of a lorry. There were few cars on the road now and there was no sign of anyone keeping their distance behind. Mavros was having to blink all the time as the wipers fought with the snow. Then the lights ahead vanished. He remembered a drive on this road with some friends during the summer vacation when he was a student – it had brought his heart to his mouth.

'Oh, shit,' he said, his knuckles white as he gripped the wheel.

'What is it?' Grace asked.

'Nothing,' he muttered, and embarked on the series of hairpin bends, nothing other than white flakes to be seen. He recalled the spectacular view across the bay to Nafplion and the mountains beyond, islands as far as Spetses to the south-east floating on the rippled dark blue. After a while he lost track of time, and found himself back in his childhood on a beach somewhere. His mother was reading a typescript under pine trees whose molten sap tickled his nostrils. Anna was playing with her dolls in the shade nearby and he was scrambling up a low rock face, head back as he looked into his brother's smiling face above. Andonis had disappeared the following winter, but he had never really left Mavros – and now there was a chance that he might at last discover what happened to his brother.

Mavros forced himself to concentrate on the

341

road. At last it levelled out. He drove along the last stretch to the sea and turned left towards Argos. The snow was much less dense now they were at sea level and the asphalt was wet rather than layered in white. Then he caught sight of a sign to Lerni and his heart thudded. Lerni, ancient Lerna, was where Iraklis, helped by his comrade Iolaos, had conquered the Hydra. They had reached the home territory of the ancient hero.

Iraklis drove slowly down the track and parked the Citroën below Kostas Laskaris's war tower. When he got out, he squatted down and examined the tyre tracks, recognising them as fresh despite the sprinkling of snow that lay on the ground. Then he walked down towards the gate and looked out towards the promontory of Tigani, remembering the meeting he had out there with Andonis Mavros. So many years ago, but suddenly it was clear in his mind again. He noticed different tracks in the mud there before he walked back to the tower.

The old poet admitted him as soon as he heard his voice. They greeted each other formally, then sat on either side of the blazing fire at the end of the long hall. They had much to discuss after so many years – the murders in Athens that had been designed to look like Iraklis red deaths, Babis Dhimitrakos, the visits of Alex Mavros and Trent Helmer's daughter. Kostas Laskaris looked worn and exhausted, lacking the sharp wit and quick tongue that Iraklis remembered, though their last meeting had been a long time ago. He said he was writing his final poem, the one that posterity would remember him by; the one that would finally set straight the record of the struggle after so many wrong turnings and obfuscations.

'I can't believe that Randos is dead,' the old man said, his voice cracking.

'He will be mourned,' the terrorist agreed.

Laskaris stared at him. 'He is already being mourned by the smart fools in Athens who think they understood him.' Suddenly the passion had returned. 'We were the only ones who could fathom his talent, we who fought alongside him.'

'I don't recall Randos on the street carrying a placard,' Iraklis said ironically. 'Or charging the police lines during the dictatorship.'

'You always had a tendency to cynicism,' the poet complained. 'You wouldn't listen to those who knew better. Randos influenced more ordinary people than you ever did with your killings and your proclamations. Randos was–'

'Let him lie in peace,' the visitor interrupted. Kostas Laskaris was changed. He was evasive, he wouldn't meet his eye. He was obviously failing. 'I must go now. The snow is getting heavy.'

'Tell your mother I was thinking of her,' Laskaris said, struggling to his feet. 'And, Michali?'

Iraklis flinched. It was many years since he'd been addressed by that name, even by his mother.

'Are you still fighting for what your parents believed in?' the old man asked, his eyes on him now, though only briefly. 'Do you remember when I took you to the place of slaughter and told you what we went through?'

Iraklis nodded.

'Your father was a great leader, a hero, Michali. I hope your struggle is the same one that he laboured for. I hope you find out what happened to him at the end.' His voice was almost inaudible. 'But perhaps the time for revenge is over.'

The man who had been Iason Kolettis looked at him. He thought the poet was going to say more, but he slumped down again, his breath rasping in his throat. For a moment he wanted to comfort his father's old comrade, but Kostas's last words had reawoken the doubts that had assailed him. Was he entitled to pursue the families of the people who were responsible for his father's death? Could it be that revenge was no longer justifiable?

'Farewell, comrade,' he said.

Back at the Citroën, Iraklis stood by the door and looked at new footprints that had appeared in the white layer on the ground. Large feet, male, shoes rather than boots. They'd come down the track towards the car, then gone back the same way. He slipped his hand into his coat pocket, removed the automatic and screwed on the silencer. Then he moved slowly back up the road, leaning forward to follow the returning prints. About twenty metres ahead they veered into the side, fallen earth showing that the person had scrambled up the bank and through the line of unkempt bushes. He took a deep breath, pulled up his scarf to cover his nose and mouth, then broke into a run and went up the same way. The bulky figure the terrorist came upon had only managed a few strides across the neighbouring field.

'Hands up, my friend,' he said, pointing the weapon at his prisoner's chest.

'Please, please,' the big man jabbered. 'I'm only hunting.'

'In a snowstorm, without a weapon, wearing city clothes?' Iraklis asked. 'Tell me your name. Better still, give me your ID card.'

The other man obliged, holding his wallet out.

'Pandazopoulos, Yiorgos,' the gunman read. 'What are you doing so far from Athens?' He looked closer at the address on the plastic-covered card. 'You live in Neapolis?' A less fleshy face from the past was flashing up before him. 'Yiorgos Pandazopoulos,' he repeated, stepping closer and examining the other man's features. 'Oh, my friend, this is very unfortunate. For you, at least. Turn round.'

'No, please,' the victim gasped. 'Don't hurt me. I don't know who you are. I didn't see your face.'

'But how can I be sure of that, comrade?' Iraklis asked softly. 'How can I trust you?'

When he had finished with the fat man, he went back down the slope to the Citroën and drove away. By the time he got to Areopolis the weather had closed in completely. The drive to Yithion was almost impossible, the big car slipping and sliding like a bar of soap. Before he reached the port on the eastern side of the mountains, he'd decided what to do. He was lucky. Beyond the main harbour road he found a new Suzuki off-road vehicle. There was no one around in the early-evening chill. It took him only a short time to open the door and start the engine, glad that the skills he'd learned decades ago were still with him. He left the Citroën where he'd parked it on the seafront road. He'd worn gloves all the time when he'd been driving and he wasn't worried about the hire company: the false identity and the credit card that came with it would stop them in their tracks, and he'd be surprised if the clerk remembered anything specific about his appearance.

Iraklis set off up the Sparta road, having bought a set of snow chains from the garage where he filled up with petrol. With any luck he'd be across the mountains and into Argolidha before the night was over. Then he'd be able to concentrate on the mission.

It was time he paid more attention to the people who had drawn him back to his native land. Soon all the debts that had been building up for years would be repaid in full. Kostas Laskaris was wrong about revenge. The old poet should have known better. He had forgotten the traditions of the Mani. Family honour could never be forgotten.

But he needed to hold his nerve. Otherwise the pallid features of the woman he'd loved, the woman whose name he couldn't speak, would drag him into the abyss before his time.

14

Mavros and Grace reached Nafplion around ten o'clock, the lights on the crag behind the town forming a beacon that drew them round the curve of the bay.

'What is that place?' she asked.

'The Venetian fortress of Palamidhi,' Mavros replied. He remembered climbing a tortuous and thigh-cracking staircase to reach it when he was a student. 'It was supposedly impregnable. Latterly they used it as a prison.'

'You know all the good stuff from Greek history, don't you?' she said ironically.

'Isn't your country the world leader in incarceration?'

'Yeah, yeah.'

The streets were unusually wide for a Greek town, the open spaces filled with trees. They found a reasonable-looking hotel and parked on the street in front of it. They were given the keys to adjoining rooms on the first floor and agreed to meet in half an hour. Mavros went back downstairs. He found a local phone directory in a booth in the reception hail. As Laskaris had said, 'Kastania, Stamatina' was listed. He took a note of the number and the address. The man at the desk gave him a photocopied town map and he located the street without difficulty – Potamianou was only a few minutes' walk.

When they met up, Mavros led Grace into the old section of the town, the buildings crammed up against the northern slopes of Akronafplia, the town's lower hill. Christmas decorations and lights had been strung everywhere. He wanted to see the street where Kyra Stamatina lived. That was easy enough. It turned out to be a stepped lane leading up from a small square with a church at the far end.

'This is Saint Spiridhon,' Grace said, holding the guidebook in the glow from a street-lamp. 'Apparently Greece's first president was murdered here in 1831.'

'That's right. Capodhistrias. He was assassinated by a pair of brothers from the Mani, would you believe?'

Grace narrowed her eyes. 'Shot and stabbed, it says here, by kinsmen of the great Petrobey Mavromichalis.' She looked up. 'Wasn't that the guy whose statue we saw in Areopolis?'

'You have been paying attention.'

'Iraklis is keeping their murderous tradition alive.'

He took in the tension in her face. 'That's the street where the old woman lives.'

She looked up the precipitous steps. 'Shall we go and knock on her door?'

'Not now. She's probably in bed. Let's go and eat. We can talk over dinner.'

There was a taverna open on the street below the church and they were ushered in by an obsequious waiter. Although the place was almost empty, there was a good selection of food. They settled on a platter of *mezedhes* and half a

348

grilled chicken. The waiter claimed the owner's wine was good so Mavros ordered a carafe, his expectations low. It turned out to be a subtle, unresinated white that went well with the assorted starters.

'All right,' Grace said, after he had refilled her glass. 'Where do we go from here? Iraklis–' She broke off and looked around. There was no one nearby, the waiter standing in the middle of the street trying to snare the few people who were about on the cold evening. 'The assassin might be here already, Alex. Why are we waiting?'

He put down his glass. 'He might be. Laskaris said he was going to visit the old woman before Christmas so there are another three days to go. Even if he's here, if he was the one coming for us with the gun, he'll only just have made it.'

'Maybe he's watching us,' she said, peering out into the street.

'In which case going to his mother's place will make him even more likely to attack.' He shrugged. 'I don't want to rush in. The chances are that the old woman will be even harder to break down than Kostas Laskaris and this time I haven't got a family connection to smooth the way.' He looked across the table at her. 'Kyra Stamatina is our trump card. He doesn't know that we know about her.'

'Unless the old poet's told him,' Grace responded. 'I don't trust Laskaris. He knows more than he said.'

'But he told us about the terrorist's mother,' Mavros countered. 'I should already have handed this whole case over to the police. They'll cut my head off if anything drastic happens because of what we've kept from them.'

Grace was staring at him. 'You're not going to do that, Alex,' she said, sliding her hand over his. 'What about your brother? You're not going to miss this chance to find out what happened to him.'

He couldn't argue with that. He'd glanced at the newspapers on a *periptero* on the way from the hotel. The government was still pretending that things were under control, but it was easy enough to discern the panic beneath the surface. The police had made no progress with the terrorist murders – the Iraklis proclamation Bitsos had told him about after the explosion that killed Stasinopoulos in the concert hall had been made public; and they were adamant, at least in public, that no one else had been involved in Randos's death. There was nothing he could tell them now that would get them any further with that. If he told them that Iraklis's mother lived in Nafplion and was expecting him before Christmas, the anti-terrorist squad would turn the town into a no-go area and the assassin would stay away. That might save Mavros and Grace from further attack, but it would put Iraklis beyond their reach, probably permanently.

'So what do we do?' Grace asked, picking up a piece of *kalamari* with her fork.

Mavros ran his fingers across the stubble on his chin. 'Can you draw?' he asked. 'Or paint?' He had remembered her mother's talent in that field.

'What? Yeah, I can sketch fairly well. My Ganma insisted I took lessons, even though my mother wasn't interested in me following in her footsteps.'

'Okay,' Mavros said. 'Here's what we'll do.' He leaned forward and started to speak in a low voice.

Kostas Laskaris tried to concentrate, his head bowed over the table. The terrorist's second visit had troubled him more than the first, the blood on his gloves a reminder of the savage struggle he was involved in. He wished he'd had the courage to ask Iraklis what had happened to Andonis Mavros after their meeting down on the promontory all those years ago. But there had always been silences between them, since the time when Iraklis was a boy and Laskaris had kept a watchful eye over him at his grandmother's house in Kitta. Even now, the assassin hadn't asked him about his father, hadn't gone over the last time the poet had seen Kapetan Iraklis in the war. And now Laskaris had put Alex Mavros and the American woman on to Stamatina. What had possessed him? Some irrational guilt about the brother who had disappeared? It was all too late, all futile.

Although he didn't have the energy to climb to the room at the top of the tower – the pain in his belly was such that he could hardly even get to the toilet on the ground floor – the inert body that had been dragged up there was making him feel like a stranger in his own home. When would the struggle be over? he asked himself, no sound coming from his chapped lips. He clenched his fists and forced himself back to the war. To the time in early 1944 when there was still a sliver of hope...

Kapetan Iraklis and his band of ELAS fighters undertook many labours in Lakonia in the final winter of the occupation. As the Germans' grip on the Peloponnese loosened, the guerrillas came down from the mountain, confining the occupiers and the collaborationist Security Battalions to the main towns. There were several skirmishes around Sparta, culminating in a bloody assault on the medieval fortified town of Mystras where detachments of the enemy were holed up.

The poet groaned when he thought of the battle. He didn't know it at the time, but that was when the last innocence was burned from his soul: it had risen up into the still air with the cordite fumes and the smoke from the grenade blasts that hung in a black cloud against the snow on Taygetos's upper flanks.

'Come, Kosta,' Iraklis said, with a wide smile, from the line of trees beneath the lower gate of the old enclosure. 'It is time for you to be my faithful helper again.'

'How many more times must I perform that role, my captain?' he asked, unable to resist returning the smile, then ducking his head as a burst of machine-gun fire ricocheted from the track a few metres in front of them.

'Not many,' Iraklis replied, his wispy beard filled with shreds of vegetation from the crawl they had made through the undergrowth. There were also breadcrumbs from the hurried meal they had taken in the village below. He glanced along the line of fighters, their tattered uniforms supplemented with sheepskins and scarves they'd been handed by sympathetic locals. 'Comrade Stamatina, Comrade Dino, are you ready?'

The hard-faced woman nodded as she slipped off the safety catch of the machine pistol she had taken from a dead German. 'Ready, my captain.' Her expression lightened for a moment as she caught his eye.

'Me too,' said the youth, his cheeks rosy and smooth but his eyes glinting mercilessly. They had seen many horrors since the massacre at the place of slaughter. He was clutching a British Army-issue Lee Enfield, a well-honed bayonet fixed beneath the rifle's muzzle.

Iraklis took in the rest of the unit, some behind him and others lined up to the north and south to stretch the defenders. Then he leaned across and squeezed Kostas's arm. 'Courage, my friend. We will prevail.' He smiled again, then raised his arm, stood up and shouted the advance. His cry was repeated by all the fighters.

The poet couldn't remember the latter part of the battle. Usually he could recall every scene, every enemy he had encountered, every man he had killed. But this time was different, this time the blood-lust rained over him in a red deluge and he became a heartless killer. Because Iraklis was hit in the first moments of the assault on the gate, his upper body jerking back like a marionette's before he crumpled to the ground.

'I'm all right,' he yelled, getting back to his feet before anyone could reach him, a dark stain spreading across his right shoulder. 'To the walls,

353

comrades.' And he staggered onwards, firing his Schmeisser with his left hand, shoving away any fighter who tried to help him.

Kostas Laskaris lost his hearing, the sound of gunfire and the shell blasts disappearing from his ears to be replaced by a loud rushing like the sea breaking over sharp rocks. He got to the barricaded gate, the grenade that looped from his arm blowing a hole in the old wood. A helmeted German's face dissolved in a spray of red when he pressed the trigger of his submachine-gun. He saw Dinos dash ahead of him, hacking through the debris with his bayonet and breaking the first line of defence. Then Stamatina was at his side, her lips drawn back to reveal blackened teeth. They cleared the gate together and found Dinos standing over a battalionist in a kilt, repeatedly burying the bayonet in his fellow countryman's chest.

Stamatina slapped his arm and pointed ahead to show him there were plenty more to be dealt with. Then a gash suddenly opened up on the left side of her face, blood welling like a mountain spring. Her eyes met the poet's for a second, then she stormed on, firing from the hip. The walls and buildings of the medieval town were lined with enemy soldiers, the flash of their guns lighting up the drab stonework. He looked back and saw Iraklis standing by the gate, his head against its shattered post. His *kapetanios* waved him on with his good arm. Then Kostas Laskaris was consumed by the slaughter.

He came back to himself in the late afternoon, sitting beneath a large, open-roofed ruin that must once have been a palace. He blinked and took in the grey sky and the skeins of cloud high above, then realised he could hear again. Small birds were chirping outside the old building and there was no sound of gunfire. He got to his feet unsteadily and walked outside, his weapon in his hand. When he checked it, he realised that the magazine was empty, as were his pockets and belt pouches. His Italian Army revolver had been completely discharged too.

'Bravo, Comrade Kosta. You survived.'

He turned his head and saw Dinos running down from a red-tiled church. Floating above him was the curved wall of the fortress on the summit of the hill. In one hand was his rifle and in the other a bulging, discoloured sack.

'What's in there, Dino?' he asked, suddenly aware that he was desperately hungry. 'Something to eat?'

The youth stopped beside him and opened the sack. 'No,' he said, with a grimace. 'I found these in the stinking collaborators' command post. They must be our boys.'

The poet had swallowed back bile as he made out a pair of severed heads with black hair. 'Take them to the *kapetanios*,' he said.

'I have already avenged them five times over.' Dinos arched an eyebrow. 'What's the matter? I saw you kill many of the pigs too.'

Laskaris walked away without replying, stopping to retch on to the cobbles. He was thinking of Iraklis's second labour, when the hero had cut off the Hydra's many heads. The myth had become reality, the horror never-ending.

Down at the gate among the corpses he found Comrade Stamatina, a field dressing on her cheek and a wild look in her eyes. She wouldn't speak to him.

'Where's Kapetan Iraklis?' he asked the men by the gate. 'Is he alive?'

They pointed down the track and he ran to the huddle of fighters, pushing his way through them.

'Ah, there you are, Kosta,' Iraklis said. He was propped up against a low wall, a medic working on his shoulder. 'I hoped you would escape unscathed. We have won a great victory.' The group muttered in approval. 'We have driven the enemy from the city that was once a Byzantine stronghold, held by the noble Palaiologi. We have proved ourselves worthy of our ancestors.'

The poet turned away, dread smothering him like a shroud. They had won a victory, but at what cost? They had become monsters, they were no better than the fascist oppressors. What was left of the struggle for a just society?

Shortly afterwards the ELAS band received orders to move to Argolidha. A few days later they heard that the Germans and the Security Battalionists had retaken Mystra.

Mavros stood behind the church of Ayios Spyridhon. In the square beyond, beneath a tall tree with a bust of a local writer, Grace was sitting with her scarf raised over the lower part of her face. They'd been lucky. The skies had cleared and the temperature was considerably higher than it had been yesterday. Walking from the hotel to the town centre earlier, he had seen the snow on the mountains across the bay. The high roads would still be treacherous, but down here by the sea it was almost balmy. Nafplion was a charming town, one of the most beautiful in Greece. By daylight, the fortifications of Palamidhi were even more impressive, the russet-grey walls rising up from the sheer hill like great dams in a complicated geometric arrangement. A partially covered staircase zigzagged up from the huddle of houses in the historical section of the town like a vein through the flank of bare rock. The seafront was that of a working port, cargo vessels alongside loading pallets full of oranges. And out in the bay a small island in the shape of a submarine floated on the bright blue water, its miniature castle – where the Turks had housed their hated executioners – standing up like a conning tower.

Grace leaned forward and shaded in a section of her drawing. At first she had resisted Mavros's demand that she sit drawing in the open air to keep watch on the old woman's street, but he eventually prevailed. He wanted to confirm that she bore the name Kostas Laskaris had attributed to her before he went any further.

Mavros moved round and glanced up the narrow lane. There were fortifications above it, but their warlike appearance was diminished by the multicoloured clothes that had been strung between the houses to dry. Stamatina Kastania lived at number three, but he hadn't been up to examine the door. Better to keep clear in case the assassin was already there, and study everyone who came up or down the steps of Potamianou. So far there had only been a couple of children wrapped up like Michelin men and a young man who gave Grace a shameless stare. The lack of action had given her the opportunity to use the pencil and pad Mavros had bought at a nearby stationery shop lower down, resting her backside on a plastic crate they'd found on the corner.

Mavros watched from the shadows of the church wall. Grace stopped drawing only momentarily when a middle-aged man walked up the street towards the lane. The guy was tall and thin, wearing an expensive green wool coat and a blue sailor's cap. He also had sunglasses over his eyes, which made Mavros suspicious. But the man passed Grace with a nod and a smile, then opened up a shop further on. No dice.

Then Mavros heard a noise from a door half-way up Potamianou. Looking out of the corner of his eye, he saw an old woman in black walk stiffly down the steps. She must once have been tall, but now she was bent, a black scarf over her silver hair. She reached the bottom and stood to catch her breath. Then she hobbled over to Grace and examined her work. *'Ochi poly kalo,'* she said dismissively, and headed down towards the town centre. There was a deep scar on her left cheek.

Mavros swallowed a smile – the judgement was that Grace's drawing wasn't much good – and set off to tail the old woman. Until he returned, his client was on her own.

Flora Petraki-Dearfield looked across the

bedroom at her husband. She could tell that he hadn't slept well. She knew it without taking in his listless form and hanging head: Geoff hadn't had a decent night's sleep since he'd started writing his memoir.

'Come on, you'll miss breakfast,' she said, making her voice as gentle as she could. The fact was that she had lost patience with her husband long ago. She had been young when she met him after the war and although she had never been impressionable – her father's piercing gaze and sharp intelligence had been passed on to her, giving her the ability to see through people and their pretensions within minutes of meeting them – she had realised that the English war hero offered a means of escape from the bitter household she had grown up in. But she hadn't expected Geoff to resign himself to a mediocre position as foreign adviser to a company run by rapacious Greeks after he'd lost his seat at Westminster. It was as if the fight had gone out of him. It was only when he fell in with the Americans in the early sixties that he had found himself again. He had contacts in the intelligence world and in the Greek armed forces from his time as a so-called observer during the civil war, and he had used them to attain an influential behind-the-scenes role before and during the dictatorship. Only recently had she realised how much guilt he had been harbouring about his past.

Dearfield got up, then sat down on the bed in his pyjamas as if exhausted by the effort. 'I don't want anything to eat. If you could ask them to send up a flask of coffee...' He kept his eyes off her. 'I can't face all those people.'

'What did Dorothy say?' Flora asked, stepping closer. 'Is she going to publish your book?' Her husband didn't answer, still avoiding her gaze. 'Geoff,' she said, 'it's all in the past now, it doesn't matter any more. Why don't–'

'Leave me alone,' he interrupted. 'Leave me alone, damn you!'

She jerked back, surprised by his vehemence. 'Very well,' she said.

Down in the dining-room, Anna and Veta were trying to inspire the children, who had stayed up late into the night and resented being forced to sit round the table. There was no sign of Dorothy or of the two husbands.

'My mother is still feeling tired from the drive,' Anna explained, after greetings were exchanged, the women's *'kali mera'* warmer than the children's – they regarded Flora with suspicion because of the impending excursion.

'And our men have gone down to the ships that Nikitas has loading in Nafplion,' Veta said. 'What about Geoff?'

'Working,' Flora said. 'He asked for coffee to be sent up.' As the order was relayed to the impassive butler, she thought about the lie. Her husband's mania with his memoir had shut him off from her, but still she was making excuses for him. The truth was that the book had her in thrall too.

When everyone had finished eating, Veta clapped her hands. 'Right,' she said cheerfully. 'The weather is better today.' She looked out of

360

the window. 'The sun is shining, so we are all going to the ruins as planned. We are fortunate to have an expert in our company. Kyria Flora will be our guide.'

'Wonderful,' Veta's son Prokopis mumbled, glancing at Anna's Lakis for support. 'We were going to play Mythical Monsters on my computer.'

His mother gave him a fierce look. 'I'm sure you'll find out all you need to know about those on our trip.'

Flora smiled at the boy across the array of cereal packets on the table. 'You know that Tiryns was the birthplace of Iraklis, don't you, Prokopi?'

The teenager scowled. 'I thought he was born in Thebes.'

'There are versions of the myth that say that,' she countered patiently, 'but Tiryns is more convincing in my opinion. I'll tell you why when we get down there.'

The children didn't look any more enthusiastic, but Veta and Anna herded them out to get ready. Flora finished her coffee, wondering what she'd let herself in for. Her students at the university were more interested in modern history than the ancient myths, but at least they didn't challenge her so insolently. She checked that she was unobserved, then went into the empty sitting room where she took out her mobile phone, made a call and spoke for a short time. Then she walked out, her face expressionless.

They made the short drive down from the hillside in two cars, Flora taking the sniggering boys in the old Rover and Veta the others in her Land Cruiser. The snow on the peaks of Arkadhia to the south-west was glinting in the sunlight, the sky pale blue, blotched with thinning clouds. From above, the acropolis was an extended oval, like an aged ship whose hull had been battered and broken by the elements. And then, as they came down on to the plain and cut through the orange groves, the vastness of the walls became apparent and any impression of weakness disappeared. The stones of the great fortifications were huge and, even though they hadn't been at their full height for centuries, they still looked impregnable, a bastion against time and decay.

The ticket-seller waved Veta's party through with a subservient smile and Flora led them up the incline to the entrance gate. The initially wide ramp narrowed when it turned back on itself and forced anyone seeking entry into a cramped space between steep walls. Now Prokopis and Lakis were silent. Even the girls curtailed their discussion of pony breeds in the forbidding enclosure. It didn't take much imagination to realise the slaughter that must have taken place here in ancient times, but Flora hammered the point home all the same. In her opinion the young weren't made sufficiently aware of the violence that underpinned so-called civilisation. Then they came up on to the flat floor of the palace, a few lines of low stone being all that remained of the royal chambers.

'In these rooms, if the myth is to be believed,' she said, giving Prokopis a tight smile, 'the great

Peloponnesian hero Iraklis was born. Appropriately enough, you might say, for such a powerful man. For the walls of this fortress were believed to have been built by giants, the one-eyed Cyclops. Only they were capable of lifting such huge rocks. Until the great hero came along.'

'It's amazing,' Anna said. 'How did the real builders manoeuvre the massive stones?'

'They used slaves,' Flora replied tersely. 'The Mycenaean regime was an élite military one, based on subjection and coercion. The ordinary people lived on the plain around the citadel, unprotected from any sudden attack.'

Veta laughed, her cheeks still red from the effort of hauling her bulk up the ramp. 'You're almost sounding like a socialist, Flora.'

The older woman pursed her lips. 'I'm a historian. I've always been fascinated by the interaction between society and myth. As you should know, Veta, politics is no less subject to mythology than any other area of human endeavour.'

The children shuffled away, bored by the exchange.

'Before we go down to see the wonderful vaults with their beehive ceilings,' Flora continued, extending an arm and swinging it round, 'breathe in the atmosphere of the place and see if you can't summon up the spirit of Iraklis. Over there' – she pointed to the south-west – 'is Lerna, where he fought the Hydra.'

'And over there is Nafplion where I'm making shiploads of money,' Nikitas Palaiologos said, from behind them. Nondas Chaniotakis was

363

chewing gum and shaking his head in embarrassment.

The boys cheered, Prokopis running to his father like a prisoner who had been granted early release.

'There you are,' Veta said drily to her husband. 'I didn't think you were interested in ancient culture.'

'I'm not,' Nikitas replied, the bald dome of his head glinting in the sun. 'We saw the cars and thought we'd surprise you.'

And what a pleasant surprise that was, Flora thought. She ran her eyes over the carpet of bright green leaves interspersed with oranges. Argolidha was one of the most fertile places in Greece, but she knew what her host and hostess's wealth was really rooted in – as did her husband. What Geoff had written was eating away at his soul. She had a strong feeling that Nikitas and Veta would not be able to stomach it either.

Mavros folded up the copy of yesterday's *Eleftherotypia* that he'd picked up from a kiosk on the way to the church, and set off after the old woman. He didn't intend to accost her, but he wanted to see if she met anyone – especially any male in his fifties. Although he wasn't yet sure that she was Stamatina Kastania, there was something about her that made him think so. She must have been in her eighties, her back bent and her legs stiff, and her face was wrinkled, though not enough to disguise the scar on her left cheek – but she exuded a curious vitality, an almost electric presence that carried to other people.

'*Kali mera sas*,' she called, in a shrill but steady voice, to passers-by and shopkeepers. They all acknowledged her with wide smiles. She went down a side-street, her body swaying from side to side, and into the main square.

It was wide and airy, the far end taken up by the impressive three-storey building with an arched passage on the ground floor and a red-tiled roof that contained the town museum. Mavros remembered seeing a stunning set of Mycenaean armour there, great hoops of green bronze surmounted by a boar's-tusk helmet. Any warrior strong enough to wear such a cuirass into combat could have taken on Iraklis himself.

'*Mia poly kali mera*, Kyra Stamatina,' a man sweeping the paving stones outside a café shouted.

Hearing that confirmation of the subject's identity, Mavros drew closer. She was talking to the man about the weather and the effect it might have on the orange crop. Then she moved on. Over the next hour she worked her way round the town centre, often stopping to converse. She bought fruit and vegetables from a stall near the front, then meat from a grinning, unshaven butcher in a back-street not far from her home.

Mavros had almost given up on learning anything significant from the surveillance when the old woman turned left past an establishment on a corner that described itself as a 'Museum of Worry-beads'. She put her bags down outside a small shop with the appearance of a kiosk built into the wall, took a piece of paper from the pocket of her black coat and went through the narrow door. Mavros got as close as he could,

365

throwing caution to the winds. He had the feeling that something significant was about to happen. Standing by the display of magazines outside, he bent his head to the right and listened.

'...use your own phone, Kyra Stamatina?' came the voice of an old man.

'It's not working,' was the brusque reply. 'Now, dial me this number. I can't see in this darkness. Why don't you turn on the light?'

'It isn't working,' the proprietor said, with a dry cackle. 'All right, let me try. Ach, this is a long one. It's a mobile, isn't it?' There was no answer to his question. 'Here you are, it's ringing.'

'Yes?' Stamatina said uncertainly. It seemed to Mavros that she was trying to restrain the inclination that many of her generation had to shout down the phone. 'Yes, I'm in old Manolis's, not at home. Are you–' She broke off and listened for some time. 'Very well. I'll be waiting. Go to the good.' There was a pause. 'There, take it back, Manoli. I've finished. How much do I owe you?'

'It's more expensive to call a mobile, Kyra Stamatina. Three hundred.'

'Pah!' the old woman exclaimed. 'You've turned into a thief like everyone else in this benighted country.'

'Do I look like I'm living a life of luxury?' the old man responded bitterly.

Mavros stepped nonchalantly away down the street as Stamatina Kastania came out, taking the newspaper from his pocket. When she passed him on her way back to the square at the bottom of her street, he leaned against the wall and studied an editorial he'd been reading about the pressure that the terrorist killings was putting on the government in advance of the Olympics. The old woman paid no attention to him, climbing the steps slowly with her shopping bags.

He walked towards Grace. She'd been keeping her eyes off him while Kyra Stamatina negotiated the steps to a large building that was in a state of severe disrepair. At the sound of a door clicking shut, she leaned back on her crate and looked at him inquisitively.

Mavros inclined his head away from Potamianou. 'Pick up your masterpiece and walk,' he said, under his breath, turning at the corner of the church. He waited for her on the other side. 'Let's have a look, then,' he said.

'Was that her?' She handed over the sketch reluctantly.

'This isn't bad, Grace,' Mavros said. 'Maybe you inherited some of your mother's talent.'

'Maybe I also inherited her impatience.' She stared at him in irritation. 'Was that her, Alex?'

'Calm down, for Christ's sake,' he replied. 'Yes, that was Stamatina Kastania.' He told her about the phone call he'd overheard.

'You reckon that was her son she was talking to?' Grace said dubiously.

Mavros nodded. 'I don't think he's in Nafplion yet. It looks like he told her not to use her own phone in case anyone's listening in.'

'We still have no idea when he might show up.'

'No,' he admitted. 'I think we need to reconsider the surveillance plan. There are some fortifications above the street.'

'The old castle?'

367

'Yes. I wonder if we can secrete ourselves up there to keep watch on Potamianou.'

'Shall we go and look?'

'Tell you what, Grace,' he said, glancing at his watch. 'Why don't you take a walk up there from the other side – over towards Palamidhi – and scout out the ground?'

'And how are you planning on spending your time while I do the investigator's legwork?' she asked suspiciously.

Mavros smiled. 'Don't worry, I'll be busy enough. I noticed that there's a war museum down in the centre. I want to see if they have any archive material about resistance groups in Argolidha during the war.'

'Why?' Grace asked. 'Do you think that the old woman fought the Germans here?'

'Could be. Laskaris said she was in ELAS. Did you see that scar on her face? She looks like she went through a lot. Besides, if the guy we're after was in his early thirties in 'seventy-six when he knew your mother, he'd have been born during or after the war. If she really is his mother, I might get some idea of what motivated him to become a terrorist by identifying her ELAS unit.'

'All right,' she said, taking the guidebook from her bag. 'I'll check out the walls. By the way, the old woman came over and took a look at my drawing. She said something like *"ocki poly kalo"*.' Grace looked at him quizzically.

He smiled. 'It means "very good". Old Communists are renowned for their aesthetic judgement.' For some reason he didn't want Grace to know what Kyra Stamatina really thought.

368

'Is that right? I'll meet you at that café down the street in an hour.' She headed away.

'Okay,' Mavros called after her. That would give him plenty of time to poke his nose into the museum. As well as to do something else that might be much more fruitful.

'Is it them?' Peter Jaeger, fair hair slicked down and white shirt pristine, was peering at the screen in the communications room beneath the American embassy. 'The woman's face is partially obscured by the guy's hair.'

'This shot was taken outside the composer Randos's place,' Jane Forster said, picking up another photograph and comparing it with the image on the screen. 'It looks like Mavros.'

'Yeah, it does. But I can't be a hundred per cent sure.' Jaeger stood up straight. 'What led them to Nafplion?'

'Shall I call Commander Kriaras?' Forster asked, her hand moving to a phone.

'No!' her superior said, his hand coming down fast on top of hers. 'No, I don't want the Greeks involved. They're already shitting themselves about Iraklis's reappearance.'

'Aren't we supposed to keep them involved, sir?' The woman's voice was tentative. 'Mavros is a Greek citizen.'

Jaeger glanced at her scathingly. 'Aren't we supposed to keep them involved?' he repeated, mimicking her southern drawl. 'We're supposed to protect our own interests, Ms Forster,' he hissed. 'How did we get this image, anyway?'

'A local freelance operative emailed it via the

369

secure server,' she said, her eyes down. 'I spread the word that we were interested in Alex Mavros. He's quite well known because of the big case he broke on that island in the fall.'

'Well done.' Jaeger's tone was little warmer. 'Is the local still on them?'

'I told him to await further instructions.'

'Good.' He turned away. 'I need to think about things.'

'What now, sir?' she called after him. 'Are we going down there?'

He stopped. 'No, Ms Forster, we are not going down to Nafplion. Not yet, at least.'

'Shall I inform Finn?'

'He knows what to do.'

'What about Tiresias?'

'I'll handle Tiresias.' Jaeger moved towards the door. 'And, Ms Forster?' He didn't turn back towards her. 'Keep all of this to yourself, you understand?'

She nodded, even though her boss was no longer in the room. She put her lower lip between her bright white teeth and bit, softly at first, then hard enough to draw blood. There was something wrong with this operation. Jaeger was her station chief, but there had been talk about him losing his touch – ever since the terrorist attacks on New York and Washington he had been obsessed with making his mark, even though Athens was no longer the major operational centre it had been when Greek governments had been more compliant. As for Lance Milroy – the man she'd been told to refer to as Finn during this mission – he made the hairs on her neck rise, for all his thirty-five years' experience in Greece.

Jane Forster desperately wanted to talk to someone, but she was on her first foreign posting and she had already seen the cost of disloyalty. Besides, she was in too deep on the Iraklis operation, even though Jaeger hadn't told her everything. Back in Langley, they joked that was all your training was good for – how to handle yourself when the shit storm set in. She hadn't expected to find herself up to her neck in it so quickly.

15

Mavros watched Grace walk down the street towards the end of the fortifications, then turned away and went down to the centre. He felt his stomach clutch when he thought about what he was doing – sending her to keep watch on the mother of the most wanted man in Greece, the man who, as likely as not, had almost blown them away in the stony valley yesterday and who, he was certain, was on their trail. It wasn't exactly responsible. But, then, he was still unsure of her background and motives. Maybe she would do something to move the case forward when he wasn't present. In the meantime, he had work to do.

The war museum was in a tall town-house, a Greek flag hanging in the still air above the steps that led to the entrance. There was a bored soldier sitting at a small table. He showed little interest in Mavros's question about the archive, replying that there was only a small collection of records in the building. As far as he knew, they referred primarily to Nafplion's role as the first capital of Greece after the War of Independence rather than to the Axis occupation. Besides, he said, with a dismissive glance at Mavros's long hair, access to the archives required written authorisation from the Ministry of Defence in Athens.

Mavros went up the stairs and made a rapid examination of the collection. There were uniforms and weapons dating from the early nineteenth century to the late twentieth. Vicious Maniate yataghans, the wide-bladed short swords that had done for so many of their fellow Greeks as well as Turks, were well to the fore. There were also many black-and-white photographs on the walls, but few cast much light on what had happened in Argolidha in the 1940s. Mavros gave the surly soldier a smile to help him through the day, then went out into the sunlight. It was warmer now, the snow that had beleaguered them on the drive from the south now a fading memory. In the open square beside a statue of the nineteenth-century King Otto, he took out his notebook and his mobile phone. The reception was good and the number he dialled rang clearly.

'Yes?' The male voice was abrupt, roughened by thousands of unfiltered cigarettes.

'Pandeli, it's Alex Mavros.'

'Aleko, my boy.' The tone became more lively. 'Where have you been hiding yourself? Wherever you are, I hope you've been skinning the rich.'

'Trying to,' Mavros replied. Pandelis Pikros was a former Communist who had worked with his father Spyros for many years. In the late sixties he'd fallen out with the hardline comrades who supported Moscow and, unimpressed by their opponents who broke away to form the Euro-Communist KKEs, had ended up as a nobody for both parties. 'Guess where I am. In the Peloponnese.'

'Are you now? North or south?'

'Both.' Mavros knew that the old man with the tobacco-stained moustache would be interested. He had been an ELAS fighter in the peninsula during and after the Second World War. 'I've been in Lakonia and now I'm in Argolidha,' he said, having first glanced around to check that he was on his own.

'Lucky you,' Pandelis Pikros said, his voice suddenly wistful. 'I was born in Neo Iraio, you know. On the plain near Argos. I haven't been back for decades.'

Mavros had heard many such stories from old fighters, unable to return to their villages because they were stigmatised by their wartime activities. The situation was worst in the traditionally monarchist Peloponnese. 'Listen, Pandeli, are you still working on that archive of ELAS members?' Pikros had started collecting data when the Party was still banned. After the socialist government's national reconciliation initiative in the eighties he had started to study the surviving official records – many had been destroyed in an attempt to dissipate the bitterness over controversial issues.

'Oh, yes,' Pikros said. 'The old woman says it's the only thing that keeps me alive. She's probably right.'

Mavros looked around the square again. People laden with shopping bags and packages in Christmas paper were heading for their cars, paying no attention to him. 'Pandeli, I need information about a woman who may have been one of yours.'

Pikros laughed. 'Careful, my boy. I had plenty of women during the war, even though it was against regulations.' He paused. 'Anyway, what do you mean "may have been"? I've got enough people who were definitely involved. If you're talking about going through the records on the off-chance, forget it. The house is full of boxes and files.' He lowered his voice. 'That's another thing the old woman can't stand.'

'Listen, do me this favour,' Mavros pleaded. 'It could be very important.'

'There you go again, Aleko.' Pandelis Pikros had always used the Greek diminutive of Alexandhros, regarding the other as a foreign affectation. '"It could be". I can't work with vague hypotheses.'

'Please, Pandeli.' Mavros had one more card to play. 'I'll pay you.'

There was a pause and then the ex-Communist grunted. 'Oh, well, if you put it that way ... give me the woman's name.'

Mavros did so, warning him that Kastania was her married name. He also advised him that Kyra Stamatina had served in an ELAS band with Kostas Laskaris.

'That narrows things down a bit,' Pandelis said. 'I'll start looking straight away. Call me in the evening. And, Aleko, how much are you going to pay me?'

Mavros told him the standard hourly rate he gave researchers and cut the connection. Earlier in his career he had often been amazed at the amounts demanded by avowed socialists. Now he saw it as just another manifestation of the free market. The West had prevailed in the ideological struggle that had dominated the twentieth century and no one cared any more.

Except Iraklis. Two of the country's leading capitalists had been executed and Mavros was certain there were more victims to come.

The terrorist had driven the stolen Suzuki up a back-street on the outskirts of Argos at two thirty in the morning and abandoned it, taking his small case and leaving the keys under the seat. The wet snow that was lying on the pavements had soaked his boots, but he was unconcerned. He had left the worst of the cold in the mountains and he was almost in position for the mission he'd returned to Greece to carry out. He found a mediocre hotel in the centre of the town and signed in under a false name, speaking Greek and paying the drowsy clerk in cash to keep him sweet. Then he dropped into a deep sleep, only waking when the grinding of a refuse lorry penetrated his room from the street below.

Iraklis shaved and showered, unperturbed by the low temperature of the water that came from the hot taps. Then, checking that the door was double-locked, he opened his bag and spread out the contents on the bed. Apart from the silenced Glock, which he had taken with him to the bathroom and now rested by his thigh, his weaponry consisted of a double-edged hunting knife that he had picked up in an outdoor-activities shop in Athens, and three pen-shaped explosive devices that had been delivered to the first hotel he'd gone to in the capital. He wondered if the person pretending to be him had used something similar on the investor Stasinopoulos in the concert hall – the newspapers hadn't been specific about the bomb. Was the impostor the man he had seen near Babis Dhimitrakos's body?

The terrorist ran his eye past the small pile of clothes to the remaining items he had taken out. Two books. A thick guide to the Peloponnese in Greek that he had used to navigate his way around the back roads of the Mani, and an anthology of Kostas Laskaris's work. He hadn't told the old man, but over the years those poems had become for him what the Holy Writ was to a monk – inspiration, comfort in hard times, a model of how to live. They were also a source of melancholic nostalgia for his homeland. He smiled as he had many times in the attic in Queens. What would the hard men in the construction gangs have thought of a colleague who read leftist poetry in his free time? But it was his secret solace, his only distraction – even though it was no diversion from the woman he had loved.

Iraklis clenched his fists to dispel the image of her and opened the anthology. The house plan he had drawn after the latest phone call to his controller was between pages in the section marked *Stichi*, Song Lyrics. As he took out the folded sheets, he saw the lines of the song called 'The Voyage of the *Argo*', and the haunting melody flooded his ears. He had heard it for the first time in years in a café in Chicago where he had gone for a break a couple of months ago – back in Queens he avoided the *kafeneia* and *tavernes* in case he was seen by anyone who had known him in the home country or who was on

377

his trail. That song, one of Dhimitris Randos's most emotional, had brought unexpected tears to his eyes. He had seen the newspapers. The composer had fallen to his death and he was sure some anti-Communist bastard had killed him. But was there a connection to the other killings – a connection to him? He would have to watch his back even more carefully than he used to in the old days.

He unfolded the papers, shaking his head to dispel the tune. This was it, the end game, the culmination of years when he had lost hope that the people who had rubbed his father from history would ever be identified. His controller had finally put the pieces together and he had to be sure of the plan: he had to memorise the location where he would finally rid himself of the family obligation he had been carrying from birth.

The house was a problem – fences and alarm systems all round, guards, security doors and windows; and people, too many people, children as well. There was a risk that the target would be obscured by innocent bystanders. But that kind of risk had never been a problem for him in the past. Why was he so reluctant to consider the possibility of accidental deaths? Had he got soft from living in the belly of the beast?

Iraklis studied the drawings for an hour, making refinements to his plan of action. Then he packed up his gear, locked the case and went downstairs without showing his face to the morning clerk. She was talking on the phone and did not break off. It was as he was walking to a car-rental office he had noticed the night before that his mobile was activated. As usual, he had it set on vibrate mode. Stopping in a doorway, he gave a monosyllabic answer. It was his mother. He confirmed that he was close and that he would be at the house late in the evening. She sounded as severe as always, but there was a waver in her voice that he hadn't heard before. She was finally nearing the end of her long road.

In an instant he was back in his childhood, seeing again the woman he had learned only in his sixth year to call Mother. It was the autumn day that she had reappeared in Kitta. He was nine years old and he was playing outside, wearing only a tattered pair of shorts and a vest, rolling in the dust with the mangy dog his grandmother tolerated in the yard behind the old tower. The sun had been blinding, glinting off the grey stone buildings and the purple-blue sea beyond Tigani. He blinked, then looked up at the figure that had materialised before him, blouse and skirt covered in dust and shoes scuffed. The woman was carrying an old suitcase tied with fraying string. She was tall, her black hair threaded with white and, although the skin of her face was not leathery like the old woman's, she looked almost as worn out. He stared at the great gash in her cheek, the edges of it pitted by irregular dots and lines.

'My son.' Her voice rang out like a trumpet, the harsh sound echoing around the enclosed space.

'Stand up, Michali,' his grandmother said. He felt the old woman's hand on his crew-cut scalp. 'Stand up, my boy. This is your–'

'I remember her,' he interrupted. 'Are you coming home to stay, Mama?' The unfamiliar word fell from his lips like a stone.

The woman knelt in front of him, her eyes burning into his. Then she glanced at the case she still held and let it drop to the stony ground. 'My son,' she said, her face coming close enough for him to take in broken teeth and smell rancid breath. She took him by the shoulders and for a moment he thought she was going to shake him. But she held him still, her dark eyes dry. 'We called you Michalis after my father when I gave birth to you behind the wire at Trikeri, but to me you will always be Iraklis.' She blinked, her eyes dry. 'Even though he left me unprotected, condemned me to years on the prison islands, my child taken from me.' Her expression softened. 'At least the comrades managed to slip you away from the camp and send you secretly to this house.' Her face hardened again as she looked up to the sky. 'Ach, my captain, was everything we gave for this? A lifetime of toil and blood for a puny, lice-ridden creature?'

'Who is Iraklis?' the boy heard himself say. 'Where is he?'

His mother gave a bitter laugh. 'Who is Iraklis? He was a teacher, a fighter, a great leader. And now I hope he has gone to a better place.' She trembled, then regained control. 'I lost him behind the barbed wire. When I ... when I woke in my agony he was gone. No one would tell me where he was, the cowards. I escaped from imprisonment to seek him as I have done now, but there was no trace.' She stood up and spoke over his head again. 'I cannot stay, Mother,' she said, to the old woman behind. 'They must not find me here. Look after the boy for me. Look after Michalis.' She bent down to pick up her case.

'I am not puny,' he said, unsure what the word meant. 'And my grandmother combs the lice out every Sunday.'

His mother laughed again, this time less harshly. 'That's good, Michali,' she said, standing up and turning away without touching him or catching his eye.

'I will become a great fighter,' he called after her. 'Like our Iraklis.'

The woman stood still for a moment, then strode off. He thought he heard a stifled sob, but he couldn't be sure.

And now, in Argos, as he went to hire a car, Iraklis found there were other things he couldn't be sure about. Had he really told the woman he loved about the place he was from one afternoon? Had she told him she was going to paint a picture of Kitta that would rend the heart of every person who saw it?

It seemed that things were becoming blurred and insubstantial. If he wasn't careful the dead woman whose name he'd been unable to say for decades would finish him. The love they had shared was like a time bomb that had been counting down since the last time he had seen her outside the apartment building in Athens, her doomed husband on his knees before them.

Iraklis forced away the image. He had to fulfil his obligation and get away from Greece before he lost himself for good.

'How are we going to handle this?' Grace asked. They were sitting in the small café near the old woman's street where they'd arranged to meet.

Mavros took a sip of unsweetened coffee. 'Well, we've already established that you're a keen amateur artist.'

'Oh, I get it,' she said, frowning. 'You want me to go up on the ramparts and do a few more drawings while you sneak off and do whatever it is you do behind my back.' She banged her cup down on the saucer. 'Am I paying you or not? I want us to stick together.'

'All right. I was going to keep you company anyway,' he said, with a loose smile. 'You haven't got a mobile so we can't keep in touch.' He pointed to the street map of Nafplion in her guidebook. 'There's a path down from the fortifications that comes out at the top of Potamianou, so if we see anyone suspicious I can get down quickly enough to tail him. I shouldn't think Kyra Stamatina will venture out again. Women of her generation tend to stay inside as much as they can during the winter.'

Grace looked at him dubiously. 'All right.' She signalled to the waiter. 'Let's get going then.'

While she was paying Mavros's phone rang.

'Alex?' came his mother's voice. 'Where are you?' She sounded out of sorts.

'Em, in Nafplion. Are you at the Palaiologos house?'

'Yes.' There was a pause. 'Why didn't you tell me you were close by? Will you come and join us?

382

It's nearly Christmas and, to tell you the truth, I'm not feeling very well.'

Mavros raised a hand to Grace and sat down again. 'Why? What's the matter?'

'It – it wasn't a very nice drive down yesterday and–' Dorothy Cochrane-Mavrou broke off.

'And?' His mother knew plenty of ways to exert emotional pressure.

'And there's something else, dear. You know Geoffrey Dearfield? Yes, of course you do, we were talking about him only a few days ago. Well, I've finished his manuscript and it's ... it's quite awful, especially at the end. I don't know what to say to–'

'Mother, I have to go,' Mavros interrupted, nodding to his client. 'I'll see if I have time to come up to the house. I'm sure you'll find a way to break the bad news to Dearfield.'

'No, it's not that,' Dorothy began. 'The problem is–'

'Got to go. 'Bye, Mother,' he said, breaking the connection.

Grace's expression was questioning. 'Your mother? What was her problem?'

He followed her out. 'I don't know,' he said, wondering if he'd been too abrupt with Dorothy. She was occasionally querulous, but this time she seemed almost fearful of talking to Dearfield. He told himself that Anna would look after her. 'She's spending Christmas at a house not far from here,' he explained.

'You should go and see her,' Grace said. 'After we've finished.'

He saw the strain in her face. One or both of the armed men would be hot on their heels, he

383

was sure. Now that they were waiting for the man she'd seen kill her father to show up at his mother's house, the tension must be getting to her. He was feeling it too, the conversation with his mother only serving to bring back the case's link to Andonis more vividly. What kind of a Christmas present would it be for his family if he found out what his brother had been doing in the month before his disappearance? The idea that it might be something that tied Andonis to the terrorists filled him with trepidation.

They found a track that led up to the battlements of Akronafplia, the great diagonal walls of Palamidhi hanging above them. The lower citadel was less spectacular, its walls and foundations bisected by a twisting asphalt road. They crossed a fence and made their way to the fortifications. There was a hole in the wall above Potamianou. The spot was sheltered from the breeze, which was fresher on the raised ground.

'The guidebook goes along with what you said about there being a prison up here,' Grace said, not bothering to take out her sketch pad. There was no one else in the vicinity.

'Glad you believed me,' Mavros said ironically. 'There were plenty of old buildings around the country for any regime that was keen on repression. Akronafplia was used by the dictator Metaxas to confine Communists in the thirties. The prisons here were used all the way through the civil war. Even though they've been demolished, they're in the collective memory of the country – there have been songs and poems written about them.'

'By Randos and Laskaris?'

'Probably. I can't think of any off the top of my head, but Kostas is bound to have used his own experience of them in his writing.'

'He was locked up here?' she asked, her eyes widening.

'Oh, yes,' he replied. 'And so was my father.'

Before he could say any more about Spyros, his mobile rang again. The caller was Kyra Fedhra, the Fat Man's mother, wondering if Mavros had seen her son in the last couple of days.

'No,' he answered. 'I'm in the Peloponnese.'

'So are we,' the old woman replied. 'Didn't he tell you?'

'Oh, yes. You're in Lakonia, aren't you?'

'I am,' she replied brusquely. 'But who knows where Yiorgos is? He left the day before yesterday. He wouldn't tell me where he was going, but I have a feeling he was heading for the Mani to see that poet who writes the songs on the radio. I heard him mention his name on the telephone the day before we left Athens.'

There were furrows on Mavros's brow. 'Why would he–' He stopped, gazing down over the array of vehicles parked down by the bus station. 'Kyra Fedhra, what kind of car was he driving?'

'Oh, he borrowed some heap of junk,' came the hoarse reply. 'One of those Russian things.'

'A Lada?'

'That's it.'

'What colour was it?'

'A kind of dirty red, like a steak that's hung too long.' The old woman paused. 'Why? Have you seen it?'

'Em, no,' Mavros said. 'Don't worry, Kyra Fedhra, Yiorgos will be back soon, I'm sure. Call me again tomorrow if he isn't.'

'Very well,' she agreed, and hung up.

Mavros put his phone back into his pocket, trying to make sense of what he'd just learned. Could that have been the Fat Man's car on the track beyond the turning to Laskaris's house at Tigani? If so, why hadn't he been inside with the poet? Could he have been in the tower but hiding from Mavros? That didn't make any sense.

'Problems?' Grace asked, her eyes on the lane below.

Mavros chewed the inside of his cheek. The idea that the Fat Man might have been near him and avoided contact disturbed him almost as much as the imminent arrival of the assassin. He had often thought that if he couldn't trust Yiorgos Pandazopoulos, devoted comrade of both his father and his brother, then the world and everything in it was lost. Had it come to that?

The politician Veta Dhragoumi-Palaiologou was lying on the king-size bed, her eyes on the dark wooden beams that ran across the ceiling. Even in winter she felt the need of a rest in the afternoons. When she was younger, she had tried to keep her weight under control – diets, exercise, nutritionists, even a charlatan of a Swiss hypnotist – but in recent years she had given up the struggle. It was another gift to the government's tame political cartoonists, who portrayed her as the elephant of the Right or as a phantom menace threatening to wrap the country in her fatal free-market embrace. That pleased her as it showed she had them on the run. But in the last few weeks she'd been uneasy, despite the Left's manifest disarray. The terrorist killings of the businessmen had been a gift to the opposition, providing clear evidence of the government's weakness – the fact that some of the cabinet had been left-wing activists when the Iraklis group first came to prominence during the dictatorship meant that they were tainted by association. It should have been an optimistic time for her party, but Veta wasn't happy.

Part of the problem was her house guests. What was going on with Dorothy Cochrane-Mavrou and Geoff Dearfield? It was bad enough having to cope with the kids' unpredictable behaviour – the boys veering between surliness and a boisterous disregard for anyone else, the girls desperately seeking attention; having to put up with a pair of elderly people who seemed suddenly incapable of speaking to each other was the last straw. At lunch they had both looked pale and drawn. Anna had tried to engage them in conversation, but they were as monosyllabic as her son was during the run-up to exams every term. Veta had stared at her husband, trying to get him involved, but Nikitas was too busy discussing the Black Sea's business potential with Nondas to notice.

Veta swung her legs off the bed when she realised that she wasn't going to sleep. She went downstairs, catching a glimpse of a muscle-bound security man beyond the fence. What was the matter with Nikitas? The house and grounds had more alarms than the prime minister's residence. She was a senior politician, but she only had one bodyguard. Nikitas had employed three – one a brainless woman – and she was pretty sure they weren't for her benefit. What kind of dirty deals had he been sticking his fingers in?

'Ah, there you are, Anna,' she said, when she went into the sitting room. 'Has Loudhovikos offered you anything to drink?' Her guest looked up from a magazine and shook her head. Veta sighed. 'That butler is hopeless. He's forever disappearing. I should never have employed him. He came highly recommended by a friend of Flora.' She looked around. 'Where are the children?'

'The men took them for a drive,' Anna replied. 'They said something about playing football on the beach at Tolo.'

'The girls will love that,' Veta said, easing her bulk into an armchair. 'Your mother?'

'Resting. Sleeping, I hope. I'm sorry, she's behaving very strangely. I don't know what's got into her.'

'Do you think they've had an argument about Geoff's script?'

Anna smoothed the fabric of her silk blouse. 'Maybe. It's not Mother's way. She's usually very good with would-be authors.'

'Perhaps my husband wrote something that insulted her.'

Anna and Veta turned their heads.

'Flora,' Veta said, her cheeks reddening. 'I didn't hear you come in.'

'I'm sorry,' the older woman said. 'I wasn't eavesdropping.'

'Don't be silly,' Veta said, inclining her head towards the sofa. 'Where's Geoff?'

Flora Petraki-Dearfield sat down and twitched her lips. 'I think he's working.'

'What's troubling him?' Anna asked. 'Is it something my mother said?'

'No, I don't think so.' Flora looked uneasy. 'He's been strange ever since he started writing that accursed memoir. Most of the time he's absent, in his own world, but sometimes he surfaces and accuses me of not paying him enough attention.'

'The older they get, the more like children they become,' Veta said. 'Don't you agree, Anna?'

The youngest of the women seemed embarrassed. 'I don't know. I think it's amazing that my mother and Geoff still have the energy to work on their various projects.'

Flora was gazing at her. 'Yes, Anna,' she said, and glanced at Veta. 'But what if those projects are harmful to themselves and those they live with?'

Veta leaned forward. 'Harmful? What do you mean?'

Flora stood up and went to the window. 'I don't know about Dorothy, but Geoff is obsessed by the past.'

'That's normal for old people,' Anna put in.

The historian turned, her face suddenly filled with anguish. 'Yes, but Geoff is haunted by it. I hear him talking in his sleep sometimes, saying terrible things – about killing and bloated corpses, slaughter and revenge.' Her eyes were bulging. 'I don't think he's got over what he experienced in the war.'

Veta pulled herself upright and went to her. 'Come, sit down, Flora,' she said softly. 'You're overwrought.'

'But that's not all,' the older woman continued, her voice low. 'There's a name he keeps mentioning, a name that frightens me.' She gave an unconvincing laugh. 'Maybe I've spent too much time studying mythology.'

'What is it?' Veta asked. 'What is this name he repeats?'

Flora looked into the politician's eyes. 'Iraklis,' she said, swallowing a sob.

'What are we going to do when it gets dark?' Grace asked, rubbing her gloved hands together. There had been no movement on Potamianou apart from a pair of children returning home.

Mavros glanced at the sky. The sun was over the western mountains, its watery light weakening further. Around them, on the low hill of the old fortress, the birds were chattering to each other as they settled down in the bushes. As the great plug of rock behind them blurred in the twilight, the bastions on Palamidhi hovered in the air like a flight of huge airships tethered to the ground by the zigzag stairway.

'Yeah, we need to rethink,' he said. 'It's getting chilly.'

'Why don't we just muscle into the old woman's house and wait for the bastard in the warmth?' his client asked, her chin up.

Mavros looked at her. 'You are joking, I hope.'

'Why?' she demanded. 'There are two of us and we'll have the element of surprise.'

'Only if we restrain Kyra Stamatina from crying out. Jesus, Grace, get a grip. The information we have is that she's the terrorist's mother. How's Iraklis going to react if he finds her tied to a chair with a gag in her mouth?'

She stared at him but didn't speak.

'The guy's a consummate professional, for Christ's sake,' Mavros continued. 'He'll be on his guard and armed. So what if we outnumber him?'

'All right, Mr Investigator,' Grace said, lowering her eyes. 'What's your suggestion?'

'My suggestion is that we get off this grassy knoll and go back to that café. I'm hungry and I'm thirsty. One of us can keep watch in the shadows by the church afterwards.'

'You want to stay up here for ten minutes while I get down there?' she said, her tone more emollient.

'I thought you wanted us to be inseparable.'

She gave a brief smile. 'Just showing you how much I trust you.'

'Charming. Okay, I'll hold the fort, so to speak.' He watched Grace head off to the right then swung his gaze back on to the stepped lane. A couple of minutes later his mobile rang.

'Aleko?'

It was the old Communist archivist. After they'd exchanged greetings, Mavros asked, 'Have you got something for me?'

'Oh, yes, my boy. I've got plenty for you.' Pandelis Pikros's voice was as throaty as ever, but there was excitement in it. 'I think you'll have to come up with a bonus.'

Mavros pressed the phone closer to his ear. 'I'll see. True enough, I'm on expenses.'

'Just as well,' Pikros said. 'I owe several people for this. You know what the official archivists are like, let alone the old comrades.' He paused. 'Right, then, Aleko. The first point is that I knew Stamatina Kastania.'

Mavros felt his heart skip a beat. 'In the war?'

'Yes. Well, I didn't know her in person, but I heard of her when I was in ELAS. I didn't realise it when you told me her name because she called herself Artemis towards the end of the occupation. Have you heard of that name?'

'I take it you aren't talking about the ancient goddess of hunting,' Mavros replied. 'No. Should I have?'

Pandelis Pikros laughed. 'You owe it to yourself to read more books about those times, my boy. The younger generations are historically illiterate and you'll pay for it, you can be sure of that. Anyway, Artemis was well known in certain circles. She was initially an ELAS fighter in Lakonia.'

'Did you find out where she was from down there?'

'No, there was no record. She was one of those who took particular care to cover their tracks – to protect her relatives, you understand. I reckon Stamatina wasn't the name she was christened with. She probably concealed her pre-war identity because she was in the Party. There are few records of her. She was in the prison camps until 1962. She was released once during an amnesty, then rearrested. She managed to escape

392

once in the mid-fifties.' There was an intake of breath as Pikros pulled on his cigarette. 'She was a brave woman.'

'There were many of them,' Mavros said, remembering the stories from the struggle that his brother had passed on when he was a boy – there had been no mention of the civil war and the persecution of the Left in his schoolbooks. 'What about her ELAS unit? You must have found some records of it?'

'Yes, I did. Her band became famous all over western Lakonia. It was led by a man who called himself Kapetan Iraklis.'

Mavros heard the name and immediately felt the tightening on his neck that he always experienced when apparently unconnected elements of a case began to come together. 'Iraklis?' he repeated.

'I hope you understand it was a real struggle to find all this out,' Pikros said. 'People on our side still keep their mouths shut, even though Left and Right are supposed to be reconciled.'

'Tell me,' Mavros urged.

'And there were dozens of *kapetanii* across the country who took their campaign names from the mythical hero,' the old man said, making clear how hard he had worked. 'Anyway, this one's real name was Rigas Zaralis,' Pikros continued. 'A schoolteacher from Areopolis in the Mani. Apparently he was a born leader and a brilliant tactician. The band was sent to Argolidha in the last winter of the occupation to strengthen the ELAS units there.' Mavros heard the rustle of papers. 'Something happened to

393

Iraklis, I haven't been able to establish exactly what. Various shit-eating Security Battalionists claim in their memoirs that he was killed in battle, but different locations are given so those may just be lies. I tracked down one old comrade who said he was captured and never seen again. Who knows? Iraklis disappears from history and Stamatina becomes Artemis. And listen to this...' There was another pause.

'Go on, for God's sake, Pandeli,' Mavros said, shivering as the cold set in.

'She joined an OPLA unit.'

Mavros recognised the acronym. 'Ah.'

'Aware of the Organisation for the Protection of the Popular Struggle, are you?' Pikros asked.

'I do know something about the occupation, Pandeli,' he replied, aggrieved. 'My father was involved, remember?'

'Of course he was, Aleko,' the old Communist said, his voice softening. 'Your father set a great example.'

'OPLA was originally set up to police the EAM-controlled territory. But later it degenerated into secret assassination squads in some places.' Mavros's stomach clenched as he saw the direction the conversation was headed. 'Shit. What else?'

'What else?' Pikros was suddenly reluctant to carry on. 'Well ... it seems she wasn't a very typical woman.'

'What does that mean, Pandeli?'

'This Artemis, Stamatina, whatever you want to call her – well, you know how the OPLA squads operated, do you?'

394

'They rounded up collaborators, black-marketeers, suspected informers for inter-rogation.'

'Correct. She wasn't involved in that side of it, though.'

'So what was her role?'

'She ... she was based in the mountains above the plain of Argos, not far from where I was born actually,' the old man prevaricated, taking a long drag from his cigarette.

Mavros sighed. 'For God's sake, tell me, before my phone battery runs out, Pandeli.'

'Fuck it,' Pikros grunted. 'All right, she was an executioner. Her comrades took the prisoners up to a cave by a ravine and she cut their throats. Then the bodies were pushed over the edge. Satisfied, Aleko?'

Mavros swallowed hard. 'What happened to her after she was released from the camps in the sixties?'

'She went back to Argolidha and married Menelaos Kastanias, a trade-union activist. He died during the dictatorship after they were both arrested again. Unlike some, they never gave up the struggle.'

'Thanks, Pandeli,' Mavros said, belatedly remembering that Grace was waiting for him. 'I'll be in touch when I get back about your payment.'

'Aleko?' Pikros's voice was low. 'There's some-thing else.'

Mavros bowed his head, fearing the worst. 'What is it?'

'I found a witness statement from a collaborator who escaped from the clutches of the OPLA unit.

This Stamatina, when she was killing those people, she – she was pregnant.'

'Did she have the child?' Mavros mumbled. 'Is there a name?'

The line was quiet, apart from a subdued electronic tone.

'There's nothing else in the records.'

Mavros thanked him again and broke the connection, then walked slowly down to join his client. The idea that the terrorist might have been in his mother's womb when she cut the throats of her victims made his stomach churn. What kind of man would such a child have turned into? Despite Iraklis's record, Mavros couldn't help feeling compassion for him. He was sure Grace would see that as unjustified. But if the woman Stamatina – the former assassin Artemis – had spent years after the war in the prison camps, could the traumatised son who had somehow survived be held responsible for the crimes he had committed? Or was he as much a victim of Greece's violent history as the people he had killed?

Geoffrey Dearfield rolled over in his bed, flitting between wakefulness and a torrid sleep that was alive with writhing forms and gouts of blood. He struggled to break out of the dream, struggled to bring himself back to present-day Argolidha, but the power of the past was too much for him. He sank away like a drowning sailor, letting out his last breath and spiralling down to the darkest depths, remembering again what he had seen in the war as vividly as if it had happened yesterday.

It was first light. There was snow on the mountains, the green canopy of the plain spattered with myriad orange dots from the fruit as he swung his binoculars over it. And on the mule-track to the village occupied by the Greek resistance band half-way up the slope to his right there was a scarcely visible line of field grey. The German column, reinforced by collaborationist Greeks, was on its way.

He had conducted a long debate with the local British liaison officers, but in the end they had had to accede to his orders. He had been promoted to regional commander two months earlier, arriving from Sparta at the same time as Kapetan Iraklis's unit of fighters. They had been exhausted after the battles at Mystras and locations in northern Lakonia. He had hoped that Iraklis would act as a moderating influence on the increasingly hardline Greek commanders in Argolidha. The leadership of the anti-occupation movement EAM and of its military wing ELAS was becoming more anti-British by the day, accusing him and his colleagues of being monarchist stooges and ignoring their orders. It seemed that Iraklis had also begun to lose the underlying rationality that had characterised his activities before the slaughter in the mountains of the Mani. That had been the start of the trouble and the *kapetanios*'s shoulder wound had weakened him, though he still retained the devotion of his fighters.

To Dearfield's surprise, it hadn't been difficult to co-operate with the Security Battalions despite official British disapproval for the anti-Communist units. As regional commander, Dearfield felt fully justified in doing so. Iraklis had only himself to blame – he had failed to prevent one of the peasant boys in his unit shooting the British guide Fivos in the back on a highland track between Sparta and Tripolis. That had made Dearfield realise how hopeless it was to imagine that EAM/ELAS could be trusted. There was no longer any question of British arms being supplied to the leftist guerrilla bands for the fight against the Germans, who would soon be on their way out. What the British had to worry about was the potential loss of Greece to the Communist front organisation EAM after hostilities ended. If the pro-Soviet resistance took over the country, the strategic balance of the eastern Mediterranean and the Middle East would be in jeopardy. The guerrillas had to be neutralised by any means.

Dearfield heard gunfire, then saw smoke rising above the village. The ELAS fighters had seen the enemy column and were attacking it. What they were not aware of was the second force that was approaching from their rear, the sentries on the ridges already neutralised. The strategy, masterminded by Dearfield and passed to the collaborationist commanders, was working. The Iraklis band was finished.

In the bedroom in the Palaiologos house Dearfield lay on his back, his mouth open and his breath short. He was suddenly unable to move, his eyes wide as a figure in tattered Greek battledress, bandoliers criss-crossing his chest, leaned over him and drove a combat knife into his chest. The man was bearded, his eyes unwavering. His tunic was soaked with blood, the smell of it burning the British officer's nostrils as he felt his heart embrace the blade.

'Traitor,' whispered his killer.

Iraklis.

16

Grace looked at Mavros in the dim light. They were standing in the small square behind Ayios Spyridhon, pressing up against the whitewashed wall to allow a young couple carrying packages wrapped in Christmas paper to pass.

'So,' she said, 'you've found out that the old woman was a Communist fighter who turned into an assassin. Now we know where her son got his inspiration.'

Mavros nodded slowly. 'It always comes back to family in this country.' As the words came out, he thought of his brother. If he wasn't careful, the case would race to its conclusion before he could establish what had resulted from the meeting Andonis had with the terrorist.

'Hello, Alex?' Grace tapped him on the shoulder. 'Anyone at home?'

He blinked. 'What? Oh, sorry. I was just trying to work out how to proceed.'

'Good,' she said, her tone sardonic. 'So was I. How are we going to keep a watch on the lane overnight? We'll stick out like pole dancers in a cathedral.'

'True. Given that the man we're after knows his trade, it's pretty likely he'll spot us. I'm wondering...' He stroked the stubble on his chin. 'I'm just wondering whether we should go in before Iraklis arrives.'

'To the mother's place?'

'Yes. It's a risk, but I think it's the only way.'

'I've been telling you we should do that all day.'

'The situation's different now. I can use the information I've got on her to gain her confidence. She'll also know who my father was.'

Grace was staring at him. 'Gain her confidence?'

'Look, all you want to do is confront the assassin about your father's death. You aren't looking for revenge?'

She wrapped her arms round her chest. 'No,' she said. 'What good would that do? And, anyway, how could I take on an expert like him?'

Mavros watched her for a few more seconds. 'Okay.' And all I want, he said to himself, is to find out if the guy who used to call himself Iason Kolettis knows what happened to my brother after they met at Tigani. 'If we convince the old woman that we're not a threat, maybe she'll let us wait with her for her son to arrive.' He touched her arm. 'You haven't forgotten the man who almost used his gun on us down in the Mani, have you?'

She shook her head, catching his eye.

'And you're prepared to give him another chance?'

'Yes.' Grace smiled at him. 'Let's just hope he decides to spare his mother an execution in her house.'

Mavros grunted. 'Nothing in her record suggests she'd be too bothered by that.'

They stepped closer together as a group of small boys came past, triangles in their hands.

'Carol-singers?' Grace asked.

'Yes,' Mavros confirmed, feeling her breath on his cheek. 'They go round the houses singing the *kalanda* and extracting money for their trouble. The problem is there's only one tune and it's a very irritating one.'

Suddenly Grace pinned him to the wall with her body. 'Are you sure you want to do this, Mr Investigator? I'm prepared to go in on my own.'

He felt a tremor of arousal, but kept his hands off her. 'Not a good idea.'

'What if she starts screaming?'

Mavros looked up the poorly lit lane with its uneven steps. The large, dilapidated house on the left was the only one with a light in the lower windows. 'Then we tie her to a chair, gag her and wait for Iraklis all the same.'

'Very funny.' She moved back when she saw his face. 'You're serious? But she's an old lady.'

'Who was once a ruthless killer, like her son.' Mavros let his limbs slacken. He didn't want to show Grace how desperate he was to find out how his brother fitted into Iraklis's history. 'It probably won't come to physical restraint.'

'Let's hope not.' She gave him a wary look. 'You got any more hidden depths I should know about?'

He smiled. 'Oh, yes. Hidden depths are my speciality.'

'Great.' She stepped away. 'Let's do it, then.'

He followed her round the corner of the church. 'Grace? I'm not going to tell her who you are, okay? That might make her suspicious about what you want with her son.'

She stopped in the street. 'Who am I supposed

402

to be, then? A female version of Doctor Watson?'

'Something like that. Unless you'd prefer to be my secretary.'

The look she gave him almost made Mavros laugh. Then he remembered that they were about to knock on the door of a woman who had cut many of her own countrymen's throats.

Kostas Laskaris let his pen drop and pushed his chair back from the table. His eyes were stinging and the stabbing in his gut was sharper by the minute. He tried to stand, but found he didn't have the strength. He wiped his sleeve across his face, then peered at the lines of writing on the pad in front of him. They were blurred, indecipherable, though he knew exactly what they said. He had spent hours crafting the section of the poem that he had been dreading most – the scene of defeat and slaughter. It was done, but he didn't know if he would be able to write any more. The horror, the pointless suffering – now that they were encapsulated in words, the work had become even more of a burden. How much longer could he bear it?

The events he had described from the spring of 1944 cascaded past him again. Grimy faces and torn bodies against a barren winter hillside. The village of Loutsa was on a small plateau four hundred metres above the plain of Argos, a dirt road climbing up the steep escarpment in repeated twists and turns. There were about a hundred houses but many had been abandoned as the occupation dragged on, the monarchist inhabitants preferring to take their chances with

403

the enemy down below than with the resistance fighters. Several locals suspected of dealing with the Germans had been taken away for questioning and none had returned. That was why the regional commander had decided to replace the unit that had used the village as a base with one from elsewhere.

Kapetan Iraklis had been uneasy when the band arrived at Loutsa, saying it was exposed to attack on more than one front. There were goat tracks leading off in several directions, including one to the west that looped round a neighbouring mountain. After the losses during the many pitched battles and skirmishes in Lakonia, there were only forty fighters left. His shoulder wound had made Iraklis terse, his face pale and drawn, but in the week they had been at Loutsa, the band had made friends with the remaining villagers, even dancing with them in the *kafeneion* one night.

'There are over a hundred of them, my captain,' Dinos shouted, as he ran into the square. 'Germans and Security Battalion dogs.' He stopped under the bare branches of the old oak. 'They are heavily armed. I saw machine-guns and flame-throwers.'

Iraklis's dark eyes glistened in the cloud-filtered sunlight. 'Very well, comrade.' He glanced round the ring of fighters that had gathered at the first cry of alarm. 'We must choose, my friends, to fight this superior force from the high ground above the road or to withdraw.'

Stamatina pushed her way to the front, the crudely stitched gash on her cheek still livid.

'Withdraw, my captain?' she said incredulously. 'Withdraw? We have never done such a thing.' She looked at her comrades. 'We must fight them, we must slaughter them as we have done over and over again.' Her voice was shrill.

'They will not follow us into the mountains,' Kostas said. 'We can return to harry them on their way back.'

Stamatina gave a harsh laugh. 'You have become weak, comrade. You no longer have any stomach for the fight.' She stepped closer to him. 'You were not raped and buggered by the devils, you did not see your sister's entrails ripped out and strung round her neck like a spring garland.'

'That's enough,' Iraklis said, moving between them. 'This is no time for arguments. I will not sacrifice any more lives needlessly.' He smiled briefly at his friend. 'Comrade Kostas is correct. We will pick them off on their retreat. To the mountain.'

Stamatina's eyes were wide. 'Retreat is surrender, my captain,' she cried. 'I will not–'

She broke off as a young fighter came into the square from the rear of the village, the nailed boots he'd taken from a dead battalionist skidding across the stones.

'The enemy!' he gasped. 'They are behind us too.' Gunfire started the second after he had spoken.

'How?' Iraklis said, as he pulled back the slide of his Schmeisser. 'The sentries...' He looked at Kostas. 'Someone betrayed us, my friend.' He shouted out dispositions, splitting the band into two sections. Then he strode away towards the

405

rattle of automatic weapons, his injured shoulder down. The fighters divided, Stamatina leading the other group to the front of the village.

And that was end for most of them. The German force that had made the long detour around the mountain to the south-west was made up of battle-hardened Alpine troops. As soon as they pinned the band down in the rough ground behind Loutsa, the column that had come up the dirt road broke through the meagre defences.

Kostas was behind Iraklis, relaying his orders to the fighters on either side. He saw Dinos, his thin face split by a frightening grin, shoot a German. Then the top of the boy's head flew off, the crack of the bullet coming after the spray of red and lumpen grey. Bitter liquid filled Kostas's mouth and he blinked hard before looking to the front again. The enemy was making relentless progress, forcing the ELAS fighters closer to each other. Grenades accounted for several comrades, their bodies thrown shattered into the air.

Iraklis and Kostas found themselves close at the last, crouching behind a low outcrop of rock that protected them from the encircling enemy. There were explosions and loud cries from the village, the rattle of gunfire getting nearer.

'We are finished, my friend,' Kapetan Iraklis said, his eyes damp. 'I hope Stamatina survives.' He swallowed. 'She ... she is carrying my child.'

Kostas nodded, unsurprised. He had seen them go off at night when the other fighters were asleep. At first he had been jealous, but then he understood that the love he felt for Iraklis was on a higher plane, unsullied by physical urges. He knew his friend returned that emotion; he had always known it even though no words had been spoken.

'The struggle will go on after us,' he said, fitting the last ammunition clip to his submachine-gun.

Kapetan Iraklis nodded, his lips parted as he fed bullets into his revolver. He leaned over and squeezed Kostas's arm. 'Farewell, my friend. Let us die like true heroes of the Mani.' But before he could clamber round the rock, a long-handled German grenade landed on the ground between them. There was only time to exchange a brief glance...

In the tower, the old poet managed to get to his feet. He would soon be going into the void. Iraklis, Spyros Mavros, Randos – so many comrades had gone before him. It would be something to share the ultimate collective experience, even though it would be over in an instant. Unlike Iraklis in the myth, heroes in the real world didn't become immortals.

But before he allowed the cancer to cut him down, there was one more thing he had to do. Iraklis's son would not return to the tower after he had visited Stamatina, Laskaris was sure of that. So it fell to him to climb the accursed steps to the room at the top of the tower. If he didn't, he would have one more senseless death on his conscience, one more comrade who deserved better.

As they climbed the steps of Potamianou towards Stamatina Kastania's house, Mavros caught a quick movement in the floodlights on the fortified wall beyond. He stopped, touching Grace's forearm.

'I think there's someone up where we were earlier on.'

She peered forward. 'You-know-who?'

He shrugged, staring up to the line of Akronafplia. It was not as well illuminated as the fortress of Palamidhi and the stars were visible in the clear night sky above the lower citadel. 'Could be. Or a couple looking for a secluded place to neck.' He moved on, thinking that if they were being observed by the terrorist, then the sooner they got into his mother's house the better – though if they had any sense, they'd turn tail and run.

The building was three storeys high: it looked as if it had once been a rich man's home but was now almost derelict. Only two shuttered windows on the ground floor were illuminated, but the street door was neatly painted in a deep shade of red, a shrivelled May wreath and a cross marked in soot above it. The old woman might have been a Communist, but she still observed the folk beliefs to bring good fortune to her house.

Mavros looked around, saw no further movement on the walls, nodded to Grace and knocked three times. After a few moments he heard uneven, shuffling footsteps and the door opened a few centimetres.

'You don't look like you're going to sing the *kalanda*,' the old woman said, only part of her face visible. The reek from a diesel stove rolled over them. Mixed up in it was the aroma of roasting meat, reminding Mavros that he had eaten little that day.

'Excuse us, Kyria Kastania,' he said. 'Can we come in? My name is Mavros. You'll have heard of my father Spyros.'

The old woman in black screwed up her eyes, moving them from him to Grace. Her mouth was working as if she was trying to enunciate a distant memory, the pocked edges of the scar on her cheek stretching. 'Spyros Mavros,' she said, surprise replacing suspicion. 'You are Spyros Mavros's son?' She stared at him, taking in the long hair and stubble. 'You don't look much like your father. The time I saw him give a speech in Athens he was perfectly turned out, his hair and moustache neat.' She opened the door a little wider. 'Andonis, that's your name, isn't it?'

Mavros felt a knife thrust to his heart. 'No,' he managed to say. 'My name is Alexandhros – Alex.'

Stamatina Kastania extended a wrinkled hand to him. 'Here, my boy, let me greet you. Your father was a great man in his way.' Her expression tightened. 'But he was not strong enough. The struggle should have been continued by force, not propaganda.'

Mavros let her have her rant. 'Can we come in?' he asked quietly. 'It's very important.'

The old woman frowned. 'No, young Mavros, I'm afraid you can't. I'm very tired. I was just going to bed.'

He had expected her to refuse them entry because of Iraklis's imminent arrival. He put his hand on the door and pushed it gently inwards. 'I'm sorry, you must let us in, Kyra Stamatina.'

409

He put his mouth close to her ear. 'I have a message for your son.'

The old woman's eyes flew wide open. 'My son?' she said. 'My son?' Her voice was suddenly tremulous. 'I have no son.'

Grace bustled in, taking her by the arm. Mavros closed the door behind them and followed them into a small living room. The diesel *somba* was in one corner, its rattling fan dispersing heat. The place was small but spotless, rough-weave blankets on the sofas and chairs, rugs on the stone floor. The only thing to distinguish it from the homes of countless other elderly Greeks was the life-size bust of Lenin in the niche that would normally have contained an icon. He wondered if it had looked the same when his brother had visited.

'What is this?' Stamatina Kastania demanded, shaking off Grace's hand. 'What do you think you are doing?' When Grace took her arm again and led her towards the single armchair, she tried unsuccessfully to break free.

'Sit down, Kyra Stamatina,' Mavros said soothingly. 'Sit down and listen to me.' He glanced at Grace. 'I'm sorry if my friend hurt you.'

The old woman gave a humourless laugh. 'It would take more than a skinny woman to hurt me. I was an ELAS fighter, I was a member of the–'

'Iraklis band,' Mavros interrupted. Stamatina Kastania was in her eighties, but her spirit was still burning strongly. She was capable of shouting for help from a neighbour unless he

410

could convince her to let them stay. Short of tying her up – which he didn't want to do – the best way of doing that was to show at least part of his hand. 'You fought here and in Lakonia.'

Grace was standing over the old woman's chair, trying to follow the exchange.

'How do you know these things?' Stamatina asked. 'Did your father tell you?'

'My father died when I was five. I didn't really know him.'

'Alexandhros,' she said, musing. 'I was sure Spyros's son was called Andonis.'

'My brother,' Mavros said, his voice faint.

'Andonis,' the old woman repeated. 'Ach, yes, I remember now. He was an activist, wasn't he? Against those bastard Colonels?' She looked up at Mavros. 'Was he involved in the siege of the Polytechnic?'

'He disappeared in 1972.' He glanced at Grace and saw that her expression was stern. He was allowing his family to hijack her case, but he didn't want to mention why she was interested in Iraklis and, besides, he needed to gain the old woman's confidence. He squatted in front of the chair. 'Kyra Stamatina, we ... I must see your son. I know he's coming here.'

'You know–' She broke off. 'I don't understand what you're saying, young man. I told you, I have no son.'

Mavros sighed. 'You must believe me, I mean him no harm.' He glanced up at Grace, who gave him an inquisitive look. 'I want to ask him about my brother Andonis. Kostas Laskaris told me that they met in the Mani a month before my

411

brother vanished.'

'You know Comrade Kosta?' Now the old woman seemed less tense. 'You spoke to him recently?'

'We visited him yesterday. He told me that Andonis stayed with you here after he saw your son.'

Kyra Stamatina stared at him blankly. 'Many people stayed with me during the stone years. I don't remember your brother any more than the others.' She inclined her head towards Grace. 'What about her? Why doesn't she speak?' She ran her eye up the American's denim jacket to her head then pointed to the blonde ponytail. 'Is she foreign?'

'Yes,' Mavros admitted.

'German?' Stamatina Kastania's voice was harsh.

'American,' Grace put in, realising she was the subject of the conversation.

An expression of loathing appeared on the old woman's face. 'A curse on the capitalists,' she hissed. Then she looked up at Grace again. 'Wait a moment, I've seen her before.' She turned to Mavros. 'And you. You've been watching me, haven't you? Following me around.' She gave a sharp laugh. 'She is no artist and you are no friend of the struggle if you are with her.' She sat back and folded her arms. 'To the devil with both of you.'

'What's going on?' Grace asked.

'I failed to convince her. She's even more suspicious of us than she was at the outset.'

'So what do we do now?'

412

'Cut and run,' he said. 'This was a mistake. She'll warn her son we're here unless we gag her and tie her up. I don't think that's a good idea. He'll realise there's something wrong if she doesn't respond in the right way when he comes to the door. You can be sure experienced underground operators like them will have some sort of password. I don't want to take on the most dangerous man in Greece in his mother's house.' He took out his notebook and wrote down his mobile number. 'Give this to your son,' he said to the old woman. 'Tell him I must talk to him. He can call me any time, day or night.'

Stamatina Kastania took the paper and dropped it on to her lap. 'I told you, I don't have a son.'

Mavros leaned closer. 'I know what you did in the war,' he whispered. 'I know you slaughtered your fellow Greeks. But I won't talk to the newspapers about that and I won't tell the police about your son, as long as he calls me by midnight tomorrow.' He gave her a look that she eventually acknowledged with an almost imperceptible nod.

'Let's go,' Mavros said to Grace. As he closed the front door, he glanced back and caught a glimpse of the old woman's scarred face.

It almost froze the blood in his veins.

Peter Jaeger came into the office in the basement of the American embassy at speed, loosening his bow-tie. There was a spot of red wine on the right lapel of his white tuxedo. Although his fair hair was smoothed down as usual, his eyes were wide

413

as they took in his nervous subordinate.

'This had better be good, Ms Forster,' he said, his tone sharp. 'The Saudi minister was not impressed when I left in the middle of his address.'

'I'm sorry, sir,' she said, her hair swinging as she pointed to the telephone on her desk. 'There was a call for you.' She summoned the nerve to look him in the eye. 'Code Red. It was—'

'I know who it would have been,' her superior interrupted. 'When's Finn calling back?'

Jane Forster looked at the digital clock on the wall. 'In four and one quarter minutes.'

Jaeger took off his tuxedo and threw it over a chair. 'Jesus, something must have got right up his ass.' He glanced at her. 'Okay, Ms Forster, you can relax. You did the right thing.'

'Yes, sir.' She picked up the jacket and draped it carefully round the back of the chair. 'Sir, if you don't mind me asking, where's this operation heading?'

His eyes met hers, taking in the bright blue irises. For a moment it looked like he was going to tear another strip off her. Then the gym-hardened muscles of his upper body relaxed. 'Where's it heading?' he said, mimicking her drawl. 'To the capture of the most wanted terrorist in Greece, of course.'

'Yes, sir, but I'm concerned about accountability here.' Jane Forster's voice was suddenly more assured. She stepped closer to him, the fabric of her grey trouser suit making a soft sound as her thighs rubbed together. 'Is the ambassador aware of what's going on? And what

414

about the Greek authorities?' She turned to her desk and picked up a yellow pad. 'Commander Kriaras called four times today. Shouldn't we brief him?'

Jaeger regarded her with a mixture of irritation and amusement, his thin lips forming into a cold smile. 'Getting a bit above yourself, aren't you, Ms Forster? Listen, fieldwork is different from what you experienced in Langley. In the field you have to allow operatives a free hand.'

'But, sir, our operative in this case seems to be more of a ghost than someone who fits into the chain of command.'

Jaeger nodded thoughtfully. 'Very well put, Ms Forster. You've read the files on Iraklis. The same word has been used about him. He's a ghost who only becomes visible when he wants to.'

'Or a chameleon,' the female operative put in. 'He was characterised that way too.'

'Right.' He caught her eye again. 'And how do you catch a ghost or a chameleon?'

Jane Forster's lips were pursed. 'By putting another ghost or chameleon on his tail.'

Jaeger clapped his hands, the sardonic expression returning. 'Very good, Ms Forster. You're learning.'

She shot him a frustrated glance, then reached for the phone when it buzzed. She listened for a few seconds. 'Yes,' she said, in a clipped voice, checking the line's security status. 'Code Red confirmed. Stand by.' She handed the receiver to her superior officer, then headed for the door.

Jaeger raised a hand. 'You can stay.' He put the phone to his ear. 'This is Ahab.' He listened for the correct response. 'Very well. Proceed.'

Jane Forster studied him as he listened and spoke, her rear against the end of her desk. She was trying to make sense of the words, at the same time affecting the air of nonchalant control affected by senior officers. Fortunately Jaeger was making things easy for her in his conversation with the undercover expert Lance Milroy, code-name Finn.

'How long were Mavros and Helmer in the house?' Pause. 'And now they are where?' Pause. 'All right, we'll put the local man on to them. You stay where you are. Is the location secure?' Pause. He smiled. 'Yeah, Ms Forster's listening in. I'm trying to teach her some fieldcraft.' Pause. 'Negative. Do not, repeat do not, engage subject. Observe only and confirm subsequent action with me before undertaking. Understood?' Pause. 'Okay. Out.'

Jane Forster took the receiver from him and replaced it. 'Did I understand that our man is in position? In Nafplion?'

Jaeger nodded.

'And he wanted to engage Iraklis?'

'Finn is perfectly capable of such action and is equipped accordingly.' He looked at her. 'He also knew my predecessor Trent Helmer – who, you'll remember, was killed by the Iraklis group – and his wife. Never disregard the power of emotion, Ms Forster. Even in organisations like ours that try to damp it down.'

'What about Tiresias, sir?' Forster asked. 'Shouldn't we advise Tiresias of these developments?'

416

'Don't you worry, Tiresias can handle things.' He stood up and held out his hand for his tuxedo. 'Time I got back to the reception.' He smiled again, this time more expansively. 'Maybe when it's finished you and I could go out for a few drinks, Jane. I think it's time we got to know each other better.'

She disguised her revulsion, but only just.

Grace stood outside her room in the Nafplion hotel and looked at Mavros. He seemed ill at ease. 'What is it, Alex? We established a line of communication with the mystery man without endangering ourselves, we had a good dinner. What more do you want?'

'I want him to make contact. Preferably by phone rather than with his weapon.'

Grace's eyes were on him. 'He'd better. Otherwise as soon as that deadline of tomorrow midnight that you gave him is up, I'm going back to his mother.' Her expression was grim. 'After what he did to my father, he can hardly be surprised if I use his mother as bait.'

'Not a good idea, Grace.'

'We're getting past the stage of good and bad ideas, Alex. I want Iraklis by tomorrow night, you understand?'

'I reckon he'll be in touch one way or another.'

'So do I.' The tension left her face. 'Get in here. I've got some whisky in my bag. The least you can do is have a night-cap with me.'

Mavros allowed himself to be ushered into the room. The shutters were open and, through the uncurtained french windows, he could see the

417

illuminated shapes of the fortifications on Palamidhi.

'It's spectacular, isn't it?' Grace said, taking a half-bottle of Johnnie Walker Black Label from her bag. 'This was the best they had in the shop,' she added. 'I picked it up when you were on the phone to your Communist archive rat. Want a glass?'

He accepted the bottle. The spirit coursed down his throat and almost immediately he felt less down. 'Sorry,' he said, handing it back. 'I haven't been very good company tonight.'

'It's all right.' She sat down on one of the beds, beckoning him to join her, then swigging from the bottle. 'You aren't required to socialise with your clients.' She smiled crookedly.

Mavros felt a crackle of sexual tension. 'Look, Grace, I told you, I'm not comfortable with getting involved during a case.'

She laughed hoarsely. 'What about the great tradition of private eyes bedding their clients?' she said, drinking again. 'I'm thinking Bogart and Bacall in *The Big Sleep*, Nicholson and Dunaway in *Chinatown*.'

'This is the real world, not Hollywood,' he said. 'We're waiting for a call from a guy who's killed a whole swathe of people.' He glanced at her. 'And who was probably the one heading up the slope with his gun pointed at us yesterday.'

Grace sat up straight. 'You think I've forgotten that, Alex?'

'You didn't seem too bothered by it.'

Her eyes dropped. 'I've been threatened often enough in the field.'

Mavros was studying her, his doubts about her motives still plaguing him.

'Besides,' Grace went on, 'I'm not scared of him. He's good at killing defenceless people.'

'And we don't fall into that class?'

She drank and then returned his gaze. 'Don't get me wrong, Alex. I'm not in this for revenge, I told you that. But I can look after myself.'

Mavros had noticed how efficiently she handled the old woman. 'I think it's time you were straight with me, Grace. What did you do before you were with the aid agency? Did you have some kind of military or police training?'

There was silence for a while. Then she said, 'You're a smart guy, Mr Investigator, but it's possible to be too smart.'

'I'll take that as a yes,' he said, shifting away from her. 'Which service?' He watched her carefully.

'It's not and I'm not,' Grace said. She let out a long sigh. 'All right, here it is. I served six years in the CIA.'

Mavros felt his stomach flip. 'What? Not in Greece?'

'Uh-uh. At first in Langley. Then in South America.'

'Field operations?'

'Yeah.'

He stood up and went towards the windows. 'You should have told me, Grace. Am I wearing donkey's ears? You've been using me. I suppose that's why you've been trying to get me into the sack.'

'I don't understand.'

419

'What is it you want from me?' he continued, ignoring her blank look. 'You want me to find Iraklis so you can nail him for the agency?'

Grace's cheeks were highlighted in red. 'I don't know what you're talking about.'

'You're telling me you're not with the CIA now?' Mavros scoffed.

'No connections whatsoever.'

'I believe you,' he said sardonically.

'Believe what you like,' she replied coldly. 'I haven't lied to you, Alex. You never asked me what I did before Meliorate until now. When you did, I told you.'

'Fucking hell,' he said, his fists clenching. 'We're careering about the country looking for a guy who's killed two major entrepreneurs, and as likely as not a leading composer, not to mention the former terrorist he drove to his death down in the Mani. He was responsible for your own father's death. Didn't it occur to you to favour me with that scrap of information about your background?' He raised a hand to the stubble on his chin, fingers moving quickly across it. He had remembered the tall man with the plastered-down fair hair and the immaculate suit he had seen outside the concert hall back in Athens following the explosion – Lambis Bitsos had hinted he was CIA. 'You saw Peter Jaeger at the embassy as well as the consular people, didn't you? Christ, now it all makes sense. The surveillance in Athens, your people were behind that. They've been on to us from the start.' He glared at her. 'Have you been giving them regular reports on our progress? Was that an American operative up on the battlements above Potamianou?'

'Jesus, don't be so paranoid, Alex,' she said, turning away. 'I told you, I have no links with Langley any more – or with anyone else in authority. I don't know any Peter Jaeger.'

Mavros dropped his hand from his face. She might have been telling the truth, but either way it didn't make much difference. He'd spent four days working for a client who had formerly worked for the agency that had supported the Greek Right throughout the post-war period and had backed the dictatorship to the hilt. His father had suffered under the regimes it had approved, he had died worn out by the struggle; and his brother had disappeared when the Colonels held power. He gave her a bitter smile.

'What?' Grace asked.

'I suppose it's the ultimate irony. The closest I've ever managed to get to Andonis has been while I've been working for an ex-CIA agent.'

She came close and punched him lightly on the chest. 'Well, be happy, Alex. I'm paying you to find my father's killer, but use the case to find out what you can about your brother. Then we'll say goodbye. Okay?'

Mavros stood motionless for a while. Then, his head angled away from her, he headed for his room.

Dorothy Cochrane-Mavrou was lying on her bed in the Palaiologos house, two pillows behind her back. Although there was a book open on her lap, she hadn't looked at it for a long time. She peered into the lines of light that were coming

421

through the shutters from the security fence outside and shivered. A feeling of paralysing dread had gripped her since the previous night, making her heart beat irregularly. Geoff Dearfield's memoir was the cause of it. She'd been unable to go downstairs and talk to the others since she finished the typescript. If only she had read it in Athens; then she would never have agreed to come to Argolidha.

She forced herself to take deep breaths and gradually regained control over the rest of her body. But she didn't want to get up, even though she had missed dinner and had eaten little from the tray that Anna had brought. Her daughter had been as impatient as ever, chivvying her along and trying to make her come down. She could see that her mother was troubled, but she put it down to the wilfulness that she herself had inherited.

'Honestly, Mother,' Anna had said, 'what will Veta and Nikitas think? The children are wondering what's the matter too.'

Dorothy had given her a pained stare and turned away. It was a shame she was casting a pall over the party, but that wasn't her fault. It all came back to what Dearfield had written. Never mind what the host and hostess would think of Dorothy missing meals – they would be appalled if they ever read what Geoff had written about their fathers. Clearly Flora knew nothing of it. She said she hadn't read the script and Dorothy believed her. If she'd known anything about the contents, she would never have accepted the invitation from the Palaiologi.

'Oh, God,' Dorothy murmured. 'I'm too old to deal with this. Spyro, where are you when I need you most? Andoni, you would know how to act now.'

She closed her eyes and instantly the scenes from the Second World War that the old British officer had described closed round her like a shroud. She could do nothing to brush them away, could only lie still and suffer the horror. If she went through it one more time, would there be some relief?

Those desperate people, the battered, bleeding men and women who'd been penned up in the wire compound round this very house. Even if they hadn't been ELAS fighters and EAM cadres like her husband, she would have felt sympathy for them. No one deserved such treatment, not even the worst collaborators. But normal human standards had been abandoned. The Metaxas dictatorship before the war, the years of repression and imprisonment, had soured the country even before the Axis forces occupied it. Spyros had seen terrible things that he would not tell her about, but they couldn't have been worse than those described by Dearfield. He had been present as British regional commander, he had watched the survivors of a joint German and Security Battalion raid on a village called Loutsa being brought into the makeshift holding camp. He admitted that he had tipped off the local collaborationist commanders Prokopis Palaiologos and Sokratis Dhragoumis, fathers of her host and hostess, about the ELAS band's location. They were a particularly renowned unit, responsible for many successful actions in Lakonia, and the anti-Communist forces were keen to make an example of them.

The images hardened before her eyes again, staying clear even when she shut them. Oh, God. There was the leader, his shoulder hanging and his face covered in blood beneath the wispy beard. Kapetan Iraklis, they called him. And there was his comrade, the man who had saved his own life and his commander's by throwing a grenade back at the Germans, killing three of them. They had been captured all the same, beaten mercilessly. The comrade, whose *nom de guerre* was Iolaos, was unconscious, his motionless body dropped like a sack in a corner of the compound. Worst of all, there was a woman, a brave fighter, her face scarred and her uniform impregnated with filth so that she looked like she had recently been dug up from the ground. She was screaming defiance at her captors, calling them jackals and traitorous scum, shouting the name of her commander shrilly until a battalionist in traditional *evzone* garb had clubbed her to the ground.

At least that meant the ELAS woman didn't see what happened to Kapetan Iraklis. Along with Palaiologos and Dhragoumis, Major Geoffrey Dearfield of the Special Operations Executive had watched as the guerrilla commander was brought to a vertical wooden frame and tied to it with barbed wire.

Then the torture had started.

17

Mavros woke early, before the light began to creep through the slats in the shutters. He got up and squinted outside, seeing little more than the dull glow of a street-lamp. The walls on Palamidhi were no longer illuminated. The great fortress had disappeared into the night like a besieging army that had suddenly given up the struggle. For some reason that thought raised his spirits, but only momentarily. There had been no call from the man they were seeking. Resisting the temptation to go straight back to Kyra Stamatina's house, he shaved and had a shower. Before he went under the lukewarm water, he put his mobile, which had been charging overnight, on a stool by the door. It still didn't ring.

Stopping by Grace's door, Mavros considered knocking. He put his ear to it and heard no sound so he decided to leave her. She wouldn't be pleased that he'd gone off on his own, but he needed to think about the case and he didn't think she'd be in too much danger while she was in the hotel. The birds in the cage behind the reception desk were quiet, the cover still over them. He gave his key to the half-awake night clerk and went out into the street. The early-morning sun was struggling to break through the clouds, but the air was dry and not too cold. There wasn't much traffic on the wide streets around the park, Nafplion being a town that serviced the tourists for half of the year and spent the other half recovering. He went into a café and ordered a *sketo* from a smiling bottle-blonde, whose accent suggested she had recently arrived from the former Soviet Union. He looked through yesterday's copy of an Athenian newspaper as he sipped the unsweetened coffee. The government was still in crisis, harried by the opposition and by most of the media for its failure to catch Iraklis. The composer Randos had been buried in the First Cemetery, his cortège followed by thousands of admirers. Mavros would have liked to be there to send off the man whose music he had lived with from childhood. The report said that the crowd had sung verses of 'Love Burns' and 'The Voyage of the *Argo*' after the committal, many of them weeping.

He leaned back in the chair and thought about the cat-loving recluse. There were still unresolved issues about his death. If Kostas Laskaris was right about the unlikelihood of his long-standing friend killing himself, that left only accident or murder as the explanation. Despite the authorities' insistence that the latter was out of the question, Mavros inclined towards it – the fact that the kittens had been found beside their owner's body almost clinched the argument for him. But if Randos had been murdered, who was responsible? Could it have been the terrorist group? There had been no miniature olive branch or proclamation from Iraklis, though the government might have suppressed those. And why would an assassin who had started out as a Communist have targeted a comrade when his last two victims had been exemplars of capitalism? Unlike many former believers, Randos had retained his political faith, despite his holiday homes. But if the terrorist hadn't murdered the composer, then who had? It all came down to the two armed men in the ravine – after Babis Dhimitrakos had fallen, one of them had come for him and Grace with what looked like evil intent, and the other had saved them. In both cases, why? And who were the men?

He glanced out of the condensation-streaked window and caught a glimpse of a nondescript man behind the trunk of a eucalyptus. He seemed familiar, but Mavros couldn't place him. Had he seen him somewhere in the town? Was he the one who'd been on the ramparts of Akronafplia above Kyra Stamatina's street? He felt his hands go clammy. He didn't think he was one of the armed men – this guy was short and thin – but he couldn't be sure. When the man started to move away, Mavros forced himself to keep thinking.

He went back to the conversation he'd had with Grace last night. Whatever game she was playing, it seemed clear that the Americans were involved in the case. Was the man part of a surveillance team? He looked outside again. This time there was no one to be seen.

Grace was right. It was easy to become paranoid in these situations. Still, someone had definitely been on their tail in Athens so why not here? But how would they have been spotted? Had Grace been keeping in touch with whoever was watching them? Had she really cut all connections with the agency she once worked for? The case had more shadows in it than an old black-and-white horror movie. If there hadn't been the lead to Andonis, he might have left Grace to it and headed back to the big city.

His phone went off, making him freeze. Was this the man they'd been tracking? The number displayed on the screen was one he didn't recognise.

'Mavros,' he said, throwing down a thousand-drachma note and moving outside quickly to ensure the signal didn't fade.

'Yes,' came an old woman's voice. 'My son still hasn't returned.'

He sighed as he reached the other side of the road. 'Is that you, Kyra Fedhra?' There was no one behind the eucalyptus. 'Yiorgos hasn't been in touch?' He pursed his lips, annoyed with himself for having forgotten the earlier call from the Fat Man's mother and wondering where the hell his friend had got to. Had that been him with the Lada down in the Mani?

Kyra Fedhra launched into a lengthy complaint about her son's lack of respect for his family, especially his long-suffering mother, stranded in her village with no one to run errands for her. Mavros thought about the distances. It must have been about three hours' drive from there to Kostas Laskaris's house at Tigani, more if the bad weather had held.

'Let me see what I can do,' he interrupted. 'I'll call you back as soon as I know more.' He broke the connection, storing the number she'd called from in his phone's memory. Then he swallowed a curse. This was all he needed right now.

Entering the park and sitting down by the equestrian statue of the War of Independence hero Kolokotronis, he called Directory Enquiries and, after a struggle, got through to the Ayia Kyriaki community president. The guy sounded like he'd been woken from a decade-long sleep, but he eventually gave him the number of the woman who cleaned for Kostas Laskaris.

'Yes?' The voice that answered was male.

Mavros had been trying to work out a coherent plan of action. He explained that he was a friend of the old poet.

'You're in luck,' the man said. He sounded young. 'I look after the tower and drive Kyrio Kosta around.' He sounded very proud of that. 'Can I give him a message?'

'Yes. It's about a mutual friend of ours, Yiorgos Pandazopoulos.' He didn't know for a fact that the poet knew the Fat Man, but he reckoned there was a good chance they'd met in the past when they were both active in the Party. 'I want to know if Kostas has seen him in the last couple of days.'

There was a protracted silence. 'All right,' came the doubtful reply. 'I can ask him that.'

'The problem is–' Mavros began, then changed his mind. 'What's your name?'

There was another pause as the young man considered the question with typical Maniate suspicion of strangers. 'Savvas,' he eventually replied.

'Okay, Savva,' Mavros continued. 'Look, this man Yiorgos, you may have seen him yourself. He's in his fifties and, well, to be frank, he's very fat. And bald.'

'Oh, yes, I saw that person,' Savvas said, less reluctant. 'He was in a clapped-out Russian car.'

'A red one?'

'Yes. But, like you say, that was a couple of days ago. I haven't seen him since.'

'Shit,' Mavros said, under his breath, then pressed the phone closer to his ear. Savvas was still talking.

'...lot of visitors recently. I can see the road from our house. There was a couple who came twice. A good-looking blonde woman and a guy with long hair – he looked like a real bender–'

'Really?' Mavros said, preparing to terminate the conversation.

'And then there was that other man,' Savvas said, his voice more expressive. 'Christ and the Holy Mother, I wouldn't have liked to meet him on a dark night. He moved like a big cat, he–'

'When was this?' Mavros interrupted.

'Two days ago, again. Let me think... Yes, the couple came on Wednesday and Thursday. So the fat man came on Thursday and the other man did too. I couldn't see so well that day because of the snow.'

'Can you describe the man?'

'The lion, you mean? That's the way I see him. He was tall, wearing a dark coat and a scarf, and he came in and out of the snow like he was hunting. Gave my mother quite a fright, I can tell you.'

'What age was he?'

'Dunno. Not young. In his fifties, judging by the lines on his face, though his hair was black enough. He had a flashy big car, silver. Do you still want me to ask Kyrio Kosta?'

'Yes. Please call me back with his answer. It's very important.' Mavros gave him the mobile number. 'You haven't seen the Lada again?'

'No.' Savvas laughed. 'It's probably fallen to pieces.'

Mavros had a worse feeling than that about the car and its missing driver. He stressed the urgency again and signed off, then put the phone into his pocket.

'Interesting conversation?' Grace startled him as she came round the statue base.

'Em, yes. Don't worry. It was nothing to do with the case.' He wanted to keep the issue of the Fat Man to himself until he heard from Laskaris.

'Are you sure? You sounded very serious.'

'Family matter,' he mumbled.

'Why didn't you wake me?' Grace demanded.

'I thought you could do with the sleep.'

She studied him dubiously. 'How many times have I got to tell you? I want us to stick together. Let's get some breakfast.'

Mavros followed her towards the café he'd just left. At least the coffee wasn't bad.

Flora Petraki-Dearfield, wife of the former British officer, slipped into the bedroom she was sharing with him in the Palaiologos house. She had finally managed to get Geoff to go out, having asked the men to take him into Nafplion for coffee. Fortunately Dorothy hadn't appeared so far this morning. She and Geoff were both on edge, thanks to his memoir. The women were

431

planning on going into the town with the kids to do the last of their Christmas shopping. Any minute now she would have free run of the house. She was sure the gloomy butler wouldn't get in her way.

The academic books Flora had brought with her were in a pile on the floor by the dressing-table. Among them was an obscure ancient text, which had some references to a sect of Iraklis worshippers in the second century AD that she wanted to check. But not now – she had more important things on her mind.

Then, at the very moment she had the house to herself, she felt the past extend its clutching hands and drag her to the place she had consigned to the dark...

Flora was back in the family house in the northern suburbs of Athens, an eight-year-old in petticoats, her jet-black hair gathered in a mother-of-pearl clasp. The German occupation was in its last months, but she had never been particularly aware of it. The Sunday rides in her father's huge American car to visit friends and relatives still went on most weekends and the food on the table was little different from that she had always been given. Since the war had begun, most days she was confined to the neo-classical house with its large fenced garden on the slopes of the hillside, her lessons provided by increasingly thin tutors whose jackets were worn through at the elbows and whose trouser bottoms were ragged. But she didn't mind the exclusion. She had her pony Snow White, a barrel-shaped creature who had never been short of fodder, the stable kept perfectly turned out by the wizened old peasant who also looked after the estate's olive trees.

Flora's only sadness was her mother. She had been a celebrated beauty in Athenian society before the war, a soap heiress from Zakynthos with piercing green eyes whose elegance had been refined in a Swiss finishing school. But since the Germans came, she had lost the irresistible charm she once had, her expression becoming haunted and her beautiful eyes ringed in black. She still attended receptions and parties with her banker husband, but they no longer diverted her. It seemed she had seen things that disturbed her, but when Flora asked her what was wrong she just sighed and shooed the little girl from her room.

And although she was young, Flora had become aware of the heavy atmosphere that was around her – not just in the house but in the city on the plain below. Sometimes smoke and dust billowed up in the distance, sometimes – more and more often recently – the sounds of aircraft and exploding bombs were carried on the wind from the docks in Piraeus. She asked her father what was happening, but he only told her not to concern herself with such things, they were not for pretty creatures like her. The tutors avoided answering too, but their sunken cheeks and nervous eyes told her that something terrible was going on beyond the wire and walls around her home. That was when she started to take refuge in the myths, the stories of the ancient heroes and gods that lifted her from the pain she knew was encroaching on her life. That was when she first read about Iraklis and his glorious deeds, his unjust fate and his eventual rise to Olympus to join the immortals...

Coming back to herself, Flora glanced around the room in the watery sunlight admitted by the half-open shutters. She located her husband's typescript without difficulty. He thought he'd been clever by secreting it behind the antique wardrobe, but she knew exactly how his mind worked. After the Mavros daughter Anna had brought it back the previous evening – a curious look on her face as she announced that her mother had asked her to return what she called 'an undesirable book' – Geoff had taken possession of it like a miser who'd lost his wallet. He had then asked Flora to give him some peace, which she'd gladly done. She had no interest in reading the dog-eared script again. She had been perusing it at her leisure ever since he'd started writing it, waiting for him to fall asleep at his desk and extracting the pages from beneath his chest every night. Once his eyes closed, they never opened for at least an hour; that was another thing she had learned about him over the years.

Flora took the block of typed pages out of their cardboard folder and started separating them – those that mentioned Nikitas and Veta's fathers to the right, the others to the left. Then she put the latter, the bulk of the pages, back in the folder and replaced it behind the wardrobe. The smaller pile she held in her hands for a few moments, then slid into a brown envelope. Waiting for the sounds of voices and car doors slamming to end, she went out of the room and walked silently down the corridor. After she had checked that there were no servants in the vicinity, she went into the master bedroom and put the envelope under the covers. She made sure it was in the middle of the wide bed so that it didn't fall out unobserved when her host and hostess got in.

Back in her own room, Flora allowed herself a smile. The die was cast. Soon the culmination of the work she'd been undertaking for years would be achieved. She pressed her hands against her thighs and regained the iron grip on her emotions that had been an integral part of her success. Then she opened her books and concentrated on Iraklis, the ancient bearer of that name. All she could think of was his final labour, the most daunting one of all: entering the death god Hades' realm through the cave at Tainaron in the southern Peloponnese and dragging the hound of hell up to the light of day.

As if to validate the course of action Flora had initiated, one of the watchdogs beyond the security fence gave a loud howl.

'So, what are we going to do?' Grace said as Mavros walked away from the equestrian statue towards the waterfront. 'Spend the day waiting for the bastard to call?'

He glanced at her, head down. 'Lighten up, Grace.' He stopped as a lorry laden with boxes of oranges ground up the road in front of them, the name of Palaiologos in large blue letters on its side. 'Have you got any better ideas?'

'Where are you going?' she asked, grabbing his arm as he set off across the wide expanse of asphalt. 'Isn't there someone you can call? Some other contact who might know something that could help us?'

Mavros stood on the quayside watching the cranes on a Russian ship hoist pallets. He made out the uneven line of Arkadhia's mountains across the gulf even though the visibility was more restricted than it had been yesterday.

'I've already rung someone,' he said, thinking of the message he'd sent to Kostas Laskaris via his driver. 'We just have to wait.' He'd been wondering about asking Lambis Bitsos if anything had broken in the big city, but had dismissed the idea – the reporter had been short with him the last time he'd called, demanding to know what had happened to the great exclusive he'd been promised. He turned, raising his shoulders, then looked beyond her. 'Oh, shit,' he said with a groan.

'What is it?' Grace followed the direction of his gaze. 'Who are they?'

Mavros swivelled his head and calculated if he had time to make a run for it. There was no chance. The open seafront provided no cover. Besides, his nephew and niece had already spotted him. They were both waving like adolescents possessed. 'My family,' he said, 'and other beasts of the jungle.'

'*Yeia sou*, Alex,' Mavros's nephew said, as the group approached. He and his overweight friend were regarding Grace with interest.

'*Yeia sou, theie*,' his sister chorused, addressing

436

him as 'uncle' even though she knew he disliked it. The girl with her gave him a supercilious smile.

'Hi, kids,' Mavros replied, English being the language he always used with them on his mother's orders. He stepped forward and kissed Anna, feeling Nondas's hand come down on his shoulder and acknowledging his brother-in-law with a wink.

'Alex, you remember Veta and Nikitas Palaiologos,' his sister said, narrowing her eyes at him – the unspoken warning was 'Don't be rude to our host and hostess, even if you don't like their politics.' 'And Geoffrey Dearfield? My brother Alex.' She watched as handshakes were exchanged.

As well as meeting the politician and her husband once at a party, Mavros had seen them often enough in the papers and on television. In real life they seemed less like wax dummies, the woman's fleshy frame and the man's bald head giving them an air of vulgar humanity for all their wealth. The bent old man with the limp hand was another story: he looked like a refugee or a prison camp survivor, his head bowed and his voice weak.

'Who's your friend?' Nikitas asked, giving Grace a lascivious look.

'Sorry.' Mavros ushered his client into the group with his arm. He introduced her without clarifying the nature of their relationship. 'Where's Mother?' he whispered to Anna, as more greetings were exchanged.

'She isn't very well,' his sister replied.

'I know. She called me yesterday, wanting me to

join you.' He looked at her helplessly. 'It's a bit difficult.' He took in a couple of burly men in suits standing a few metres behind the group. 'Who are they?'

'Security guards,' Veta Palaiologou put in. 'Now we can't even go for a walk without scheduling a military operation.'

'You must be used to it,' Mavros said.

'In the city, yes. But down here? It's ridiculous.' She raised an eyebrow. 'You're in that line of business yourself, aren't you?'

'Not exactly. I look *for* people, not *after* them.'

'It appears you've found one,' Veta said, inclining her head towards his companion. 'Helmer. That name means something to me.'

'My father was in the US embassy back in the seventies,' Grace said.

Veta's eyes sprang open above her puffy cheeks. 'My God, not Trent Helmer?' She glanced at her husband – he was making expansive movements of his arms as he tried to impress the children and Dearfield with his business operations. 'We – we knew him. My dear, I'm so very sorry. How old were you when he ... when it happened?'

'Five,' Grace replied.

'It was a disgrace. Those terrorists, they are scum, and our pathetic government is doing nothing to catch them now they have started killing again.' She gave a weak smile. 'I'm sorry. I am a shadow minister so you must forgive my intemperance.'

Anna was following the conversation avidly, scenting a story. 'What are you doing in Nafplion?' she asked Grace. 'I don't imagine my

438

brother is showing you the sights.'

Mavros glared at her.

Grace spoke before he could formulate a response. 'I'm trying to locate the woman who looked after me back then.' She lowered her eyes. 'My mother died recently and I ... I felt the need to reconnect with my childhood.'

There was a silence, broken by Nikitas yelling at his son to get out of a forklift's way.

'And this woman, she is from Nafplion?' Veta Palaiologou asked.

'We thought so,' Mavros put in, trying to help his client out with the story she'd come up with. He was impressed by the fluency of the lie. 'But unfortunately she seems to have moved away.'

'Perhaps I could help,' Veta said. 'I have many contacts in the area.'

'That's very kind of you,' Grace said, 'but we have a couple more people still to talk to.'

The politician gave her a thoughtful look. 'Well, if you're sure...' She moved away towards her family, a security guard close behind.

'Quite a coincidence, you being down here, Alex,' Anna said. 'I hope your case has nothing to do with the Palaiologos family.'

Mavros stared at her. 'With the Palaiologos family? No. Why should it?'

Anna drew closer. 'Veta rather understated her standing in Argolidha. Her and Nikitas's families have run the place for decades. I get the impression that nothing goes on around here without her knowing about it.' She pointed at the ships and trucks. 'Look at all this, for a start.'

'We're only trying to find a retired nanny,'

Grace put in.

'Are you really?' Anna said, her tone suggesting how much credence she gave that. 'Come up to the house later, Alex,' she said. 'Mother wants to see you.'

'I'm working, Anna,' he insisted.

'I can see that,' his sister said, and went to join the others.

'Why the lie about your nanny?' Mavros asked.

Grace ignored the question, her eyes on Veta and her husband. 'Who are those people? She said they knew my father.'

Veta Palaiologou's voice carried to them across the asphalt. 'We're going for coffee, if you'd like to join us.' It was more of a command than an invitation.

'Sorry,' Mavros shouted back. 'We're meeting someone.' He didn't want to be overheard if the terrorist rang.

'Come up to the house in the evening, then. I'll expect the two of you for dinner.' The politician turned away, her demeanour and Anna's look making it clear that another refusal was out of the question.

'Christ,' Mavros said. 'Families.'

Grace looked unconcerned. 'Maybe we'll have heard from our man before then. Even if we haven't, going there might keep our minds occupied. How far away is the house?'

'Not far. Five kilometres at the most.'

'Fine. We can get back here quickly enough if we have to.' She nudged him. 'Have you done your Christmas shopping, Alex? Only two days to go. Tonight will be an ideal opportunity to hand over your gifts.'

'I hate Christmas shopping.'

'Don't worry,' she said, taking his arm. 'I'll help.'

'Anyway, we can't,' he protested. 'We have to go in search of your old nanny.'

Grace jabbed her elbow into his ribs. 'What did you expect me to say? Actually, we're looking for the guy who killed my father and is currently assassinating prominent businessmen?'

'No, of course not,' he replied, wondering if his client had experience of assuming false identities from her time in the CIA.

He watched as the group filed into a classy café. Geoffrey Dearfield was hanging back, his head still down. Mavros remembered what his mother had said about the old man's book and wondered if that was why he looked like a prisoner on Death Row.

That thought made him glance up at the ramparts of Akronafplia. Many Communists had been executed after the war in the now demolished prison. The town where Veta and Nikitas Palaiologos held sway might be one of the most attractive in Greece, but it had been a place of slaughter in the recent past. The ancient hero Iraklis had been born nearby too. Would those aspects of the town make his modern counterpart feel at home?

Iraklis drove across the plain of Argos in the four-by-four he had hired, keeping to the back roads that cut the orange groves into regular shapes. Groups of defeated-looking men were walking up

441

the asphalt, modern equivalents of the slaves and bondsmen who had cultivated the land since prehistoric times. Under the Ottoman Empire, droves of Albanians had come down to the fertile land of the Peloponnese and, until recently, the local dialect, with many traces of their native language, had been widely spoken. The men he was passing – a new generation of Albanians, but also Russians, Bulgarians, the dispossessed of the Balkans – were doing the jobs that Greeks no longer lowered themselves to carry out. Or so his mother had told him in the letters she occasionally sent via an intermediary, an old comrade in exile in the Caucasus, to the apartment in Queens.

He drove through a small village and followed the road up to an old monastery. He left the car about a hundred metres from the building with its red-tiled dome and struck out over the foothills of Mount Arachnaio. The vegetation was damp, but there was a goat track and his feet didn't get too wet.

As he walked, he thought about his mother. She had kept her faith, both in the Stalinist ideals she had grown up with (none of the pallid trash peddled by the modern Party for her) and in her son. They hadn't met for nearly eleven years, when he was first becoming suspicious of his fellow terrorists. He had come down to Nafplion from the city to visit her. His stepfather had recently died and he had wondered how she would be, but there was no sign of grief. She was still a striking woman, though her hair was now heavily streaked with silver and the scar on her cheek was as prominent as ever. He'd even wondered if she used makeup to emphasise it; she was like a Soviet war veteran sporting campaign medals every day. She didn't ask him about the Iraklis group's activities, though she knew he was involved in it – she knew enough about clandestine activities to keep her distance. She was proud of him; she told him never to give up the struggle and to remember that his father was the greatest hero of them all.

It all came back to his father. The ELAS *kapetanios* had suffered on these very hills, along with his fighters and countless other comrades who had made the final sacrifice in the wars and against the bullet-pocked walls of the prisons. But no one knew exactly what had happened to him, not even his mother. She had lost contact with him at the very end and he had disappeared into the void. Now, at last, the assassin was about to find out who had despatched him there and the debt of family honour would be repaid.

Iraklis came over a ridge, then pulled back a few yards. There it was, the building he had come to inspect. An ugly block like a factory or a warehouse, the modern extensions that had been built against the sides alleviating the ugliness only slightly. The Palaiologos house. He took out his binoculars and focused on the lower walls, registering the metal posts between which barbed wire was strung and the lights, turned on even during daytime. It wouldn't have been so different when his mother had been here in the war. There were guards and dogs then as well, though no electronic alarms. He took the plan

443

from his pocket and checked the locations of the sensors. It wouldn't be easy to get in unobserved, but he knew he could do it – and get out again too. He swung the binoculars round and picked up the road that led down from the house to the walls of ancient Tiryns.

He confirmed the line of the smaller track on the other side of the citadel that he planned to use on the way in, then moved back behind the ridge. Tiryns. When he was a kid, he'd paid little attention to ancient myths and heroes. From the time he first saw his mother, he had concentrated on modern history, pestering his grandmother and his teachers to tell him about the war. He had earned himself many beatings at school and in the streets of Kitta – most of the adults wanted to pretend the civil strife that followed the Axis occupation had never happened. There was a collective amnesia that spread even to his grandmother, though she did let slip some things about his mother and his wretched, murdered aunt. The rest he found out from Kostas Laskaris, when the poet returned to the Mani to refurbish his family's tower. He was the one who had spoken about his father, the idealistic schoolmaster who had been transformed into the master-tactician and guerrilla captain known as Iraklis. Laskaris had wept when he had spoken about his leader, and the assassin had finally discovered that they had been friends from boyhood – friends and maybe more than friends before his mother had got involved. When he was old enough, the poet had taken him up to the place of slaughter and told him what had happened during the war.

He stood up and started to walk back to the car. Soon it would be dark and he would make his way to the tiny ground-floor flat in the steep lane to see the old woman one last time. Then he would go to the Palaiologos house and regain his family's lost honour according to the traditions of the harsh land where he had been reared. His father had been betrayed at the last, he was sure of that – just as he had been. Since he was a boy, he had felt the need to avenge his father. That urge had been behind the acts of terrorism, the killings, the violence that had destroyed the lives of many more than the victims – it had destroyed the families of the victims and it had destroyed the woman he had loved, the woman whose name he couldn't speak.

Iraklis stopped, his head down. He had come to the final labour, the culmination of his career, and the weight of it was crushing him. He was no longer sure that he had the strength to prevail. But then he thought of his controller and shuddered. He couldn't stand up to an iron will like that, not now after so many years. There was no option. He would be given the last pieces of information, which had only recently come to light, and he would do what he had been trained for. Then, perhaps, he could slip away into the darkness one last time.

Mavros bought gifts for his family in the well-stocked shops of Nafplion, allowing Grace to guide some of his choices. They had lunch in a *taverna* after dropping off the parcels at the hotel.

The phone stayed resolutely silent and eventually he couldn't take it any more.

'I'm going back up to the ramparts above the old woman's place.'

'Are you sure?' Grace sounded doubtful. 'Remember the men with the automatics.'

'The waiting is driving me crazy.' He glanced at his watch. 'There's only about an hour till dark. I won't stick out too much in that short time.'

'I'm coming with you.'

Mavros would have preferred to go alone, but it made sense to keep her in tow – he didn't want to leave her as easy prey for the terrorist, and this way she wouldn't be able to act independently. His suspicions about his client wouldn't go away.

They walked up the long way round, skirting the Venetian bastion on its eastern side. The sun was dropping behind the distant mountains and lights were glowing across the town. The call of a nocturnal bird preparing for the hunt echoed round the old walls. As they came round a bend in the road, the impending darkness making it difficult to see clearly, Mavros grabbed Grace's arm.

'What is it?'

He raised a finger to his lips and craned his head forward. 'Do you see that figure?' he whispered. 'By the wall at the top of Potamianou?'

She screwed up her eyes in the gloom. 'Do you think it's our man?'

'Why would he be hanging around above his mother's front door?' He paused. 'Unless he thinks the place might be staked out. No, I saw a movement up there last night, remember?'

'Someone else on the terrorist's trail?'

He stared at her. 'Maybe it's the guy who saved us.'

Grace met his gaze. 'Or one of the people who were tailing us in Athens.'

Mavros led her to a low wall. 'Shit,' he said, under his breath, as he crouched down. He looked quickly over his shoulder. A man was walking his dog about fifty metres away. Further off, a pair of noisy boys were belting a football across the road that bisected Akronafplia.

'Perhaps he's just a local voyeur,' Grace said. There was a guest-house below the ramparts, some of the shutters open.

Mavros had his lower lip between his teeth. 'Let's leave him to it, then.' He stood up. 'I don't suppose he'll put our man off calling us.'

On the way back down to the lower town, Grace nudged him. 'We don't have to go to that politician woman's house if you don't want to. Maybe it's better to stay in Nafplion in case Iraklis wants a meet.'

He thought about that. 'No, let's keep to the plan. It's close enough for us to get back quickly. Besides, I want to check out that house party.'

'Why?'

He held off answering until they had cut through a disorderly line of people boarding the Athens coach. 'It was something my sister said – about the families of the politician and her husband running this area for decades.' He glanced at her. 'Could there be some connection between them and the assassin? After all, Stamatina Kastania's been living here for years.'

447

Grace brushed away some hairs that had escaped from her ponytail. 'And the woman Veta said they knew my father.'

As Mavros turned to look at her, his phone went off. They both jumped. Going into a dark alcove he raised it to his ear.

'This is Alex Mavros,' he said clearly, in Greek.

'Hallo,' came a rough voice. 'This is Savvas.'

It took Mavros a few seconds to connect the name with Kostas Laskaris's driver. 'Ah,' he said, stifling his disappointment. 'You have some news?'

'Yes. I gave Kyrio Kosta your message and ... you know, he really isn't very well. You shouldn't have made me bother him with this. He's trying to finish a very important—'

'Get to the point, will you, Savva?' Mavros interrupted. 'Has he seen Yiorgos Pandazopoulos?'

There was a pained silence before the Maniate spoke. 'No.'

'Fuck it, that's all?' Mavros said, his voice rising in frustration.

'You should be careful how you speak to people, my friend,' Savvas said, his tone menacing now. 'Kyrios Kostas says he doesn't even know any Yiorgos Pandazopoulos. Goodbye.'

Mavros lowered the phone from his ear and swore again.

'Bad news?'

'No news, more like,' he replied. Then his anger turned to unease when he realised that the call from the Mani had told him more than he'd initially thought. Even though Kostas Laskaris

448

was aged and failing, his mind had been working well enough when they saw him. The chances of him not knowing and not remembering the Fat Man struck him as minimal – as did the chances of Yiorgos parking his car in the shadow of the Communist poet's tower but not knocking on the door.

Something very strange was going on above the rugged headland where his brother had met the man who became Iraklis.

Geoffrey Dearfield closed the door behind him and staggered to his bed, his strength almost gone. Why had he agreed to go to Nafplion with the other men? Why had he acceded to Flora's demands? As soon as they got out of the Range-Rover, Veta and Anna had arrived with the children and his spirit had almost cracked. This was no time to be carousing with children who knew nothing of the past, who were innocent of the crimes their ancestors had committed in the name of king and country.

God, the lies that had been told. And would continue to be told, now that his only hope of seeing the memoir in print had been dashed. Not that he could blame Dorothy for rejecting the script; it was too divisive and corrosive a text for any publisher to accept – he'd known that from the start. Nor could he blame her for being so hurt, for refusing to speak to him about it. Her husband had been through similar horrors: reading the memoir must have brought that back to her. But it was unjust to treat him like a pariah. He was not responsible for the evils that the ELAS band had committed and, at the last, he had done as much as he could to lessen the suffering of its leader. He swallowed the bile that had risen to his mouth. He was kidding himself. He had made the fatal disclosure that the band was holed up in Loutsa, exhausted after the long trek across the mountains from the south. He was the one who had told Palaiologos and Dhragoumis. He could never forget the smiles that had spread across their faces.

He turned towards the window, security lights casting the shadows of fence-posts and branches across the floor of the room in the late-afternoon gloom. And suddenly he was back in the compound on that terrible day when Kapetan Iraklis had been crucified on the St Andrew's cross, his wrists and ankles bound tightly with rusting barbed wire. Prokopis Palaiologos and Sokratis Dhragoumis were standing in front of him, the former in a Greek Army uniform and the latter in a traditional tunic and kilt – he thought it gave him the look of a War of Independence hero, but it only emphasised his corpulent build and would have made his men in the Security Battalion snigger if they hadn't been so terrified of him. They had been beating their prisoner for what seemed like hours.

'Where are the other bands?' Palaiologos shouted, bringing his cane down across the prisoner's face. He stepped closer. 'You traitor, you Communist snake, don't you realise that your surviving fighters have all been captured? If you tell me where the neighbouring ELAS units are, you can save them.' He drew closer. 'Come, now, a commander's responsibility is to his men. Or are you too much of a peasant to understand that?'

The guerrilla chief raised his head with difficulty and spat blood, making Palaiologos step back and curse. He blinked, his eyes focusing on the comatose form of the woman in tattered fatigues. 'Stamatina?' he gasped. 'Comrade Stamatina, can you hear me?'

Palaiologos glanced at Dhragoumis and nodded. The heavy man in the kilt went over to the woman with the livid scar on her cheek and hauled her up. He took a knife from his belt and held it to her throat.

'So,' the interrogator said, 'you have feelings towards this she-fighter?' He spoke the last word as if it were unclean. 'I thought that kind of thing was illegal in your rabble army. No matter. My friend here will cut her, do you understand? Cut her slowly and often if you do not speak.'

'No,' came a faint voice from the other side of the compound. 'Let her be.'

Dearfield watched as a young battalionist stepped up and slammed his rifle butt down on the bare head of the sad-eyed ELAS fighter who had spoken.

'A pity,' Dhragoumis said, over his shoulder. 'You should have let him watch. No matter. If the pig on the cross doesn't speak, use your bayonet on him.'

'Yes, sir,' the young recruit replied keenly.

'Are you ready to speak now, *kapetan?*' Palaiologos asked, mocking.

The bearded man's eyes moved from the

451

woman to the man on the ground beyond. 'Kosta,' he gasped. 'My Kosta...' He ran his tongue over broken lips. 'I cannot,' he gasped. 'I will not—'

A shot rang out and his eyes sprang wide open, the last of the sun flaring in them for a second. Then his head slumped over the ruin of his chest.

Dearfield lowered his service revolver slowly. He was aware of Palaiologos's eyes burning into him as Dhragoumis dropped the woman and stamped through the mud towards him.

'What the hell did you do that for, you stupid bastard?' he screamed, in coarsely accented English.

Palaiologos appeared beside him, his face red.

'You were going to kill him anyway,' Dearfield replied. 'He wouldn't have told you anything that we don't already know. And I would remind you that torture is contrary to the Geneva Convention.'

'What Geneva Convention?' Palaiologos scoffed. 'These people are animals, not soldiers. You know how they treat their prisoners.'

Dhragoumis stepped over to the unconscious male captive on the ground and started to kick him in the chest.

Dearfield pulled him away. 'Stop it, Sokrati! This is savagery, not war.'

'They are the same thing, fool,' the man in the kilt said. He looked at Palaiologos and laughed. 'We shall take the woman inside. Since we can't torment her leader any more, we'll satisfy ourselves with her.'

The two men went over to the unconscious

female guerrilla. Dearfield tried to intervene but a pair of battalionists prevented him following them into the blockhouse.

So he had listened from outside as they violated Comrade Stamatina; he heard the grunts and groans of two men he had once thought were worthy allies. She made no sound at all. Afterwards they boasted that they had defiled her every orifice, even though the curve of her belly suggested she was carrying a child.

Geoffrey Dearfield came back to himself, shivering uncontrollably. Suddenly he had a desperate need to see the memoir he had written, to convince himself that at least he had tried to save the woman; that even though he had remained in contact with Palaiologos and Dhragoumis, he had always despised them. Pulling the package from behind the wardrobe, he unwrapped it and ran his fingers shakily through the pages.

It only took him a short time to realise that the worst of it, the episodes that brought most shame on Veta and Nikitas's families had been removed. His heart was pounding. Who could have taken them? And where were they now? The idea that his host and hostess might learn how low their fathers had sunk while he was in their house went through him like a bayonet thrust.

But even worse was the realisation, long suppressed and never substantiated, that his wife had betrayed him.

18

When they got back to the hotel, the last of the sun gone from the waters of the gulf, Mavros headed for his room to get ready for the dinner at the politician's house. He thought about shaving – his mother would no doubt appreciate that – but decided that was too much of a capitulation to the standards of the rich and powerful. His jeans weren't too clean but they were all he had. The best he could do was shower and wash his hair. It was while he was under the lukewarm water that he heard the knock on his door.

His breath caught in his throat. He grabbed a towel and crossed the tiled floor, water dripping everywhere. He blinked hard and opened the door. 'Grace,' he gasped.

'Oh, sorry,' she said. 'Sorry, Alex. You thought I was Iraklis, didn't you?' She handed him a plastic bag. 'I thought you might like a fresh shirt.' She ran her eyes down his torso. 'Want me to rub your back?'

'Jesus.' He grabbed the package and closed the door in her face, then went back to the bathroom. The look on Grace's face had suggested that she was still interested in getting him into the sack. He was attracted to her, there was no doubt about that – most men would be – but he couldn't give in to her, and not just because it would complicate their working relationship: he was apprehensive about Grace – beneath the controlled surface, he had seen evidence of strong emotions and he didn't want to unleash them. Then there was Niki. He couldn't let her down, even though their relationship wasn't in good health. Maybe he was letting his imagination run away with him over Grace; maybe she really had severed all connections with the CIA and just fancied him. He'd never had any problem attracting women: he had the good looks he'd inherited to thank for that, but he had trouble responding to their emotions – women seemed to feel things that were beyond him.

Mavros came out of the bathroom and put on the shirt Grace had bought him. It was a tasteful dark blue number with a button-down collar. At least the top half of his body wouldn't look too out of place in the Palaiologos house, apart from the length of his hair.

He picked up his phone and, after he'd locked his door, went to the adjoining room.

'Hold on,' Grace called, when he knocked.

Mavros put his ear to the door. He thought he could hear her voice faintly. Was she speaking on the phone? If she was, she was making an effort to keep the volume down.

After a while she opened up. 'Sorry,' she said, her face slightly flushed.

'Keeping in touch with your nearest and dearest?' Mavros asked, stepping past her and looking round the room. The bathroom door was open, the confined space unoccupied. It had occurred to him that perhaps she was not alone.

455

'What do you mean?' she said.

'I thought I heard you talking.'

'Not me. Must have been from another room.' She turned away, stretching for her jacket.

Mavros watched her. 'Look, Grace,' he said, feeling the worry-beads in his pocket and taking them out. 'This isn't the time to keep things from me. We're up against a killer who's–'

'I know what he's done,' Grace said, flashing an angry glare at him. 'Oh, for God's sake, put those stupid beads away. What are you? A kid who needs something to play with all the time?'

He looked at the *komboloï* distractedly, then slipped it back into his pocket. 'No, a reformed smoker.' He stepped towards her. 'I just meant we need to be straight with each other. There's a lot at stake.'

'Your brother, you mean,' Grace said, still aggressive.

'Your case has priority but, yes, my brother's part of it.'

'Don't worry,' she said, 'I'm being straight with you.'

'All right.' He moved away. But doubts were still nagging him. He was sure he had heard Grace talking. Why hadn't she come clean about that? What the hell had happened to the Fat Man? And, worst of all, by going to the Palaiologos house, was he running the risk of bringing not only his client but his mother and the rest of his family into the assassin's sights?

Before Mavros got to the door, the ring tone of his mobile phone made him catch his breath once more.

Veta Palaiologou was sitting on the edge of the bed, her heavy haunches sunk deep into the mattress. Sheets of typescript were on her knees and on the floor before her. The shutters and curtains were still open, though night had fallen and the lights in the garden were on. She could hear the shouts of her husband and Nondas Chaniotakis, interspersed by the shriller tones of the children. Despite the chill, they were playing basketball on the outside court.

The outside court, Veta thought. That was where the horrors had taken place, concrete laid over the blood-soaked earth and sharp-edged stones that once surrounded the house her father-in-law had built. She'd always known that awful deeds had been committed there, but the details had been spared her. That was no defence. She could easily have found out if she'd wanted to. Prokopis Palaiologos had been proud of his actions during the occupation and the civil war; he would have told her if she'd shown an interest. Her own father had been more reserved, especially later in life when he would often fall into a reverie, his hands shaking and the sallow skin of his face coated in sweat. Had he felt remorse? Veta found that hard to credit. Her father was as hard as a bare-knuckle fighter beneath the layers of fat, his commercial acumen rooted in a contempt for the rest of humanity that had poisoned many members of his family. More likely, as he lost his strength, he had become afraid. The Iraklis group had been targeting prominent businessmen and Junta supporters throughout the last decade of his life.

Veta glanced down at the pages with their compact, single-spaced lines of text. They must have come from Geoff Dearfield's memoir. Reading it must have been terrible for Dorothy Cochrane-Mavrou. No wonder she couldn't bring herself to face the author. Her husband Spyros would have passed through similar blockhouses on his way to the brutal prisons and island camps where he spent so much of his life. At least he had escaped the fate of the ELAS commander Iraklis and the poor, ravaged female fighter. How could her own father and father-in-law have treated a woman, a fellow Greek, like that? She felt defiled, her veins running with tainted blood.

'No,' she heard Nikitas shout angrily, 'not like that! Are you a girl? Put your back into him, Prokopi.'

And what about her husband? Veta thought. Did he know what had gone on in the house he inherited? She didn't have to ask: she was sure he did. There was a harshness about Nikitas, a crude certainty that his family had always acted for the best – old Palaiologos had drummed that into his only son, at the same time as pampering and spoiling him. She was certain that he would have boasted to Nikitas about his deeds in the war when the pair of them drank brandy late into the night. That was what had destroyed the country in the forties – people on both sides, the Right and the Left, knowing without any doubt that they were right. It was the crazed polarisation that had led to the murders and the massacres, the rapes and the mutilations that had gone on until the civil war finished in 1949. But that hadn't been the end, Veta understood that now. Glib historians said that the fraternal hatred hadn't run its course until the dictatorship fell in 1974, but the recent terrorist killings showed that the horror was still alive in the twenty-first century. And she was in the middle of it. Two businessmen whom she knew, supporters of her party, had recently been laid in the cold earth. Who would be the next target?

The knock on the bedroom door made her start.

'A moment,' she called, leaning forward awkwardly to gather up the pages.

The door opened before she had finished.

'Veta,' Dorothy began, 'I–' She broke off when she saw what was in her hostess's hands. 'Oh, my God,' she said faintly. 'How...? Surely Geoff hasn't given you his book to read?'

Veta raised her shoulders. 'I don't know. I found these pages under the covers when I came to lie down. They – they are about what went on at this house in the spring of 1944.'

Dorothy stepped forward and took the script from her, running her eyes over the top page. 'I see,' she said, her voice growing stronger. 'Veta, this is ancient history. You mustn't – you mustn't let it hurt you and your family.'

The politician looked up in bewilderment. 'How can you say that, Dorothy? My father and my thug of a father-in-law weren't human, they raped, they–'

The Communist leader's wife sat down beside

her and took her hand. 'It's all in the past,' she said gently. 'There's nothing you or anyone else can do to change the course of the last century.'

Veta gave her an agonised look. 'But, Dorothy, don't you understand? That woman was pregnant. What happened to her unborn child? It might have survived, it might still be alive. I might be able to help...' Her words tailed away in a long sob, her chin sinking on to her chest.

Dorothy smoothed the fleshy hand and searched for comforting words. She had knocked on Veta's door because she had managed to come to terms with Dearfield's soul-destroying script and she wanted to reassure her hostess that she was all right. Thinking of Spyros and Andonis had brought her through. She knew they would have wanted her to see beyond the foulness to the strength of human spirit contained in the memoir – Kapetan Iraklis's dogged bravery, his concern for his comrades in his agony on the cross, even Geoffrey Dearfield's brave decision to act as executioner. She wanted to tell him she understood how much that must have cost him, that she knew the decision to betray the ELAS band and to kill its commander had given the Englishman a lifetime of pain for all his good intentions. But he wasn't in his room or downstairs, and neither was Flora. No one seemed to know where they'd gone.

'You're a good woman, Veta,' Dorothy said. 'You have worked to improve the lot of your fellow men and women.' She gave a light laugh. 'Even though your politics are on the wrong side of the great divide, if such a thing exists any

460

more.' She pressed the younger woman's hand again. 'You mustn't let this knock you from your chosen course. The past can only hurt us if we refuse to let it go. I, of all people, should know that.'

Veta looked at her quizzically. 'Your Spyros, your Andonis, you have let them go?'

Dorothy smiled sadly. 'Yes, I have. My younger son Alex has not. He still searches for his brother. He clutches at the hopeless belief that Andonis might still be alive. But eventually he will learn to forgive and forget, as Anna has done.'

Veta looked at her, feeling tears well up. 'You're an extraordinary woman,' she said, between sobs. 'Your husband would have been proud of you.'

Dorothy patted her hand and stood up. 'You need to get ready,' she said encouragingly. 'I gather my son is coming to dinner with a beautiful American woman in tow. How interesting.' She smiled again and left the room.

But Veta Palaiologou stayed on the bed, her head bowed as it had been before Dorothy had tried to comfort her. Alex Mavros and Grace Helmer were coming to the house. Why had she invited them? Grace Helmer, daughter of blind, idealistic Trent who had been slaughtered by the Iraklis group. There really was no end to the torment, whatever the old woman thought. Iraklis was operating again, killing the kind of people who had been in their sights when they started thirty years ago.

What kind of a Christmas was this going to be in the house that looked down on the citadel of Tiryns, birthplace of the relentless ancient hero?

'Yes,' Mavros gasped, after he'd fumbled for the phone in his jacket pocket.

'Alex Mavros?' The male voice was deep and level, the name pronounced by a native Greek speaker.

'Yes,' Mavros confirmed.

'You have made a mistake,' his interlocutor said. The tone was neutral, but there was a threatening undercurrent to the words.

'Have I?' Mavros asked, his mouth dry. He raised a hand to keep Grace at bay. She was staring at him frantically, unable to follow the one-sided exchange in Greek. 'You mean by going to your mother?'

'Yes. She should not have been brought into this. Her home should not have been invaded.'

Mavros was trying to work out a way to keep the terrorist on the line for as long as possible. 'I can explain,' he said, willing the tension from his voice. 'We need to meet you. It's very important.' If the assassin had been talking to his mother, Kyra Stamatina, that probably meant he was in Nafplion.

'Who is the woman?' The man sounded close and, without thinking, Mavros went to the window. There was no one in the street below.

'Can we meet?' he asked, realising that he sounded desperate.

'I repeat, who is the woman?'

Mavros gazed at Grace, wondering what the effect of revealing her identity would be. 'Grace Helmer,' he said, deciding that openness was the best policy. 'Daughter of the American diplomat

462

you murdered in 'seventy–six.'

There was a pause. 'What does she want with me?' The voice was less confident.

'To see you,' Mavros answered. 'To find out why you killed her father.'

There was another pause. 'And you, Alex Mavros?' the man continued. 'This isn't only about her. What do you want with me?'

Mavros was impressed by his perspicacity. 'No, it isn't,' he admitted. 'I believe you knew my brother, Andonis Mavros. You met him at–'

'The peninsula of Tigani in the Mani,' the man said. 'Yes, I did. In ... November 1972. What of it?'

'Help us,' Mavros pleaded, running out of options. 'I guarantee there will be no involvement of the authorities.'

The laugh was tired, even sad. 'How can you be sure of that? Would you like to know what I did to the last man who was on my tail?'

Mavros felt his stomach leap as he remembered the tall gunman who had saved him and Grace. 'Where? In the Mani?'

'Maybe. Why do you want to meet me? You, Alex Mavros, not the woman.'

'Because ... because I want to know what you discussed with my brother.' Mavros could hardly get the words out. 'For my own purposes. I won't tell anyone else.'

'What I discussed with him?' The terrorist sounded puzzled. 'Why?'

'Because Andonis disappeared the following month. He hasn't been seen since and I – I wondered if you could cast any light on that.'

The man did not speak for what seemed to Mavros like a very long time. 'You made a mistake,' was all that he said. 'Mistakes are costly in this business. Make sure you don't make any more. Stay away from my mother.'

'No, wait!' Mavros shouted. 'Yiorgos Pandazopoulos, do you know him?'

The disconnection he had expected didn't happen: the man's voice returned with a questioning edge to it. 'Yiorgos Pandazopoulos?' he repeated. 'Now, why would you be interested in that overweight comrade? Did you put him down at Tigani to watch out for me?'

'No, I didn't.' Mavros felt his heart somersault. 'For Christ's sake, you haven't hurt him, have you? Did you visit Kostas Laskaris?'

This pause was the longest of them all.

'There is nothing more to be said,' the terrorist said at last. 'If you or the woman go near my mother again, you will be sorry. Let me be, Alex Mavros.'

There was a buzzing in his ear. Mavros threw down the phone with a curse.

'You lost him?' Grace said dully, her eyes following him across the room. 'He won't see us?'

Mavros told her what had been said. Then he picked up the phone again and called the Fat Man's mother. Kyra Fedhra had still not seen her son. He comforted her as best he could, trying as he spoke to imagine what might have happened to his friend and what he could do to help him. Short of driving through the night to the Mani to check the area around Kostas Laskaris's tower, he couldn't come up with anything. No policeman

464

would go out on a winter's night unless Mavros came clean about what was going on and that would be the end of the case.

Grace was pulling on her jacket. 'I'm going to the old woman's,' she said.

He managed to get to the door before she did. 'Don't, Grace. I told you what he said. Anyway, he's too much of a professional to have called from there, I'm sure of it.' He looked into her eyes. 'Please, let it go.' He pressed buttons on his phone and wasn't surprised to find that the last incoming call showed 'Caller Identity Withheld'.

Grace sat down on the bed, one hand to her forehead. 'We're so close to him,' she said. 'He's here, I know it.'

'We can't make him see us,' Mavros said, as a wave of hopelessness washed over him. 'I tried, but he wouldn't go for it.' He had a glimpse of Andonis's face: it was fading into the darkness. 'Let it go,' he repeated, to himself as much as to Grace.

They sat next to each other on the rumpled covers facing the windows, a gap between their bodies, the lights from the fortress of Palamidhi streaming through the windows. The great walls and bastions hovered above the town in the still air like a wreath on the brow of a fallen warrior.

Peter Jaeger stood in the door of the small office, beads of sweat on his forehead. His tuxedo was slung over his right shoulder and his expression was stern as the woman at the desk spun round in her chair. 'You're beginning to make a habit of this, Ms Forster. The ambassador must be

465

wondering what we're cooking up in the bowels of the building.'

'Yes, sir. Sorry, sir.' The words came in a rush. 'But this is a hot one. I've taken a message from our man on Iraklis.' Jane Forster's face was taut, her expression showing barely contained excitement.

Her superior raised a hand. 'Slow down. By "our man", you mean Finn, not the Nafplion stringer?'

She nodded. 'Our own man.' She handed him a yellow pad.

'Target observed and under surveillance,' Jaeger read. 'He is proceeding Palaiologos house. Local back-up uncontactable. Tiresias still on site. Advise course of action soonest.' He looked up from the message. 'And you took this at nineteen fourteen, that is...' he checked his watch '...Five minutes ago. Shit.' He handed back the pad and smoothed his hair with the fingers of his right hand. 'Shit. We've got to get Tiresias out of there.'

'Tiresias?' The young woman's eyes were wide open. 'Tiresias is at the Palaiologos house?'

'Sure,' her superior replied in a scathing voice. 'Where did you think Tiresias would be?'

Forster dropped her gaze, her cheeks reddening. 'But, sir–'

'Let me think,' Jaeger ordered. After a few moments, he glanced at his subordinate again. 'What's this about the local guy being out of the loop?'

Jane Forster shrugged her shoulders. 'I tried him myself while I was waiting for you. There was no answer on his cellphone or his land-line.'

Jaeger pursed his lips. 'All right. We have to assume Iraklis has taken him out. It looks like things are moving ahead faster than we expected. We'd better get down there.' He felt in his jacket pocket and handed her a key. 'Go get my car up and wait for me at the gate. And, Ms Forster, bring your weapon.' He watched as the young woman stood up.

After she had left the office, Jaeger sat down at the desk and called a number from the secure phone. 'Finn, this is Ahab,' he said, after he heard the response. 'We are *en route*. Advise any change of location. Do not, repeat do not, advise any security personnel on site of target's proximity. And do not, repeat do not, engage target.' He listened for a few moments. 'Yes, I am fully aware of that danger. Keep target under surveillance and keep me advised. Confirm.' He listened again, his brow furrowing. 'That is not acceptable at this time. Await my arrival. Out.'

Jaeger replaced the handset and went to his own office. He unlocked the door, then the bottom drawer of his desk, removed a holstered automatic pistol and a set of ammunition clips. Then he exchanged his tuxedo for the leather jacket that was hanging on the back of the door and headed for the elevator.

It looked like Iraklis was about to do as he'd been told, but there was no point in taking any chances.

Mavros drove the Fiat up the narrow road past ancient Tiryns, the floodlights on the ruins

467

making the titanic blocks of stone look unreal. He pointed them out to Grace but she showed little interest. He'd had a struggle to get her to accompany him to the Palaiologos house, the terrorist's call making her change her mind. But he wasn't going to leave her alone in case she took independent and potentially suicidal action. Eventually Grace had agreed, won over by his suggestion that she should find out how well the politician had known her father. For his part, he wanted to find out if Veta or her husband knew the terrorist's mother, however unlikely that seemed. The region's most powerful family had provoked his curiosity, as had the broken old man Dearfield, whose book had disturbed his mother so much.

'Listen, we don't have to stay long,' Mavros said, as they came to a junction at the end of the orange groves. Ahead of them a road snaked up the hillside, leading to the large patch of light that marked the politician's country residence. 'We'll eat and then leave them to it, okay?'

Grace, lost in thought, didn't reply and he drove on without pressing her. The road got even narrower, the raised part between the tyre furrows scraping the hire car's chassis. At the last hairpin before the compound, Mavros stopped and looked down over the plain. Beyond the prow of the Mycenaean citadel, the lights of Nafplion shone brightly in the distance, Palamidhi floating above the town in its tangle of ramparts. On the other side of the gulf, a line of street-lamps and villages led down the coast to Astros and the coastal section of Arkadhia.

Grace roused herself. 'Christ, this country's beautiful,' she said, 'but why has it always been so violent?' She looked down at the glow of Tiryns. 'Fortifications everywhere, walls to keep out the enemy, tombs and destruction in every part of the country.' She turned to him. 'Why, Alex? Why have people never been able to live here in peace?'

'Big question, Grace. Maybe they'll finally manage to achieve that in the twenty-first century. Maybe they'll finally learn something from the divisions of the past.'

'Oh, yeah?' she said ironically. 'It's twenty-five years since my father was executed on the street in Athens. And it's only a few days since the same bastards who killed him blew that businessman to pieces.' She looked down again. 'People haven't learned a fucking thing.'

Mavros wanted to explain that Greece had been torn apart for centuries, the people enslaved and tyrannised first by external powers and then by their own leaders, but he didn't think Grace would understand. He had the impression that her life had been defined by the horror she had witnessed from her bedroom window as a child. Was her need to meet the man who murdered her father really inspired by a desire for understanding? He was afraid that she had a bitter heart, like the old Communists he'd met as a child – the ones who had rotted on the prison islands and could never forgive their tormentors.

He drove on towards the house and saw that there was a barrier across the road in front of the lights. When he slowed to a stop, a heavily built guard in a dark anorak stepped up to his side of the car. 'Your names, please,' he asked, one hand on his belt as he looked in.

Mavros saw a holster and a walkie-talkie at eye-level, a bulletproof vest above. He identified himself and Grace, wondering how many security personnel there were around the compound.

The guard asked for ID, scrutinising Mavros's card and Grace's passport before he pressed a button on a remote-control handset. 'Park to the right of the buildings,' he said. 'My colleagues will search you and your vehicle.'

'Jesus,' Mavros said, as they passed into the compound. 'This is like a fortress.'

'What did I tell you?' Grace said, looking up at the imposing house with its tower-like main block and whitewashed annexes. 'The war's still going on.'

They got out and watched as another security man checked the Fiat's boot and interior.

'What's in the packages?' he asked.

'Christmas presents,' Mavros said, pointing to the wrapping paper.

The guard started running a portable scanner over the parcels. A woman joined him.

'They're going to search us as well,' Mavros said.

Grace shrugged. 'I've got nothing to hide.'

The dark-uniformed guards ran the scanner and their hands over them, nodding when they'd finished. 'That entrance over there,' the female operative said.

Mavros picked up the presents and led Grace towards a heavy oak door at the front of the main building. In the area enclosed by a high fence he made out a swimming-pool, covered for the winter, and a full-size basketball court, as well as tables and chairs in a sheltered alcove.

'Good evening, sir, madam,' said the funereal man who opened the door. 'Can I take the packages? Your ... coats?' He gave Grace's fleece a cursory look, then turned an even more supercilious eye on Mavros's leather jacket.

'No, thanks,' Mavros replied, glancing around the wide hallway. The house was warm, but he didn't want to lose track of the mobile in his jacket pocket. 'Where do we go?'

'I was coming to that, sir,' the servant replied impassively. 'The family and their guests are in the–'

'Don't worry, I can hear them,' Mavros said, beckoning to Grace and walking past him. Butlers were rare in Greece and he felt uncomfortable with this representative of the species. He wasn't surprised that a notorious snob like Nikitas Palaiologos would employ one.

They entered the large drawing room and the volume of voices dropped for a few seconds, then went up again as Mavros's niece and nephew greeted him with squeals when they saw the presents in his arms. It took him some time to fight them off and introduce Grace to his mother. The only person in the party whom he didn't recognise was a well-preserved older woman.

Geoffrey Dearfield still looked tormented. 'My wife Flora,' he said, in a low voice.

'So, Alex Mavros,' the woman said, as she

471

shook his hand, 'you are the famous detective.'

'Neither famous nor a detective,' he replied. 'I prefer infamous private investigator.' He switched to English. 'This is Grace Helmer, Mrs Dearfield.'

The two women shook hands, Flora looking thoughtfully at the American before asking her what she thought of Argolidha in winter.

'She's very pretty, Alex.'

Mavros, dumping the packages by a large and sumptuously decorated tree, turned to find his mother behind him. He kissed the cheek she presented then took her to an armchair. 'Are you feeling better now?'

'I'm all right, dear,' Dorothy said, smiling at him. 'A little trouble that I'll tell you about another time, but that's all over now. Don't you agree that she's very pretty?'

Mavros gave her an exasperated look. 'She's a client, Mother.' He watched as Anna went up to Grace and Flora, and started talking animatedly. Behind them Nikitas and Veta were conversing in a curious huddle, paying no attention to their guests. The children had gone back to the Monopoly board on the carpet behind the sofa, less interested in Alex since he'd told them that the presents were not to be opened till Christmas Day. Finally Veta looked at him and came across, stopping to greet Grace on the way and bringing her over.

'Good evening, Alex,' the politician said smoothly. 'Forgive me, I had some arrangements to finalise with my husband.' Although her voice was level, her eyes were restless and she looked

472

much less at ease than she had in Nafplion that morning. 'Dorothy, have you met Alex's friend Grace?' she said, in English. 'Please forgive me, I must talk to the butler about the arrangements for dinner.'

They watched Veta's bulky form, in an expensive evening gown, move away. Mavros wondered if she was always so short with her guests – probably not if they were well-heeled potential donors to her party rather than scruffy passers-by.

'Sit down, Grace,' Dorothy said, indicating a neighbouring chair. 'I hope my son has been looking after you.'

'Oh, yes,' Grace replied, giving Mavros a sharp smile. 'He's been doing that all right.'

'And what exactly is it that Alex has been doing for you?'

Mavros looked beyond his mother towards the works of modern art on the far wall. 'You know that my cases are confidential,' he said wearily.

'No, no,' Grace said to Dorothy. 'I don't mind talking about it.'

Mavros turned his eyes on her. 'I don't think–'

'We're trying to track down the man who killed my father,' his client said, talking over him. 'My father Trent was at the US embassy in Athens in the seventies.'

'Oh, my dear,' said Dorothy, clutching the younger woman's wrist. 'I think I remember him. He was – he was assassinated by the Iraklis group, was he not?'

Grace nodded slowly. 'And we thought we had him,' she added, glancing at Mavros, 'but he slipped away.'

473

Dorothy turned to her son. 'Is this right, Alex? Surely you haven't been getting close to those madmen.'

Mavros paused as his brother-in-law Nondas let out a loud cheer from the Monopoly board. Nikitas Palaiologos was also there, his bald head visible above the sofa. 'I told you, Mother,' he said, 'my work is confidential, whatever the client thinks.' He gave Grace a pained look.

'The client's paying so the client thinks what she likes,' Grace observed caustically.

Dorothy was following the exchange closely but, before she could speak, her daughter arrived on the scene.

'Is everything all right?' Anna asked, her eyes moving between Mavros and Grace. 'Dinner should be ready soon. Veta's gone to see what's happening in the kitchen. Loudhovikos, the cheerful butler, seems to have absented himself.'

Mavros turned towards the door, a frisson of uncertainty that he couldn't explain running up his spine. The windows were unshuttered, the glass covered by criss-crossed metal strips, and it struck him that he hadn't seen the security guard, who had been pacing up and down in the compound, for some time.

Before he could take a step forward, the lights dimmed, both inside the house and in the fenced area outside. The power was reduced for only a few seconds before it came back on at full strength, but that was long enough for the atmosphere to change.

Veta Palaiologou appeared haltingly at the door of the *saloni*, her face pale and her mouth open.

474

Behind her, almost obscured by her portly frame, stood a tall man. There was a black cashmere scarf round his neck. The eyes that quickly took in every occupant of the room were dark and empty, the smile as cold as the moonlight on a ruined mountain redoubt.

Kostas Laskaris knew that he had reached the last stage of his journey, that after this effort there would be no more agony to bear. He had got to the bottom of the staircase without too much difficulty, managing to drag his legs across the stone slabs. Then the weight began to crush him, the breath rushing down his airway but seeming not to reach his lungs. He felt himself suffocating as he hauled himself to the first floor of the tower. Pausing there for a length of time he could not calculate, he regained control of his breathing. He started the crawl to the second storey, aware of splinters from the wooden steps needling into the skin of his fingers and palms. But he felt no pain – the pills he had swallowed with a gulp of Savvas's wine were doing their work. No pain, only a cascade of images that he seemed to be swimming through, his arms feebly trying to bat them away as he pulled himself to the next level.

Kapetan Iraklis gone from the cross, nothing left of him but the blood on the wood and fragments of battledress on the wire: that had been the sight before him when he came round from the beating he'd been given by the battalionists. My Irakli, he was thinking. That it should have come to this, all the fighting, the brilliant leadership, the victories. A Communist on a cross, then nothing, only the absence of a god who has left the world of men. No doubt the bastards found the irony irresistible. My Irakli, I had so much to say to you, I wanted to tell you that I loved you from boyhood, that I didn't care what you did with the woman Stamatina, that you were more to me than just a man with the needs that other men have. You were a hero to me, I wanted to tell you that, a hero as great as your ancient namesake, a hero who fought against oppression and injustice, and who didn't deserve to disappear into the void.

Kostas Laskaris made it to the top floor of the tower, too exhausted to raise his hand to the door. Despite the pills he had taken, the familiar lancing in his abdomen had now returned, making him roll desperately against the wall. Iraklis, he told himself, concentrate on Iraklis. You succeeded, you finished the poem: you have given the hero eternal life. The original Iraklis died on the pyre in a shirt of fire, a red death like those for which his modern counterpart was responsible. His betrayed wife Deianeira sent him the garment as a love charm, having soaked it in the blood and semen of the treacherous centaur Nessos, unaware that the centaur, dying from one of Iraklis's own arrows that had been soaked in the lethal gore of the Hydra, had woven a web of deceit around them. So the great hero died in agony, burned by the blood of his victims; as Kapetan Iraklis had suffered at the hands of his fellow countrymen, enraged by the violence and hatred caused by decades of oppression and fear. 'The Fire Shirt'. The poem was finished, but would anyone read it? Would anyone understand its message, that love is stronger than war, stronger even than death itself?

Laskaris dragged himself to his knees, taking the key from his pocket with a shaking hand. With the last of his strength he turned it in the lock, then fell to the floor. As the light faded from him, he was vaguely aware of a heavy form bending over him, mouthing inaudible words. At least the captive would go free now; at least he would escape an unjust fate.

The light was gone, the rush of air that was filling his ears had receded. Silence, cold stone all around. He was alone, as he had been after Iraklis had vanished from the cross. When he came round he and Comrade Stamatina had been taken by a fresh-faced Englishman with tortured eyes from the compound, then consigned to the prisons with thousands of other resistance fighters, thrown into the maelstrom of repression for years without word of the man they had loved and followed – but alive. Stamatina's single scream from inside the blockhouse – as if she had awoken from a nightmare into a world that was even more horrific – had haunted him for years. Until she contacted him in the fifties during a brief spell of freedom and told him about her son, the son by Kapetan Iraklis who had been born in the prison camp and whom the Party had managed to spirit away to Kitta. Comrade Stamatina, her face marked and her eyes hard, rejoiced that the boy had a lifetime of struggle before him; she called on Laskaris for the sake of their lost *kapetanios* to watch over young Michalis until he had made his way in the Party. And he had done so, had kept the son's identity secret, despite all the crimes that he went on to commit...

Suddenly there was a host of empty war towers around him, their grey stone walls taking on a reddish hue as the last sun erupted across the gulf.

Then a deeper silence took him down.

Yiorgos Pandazopoulos, the Fat Man, stood outside the room where he'd been confined. Blinking away tears, he bent over the motionless body and closed the old poet's eyes with his fleshy thumbs.

19

Silence fell as the occupants of the drawing room took in the scene at the door. Then Veta Palaiologou moved forward slowly, blinking in time with each step. As she and the man close behind her came further in, Mavros realised there was another figure – one he couldn't make out – bringing up the rear, a heavy revolver in his hand. But he had recognised the first armed man immediately: he was the one who had fired the shots to scare off Grace's and his assailant near Babis Dhimitrakos's village in the Mani.

'Are they all here?' the man in the scarf asked over his shoulder.

The butler stepped up and ran his eye round the *saloni*. 'Yes,' he said, with a nod, his voice low. 'Those two are the latest arrivals.' He pointed out Mavros and Grace.

'He's got a gun,' Veta said, her voice hoarse. 'He says he'll kill me if anyone moves.'

The man in the scarf moved his arm quickly round the politician's neck, then held up a black automatic pistol. 'In case anyone's wondering,' he said, almost apologetically, 'I am Iraklis.'

There was a series of gasps around the room, Mavros's niece, Evridhiki whimpering as she buried her head in Nondas's chest.

'Let my wife go,' Nikitas Palaiologos demanded, his voice weak and his face ashen.

'Certainly,' the assassin said. 'If you are prepared to come over here and take her place.' The prisoner's husband stayed where he was. 'Rich and afraid. The combination has never been unusual.' He glanced behind him. 'Take their mobile phones. And make sure they aren't concealing anything like Swiss Army knives or keys.'

Loudhovikos the butler, the armed man behind him, moved around, feeling in pockets and on belts. Mavros, Nondas and Nikitas had phones, as did all the children, but the women – Flora, Anna, Dorothy and Grace – were not equipped. That didn't stop him running his hands over the two younger women's bodies.

'You pathetic creep,' Grace said, her eyes locked on the man as he dropped the phones into a plastic bag.

'Sit down and be quiet,' Iraklis said, in English, staring at her. He nudged Veta forward and pushed her into an armchair, putting the muzzle of the automatic against her head. 'I'm going to continue in English so that you understand what's happening, Ms Helmer.' His accent was American, the pronunciation precise.

'Here are the phones,' his accomplice said, brandishing the bag. 'No weapons.'

'Turn them all off,' the assassin said. He looked around the company. 'Be aware that shouting for help is useless. I have neutralised the alarm system and the security guards.'

Nikitas translated the words to his children. 'How did you do that?' he demanded. 'There are three of them, for Christ's sake. And what

480

happened to the dogs?

'Loudhovikos took care of them, and the chef. Your highly trained fools are currently locked in the cellar, having been relieved of their weapons and communication equipment. And the meat we gave the dogs will keep them asleep till morning.'

'How did you disable the alarm system?' Palaiologos asked.

'That does not concern you.' The terrorist put his hand inside his jacket and took out what looked like a pen. He looked around the occupants of the room again. 'You,' he said, pointing to Anna, 'come here.'

Mavros watched as his sister walked slowly towards the man with the gun, a disdainful expression on her face. He was hoping that she wouldn't goad the assassin into violent action – she was certainly capable of it. Fortunately she caught Dorothy's eye as she passed and held her tongue.

'This is a highly sophisticated device,' Iraklis said, giving his weapon to the butler and turning the casing of the silver tube carefully. He held it upright when he'd finished. 'The security people downstairs are looking after one for me too.'

'You used another to kill the entrepreneur Stasinopoulos at the concert hall in Athens, didn't you?' Mavros said.

There was another shocked intake of breath around the *saloni*.

Iraklis looked at him curiously. 'That's what you were meant to think, certainly.'

Mavros tried to make sense of that. He took a

481

step forward, stopping when the muzzle of the automatic turned towards him. 'Leave my sister out of this,' he said. 'I'll do whatever it is that you want.'

The assassin studied him for a few moments. 'Oh, you'll do what I want, there's no question about that, Alex Mavros. But I prefer someone without experience as an investigator to act as guarantor.' He held out the metal object to Anna, taking care to keep it vertical. 'Do not be deceived by its size. This device contains enough explosive to kill everyone in this room. It is equipped with a tilt fuse. All you have to do is hold it upright and nothing will happen.' He ran his eyes round the room again. 'I strongly recommend that no one does anything to distract our friend here.'

'At least let my daughter sit down,' Dorothy said, her voice cracking. Mavros watched as Grace touched his mother's arm to comfort her.

'It will concentrate her mind and everyone else's if she remains standing.' Iraklis waved his hand at Anna. 'Go into the centre of the room,' he added, watching as she backed slowly away. 'Good. Stop there.'

Silence fell again, broken only by swallowed sobs from Mavros's niece.

'All right,' Mavros said. 'You've got us where you want us. What next?'

The assassin looked at him, his lips set in a tight line. 'Indeed, Alex Mavros, what next?' He took the automatic back from the butler. 'The simple fact is that I have come here tonight to kill someone.' He raised the weapon to Veta's head again. 'If you all keep quiet, I will explain why.' He gave a vacant smile. 'In fact, I will give the object of my attentions the opportunity to justify the crimes that were committed before I proceed.' He raised his shoulders. 'Let no one say that Iraklis kills indiscriminately.'

The terrified expressions on most of the company's faces suggested the assassin hadn't come close to convincing them of that.

'How long till we reach Tiryns?' Peter Jaeger demanded from the wheel, his eyes on the tail-lights of the car on the motorway ahead.

'Um, I estimate thirty minutes,' Jane Forster answered, her head bent over a map that she was lighting with a small torch.

'You estimate?' her superior said acidly.

She glanced at him, taking in the sweat-drenched features that had turned green in the dashboard light. 'Well, it's difficult to be sure, sir. The highway leading from the motorway is single track. We might meet slow-moving traffic.'

Jaeger grunted. 'Still no contact with the local man?'

'No, sir.'

'He's gone, definitely.' He looked at a large sign. 'Two kilometres to the exit. Let's just hope that Finn is on top of his game.'

'Shall I call him to confirm his position?' his subordinate asked.

'No, Ms Forster, you will not call him to conirm his fucking position. He is in close proximity to the target. Do you want to compromise him?'

She looked from the side window into the

darkness. 'I assumed he had his communication device on vibrate mode.'

'Well, good for you, Ms Forster,' Jaeger said, with a mocking laugh. 'Do me a favour. Let me do the assuming around here, okay?'

'Yes, sir,' she replied, sounding dispirited. Then she turned back to her superior. 'Sir, what exactly are we going to do when we arrive on the scene?'

This time Jaeger did not answer immediately. He took his foot off the accelerator as he approached the exit. 'Good question,' he said, giving her a quick look. 'Keep cool. I know what I'm doing.'

The expression on his subordinate's face suggested that she didn't.

Shortly afterwards they ran down the slope on to the plain, the lights of the fortifications above Argos and Nafplion shining out like beacons welcoming home a victorious army. Jane Forster had read up on the ancient myths. She was thinking that Mycenae, where King Agamemnon had been slaughtered in his bath by his wife and her lover, lay only a few kilometres to their left.

What was about to go down at the ancient stronghold on the other side of Argolidha where Hercules had been born?

Iraklis nodded as they sat down slowly, the children on the floor with their fathers beside the sofa where Geoffrey and Flora Dearfield were, the old man staring at the captive Veta with his mouth open. Mavros and Grace were on either side of the armchair where Dorothy sat. Only

Anna and the two armed men remained on their feet.

'Very good,' the terrorist said. 'Now, where shall we begin?'

'How about during the war?' Mavros said. He had been wrestling over how to handle the confrontation. His family's safety was paramount, but the fact was that they were already in mortal danger – he was praying to the God he didn't believe in that Anna would keep a steady hand – and he reckoned that if he didn't take the lead, then Grace would: he couldn't be sure how much she would antagonise the terrorist. His strategy was to draw Iraklis away from the present to the historical background – that way maybe he could distract him enough to give them a chance. 'This nightmare you're putting us through has its roots in the occupation, doesn't it?' he said. 'Kostas Laskaris told me your mother was in the resistance with him.'

'I told you before to keep my mother out of this,' the assassin said.

'Okay, okay,' Mavros said, raising his hands. 'What I mean to say is that your family suffered during the war and its aftermath.'

'Everyone suffered during the war,' Geoffrey Dearfield said.

'What's that, old man?' Iraklis said, leaning forward. 'Is there something you want to say about the war?' Suddenly there was tension in his voice.

Flora nudged her husband. 'Go on,' she said. 'This is your chance to set yourself free from the memories that have been tormenting you.'

Mavros looked up at his mother, trying to catch

485

her attention, but she was staring at the couple on the sofa, an expression of deep foreboding on her wrinkled face. 'Maybe this is a blind alley,' he said, realising that his tactics had been counter-productive. 'Let's leave the ancient history alone.'

The terrorist glanced at Mavros, then turned his gaze back on Flora and her husband. 'History is what this country is all about, my friend. I will come back to it.' He looked at his watch. 'But now we must move on.' He pushed the automatic into the side of Veta Palaiologou's head. 'It's time to discuss my prisoner. A leading opposition spokesperson, daughter of a family that made its money from the black market during the war.' He glanced at Mavros. 'You see, there's no getting away from the past.'

'Leave my mother alone!' the teenager Prokopis shouted, pulling his arm away from Nikitas's ineffectual grasp. 'Let her go!'

The assassin gave another sad smile. 'I like your spirit, boy,' he said, in Greek. 'But the next time you raise your voice your mother will suffer, do you understand?'

'It's all right, Prokopi,' Veta said, her voice steady.

'As I was saying,' Iraklis continued, in English, 'my prisoner, my target. Who could be more appropriate than a major conservative figure, a figurehead – if I can put it that way – of the thieving ship-owner class that has ruined this country?' His tone hardened. 'A person whose father was something worse than a war criminal.'

'And that gives you the right to go around kill-ing people, does it?' Grace was leaning forward,

486

ignoring Mavros's warning look. 'That gives you the right to cut people's throats in front of their children?'

The assassin kept his gaze off her. 'I tried to make amends to you by saving you from the gunman in the Mani, Ms Helmer. This is not the time to discuss your father. He represented the imperialist foreign power that exterminated thousands of Greeks during the so-called civil war.' He looked at Dorothy and Anna, then at Mavros. 'You people can understand this, can't you? Spyros Mavros was a brave fighter for the rights of the people.'

Dorothy gave him a withering stare. 'My husband was a revolutionary, not a killer. He never advocated violence outside wartime.'

'And that's why the revolution failed.' Iraklis turned back to the woman beside him. 'But enough of this. Veta Dhragoumi-Palaiologou, defend yourself. Convince me that you are not an enemy of the people. I have learned that your father certainly was.'

The politician gave a long sigh. 'What would be the point?' she asked, her eyes on her children. 'Why don't you just get it over with? But, please' – she looked round with an agonised expression – 'don't do it in front of them. Please.'

The girls Klio and Evridhiki couldn't contain their weeping any longer, their tear-stained faces turning desperately to their fathers. The boys were crying too. Mavros opened his eyes wide at Nondas and shook his head to forestall any reaction.

'She's right,' Mavros said to Iraklis. 'What's the

487

point? What's the point of her defending herself and her father? But what's the point of you going on with your campaign?' He took a deep breath. 'You might as well admit it's been a failure.'

The assassin blinked. 'A failure?'

Mavros shrugged. 'Of course. Greece has changed. I can just about understand the rationale behind terrorist attacks during the dictatorship, but now? The country's moved on. No one cares about the old ideologies any longer. People just want to make money and have a good time.'

'Those are poisonous lies and you know it, Alex Mavros.' The shrill voice came from the far side of the room.

Everyone's gaze settled on Flora Dearfield. She had risen to her feet, her left arm extended in Veta's direction. 'Here is the final instalment of the truth I promised you, Irakli. Her father raped your mother. Her father and this bastard's.' She broke off and swung her arm towards the cowering Nikitas Palaiologos. 'They were the battalionist commanders who tortured your father.' She looked back at her husband. 'You want proof? Ask Geoff. He was there when your father died.'

There was a shocked silence. Mavros put his hand cautiously on his mother's knee and she nodded, lips apart, breath coming quickly.

'Oh, no,' Dorothy said faintly. 'Oh, no.' She sat forward. 'Don't, Geoff. Don't tell him.'

Dearfield stared ahead, the dark blue veins on his hands pulsing.

'Well, old man?' the terrorist asked. 'What is this?'

Dearfield stood up unsteadily, glancing at

488

Dorothy, then at Veta. 'I was present, it's true.' Then he looked at his wife. 'You're saying that the woman Stamatina was this man's mother? That the guerrilla leader was his father? How do you–'

'Never mind that now,' Iraklis interrupted. 'Tell me, old man. What happened there?'

Geoffrey Dearfield bowed his head, then seemed to summon a last reserve of strength. He began to speak, slowly at first then faster, as if the words were taking control of him. He described his role as liaison officer, the betrayal of the ELAS unit to the Germans and the Security Battalions, and the final scene in the compound. He raised his head, stared into the assassin's eyes and said, 'I executed Kapetan Iraklis on the cross.'

Anna looked over her shoulder at Dearfield, the explosive device wavering in her hands. Mavros felt his heart pound.

'Be careful,' the terrorist said to her. 'I am not ready to die yet.'

Anna turned to the front again, her face pale. Mavros could see that the tension was close to overwhelming her. He was struggling to find a way out for her and the rest of them.

Dearfield explained how horrified he'd been by the monarchist Greeks' maltreatment of their countrymen. He had seen several other ELAS fighters killed after brutal torture over the previous days and he wanted to spare the brave Kapetan Iraklis that fate. But he had also seen the ELAS band slaughter prisoners; and he felt bitter about his guide Fivos's death. He couldn't be sure that a desire for vengeance hadn't blinded him, driving him to disclose the fighters' dispositions at Loutsa to the enemy. Over the years he had managed to block out the guilt and shame, he had even continued to work for the anti-Communist side, had shared information with the Americans. But since he'd retired the pressure to make some atonement, to admit the mistakes he and his superiors had made, had led him to write a memoir.

Mavros looked at his mother again. What she had told him about the manuscript Dearfield submitted to her had fallen into place.

'Ach, Geoff,' moaned Veta. 'That accursed memoir. Why couldn't you have left everything undisturbed? Why did you have to leave me those pages to read?'

The old man was staring at her, as if he had suddenly woken from a deep sleep. 'Leave you pages to read? I didn't–' He looked at his wife. 'How is it that you know about all this, Flora? Have you been meddling with my papers?'

'Your wife is good at meddling, old man,' the assassin said.

'What do you mean?' Dearfield asked.

She was gazing at him contemptuously. 'Sit down, you old fool,' she said, stepping forward. 'You know nothing about me. You have never taken the trouble to look beneath the surface of my life. Did you really think I was fulfilled only by studying history?'

'What ... what...' The old man slumped on to the sofa. 'Why didn't you let me leave earlier?' he asked, then looked up again. 'My God, you knew he was coming.'

Flora moved closer to the terrorist and his captive, showing no fear. 'I was the one who put the pages under your covers, Veta.'

'But why?' the politician asked. 'Why?'

'Because she is the one who directed Iraklis to you,' Mavros said, standing up slowly and addressing himself to Flora Dearfield. 'What are you? His leader? The one who controls him?'

The woman's face had remained pale. 'What do you know of such things, young man? Your father was weak. People like him were responsible for the defeat of the Left. You yourself are nothing but a lackey of the rich.'

Mavros looked at the assassin. There was a weakness about him, a sadness that seemed to be taking him over. 'So why don't you explain to me, Kyria Flora, explain to my mother and my sister, what you and your pet gunman have achieved that Spyros Mavros didn't?' He raised a hand to keep Dorothy and Anna quiet.

Flora Dearfield glanced at Iraklis, then inclined her head towards Mavros. 'Very well. I will make things clear to you and to everyone else.' Then she began to speak, in the style of a lecturer who was certain of her subject beyond all possibility of doubt.

In the *saloni* of the Palaiologos house, Flora saw the puzzled expressions of the people around her. Her husband had never heard her talk about her childhood with so much candour. The terrorist was staring at her, the black pistol pressed loosely to Veta's head. And young Mavros, the hound who dug up information to use against people, he

491

was watching her avidly, no longer paying the slightest attention to the American bitch he was working for. She heard herself speaking, but deep down she had gone back to her childhood, back to the day that had made her what she was...

Eight years old and the life she had known slipped away from her, quicker than a fish from fingers clutching in the shallows. It was early spring, the clear sky cut by trails from aircraft. She had been out on Snow White, taking her over the low jumps laid out in the meadow below the house. She ignored the glass of lemonade that the butler offered, running up the ornate staircase to her mother's room, anxious to tell her how well she had ridden.

'Mama!' she called, opening the heavy door. 'Mama, Snow White has–' She stopped when she saw the blood on the bed. It took her a while to realise that her mother's body was there too, so hard was it to make out the alabaster skin below the slick of crimson. She went closer, watching for a movement of the chest. There was none. Then the object in her mother's right hand glinted at her dully. It was a razor like the one the old groom used to shave Snow White's mane.

Little Flora opened her mouth but no sound came out. She brought her lips together, feeling the breath coursing through her nostrils and aware of a warm, metallic smell. The realisation that she was the only person in the house who knew about this scene gripped her, seemed to give her a new kind of power, greater than the one she had become used to exerting over the servants. She looked at her mother's death-bed

492

for the last time, then turned away and marched downstairs to her father's study. Normally he locked it when he was working, but she was sure he would let her in this time. In the wide hall downstairs she saw the butler. He was talking in a low voice to a damp-eyed man holding a briefcase tied together with frayed string. When she walked past them towards the study, they tried to stop her. But she was too quick for them, evaded their arms and reached the door. The gilt handle turned and, to her surprise, the great oak panel swung open. 'Baba!' she cried self-importantly. 'I have something to tell–'

Her father had his back to her, his trousers round his ankles and his heavy behind bare. He seemed to be exercising himself over the armchair in front of his desk, his arms supporting his weight. At the sound of her voice, he froze. Then his face, sweat drenching the loose cheeks and carefully sculpted moustache, appeared over his shoulder.

'Get out,' he hissed. 'Get out, you little fool.'

But Flora stayed, she drew closer. She had seen the pair of thin legs, one outside each of her father's, the feet in scuffed and ill-fitting shoes. She went to the side of the chair and looked round her father's bulk, briefly aware of a thick rod with a sticky red head as he pulled back. The girl was sobbing, her blouse parted to reveal the bumps of undeveloped breasts, her skirt above her waist. Flora put out her hand to the thin wrist that lay on the armrest, looking into the ravaged eyes in the second before her father's hand slapped the side of her head and sent her flying

493

across the tiles.

The girl's shrunken frame was little bigger than her own.

The room was quiet, only the muffled noise of the two girls' sobs audible. Mavros glanced at Grace and then at his mother. Both returned his gaze, their faces damp with tears.

'Why – why did you never tell me about this?' Geoffrey Dearfield stammered. 'What has this to do with' – he looked at Iraklis – 'with this murderer?'

Flora shook her head at him. 'You still don't understand, do you? Maybe it's something in the British soul – take everything at face value until you know otherwise. Was that a regulation in your stupid army?' Her eyes were wide now, her lips glistening.

'I don't get it either,' Grace said. 'Your mother committed suicide and your father was a child-molester, right? Are you telling us that's why you got involved with terrorism?'

Flora turned to the assassin and gave him a knowing smile. 'You see? I always told you that we had to make our own rules. Everyone else is blind.' She glanced back at Grace. 'You understand everything and nothing. That's the curse of your country. You have the best universities and research centres in the world, but you destroy every country you touch with your uncaring foreign policy, your wars and your filthy capitalism. Yes, of course I rebelled against my family after that day. Of course I wanted to destroy everything my father stood for. He was a

494

dedicated collaborator, he operated in the black market, he exacted payment for debts in the form of underage girls. Rebelling against him and his degenerate class wasn't difficult.'

'But you never joined the Party,' Dorothy said sharply. 'You preferred to operate secretly, like a thief in the dark.'

Flora glared at her. 'And your husband didn't operate that way all those years when the Party was banned?'

Mavros was studying her. 'You couldn't have set up a group like Iraklis on your own,' he said, watching the terrorist out of the corner of his eye. 'You must have had outside help.'

'Oh, yes,' the historian said. 'I had outside help, all right.' Her eyes were on Dorothy again. 'Not that your husband and his squabbling comrades knew anything about it.'

'The Soviets,' Mavros said, putting his hand on his mother's arm to restrain her. 'They financed you separately from the main party?'

'At the beginning. Though I also had my inheritance to give to the cause. I sometimes wish my father had survived the assassin's bullet to see what I did with my dowry.' She looked at Grace. 'Now perhaps you can understand why your father was a target, a legitimate target. The Americans supported the right-wing regimes who persecuted the Left for decades after the war and those regimes contained many men like my father.'

Mavros saw that his client's jaw was hanging loose.

'And you,' Flora said, turning to her husband,

'why do you think I encouraged you to write your guilt-ridden, self-pitying memoir? I needed the material to convince Iraklis to come back for one last, devastating strike.' She snorted disdainfully. 'You poor fool, Geoff. You wrote that book to absolve yourself of guilt and all it did was lead to more deaths. Even this afternoon when we walked down to the old citadel and I hinted at my real life, you were too self-obsessed to pick up the thread.'

The terrorist roused himself, giving Geoffrey Dearfield a surprisingly sympathetic look. 'How did you find out about my parents, Comrade Tiresias?'

Flora smiled at him. 'I have been going through the records that began to appear after the so-called national reconciliation in the eighties. They were misleading and incomplete. Scum like Dhragoumis and Palaiologos who took part in atrocities made sure their names never appeared. But it turned out that my own husband held the key to your past. And he thought I wasn't reading what he wrote.' She gave Dearfield a pitying look, then turned back to the terrorist. 'You understand what I did, don't you, Irakli?' she said, now slightly less certain. 'You understand that I had to delve into your family's past to bring you back. You must agree, this woman is the perfect choice as your final victim. Execute her leech of a husband, too, if you like.'

Iraklis straightened his upper body with what looked like a great effort and moved his head forward to signal his assent. Then he pressed the automatic harder against Veta's head. 'That's

496

enough of the past.' He sounded almost exhausted. 'It is time for my last victim to–'

Before he could complete the sentence, the butler appeared at the door from the hall where he'd been keeping watch. 'There's someone outside,' he said, 'a man, and I think he's armed.'

The assassin drew himself up. His languor disappeared. 'All right,' he said, resignedly. 'If that's the way they want it...' Then he hauled Veta Palaiologou to her feet and dragged her to the door. 'If any of you moves, she will die instantly.' He glanced at Anna. 'Now, more than ever, daughter of Spyros Mavros, you must keep still.'

Motioning to the butler to lead the way, Iraklis went out with the politician, closely followed by Flora. The rest of the company sat motionless, their faces paler than a hunter's moon.

'Oh, my God,' Jane Forster said, lowering the phone from her ear. 'He's moving in. Finn's moving in.'

'What?' Peter Jaeger gasped. 'Why? Did he end the transmission?'

'He said he'd scoped a secure access point. Apparently there's been no movement inside for fifteen minutes. He said he was concerned that innocent people were in danger.'

'Finn's concerned about that?' her superior said, swerving past a lorry on the Argos–Nafplion road and accelerating hard. 'I don't think so. Finn's taking the initiative when he shouldn't. Re-establish contact and tell him to stay the hell out of there till we arrive.'

Forster ducked her head as a car flashed past

them, its horn blaring. She pressed buttons and raised the phone to her ear again. 'Nothing, sir,' she said, after a pause. 'He's not responding.'

'Fuck!' Jaeger yelled. 'Try Tiresias.'

Jane Forster pressed more buttons and listened. 'No answer there either, sir.'

'Jesus. Why is Flora still at the house? That wasn't the plan. We should be there in five minutes. If the idiots screw up the operation, I'm not authorising any fucking pension payments.' Jaeger glanced at his subordinate. 'Prepare your weapon, Ms Forster. This could get bloody.'

The lights on the ancient fortifications of Tiryns were visible now, spreading over the green canopy of leaves in the orange groves between the citadel and the hill inland. Jane Forster slapped the clip into the grip of her automatic and racked the slide. She'd trained for this moment for years, swallowed the insults of drill masters who thought she was a fader, conquered her emotions over and over again, and still she didn't feel ready. The fact that her boss was leading her into some weird alternative dimension that only he seemed to understand didn't help at all.

Mavros got slowly to his feet when he saw the terrorist's party clear the immediate vicinity. He went over to Anna and carefully removed the metal tube from her grasp.

'Let's hope there isn't a timer in it as well,' he muttered to her, smiling to show that he didn't think there was. He glanced around and saw a pot containing a spider plant. He went over and, ascertaining that the earth was reasonably soft, slid the device in with the bottom half obscured. 'As long as no one knocks this pot over, we're all right.'

'Where have they gone?' Grace said, joining him.

'That's what I'm going to find out,' he said. 'Everyone stay here. I'll be back when the coast is clear.' He kept his eyes off his mother and headed for the door.

'I'm coming too,' Grace said.

'What a surprise.' Mavros slipped his head round the door and saw that the hall was empty. Further down another door was open, a cold breeze blowing through it. 'Looks like they've gone outside.' He moved forward cautiously and entered a long, well-equipped kitchen. The external door at the far end was the source of the draught.

'I can hear voices,' Grace said.

Mavros crouched down, moving past cupboards and the oven. As he approached the door he could make out words from beyond.

'...gun down,' said a male, the accent American.

'Don't be foolish,' replied Iraklis. 'You see where I'm pointing it? In case you're not aware, this lady is a senior politician.'

'I know who she is and I know who you are, pal. Drop the gun and we can all walk away from here.'

'Kill her,' said Flora, in Greek. 'Kill her, Irakli.'

'Finn!' Another American male.

Mavros looked at Grace. He didn't have a clear idea of what was going on. The latest voice had come from across the compound. His client was looking equally confused.

'What the hell's going on here?' The new voice was closer.

'That you, Jaeger?' said the first speaker. 'I mean Ahab.' He gave a dry laugh.

Mavros nodded slowly when he heard the name of the embassy official. He watched as Grace registered it too.

'Who the fuck do you think it is? Back off, you lunatic, Milroy. This isn't the way it's meant to be.'

'Things are well out of control here. I thought–'

'You thought you'd get involved, huh? Well, screw you. This isn't the time for you to play the masked fucking avenger.' There was a pause. 'Ms Forster, keep your pretty head down and cover me.' He didn't sound confident that the woman he was addressing was capable of that.

'What's going on?' Mavros heard the terrorist whisper to Flora. They were gathered in the space outside the kitchen, their feet visible from the door. Veta Palaiologou was pushed up against the wall by Iraklis, her legs splayed.

There was no reply from his controller.

'Well, well,' Jaeger said, from nearby. 'This is your man, eh, Flora?'

'Keep your distance,' Iraklis said, in English. 'I'll blow the politician's head off.'

'Wish you would,' came the reply. 'Tell you the truth, I was kinda hoping you'd have done the deed already.' He laughed. 'That was our deal, wasn't it, Flora?'

'What?' The assassin's voice was hoarse. 'What is this he's saying? Who is he? CIA?'

Another laugh. 'Tell him, Flora, why don't you? It's about time he found out how you've been playing him.'

'Talk,' Iraklis said, in Greek, his tone iron-hard. 'Talk now, comrade.'

During the silence that followed Mavros moved closer to the door, feeling Grace's presence behind him. He could see a pair of upright forms, a male and a female, about five metres apart in the garden, both with handguns raised. Further towards the covered pool, a shadowy form behind a palm tree was in a crouch, holding a weapon in both hands.

'I... Oh very well,' Flora replied. 'I have been working with Peter Jaeger on this operation.' Her words were rushed. 'Yes, he's CIA. The Athens station chief. I ... we decided to entice you back with the material I had learned about your parents. We wanted to use you to destabilise the government. That's a reasonable aim, isn't it? One that's in line with the original aims of the Iraklis group. To destabilise regimes, whether democratically elected or not, to facilitate the rise of a true government of the people.' She stopped to catch her breath.

'So Milroy here took out the two investors,' Jaeger said, 'in your style. They were obvious enough targets for left-wing terrorists. And the lady you're holding now is an even more logical victim – conservative spokesperson, shipping-family heiress, wife of a prominent businessman.' He gave another empty laugh. 'What are you waiting for, Irakli? Or should I call you Iason Kolettis? Or Michalis Zaralis?'

'Kill the Palaiologou bitch,' Flora pleaded. 'Kill her before it's too late.'

After a brief silence the assassin spoke: 'Too late? It is already far too late. You have duped me, and by doing so you have betrayed our group and all we have fought for.'

'Everyone betrayed your group over the years,' Jaeger said. 'Even the ones you called Markos and Thyella. Milroy here got rid of them to make sure the press didn't find out about them after you escaped. The other guy Dhimitrakos, Odhysseas as he was known, was scared shitless and he was useful to us.'

'Is that why you drove him to jump from that rock?' Iraklis demanded bitterly.

'He was already finished, his heart was shot,' Milroy said, dispassionately.

'Everyone betrayed your group, including your beloved controller,' Jaeger continued, his tone ironic. 'How else do you think she's stayed out of jail and alive these last ten years?'

'Is it true, Flora?' Iraklis's voice cracked.

There was no reply.

'Except you, of course,' Jaeger called. 'You were the only one who stayed true to the cause. The high-minded revolutionary who escaped to continue the struggle. Where did you go? Latin America?' He gave a mocking laugh.

'New York,' came the reply.

'Bullshit.'

'It's true enough,' Iraklis said, his voice steady now. 'I worked on a construction gang. But what I did before I left Greece was right. I killed Americans in the old days because they were

502

interfering in my country. When I went to your country I thought I would carry on the fight. But I soon realised that the world had changed.'

Mavros looked at Grace. Her lips were tight, her limbs tense like those of a tiger about to pounce. He put his hand on her arm.

'And you, my Tiresia,' the terrorist said, 'you went along with this plan of the Americans, you sanctioned the murders of the Greek business-men?'

'They were bloodsuckers,' Flora said. 'No different from the ones you slaughtered in the past. And where do you think the equipment you received came from?'

'The explosive pens, the details of this house, this automatic came from the CIA?' Iraklis asked disbelievingly.

'Sure they did,' Jaeger said. 'Though it would be fair to say that the decisions have been taken at a local level rather than in Langley. Don't look at me like that, Ms Forster. Our masters will get behind us quickly enough when we dispose of the notorious Iraklis.' He paused. 'As long as Milroy here can keep a grip on himself. Christ, Lance, why did you have to rush things? How come Trent Helmer meant so much to you? How can you still have the hots for his wife after all these years?'

Mavros glanced at Grace. Her expression was rigid, giving nothing away.

'Be quiet, you bastards!' Iraklis shouted. 'Who killed Randos? Who killed the composer?'

'Ah,' Jaeger said. 'That was Milroy again. He decided to take the old Communist out when he came into the frame. He's been bugging us for decades. That asshole Mavros put us on his trail.'

'Mavros?' The terrorist sounded surprised. 'What has Mavros got to do with this?'

Jaeger grunted. 'Nothing. He just gets in the way. That's how he works. We hoped he and his client might pique your curiosity. We know about you and Laura Helmer, Irakli. The Filipina nanny talked after the murder, she saw how her mistress was. God, that woman must have been something special. Guys falling over each other to get a sniff of her.'

Mavros squeezed Grace's arm. She gave him a cold stare.

'Do it, Irakli,' Flora said. 'Execute the politician. The others will have called the authorities by now.'

'No, they won't,' came the voice of the butler. 'The phone lines have been cut and I still have all their mobiles.'

'You snake,' Veta Palaiologou gasped. 'You have been in my house for months. Have you been waiting for this night since you arrived?'

'There are plenty of us with time on our hands since the end of the Cold War,' Loudhovikos said. He grunted. 'Fuck the rich!'

Silence fell again.

'Kill her,' Flora said desperately. 'It will be the end of a glorious career. If you don't, I will.'

There was the sound of quick footsteps across the yard, then a moan.

Mavros tensed and edged his head round the door jamb. The shot reverberated in his ears before he had a clear line of sight.

20

'Shit!' Grace gasped. 'This has gone far enough.'

Before Mavros could stop her, she was past him and through the doorway on all fours. At first he thought she was heading for the gunman, but then she veered towards the woman who had been hit, a spatter of blood on the white wall above her slumped form. There was a patch of red at the centre of the white blouse. He watched as Grace leaned over Flora Dearfield, fingers feeling for a pulse on her neck. She glanced back at him and shook her head.

'Jesus,' came Jaeger's voice. 'He's shot Tiresias.'

'Be quiet, can't you?' Grace screamed.

Mavros swallowed hard and got to his feet. This was his chance to get close to the terrorist, whose face was pale. Maybe he could do something to help the woman who was still being held captive. He raised his arms and walked out into the light in the enclosed space outside the kitchen. The assassin had taken cover behind a large plastic waste-bin, his pistol held in one hand. The other arm was around Veta Palaiologou's neck. Jaeger and his companions had retreated into the bushes inside the fence. The butler was nowhere to be seen.

'Over here, Grace,' Mavros called, from behind Iraklis.

The assassin gave him a restrained look as she

came across the yard in a crouch.

'Suddenly I've become very popular,' he said. 'I can finish her before you can do anything, I hope you realise that after what happened with ... with Comrade Flora.' He shook his head. 'I didn't want to kill her. She tried to take the gun from me. She–' He broke off, eyes fixed on the dead woman.

'Let the politician go,' Mavros said. Despite the chill air, her face was drenched in sweat. 'I'll take her place.' The terrorist's calm manner made him sure that he had an escape plan.

'I don't think so,' Iraklis replied. 'I prefer female hostages. They make pursuers think twice before pulling the trigger.'

'Take me,' Grace said, before Mavros could stop her. 'I can move a lot faster than your present victim.'

The terrorist turned his eyes on her and thought about it. 'All right. If you're crazy enough to volunteer.' He beckoned her forward. As soon as she was in his reach, he stretched out a hand and grabbed her, dragging her close and wrapping an arm round her neck. At the same time he pushed Veta away with his legs. Mavros bundled the politician past him to the rear of the waste-bin. She was panting for breath.

'Very well,' Iraklis said to the politician, 'your father and your father-in-law committed terrible crimes against my family, but I am setting you free. The old man Dearfield killed my father, but he was right to do it. He is suffering for his actions still. I have no right to exact revenge from you or from him. My controller and I are as

506

guilty as anyone on the other side.' Veta stared at him but didn't speak. For a few moments he looked as if he was about to drop his weapon.

'Let the Helmer woman go,' came the American Lance Milroy's voice, agitated now. 'Let her go, you bastard.'

The assassin tightened his grip and turned to Grace. 'I admire your nerve,' he said, 'but I wouldn't recommend trying to jump me. The same goes for you, Alex Mavros.'

'Nothing could be further from my mind,' Mavros replied, eyeing first the weapon and then Grace. She had gone limp, the veins on her forearms pulsing. Mavros's heart was pounding in his chest. He knew that the crucial moment was near, but he wasn't sure how he was going to react.

'Give it up, Iraklis,' came a loud shout. The voice was Jaeger's. 'You'll get a fair trial. We're not going to kill you in front of witnesses.'

'Of course you aren't,' the terrorist said, under his breath. 'And Nikitas Palaiologos will give all his profits to the Party.' Iraklis took a mobile phone from his pocket, squeezing Grace harder as he did so, then pressed buttons. 'Loudhoviko? Are you where I hope you are? Good. Do it when you hear my shot.' He slipped the phone back into his jacket and leaned his head against his prisoner's. 'If you want to live beyond the next few minutes, sit up slowly.' He released the pressure from her and the two straightened up.

'Come on!' Jaeger yelled. 'We can't wait all night.'

Iraklis turned to Mavros. 'I'm taking her with me. Don't try to follow.'

'Take me as well,' Mavros said. 'You can trust me. I need you.' He felt Grace's eyes on him. 'There are things that only you can tell me about my brother. I swear I won't make any trouble.'

Iraklis looked at him. 'You really are obsessed, aren't you? All right. If you keep up, you can stay with us. Two hostages are better than one.' He tightened his grip on Grace's wrist and raised the automatic.

As soon as the sound of the shot echoed around the walls, all the lights went out. Mavros heard muffled cries from inside the house, then a shout from the Americans ahead. He tried to concentrate on Iraklis and Grace, listening for the sound of their feet on the flagstones. The moon had disappeared behind a layer of cloud and it was hard to make anything out. Then a thin torch-beam swept across the yard, missing them but illuminating the ground enough for Mavros to catch a glimpse of his client's shoes. She and the terrorist were over to the left of the compound, crawling behind a thick line of oleanders. He followed, keeping his head down even though no more shots had been fired.

'Still here?' Iraklis whispered, from close to ground level. 'All right, I've got excellent night vision. Anyone who cries out gets a bullet. Clear?'

'Clear,' Grace and Mavros responded in unison.

'This way,' came the low voice of the butler. 'The side gate's about thirty metres further on.'

They started moving again, the leaves of the bushes whipping against Mavros's face and the ground damp beneath his feet. Extending his right hand, he felt the close mesh of the security fence that had failed to protect the occupants of the Palaiologos house but was now hampering their assailants' escape. Then he became aware of a thick metal post and, beyond it, an open space.

'Through here,' Loudhovikos whispered. 'The Range-Rover's about fifty metres down the track.'

There was asphalt under their shoes now and Mavros quickened his pace, hearing the steps of the others move ahead. The shape of a large vehicle loomed up in the murk.

'In the back,' Iraklis said to him. 'You too, Loudhoviko. Grace Helmer, you're in the front with me. Close the doors quietly if you want to stay alive.'

They climbed in, following his instructions. Then there was a pause as he checked that the key was in place.

'All right, keep your heads down.' The terrorist's voice was level. 'I'm going to drive without lights.'

'Jesus,' Grace hissed.

The engine fired immediately and they started moving down the slope from the house. Branches scraped along the sides, Iraklis straining to pick up the line of the road. Then the clouds parted and the moon shone through, giving enough silvery light for him to make out the asphalt surface. Immediately they heard shouts.

'On the road!' came a female voice.

'Get to the car!' Jaeger yelled.

Loudhovikos was laughing quietly. 'Unless they hid a spare vehicle in the orange groves, they've got no chance of catching us.'

'You took out all the cars?' the assassin asked.

'Every one I could find. They'll have trouble keeping up on flat tyres.'

Iraklis hit the lights and accelerated after they crossed the junction at the bottom of the slope. The ancient citadel was ahead of them, the agricultural prison to the left and, not far beyond, the Nafplion–Argos highway.

'Where are we going?' Mavros asked.

'Wait and see.' Iraklis leaned forward. 'Is that one of them?' He stood on the brakes as the full beam of an approaching vehicle swerved, presenting its doors and side panels to them. The Range-Rover stopped a few metres in front of it with a loud squeal, the driver's door opening immediately. 'Stay with them, Loudhoviko,' Iraklis ordered.

Mavros clenched as he felt a sharp point in his ribs.

'I've got a knife on him,' the butler said to Grace. 'Sit still and I won't push it in any further.'

Grace turned to Mavros. The look on his face made her nod in acquiescence.

Then a single shot made all three of them start.

'Another one goes to hell,' Loudhovikos said, running his tongue across his lips. He watched as Iraklis put his shoulder to the car and shoved it into the unfenced orange grove at the side of the road.

The terrorist ran back to the Range-Rover and slammed the door. 'Madman. How did he get down so quickly?'

'Who was it?' the butler asked, as the vehicle started to move again.

Iraklis glanced at Mavros and Grace. 'The guy

510

I scared off down in the Mani, the one who did for my old driver.'

'You put a bullet in his head?' Loudhovikos said avidly.

Iraklis stopped at the main junction, then pulled out to the right. 'No, I didn't. There's been enough killing. I knocked him out and blew away the ignition unit. Satisfied?'

Loudhovikos was shaking his head slowly. 'No, this can't be. The great Iraklis letting a CIA bastard off the hook? You must be losing your touch.'

Mavros sat back as the knife was withdrawn, seeing the lights of the fortress above Argos in the distance past Grace's head. If this was the terrorist losing his touch, he was glad he hadn't met him when he was at the height of his powers – as his brother Andonis had.

Veta Palaiologou made her way through the kitchen in the darkness, feeling the surfaces with her hands. The moonlight wasn't penetrating the low windows. She could hear sobbing and hushed voices from the *saloni*.

'Nikita?' she called. 'It's me. I'm all right.' She listened for a few moments. 'I think they've gone.'

There was a rush of feet and a mounting clamour ahead of her. Then a torch came on and she had to raise her hand to shield her eyes.

'Mama,' Klio moaned, burying her head in her mother's abdomen.

'My love,' Veta said, admitting Prokopis to her embrace as well and screwing up her eyes. 'Lower that torch, for God's sake, Nikita. I think the worm Loudhovikos did something to the fuse box. Go and see if you can fix it. Then you'd better let those idiot guards out. Make sure they're very careful with the explosive device.'

Nikitas came up and handed her the torch, switching on another that he had found in the hall. 'What happened?' he asked. 'Where are the others?'

'Flora,' she whispered. 'The terrorist shot Flora.' She paused as she saw Anna appear in the doorway beyond. 'He took Alex Mavros and Grace Helmer with him.'

'Christ and the Holy Mother!' her husband gasped. 'We'd better call the police. Nikos Kriaras in Athens will know what to do.'

'Call them with what?' Veta asked. 'They have all our mobiles and I think the land-line is down. The butler again.'

Nikitas had picked up the receiver on the hall table. He shook his head. 'What about Flora? Shouldn't we get an ambulance? We could send Prokopis down to the main road.'

'She's beyond help,' his wife said, glaring at him. 'And I'm not sending our son anywhere tonight.' Her voice softened. 'We must be careful, Nikita. There are political considerations here. Go now.'

She watched him move off, then pushed her children away gently. 'Let me talk to Geoff and Dorothy,' she said to them. She smiled briefly at Anna as she made her way into the sitting room. She knew where the candles were and soon the place was well illuminated. When she saw the fearful faces of her guests she almost wished

512

she'd left the room in darkness.

She went over to Geoffrey Dearfield. He was sitting on the sofa as he had been earlier, his chin lolling on his chest. She sat down beside him. 'Geoff, I'm so sorry. Flora ... Flora has been shot. She–'

'I can't believe she hid so much from me,' the old man said. 'She betrayed everything I worked for, she lied, she directed assassinations. I... Oh, God...' His head went down again and he started mumbling to himself, his lips slack and wet.

Veta touched the parchment of his hands briefly, then got up again. There was nothing more she could say to him. Flora's revelations had shocked her to the core, but not as much as Geoff's memoir. Even the sight of the woman she'd regarded as a friend being shot in the struggle with Iraklis had shaken her less than the confirmation that her father and her father-in-law had been rapists and murderers. She could hardly bear to look Dorothy Cochrane-Mavrou in the eye, but she forced herself to go over to her.

'Alex is all right?' the old woman asked, when the politician approached her. Anna was kneeling before her, Nondas and the kids around the armchair.

Veta shrugged. 'I think... I hope so. The American woman, Grace, she volunteered to take my place. And Alex ... he went with her. I don't know where the terrorist's taking them.'

Dorothy was nodding. 'Alex knows what he is doing,' she said, with a bright smile that surprised the politician. 'And so does that young woman.'

Anna grimaced. 'How can you say that, Mother? We've just been within an inch of our lives, your grandchildren as well as the rest of us, and you sit there giving Alex and his peculiar client a vote of confidence.' She got to her feet, ignoring Nondas's hand. 'Honestly.'

'That Iraklis,' Dorothy said. 'He's finished. I saw it in his eyes.'

'I don't suppose Flora would agree,' Anna said.

Dorothy looked up at her. 'On the contrary,' she replied, 'Flora knew Iraklis had reached his limit. That was why she kept exhorting him to do what he came here for.' She glanced at Veta. 'He may be a terrorist and a murderer, but he knows his career has run its course. Shooting the woman who manipulated him will only have made that clearer.'

'I hope you're right,' Veta said. 'All these years, all the horror. It has to end now.'

'It will end,' Dorothy said. 'My husband was a man of peace. Most fighters were, whatever side they were on. People have learned to put their faith in peaceful methods in this country now. Iraklis and his kind are an anachronism.'

The others looked at her, their faces racked with uncertainty. Only Geoffrey Dearfield kept his eyes off her. He was weeping quietly, a prisoner of the past who had thought he could find redemption by writing down his story; instead he'd handed himself a life sentence in solitary confinement.

About two kilometres further on, Iraklis turned the Range-Rover off the highway. A side-road led down to a canning factory and he pulled up between a pair of thick-trunked eucalyptuses. The Suzuki he had hired earlier in the day was parked to the right.

'We'll change vehicles,' he said. 'You and me first, Grace Helmer. Loudhoviko, lock up and lose the key.'

The butler watched as the occupants of the front seats left the Range-Rover.

'What's your interest in this?' Mavros asked, instantly feeling the knife-point jab into his side again.

'My interest?' Loudhovikos replied, in a mocking tone. 'My interest is the same as your father's. The overthrow of an unjust system and its replacement by one that treats all citizens in the same way.' He looked to his left. 'Out. And slowly.'

Mavros opened the door, the butler sliding after him. He could have risked slamming the door into him and making a run for it, but that would have left Grace alone in Iraklis's hands. Besides, he'd given his word that he wouldn't cause any trouble. Loudhovikos activated the central-locking system, then lobbed the key into the darkness beyond the trees.

'Who will you work for now?' Mavros asked, as they reached the Suzuki. 'I presume you took orders from the dead woman.'

'Shut up and get in,' the butler said. 'What do you care? At least your father and brother were in the struggle. You just suck up the crumbs from the rich man's table.'

'The struggle's over, my friend,' Mavros said, as

515

he sat down in the back. 'The Soviet Union's gone. There's no need for undercover operatives like you any more.'

Loudhovikos closed his door and sniffed. 'If you believe that, you're even more of a fool than you look.'

Iraklis started the engine and drove back up to the main road. He took a long look to right and left, then pulled out and accelerated towards Argos, but at the first left turn he braked hard without indicating and got off the highway. A narrow road led down to the bay. There was little traffic around. The lights of Nafplion were dancing on the still water to their left, while away to the right a line of small towns stretched down the Peloponnesian coast. The road they were on cut through a couple of villages, one consisting mainly of garish *tavernes* and nightclubs, before it reached the highway that led south from Argos. Iraklis stopped about fifty metres from the junction. 'Will this do for you?' he asked the butler.

Loudhovikos nodded, his hand on the door catch. 'Are you sure you don't need my help any longer?'

'Like you said, I'm losing my touch. I trust these two not to make a move on me.' The terrorist turned and gave him a soft smile. 'Go to the good, my friend.'

'The mobile phones are in the bag on the floor,' Loudhovikos said, as he got out. 'Long live the struggle,' he added. 'Whatever anyone says, you are still a great hero, Irakli.' He closed the door behind him and disappeared.

The assassin drove on past a brown sign

516

pointing to the early Bronze Age site at Lerna.

'Great hero,' scoffed Grace. 'Great murderer, more like.'

'This is where your namesake defeated the Hydra,' Mavros said, trying to distract Iraklis from Grace's verbal assault.

'Yes, how symbolic,' his client said, giving him a sharp glance, then looking at the driver. 'You've spent your life cutting off the heads of the people you think are your enemies, but still they keep coming.' Her shoulders dropped. 'What's driving you? All that killing, all that blood. What's the good of it?'

Iraklis looked in the rear-view mirror. 'They aren't coming now, Grace. Don't imagine they will rescue you. Not tonight, at least.' He shook his head. 'You don't understand. No one who hasn't grown up with the horror, no one who hasn't seen what happens to people when power is wielded unchecked can understand.'

'So, help me understand,' Grace said, her eyes glinting in the glow from the dashboard. 'You think I didn't grow up with horror? I saw you cut my father's throat, you bastard. How much worse was what you experienced?'

Iraklis glanced at her, his jaw jutting. 'I never even knew my father. You heard how he died on the cross. My mother was raped when she was carrying me, her sister was ripped open by the Right's jackals. Why are you surprised that I could act as I did?'

Mavros leaned forward, catching sight of the automatic between the assassin's knees. 'What are you saying? That there's a genealogy of terrorism?

517

That people who grow up with the sufferings of the previous generation are turned into unthinking avengers? If that was the case, Greece and most other countries would be full of people like you.'

Iraklis was nodding slowly. 'You're right. I'm not talking for everyone, just for the few of us who had some kind of ability to shut off our emotions. That's a curse. I didn't ask for it. But there are a few like me, like Loudhovikos. His parents were in EAM, they fought in the Democratic Army in the civil war. They were starved and beaten in the camps throughout the fifties. Their health was ruined. And then, when the Colonels came to power, they were immediately taken back into custody and returned to the prison islands. They died within a month, separated from each other. They were both over sixty years old. My mother was lucky to survive the same experience. My stepfather was crippled by it.'

Mavros sat back. The story wasn't uncommon, he'd heard similar ones throughout his childhood, but that didn't make it any easier to accept. If his own father hadn't died before the dictatorship, that would probably have been his fate too. Fighting with the memories that were suddenly stirred up, he was only vaguely aware that Iraklis had turned right on to the road that led over the mountains to Tripolis.

'But you weren't just a killing machine, were you?' Grace was saying. 'You knew my mother – you were the Iason Kolettis who seduced her. I suppose that crazy Flora gave you instructions to target an American diplomat. But then you fell in love with her, didn't you? You felt the same way as Laura did.'

The terrorist's head shot back as if acid had been dashed into his eyes. He wrestled with the wheel as they went into the first hairpin of the ascent, then accelerated as the Suzuki cleared the corner. Shortly afterwards he pulled into the side.

'Yes,' Iraklis said, his voice almost inaudible. 'Yes, I loved her.' He glanced at Grace, his face a ruin. 'I loved ... I loved Laura.' The instant he spoke the name, his face slackened and he gripped the wheel hard, like a man trying to resist a tidal wave.

Grace was driving, Iraklis holding the automatic loosely, its muzzle pointed to the floor. He had his eyes locked on the road, which was twisting up the mountain in the beam of the headlights, but his mind had slipped on to another plane. He was aware that he should be paying more attention, that Grace or Mavros might make a move on him, lunge for his weapon, but he couldn't fight his emotions any more. It had finally happened. He had said her name.

For so many years he had kept out of his thoughts the name of the only woman he had ever loved even though her form – her joyful face and her soft, freckled skin – often slipped through his defences like a ghost. Laura. Oh, God, Laura, he said to himself. What did I do to you? Is it too late to lay you to rest, now that your daughter – her features and her lithe body so like your own – has found me? Oh, Laura.

'Tell me about you and her,' Grace said, her

voice unwavering. 'Tell me what it was between you that filled her life even after you killed my father, that eventually drove her to kill herself.' She glanced at him. 'Tell me!'

Iraklis's thoughts were running out of control. It seemed that someone else was talking, he hardly recognised the voice, but the words came from deep inside himself.

'I wanted to find Laura,' he was saying, 'even though it was too late. That was why I went to the US. I thought I could see where she had lived, I thought I could bring her back from the grave by visiting your home. It wasn't hard to track down your mother's address. And I went there one Sunday. It was fall, the trees in the countryside turning red and gold. I parked a couple of streets away and walked to the house, a baseball cap pulled low over my face. I hoped to make some kind of contact with her, I hoped to raise her shade like Odysseus did with his mother's in the myth. And then I saw the woman I thought was Laura. I couldn't believe it. She was alive, her face younger than it had been the first time I met her in the museum in Athens, her hair tied in a ponytail and her beautiful face caught in the soft light as she walked across the lawn. I started to run towards her – opened my mouth to call her name.' He stopped, panting. He looked round at Mavros, and then at Grace, whose expression was impassive, her eyes on the road.

'And then ... and then I realised it wasn't Laura. There was something hard about the face, a terrible bitterness in the eyes of the woman before me. She was Laura's daughter, the little girl who had looked down on me the night I killed her father.' He leaned towards Grace. 'She was you.'

Still Grace made no response, her lips set.

'I managed to regain control of myself before you noticed me,' Iraklis continued. 'I walked past the house, never looking back, my heart almost wrenched from my chest. And I finally understood what I had done. Laura's life had been ruined by what I did and she had killed herself, but her daughter was still carrying the burden of the pain. I realised then that love isn't everything, that there are emotions stronger than love, places where love cannot survive. I should have known that earlier, much earlier. Perhaps deep down I did know it, but I was beguiled by the vain hope that I could get beyond the hatred and bitterness of my parents' generation, beyond the violence it had spawned. False dreams and deception.'

Grace turned to him. 'Is that what you believe in, then?' she said. 'The triumph of hatred over love?' She gave a bitter laugh. 'Yeah, I guess that squares pretty well with what you've done in your pathetic life.'

But Iraklis had sunk into himself, the words he was mouthing audible to no one.

Laura, I could never have explained my actions to you. I could never have made you understand that hatred can only be matched, can only be beaten by greater hatred, force by greater and more pitiless force. I believed that, we all did. Flora died believing it. My mother still believes it in her scarred, unyielding soul. But now, my Laura, now I am tired and it's far too late to make amends. Even the memories of our love – the museum's cool halls, the statues' vacant eyes, your shocked acceptance of the emotions that swept us away on an irresistible tide, your desperate screams as we surged to a climax – even those memories have receded now.

All that remains is the awful emptiness in the eyes of the little girl, the girl who has grown into the woman sitting beside me, her pale, immobile face at the window above. That and the spray of blood from your husband's throat, his body slumping and the light extinguishing in his eyes as he became another in the long line of red deaths.

They had reached the plateau beyond the ridge, the lights from the gulf now gone. Grace increased her speed, her eyes flicking up to the rear-view mirror continuously. Beside her, the terrorist was sitting up straight. He didn't look sleepy; rather, it seemed to the others, he was fighting to keep his emotions in check.

'How could you do it?' Grace asked. 'How could you kill your lover's husband in front of her? In front of me?'

Iraklis glanced at her. 'Believe me, I never thought that you would be awake at that time, that you would come to the window.'

She looked to the front and Mavros could see the muscles on her face clenching. 'But you killed him anyway. You would have killed him if you hadn't seen me. What did you think? That my mother would rush into your arms and congratulate you? That you would ride off into the night with her?'

'I knew I would never see her again. I wasn't a romantic.'

'Ah, but you were,' Grace contradicted him. 'She wrote to me about you, she told me how you behaved when you were together. Don't tell me you were faking that. My mother wasn't a fool.'

Iraklis was silent for a while. 'No,' he admitted, 'I wasn't faking what I felt for her. But the struggle was more important than the individuals caught up in it.'

'Bullshit!' Grace shouted. 'You just killed the woman who was behind your band of murderers. You wanted her to pay for what she'd made you do back in 'seventy-six.'

'That was an accident. Besides, she went over to the Americans.'

'But she was the one who told you to execute my father. She was the one who separated you from my mother.'

The assassin didn't answer.

Mavros leaned forward. 'Where are we going?' he asked, raising his hand to secure Grace's silence.

'You'll find out.'

'Tripolis?' Mavros hazarded. 'You could let Grace out there. I'll stay with you for as long as you want.'

'No way,' his client said. 'I haven't finished with this guy yet.' She glanced round. 'There's more that I have to ask him.'

Mavros looked at Grace. He was still unsure of her motives.

'You're both staying till the end of the road,' Iraklis said.

Mavros sat back. 'Good. I've got some questions for you too.'

The terrorist sighed. 'About your brother?'

'Yes, about Andonis. Among other things.'

'Jesus.' Iraklis looked round at him. 'What makes you think I'm going to open up to you?'

Mavros gazed back at him. 'Everyone needs to communicate.'

'You want a confession?'

'If you like.'

'You've got enough sins to confess,' Grace put in.

'All right, all right.' The assassin sighed again. 'Andonis Mavros. I only met him once.' He was aware that he was talking, but he suddenly found himself in another Peloponnesian location – one that he had visited recently and that was only a few kilometres from the village where he grew up.

From the ridge they could see the towers of Kitta, the mist rolling up the hillsides as the breeze set in from the sea that November morning of 1972. The poet Kostas Laskaris closed the door behind them and the pair of anti-Junta activists walked towards the peninsula of Tigani, their heads down.

'So, Andoni, will you join us?' Iraklis asked.

The young man with the piercing blue eyes turned to him. 'Maybe. If you tell me your real name. All this messing about with code-names and pseudonyms. How can you trust someone if you don't know their identity? For me Iraklis is a mythical strongman who went around kicking

524

hell out of gods and monsters, not flesh and blood.'

'How do you know Iraklis isn't my name? There was a boy in my class at school called that.'

Andonis Mavros swung his leg over the gate that blocked the path leading to the headland. 'Because everyone in the underground uses false names.' He smiled. 'Except me.'

'You're a fool, then.' Iraklis stepped past him and headed down the rough track, the dew soaking into his boots. They didn't talk again until they were on the narrow handle of the frying-pan, surrounded by salt pans and sharp-edged boulders.

'Tell me more about your group,' Andonis said. 'The comrades don't approve of it. They told me to stay away, which is why I had to come all the way down here. Kostas Laskaris is the only one who seems to like you.'

'Kostas has been a friend of my family for many years. But the rest of the old comrades have lost sight of the struggle. They think that leaving the Colonels to self-destruct is the safest policy.' He caught his companion's arm. 'That could take years. We aren't going to wait.'

They looked ahead as a seagull rose up, its harsh cry echoing around the rock surfaces.

'I don't want to wait either.' Andonis Mavros was springing from boulder to boulder, as sure-footed as a goat. 'But I need to know what you're intending to do.'

So he told the blue-eyed boy; told him about their determination, about their weapons and their training, about their list of targets. By the time he'd finished they were under the surviving bastion of the citadel.

'How did they build this?' Andonis Mavros mused, the question directed at himself as much as at Iraklis. 'No wonder the myths say that Titans and Cyclops were responsible for walls like these. And now they're undefended and irrelevant, the men who fought here forgotten by history.'

Iraklis knew then that the young man wasn't going to join the group, and that he wasn't going to allow anyone he knew to do so either. They went up the narrow track to the ruined castle and wandered around the foundations and shattered cisterns.

When they were inside the remains of a basilica, Andonis Mavros turned to him. 'There are bones in here,' he said, indicating a broken tomb. 'Do you think they belong to some illustrious warrior?' He looked out to the grey sea then back to the last summits of Taygetos, shrouded in mist. 'You're wrong, Irakli, or whatever your name is. Violence is not the way to proceed. Our parents learned the cost of violence and hatred. You should listen to the old men.'

Then Andonis Mavros walked away, his figure gradually shrinking to a dot among the razor-stones of the crossing.

Iraklis was sure that the young man with the blue eyes and the solemn voice was wrong. He hadn't been surprised when he heard that Andonis Mavros had disappeared soon after. He was brave but he had no guile. There was no gravestone marking his time on the earth, as there was none for the thousands who had breathed their last on the barren, wind-ravaged headland of Tigani over the centuries. His father and his ELAS comrades had gone unremembered into the abyss as well.

'So Andonis would have nothing to do with the Iraklis group,' Alex Mavros said, his voice little more than a murmur. The unworthy suspicion that his brother had been involved with terrorism loosed its hold on him and was gone. 'Did you ever hear anything more about him?'

The assassin's head rocked back in a negative movement. 'No. He has still not been found?'

Mavros didn't answer. Initially relief had flooded through him, but now he was stricken with bitter disappointment. He had been hoping that Iraklis would have some unique information to give him, something that would finally put him on Andonis's track after all the empty years of searching. But there was nothing. The trail was as cold as ever.

Grace looked round at him. 'Alex?' she said softly. 'I'm sorry.' She reached a hand out to his. 'It was always a long shot. You said so yourself.'

Mavros sat for a while with his head bowed, then pulled himself together. Ahead of them, the lights of Tripolis were glowing in the distance. 'You have more to tell, Irakli,' he said, his tone firmer. 'What happened to Babis Dhimitrakos? He was a member of your band, wasn't he?'

'He was. As the American said, he betrayed me along with the others a decade ago. They were caught and tortured. So was I, but I managed to

527

escape. I thought Flora had eluded them, but I was a fool.' He shook his head. 'I visited my old comrade in that hovel up in Kainourgia Chora. I didn't do anything to him. I wanted to know if he'd been contacted recently by the Americans or their Greek equivalents. Something about the way Flora drew me back to Greece made me suspicious, though I never thought she'd gone over to the Americans. I left, but then I saw the American operative in the village and doubled back to see what he was doing. It looks like he was making sure that Babis's mouth was permanently closed.'

'And why did you save us from him?' Grace demanded. 'What was in that for you?'

'I'd recognised Milroy,' Iraklis said, his voice low. 'Whatever that bastard was doing needed to be stopped.' He glanced at her. 'Besides, I'd also recognised you, Grace.'

There was a long silence.

'Thank you,' Grace said finally, her eyes on the road.

'Yes, thank you,' Mavros echoed, recalling the crazed glint in the American's eyes as he had approached them.

'What was it the guy called Jaeger said about my parents?' Grace said. 'Milroy was a friend of my father, but it sounded like he had a thing for my mother.'

Iraklis gave her an agonised look. 'That animal? I don't think he has emotions.'

'No doubt he feels the same about you,' Grace said.

'He killed the composer Randos on a whim,'

the terrorist said, his voice filled with indignation. 'I never killed anyone without just cause.'

Mavros decided to ratchet up the pressure. 'You visited Kostas Laskaris after you found Dhimitrakos, didn't you?'

'How do you know that?'

'Never mind,' Mavros replied, his tone hardening. 'What did you do to Yiorgos Pandazopoulos?'

'The overweight comrade who was down there? Don't worry about him. I locked him up in Kostas's top room. He should be out by now. I didn't want him blabbing about me. There was another guy on my tail in Nafplion. Anything to do with you?'

'No.' Mavros remembered the shadowy form he'd seen on the ramparts above Kyra Stamatina's street.

'He must have been with the Americans.'

'Did you hurt him?' Grace demanded.

'Not much. He's in my mother's cellar,' Iraklis replied. 'If he's lucky, she'll have left him alone. I told her to let him go tomorrow.'

Mavros stared into the back of the terrorist's head, the hair still dark despite his age. 'Loudhovikos was right. You have lost your nerve.' He was taking a chance, but he wanted to see how much fight there was left in the man.

'Look at it this way,' Iraklis said, after a long pause. 'If I hadn't, you two would already be dead. As it is, you're safer with me than you would be in the open. You can be sure the Americans are after me. If this is an operation that Jaeger's superiors don't know about, they'll be planning to dispose of me as spectacularly as they can and they won't want any witnesses.' He laid his hand on the butt of the automatic. 'Now, be quiet and let Grace drive. We've a long way to go.'

Mavros sat back and watched as the lights of the town grew closer, then slipped past on their right. They were on the bypass, aiming south into the cold, dark heart of the Peloponnese.

'How do you know he'll be heading there, sir?' Jane Forster asked, her eyes on the surface of the Argos–Tripolis road. They had found a Land Rover parked near the entrance to the site of Tiryns and Milroy had hot-wired it.

'Never fucking mind,' Jaeger said, blinking hard. His nerves were at breaking point, his plans turning to shit. Fortunately the Palaiologou woman was playing ball, agreeing to keep quiet until Nikos Kriaras arrived to smooth things over. He reckoned it would be possible to secure the police commander's silence – there were some old debts Jaeger could call in. Christ knows how he'd keep the rest of them quiet. Alex Mavros's sister was a journalist. Hopefully Kriaras would put the fear of God into her. 'You all right?' he asked, looking over his shoulder.

'Yeah.' Lance Milroy was stretched out on the back seat. The handkerchief he had spread over his face obscured livid bruises on his cheek and temples. 'I'm going to tear that shit-eater apart.'

'All in good time,' Jaeger said. 'You should never have gone near the house and you shouldn't have tried to block his escape. All that because you couldn't wait to get even with the guy who screwed a woman you had your eye on twenty-five years ago.' He gave a hollow laugh. 'Besides, you should be grateful to him. He could have blown your brains out.'

'Fuck you. We shouldn't have trusted Tiresias. There were things she set up with him that she kept from us, I'm sure of it.'

'Like how he was going to get out of the country?' Jaeger asked. 'Don't worry. Flora thought I didn't know about the letters she sent Iraklis via the old Communist they used in the Caucasus. Stupid mistake.' He glanced at the driver. 'Ms Forster, I hope you're not thinking of telling anyone about this conversation.'

She shook her head, keeping her eyes on the road.

'Good, because that would be detrimental to your career.' Jaeger watched as the lights of Tripolis loomed up, a bitter taste in his throat. The operation had almost been blown at the house above Tiryns. Langley would have his balls unless he could deliver the head of the most wanted man in Greece. At least there was still a good chance of that. Iraklis looked like he might have lost it after Flora had tried to take his gun from him. The fact that she'd ended up dead meant she wouldn't be talking.

Jaeger smiled. Maybe the set-up was going to work out after all.

21

Mavros woke with a start, his eyes gummed together. The sound of the car's engine was still in his ears, but it was labouring more than it had been on the fast road south of Tripolis. He sat up and rubbed away the sleep. Iraklis and Grace had swapped seats again. 'Where are we?' he asked.

'Almost there,' Iraklis replied.

'Almost where?' Grace said. She seemed to be fully awake. 'We're going to run out of land soon.'

Mavros could see nothing outside the Suzuki – no lights, no other vehicles, no sign of civilisation. 'Are we in the Mani?' he asked.

'Even in his sleep the great detective has his finger on the case,' his client said, her tone mocking. 'The last place we went through was that vampire town Vatheia.'

'Shit,' Mavros muttered, straining his eyes outside again. 'We really are going to hit the sea soon.' He looked into the rear-view mirror. 'Are you being picked up by boat?' he asked the driver.

'Wait and see, young Mavros,' Iraklis replied. His head was moving from side to side and it looked like he was wrestling with exhaustion.

They went over a series of low hills, a few lights below, and then continued in a straighter line, the first flecks of dawn appearing in the eastern sky.

By the time that Iraklis had driven down an incline and stopped the car, there was enough of a glow to make out a great finger of land stretching away to their right. Ahead was a wide expanse of open, white-flecked water.

'This is it,' the assassin said, raising his weapon. 'Get out, both of you.'

Mavros and Grace followed his instruction, stamping their feet on the reddish mud covering a makeshift parking area. The place was silent, the pale green mounds of the hills dotted with scrub. Behind them was a boarded-up restaurant, its terrace festooned with unpruned vines. An icy wind was blowing from the north.

'Jesus,' Grace said, from in front of a brown sign. 'What is this? "Sanctuary and Death Oracle of Poseidon Tainarios"?'

'So that's it,' Mavros said. 'This is where it ends.'

'You know your mythology?' Iraklis asked, herding them with his automatic past a low ruin of roughly hewn stone blocks with an arched roof.

'It was drummed into me at school,' Mavros replied. 'This is Tainaron. The cape down there is the furthest southerly point of mainland Greece. And somewhere around here is the entrance to the underworld.'

'That's right.' Iraklis stopped above the end of a narrow inlet, a yacht bobbing at anchor, and pointed to a cave shrouded by the leafless branches of a dead tree. The entrance was marked by a couple of low gateposts, a wall of piled stones to the right. 'The local fishermen, the few who remain, use it to store their gear now, but in the myths this was the way that Iraklis went to the death god's kingdom on his twelfth and final labour.'

'To haul Cerberus up,' Mavros added. 'Did Flora teach you all this?'

'Uh-uh. I'm a local. And I read more about the history when I was in New York.' He looked around and pointed to a scarcely discernible line of foundation stones by the tiny beach. 'That was the temple of Poseidon. Mercenaries came from all over the Greek world to be hired here.' He looked at Grace. 'Killers with a blood-curse on them could seek asylum at the temple and summon up the souls of their victims to absolve themselves of guilt.'

Grace's mouth was twisted in disgust. 'Did you bring me here to ask for forgiveness?' she demanded. 'Do you really think I'm going to give you that?'

Iraklis held her gaze. 'If I thought it would help you,' he replied haltingly. 'For me there can be no forgiveness, I know that well enough.' He stepped away. A small green-bottomed rowing-boat was lying upturned on the stony beach. 'Help me with this, Alex Mavros,' he said, slipping off his coat and rolling up the sleeves of his white shirt. He kept the automatic within his reach on the wooden hull. 'The yacht is chartered to me. I will leave you the Suzuki.'

Mavros stepped forward. 'How did you arrange the boat? It wasn't through Flora, was it?'

The terrorist nodded. 'I'm taking a chance that she didn't tell the Americans. That's why we

534

should hurry.'

Grace stood stock-still, her eyes burning as Mavros put his shoulder to the boat and manhandled it to the water with the terrorist, the automatic now in his belt. Then he turned back, went into the cave and reappeared with a pair of oars.

'Don't worry about the dinghy,' Iraklis said. 'The fisherman has been paid over the odds for it.'

'You ... you can't let him leave,' Grace said to Mavros. 'You can't.' She ran forward, to be pushed immediately on to the stones by the assassin with a weary grimace.

'It's finished,' Mavros said. 'You told me you wanted your father's killer to explain himself and he's done that.' He watched as Iraklis took the automatic from his belt. 'I don't think he's going to kill again. Unless you drive him to it.'

Iraklis glanced at him, then shouldered the oars. 'No,' he said. 'I'm not going to kill again.'

The shot surprised them, the enclosed space making the reverberation boom into their ears. Suddenly the assassin was lying on his back beside Grace, crimson flowering on his right shoulder. The weapon had spun from his hand and Grace scrabbled for it, taking hold before he could.

Mavros crawled towards the boat and looked around the surrounding slopes, trying to pinpoint the shooter's location. Then he turned to his left when he heard Grace speak: 'They never give up,' she said, the muzzle of the Glock against Iraklis's temple.

He was gasping, his left hand over the wound

535

and the veins on his forehead protruding. 'I was almost certain the Americans would come,' he said.

Mavros swivelled round and saw a tall figure he recognised walking slowly down the hillside. There was a woman about ten metres to his right and further down another man, hair close cut and grizzled, his face and the side of his head discoloured by livid marks. All three had pistols raised in a double-handed grip.

'Grace?' Peter Jaeger called. 'Grace Helmer? Take the shot, why don't you? The guy killed your father. Now's your chance to make him pay.'

Mavros looked round and took in the scene beyond the boat. Grace was on her knees, her ponytail dangling over her shoulder. Iraklis had stopped writhing, his lower lip between his teeth and his eyes narrowed. Blood was seeping through the fingers he had placed over his wound. 'Kill me,' he gasped. 'Kill me before they do.'

Grace shifted the weapon round till the muzzle was in the centre of his forehead. Her breathing was steady, but there were drops of sweat on her brow. 'You loved my mother,' she said. 'But you killed my father.'

Iraklis turned his head away. 'Laura,' he said, the skin on his face beaded with sweat. 'Laura...'

Grace leaned closer, her finger tightening on the trigger.

'Don't!' Mavros yelled. 'Don't let them suck you into their world!'

She gave him an agonised look, her eyes damp, then turned back to the man on the stones beside

536

her. For a moment Mavros thought Grace was going to fire and so did Iraklis – he closed his eyes and lay still. But then she stood up in a quick movement and tossed the automatic towards the cave entrance, stepping to the boat.

Before Mavros could say anything to her, before he could comfort her, his ears were blasted by a succession of shots. When he looked back at Iraklis, he saw that his chest had been torn apart, his shirt perforated and bathed in blood. The crew-cut man stepped up and fired one more time into the terrorist's head from close range.

'The last red death,' Jaeger said. He nodded to Lance Milroy, who had ejected his ammunition clip and slapped in a replacement. 'At least, that's how it will seem.' He glanced round. 'Ms Forster, go find Iraklis's weapon. We'll need it to dispose of our two witnesses.'

Mavros and Grace exchanged looks as the American woman headed towards the cave mouth. The enclosed bay was silent, waves lapping against the unmanned yacht. Further out, a deep-sea vessel was cutting through the chill grey water at the very end of Greece.

22

Mavros took a step forward. 'You know Grace was CIA,' he said to Jaeger. 'She was one of yours.'

'Alex,' she said, grabbing his arm. 'Don't–'

He shook himself free. 'She won't talk. You can't...' He let the words trail away when he saw the look on Jaeger's face.

'Give it up, Mavros,' the American said. 'You know you're whistling in the wind. It'll look even better that Iraklis took out the daughter of one of his victims before we got to him. Took her out along with the cretinous investigator who brought her into contact with the terrorist.'

Milroy ran a hand over his hair. 'I don't like it. She's Trent's daughter, for Chrissakes. She's ... she's Laura's daughter.'

Jaeger shook his head. 'There you go again, Lance. Still harping on about your old friends.' He laughed. 'Still obsessed by a woman who didn't return your lust. If you'd been professional at the Palaiologos house, we'd never have ended up in this shit.' He glanced over to the cave. 'What's going on, Ms Forster?' he called in a mock-southern drawl. 'Can't you find the weapon? Don't tell me you're afraid of snakes in the grass?'

The female operative's back remained turned towards them as she scoured the ground for

Iraklis's Glock.

Mavros felt the chill wind on his face as he played for time. 'What were you trying to achieve with this complicated scheme, Jaeger?' he asked. 'Is this how the agency's acting after September the eleventh? Catch all known terrorists no matter the cost?' He took another step forward and stopped when Milroy raised his automatic.

'Something like that,' Jaeger replied, with a grin. 'Except this is my own little plot. No one in Langley knows about it yet.'

Mavros saw Jane Forster look anxiously over her shoulder as she leaned forward into the new grass outside the entrance to the underworld. 'So you put the squeeze on Flora Petraki-Dearfield to get Iraklis back into the country. How did you manage that? From what I saw, she was committed to the struggle with a will of iron. Even Iraklis was in her power.'

'You haven't got a clue, asshole,' Milroy said. 'We identified her back in the early nineties before we caught the gang. We let her think she was in the clear, then we tightened the screw on her.' His weapon was still pointed at Mavros's chest. 'She gave us some useful stuff on certain other underground cells so we let her stay out of jail.'

Grace came up to Mavros, ignoring the weapon that Jaeger levelled at her. She glared at the station chief. 'You guys are really something, aren't you? Do you seriously imagine Langley's going to go along with the murder of the composer Randos?' She turned her gaze on Milroy, her expression one of loathing. 'It was you, wasn't it? Christ, you even threw the kittens out of the window with him, you sick fuck.'

Mavros squeezed her forearm, fearful of the response her words might provoke.

Milroy raised his shoulders. 'They were making a hell of a noise.' He returned her stare. 'Anyway, what are you complaining about, Grace? We killed the man who slaughtered your father like an animal.' He nodded at her. 'You wanted to do it yourself, I saw the look on your face. Why didn't you?'

'You also killed the businessmen to make it seem like Iraklis had returned to the scene,' Mavros said, nudging Grace away. 'Your superiors are hardly going to raise a cheer for that.'

Jaeger looked unconcerned. 'Who'll believe that, whatever Iraklis said at the Palaiologos house? We'll produce all the evidence anyone needs to prove that he was the perpetrator.'

'Wait a minute,' Grace said, raising her hand. 'What exactly was your smartass plan at the Palaiologos house? You said that this piece of slime here lost his grip. So what were you expecting to happen?'

Mavros turned to her. 'Christ, that's right.' He looked back at Jaeger. 'You were hoping that Iraklis would shoot Veta, weren't you?'

'That was the general idea,' the American confirmed.

'But what about the effect that would have had on this country?' Mavros said.

Jaeger glanced over towards Jane Forster, who was now on her knees in the undergrowth, her head averted. 'The effect?' he said, his tone hardening. 'Nothing but good. The socialist buffoons in government would have been terminally discredited by the assassination of such a major opposition figure on their watch. It wouldn't have been long till the other side won power in elections.' He shook his head at Mavros. 'The Left is a spent force, my friend. You should know that better than most.'

'That may be true,' Mavros said, his fists clenched. 'My father struggled for years and Greeks still chose the free market, but that doesn't give you the right to meddle in other countries' affairs. That doesn't give you the right to play God.'

Milroy's face flushed. 'And what about the innocent victims like Trent Helmer?' he yelled. 'What about Laura, her life ruined? There's a twenty-year statute of limitations in this fucking country. Even if Iraklis had been caught, he wouldn't have stood trial for that killing.' His eyes were locked on Grace. 'Don't you get it? I did this for your parents.'

She looked back at him without flinching. 'Go to hell. You can't treat people like you do. You can't use my parents to justify the murders you've committed.'

'That's right.'

The female voice made them all turn towards the cave. Jane Forster was striding to them, both arms raised, an automatic in each hand. They were pointed at Jaeger and Milroy.

'Ms Forster,' Jaeger began, his eyes wide.

'Drop your weapon,' his subordinate shouted. 'You too, Finn.' She stopped, her arms straight and her eyes flicking from target to target. 'You've got five seconds to comply.'

The CIA men looked at each other.

'Ms Forster,' Jaeger said, his tone soft, 'don't do—'

'The five seconds are up,' Jane Forster said. She changed the angles of her arms and loosed off two shots in quick succession.

Milroy's automatic flew from his grip, his fingers suddenly wreathed in red, while Jaeger's dropped to the ground when the round entered his forearm.

'Jesus!' the station chief gasped. 'You shot me.'

'And I'll shoot you again – you, too, Finn – if either of you makes another move.' Forster smiled. 'You've probably forgotten, but I passed out top of my marksmanship class.' She turned her gaze on Mavros and Grace. 'You might want to pick up their weapons, though I reckon they're too gutless to try anything now.'

Mavros complied, while Grace stepped up to Milroy.

'You choose,' she said, glancing at the two wounded men. 'The benefit of my agency unarmed-combat training or the course we did in field first aid.'

They chose the latter.

'Thanks,' Mavros said to the woman who had saved them. 'I take it you were kept in the dark about a lot of this scam.'

Jane Forster nodded, the automatics still trained on her colleagues. 'But not enough to save my ass.'

Mavros grinned. 'Don't worry. We'll put in

several good words for you.'

On the horizon another ship was bisecting the space between the low headlands. In the east the sun had broken through the grey cloud cover. A solitary seagull was soaring on the updraughts above the narrow inlet, looking down on the red shirt of the terrorist: Iraklis was lying on the stony ground by the temple foundations where ancient blood crimes were expiated, beside the cave where his mythical counterpart had entered the realm of the dead.

23

Mavros walked out on to the narrow balcony and pulled the french windows to, looking up the street to the tree-covered hill of Strefi beyond. The noise of traffic from the lattice of roads between the raised ground and the central avenues of Athens was jarring, motorbikes revving and horns blasting every few seconds. The sun was bright and, though the air was chill, the snowstorms of the previous days were a distant memory. Then the stark beauty of the southern Peloponnese came back to him in a rush – the wind whipping off the rocks of the Tigani peninsula, the grey sea running gently up the bay at Tainaron. He caught his breath as he heard again the shots that had despatched Iraklis and stepped rapidly back into the hotel room.

Grace was sitting on the bed, towelling her hair. 'Jesus, Alex, close the door. It's freezing in here.'

'Sorry.' He sat down on the opposite side from her and glanced at his watch. 'They'll be wanting you in a quarter of an hour.'

'I know.' She dropped the towel on the floor. 'Are you coming to the airport?'

'I don't think so. It isn't part of the deal.' The Greek authorities had decided to ignore Mavros's failure to pass on information about the terrorist, provided that the American embassy spirited Grace out of the country; and provided that the two of them had no further contact.

'Screw the deal,' Grace said, her eyes wide. 'After all those bastards have done...' She let the words trail away, stood up and undid her robe.

Mavros looked outside again: the balcony on the apartment across the street was covered in plant-pots strung with Christmas decorations. It was ironic that the hotel they'd been put into by the embassy was in Neapolis, the area of Athens where he had grown up and where the assassin had lived when he was involved with Grace's mother. The Fat Man was still a local resident.

'What is it?' Grace asked, pulling up the zip of her jeans.

Mavros stood up, keeping his eyes off her. 'I was just thinking. Everything seems to come back to these streets around here. All that's missing is any trace of my brother.'

She came over to him. 'I'm sorry, Alex. Maybe ... maybe there are some things that can never be found.' She squeezed his arm. 'It could be that it's better that way.'

'You're probably right,' he muttered. 'Even though you sound worryingly like my mother.' Dorothy and the rest of his family had been brought back to Athens from the Palaiologos house by a squad of plain-clothes police, Nikos Kriaras directing operations. The Fiat Mavros had hired from the dubious operator in Corinth had even been returned on his behalf. The government was involved behind the scenes and it had become apparent that a major cover-up operation was under way. The cabinet members who'd been involved in the anti-dictatorship

545

student resistance had no interest in the press digging into that period. Peter Jaeger and Lance Milroy had been sent back to the US under armed escort, their existence denied. The conservative opposition was also keen to keep the issue under wraps on Veta Palaiologou's recommendation – neither she nor her fellow leaders wanted the Right's historic links with the Americans excavated. The general feeling was that the old battles were over and should not be allowed to resurface. What the families of the entrepreneurs murdered in Jaeger's conspiracy would have thought of that, Mavros tried to put from his mind.

Grace zipped up her bag and turned to him. 'Your sister,' she said, catching his eye, 'won't she want to write an exclusive about all this?'

'It's been made clear to her that this is a matter of state security, both Greek and American,' he replied. 'They aren't messing around. And remember, she has kids.'

'Shit,' Grace said. 'Can they get away with that? What about Geoffrey Dearfield? Won't he talk? He's written a book, for God's sake.'

'His typescript's been confiscated.' Mavros shrugged. 'Anyway, who would believe him? Since his wife died – the story that's been put about is that it was a heart-attack – he's been a wreck.'

'And Jane Forster? I wanted to see her again to thank her properly.'

'She'll be all right. But it's obviously in the interests of her career to stay away from us and to keep her mouth shut.'

Grace caught his eye. 'Why do you think she did it? Why did she save us?'

Mavros smiled. 'Not all your former colleagues in the agency are crazy conspirators. I guess she finally realised how far out on a limb Jaeger and Milroy had gone.'

'And that stone killer Milroy supposedly loved my mother.'

'Even stone killers have feelings,' he said, stepping closer. 'Iraklis died thinking of Laura, I'm sure of it.'

'But what good does a love like that do?' Her voice shook. 'He kept on assassinating people after my father. He never stopped believing in the cause.'

Mavros breathed in her scent. 'I think you're wrong, Grace. Despite what he said, I think he realised that your mother meant more to him than the struggle. That's why he went to the States – to be near her even after she was dead. He came back here for the family honour and because of the hold Flora had on him.'

She looked unconvinced. 'You reckon?'

'I reckon.'

Grace stepped away and pulled on her denim jacket. 'Alex, I owe you.'

'Don't worry about that,' he said, bowing his head. 'I had a personal interest in the case.'

'I don't just mean the money,' she said. 'I'll send that to you. If you don't want it, give it to the old woman Stamatina.'

'Are you serious?'

'Only don't tell her it came from me. She wouldn't accept it.' She touched his hand. 'Won't she talk to the press? Won't she wonder what happened to her son?'

'She would have known he was leaving the country. I think they'd have said their farewells. Besides, an old Communist like her would be easy enough for them to discredit.'

Grace's expression was grim. 'This place is a fucking police state, Alex.'

'Your people showed them the way after the war.' Then he relented, opening his hands. 'Now, maybe, we can begin to get beyond that.'

There was a knock on the door. 'Two minutes, Ms Helmer.' The voice was male and American.

'I hope you're right,' Grace said, moving close to him and putting her hands on his shoulders. 'Screw this deal. Now we're no longer bound by your strict client code, you could come with me, Alex.'

'What, to the jungle?'

'Actually, I'm going to the western Sahara.'

'There's someone waiting for you, isn't there?'

Her eyebrows shot up. 'You're a quick one, aren't you?' She put her mouth to his ear. 'Yes, there is. He's been on my case for over a year, calling me when we're apart, insisting that I call him when he's off-duty. But that doesn't mean I didn't fall for you. In different circumstances, we–'

'It's all right, Grace,' Mavros interrupted. 'There was too much going on for us to find each other properly.' He pushed her away gently. 'You know, I was suspicious of you right up to the end. I was never sure that you didn't just want revenge on the man who killed your father.'

548

'You were right to have suspicions, Alex,' she said, looking into his eyes. 'I did want revenge. But – but at the last, I couldn't do it. What I heard from Iraklis hasn't made it any easier to understand what happened when I was a kid, though. Getting some insight into why people resort to violence doesn't do anything to reduce the pain.' She blinked back tears. 'The genealogy of terrorism, you called it when we were in the car with Iraklis. Nice phrase, my friend, but it's written on air. The pain doesn't ever stop.'

'But at least we stand more chance of averting the same in the future if we understand why people are driven to kill. Don't forget, Iraklis was in pain too.'

She nodded. 'That's why I couldn't pull the trigger. Even though the bastard deserved it.'

There was another, heavier knock. 'Time, Ms Helmer.'

'Grace,' he said, as she pulled away, 'don't talk to anyone about this. People's lives are at stake. My family...'

She picked up her bag. 'I won't, Alex. Make sure you keep that smart mouth of yours shut too.' She headed for the door.

Mavros watched her go, then went back out on to the balcony. Grace appeared on the street, dark-suited minders in front of and behind her. She got into the unmarked car without looking up. As it moved away, Mavros heard music peal out from an open window across the road. The song was instantly recognisable. It was 'The Voyage of the *Argo*' – the creation of Kostas Laskaris and Dhimitris Randos, both recently

549

departed to the Kingdom of the shades.

Looking through the dusty windows of the café, Mavros could see that there was only one person inside. He pushed open the door and stepped in before the figure behind the chill cabinet could raise his head.

'No customers as usual.'

'Alex!' For a few seconds the Fat Man looked like he was going to burst into tears. 'You're alive, you wanker,' he said hoarsely.

'Good morning to you, too,' Mavros said, going up to the café-owner and putting his arms round him. 'Are you all right, my friend?'

The Fat Man shoved him away. 'Yes, I'm all right,' he said, with a glare. 'No thanks to you. I was sure that madman had caught up with you. What happened?'

Mavros took a couple of paces back. 'Any chance of a coffee? I haven't had anything all morning.'

'No way,' Yiorgos Pandazopoulos said, his expression malevolent. 'Not until you tell me everything that's been going on. Christ and the Holy Mother, I almost got myself killed by that bastard you were after.' He shook his head. 'It would have been better if I had. My mother's been gnawing my guts ever since I got back to the village.'

'I thought you were going to spend Christmas there,' Mavros said, sitting down at his usual table.

'That's been the only good thing that came out of all this,' the Fat Man said, with a rueful smile.

550

'The old woman decided she wanted to come back to the big city. Apparently the villagers made some poisonous comments about my politics. Amazingly enough, she actually took exception on my behalf.'

Mavros had spoken to Kyra Fedhra after the assassin's death and had been told that her son had reappeared. Her voice was more scathing than he could remember, but he could tell beneath the bluster that she was relieved. 'Look, here's the deal. Make me a coffee and I'll tell you what happened.' He caught his friend's eye. 'But you have to promise to keep your mouth firmly shut about the whole story.'

'Who am I going to tell?' the café-owner asked ironically. When he saw the look on Mavros's face he raised his hands in surrender. 'All right, all right, I won't say a word to the comrades or to anyone else. I've learned my lesson.'

'I don't want any *galaktoboureko*, though,' Mavros said. He flinched as the terrorist's body filled his eyes again. 'I haven't felt up to eating the last couple of days.'

'Just as well,' Yiorgos said, with a sardonic smile. 'I had the last piece five minutes ago.' His expression grew more sombre. 'You heard about Kostas Laskaris?'

'When I saw him in the tower, I knew he was close to the end.' He looked up. 'That wreck of a Lada was yours, wasn't it? What the hell were you doing down there? It seems to me that you've got some explaining to do, too.'

The Fat Man brought his customer's coffee, locked the door and sat down opposite him.

Then they started to talk.

'This is amazing,' Mavros said, looking up from the sheaf of paper covered in spidery handwriting. '"The Fire Shirt". I saw him writing it when we were at the tower.' He caught Yiorgos's eye. 'What gave you the right to take it?'

The Fat Man snorted. 'I wasn't going to leave it for that peasant Savvas and his mother. It's a significant historical document. I was going to give it to the comrades.'

'The same comrades who sent you to keep an eye on one of their own?' Mavros said sharply. 'The comrades who were shitting themselves that Iraklis might do something that would rebound on them? Screw the Party, Yiorgo.' He dropped his gaze. 'Besides, I told you. The authorities aren't messing about. This is the cover-up of the decade and people's lives are at risk.'

The café-owner's face gradually slackened. 'All right,' he said, in a low voice. 'You'd better take the poem, Alex. I couldn't make much sense of it anyway. It's all about the Second World War and the sufferings of an ELAS group. There's even a character in it called Vladhimiros. That was my old man's name.' His heavy chin jutted forward. 'Maybe it's him. He never told me what he did during the occupation.'

'Perhaps it can be published some time in the future,' Mavros said. 'When the war and the horrors that followed it finally lose their power over people.' He reckoned he'd give it to his mother. She'd been keen enough to publish Laskaris's other work, though if this one contained the background to Iraklis, as he suspected it did, she'd have to be careful.

'And when will that be?' the Fat Man demanded, with a scowl. 'In five hundred years?'

'Maybe.'

'That Flora Dearfield woman. I can't believe a history professor was working for the Soviets without any of us knowing.'

'It's not exactly unheard-of. Everyone told lies back then.'

'You realise that in effect we're telling lies by keeping silent about all this,' the Fat Man observed.

'Yes, but we're also staying alive.'

'And the murderer Dearfield,' Yiorgos said, his voice rising. 'He should be strung up for what he did. He betrayed the ELAS band to the enemy, the fucker.'

'Let it go,' Mavros said, with a sigh. 'The British thought they were doing the best for Greece by supporting the king against the Communists. The Americans continued the policy. The fact is, whatever you and the comrades think, most Greeks never wanted to live in a hardline socialist state.'

'What happened to the American woman?' the Fat Man asked, after a sulky silence. 'When I saw you outside the Laskaris tower, I got the impression she had her eye on you.'

Mavros glanced away. 'It was too complicated.'

'She was quite a looker,' Yiorgos conceded. 'But it would never have worked. You can't sleep with the enemy. Are you seeing her again?'

'She's gone for good, my friend.'

The café-owner hauled himself to his feet. 'Just as well. That mad woman Niki Glezou came round here this morning. I think she may have got over whatever it was you did to her.'

'Jesus.' Mavros didn't know whether to laugh or cry. 'Anyone else on my tail?' His mobile phone had been returned to him by the police commander Kriaras, but he hadn't switched it on. He was sure the authorities would be scanning his calls for some time.

'Lambis Bitsos. He looked like he wanted to eat your balls.'

Mavros groaned. The exclusive he'd promised the crime reporter was now locked up tighter than a miser's hoard. He'd have to keep his head down till Bitsos was distracted by another story.

'Alex?' The Fat Man's voice was softer. 'I'm sorry I got in the way down in the Mani. I shouldn't have agreed to watch the Laskaris tower. But I didn't tell the comrades that I saw you or Iraklis.' He bent over the table. 'I know my mother was hassling you about me. I hope that didn't distract you from more important things.'

'More important than you?' Mavros got up and slapped his friend's shoulder lightly. 'Stick to what you're good at,' he said, heading for the door with a smile on his lips. 'Making your customers deliriously happy. And, Yiorgo? Don't ever send a woman round to my place again, okay?'

The Fat Man grunted and started loading his tray.

Outside, Mavros breathed in the Athenian air, a fresh northerly blowing the pollution cloud away over the Argo-Saronic Gulf. Walking towards his flat, he passed a group of men whose cheap clothes marked them out as refugees or illegal immigrants. They were engaged in muted but intense conversation, the language sounding like Arabic. The sallow skin of their faces was in contrast to the scarlet-and-white check scarves they wore on their shoulders.

Mavros found himself thinking of the words that the renegade CIA man Peter Jaeger had spoken after the terrorist had been despatched without mercy.

The last red death.

If only.

Afterword

The Iraklis group does not correspond to any real terrorist organisation; nor should its victims be identified with the casualties of terrorist attacks in Greece – the author has the deepest sympathy for them and their families.

The following books in English proved particularly useful:

On history: David H. Close, *The Origins of the Greek Civil War* and *Greece since 1945*; George Kassimeris, *Europe's Last Red Terrorists: The Revolutionary Organisation 17 November*; Mark Mazower, *Inside Hitler's Greece: The Experience of Occupation, 1941–44*; Mark Mazower (ed.), *After the War Was Over: Reconstructing the Family, Nation, and State in Greece. 1943–1960*; C. M. Woodhouse, *Something Ventured* and *The Struggle for Greece 1941–49*. None of the writers should be held responsible for this fictional portrayal of life and death in modern Greece.

On locations: No traveller to, or student of, Greece should be without the *Blue Guide*. Visitors to the southern Peloponnese are fortunate to have Patrick Leigh Fermor's legendary *Mani*; *Deep into the Mani* by Peter Greenhalgh and Edward Eliopoulos is no less essential. Lakonia features substantially in Kevin Andrews's moving civil war memoir *The Flight of Icarus*. Apart from Henry Miller's effusions in *The Colossus of Maroussi*, Argolidha – heartland of Greek myth and history – has surprisingly escaped the attention of major modern writers. John Fowles's *The Magus*, a benchmark for writers of fiction set in Greece, includes a magnificent description of the view from Athens to the Peloponnese (admittedly in pre-pollution times).

Further information about the background to *The Last Red Death* can be found on the author's website, *www.paul-johnston.co.uk*

The publishers hope that this book has given you enjoyable reading. Large Print Books are especially designed to be as easy to see and hold as possible. If you wish a complete list of our books please ask at your local library or write directly to:

Magna Large Print Books
Magna House, Long Preston,
Skipton, North Yorkshire.
BD23 4ND

This Large Print Book for the partially
sighted, who cannot read normal print, is
published under the auspices of

THE ULVERSCROFT FOUNDATION